Mad Grass: A Warrior Returns

Daniel Sobieck

Mad Grass

Copyright © 2020 Daniel Sobieck

Mad Grass

The following work of fiction is based on actual events that occurred on July 13-14, 1851, near present-day Butte, North Dakota.

This book is dedicated to the memory of those who fought at the Battle of the Grand Coteau and to those who have endeavored to keep the story alive.

Mad Grass

Chapter 1

She felt a tug on her right calf, around the calf thin arms, within those arms a desperate clench, as tight as life. They were depending on her. In her left hand, the knife.

The steel penetrated his flesh easily.

She thought there would be a gasp or a gurgle, but the blade entered silently and she felt warm fluid pulse over her hand as it hit home. Then she heard the noise—pounding—again and again. What was that pounding? Refocusing, she watched herself pull back, swing, and cut once more, like a fresh dead spirit observing its departure from high above a hospital bed. She knew this must be a dream; she couldn't watch herself kill someone. The rifle dropped and he fell forward through the doorway, hands reaching for his throat. Then he began to turn. More pounding, louder now. She looked away and forced herself to consciousness, eyes open.

A soft morning light filled her room and she knew instantly this was another dream—no broken concrete, no crying children, Kristal was not there. She smelled coffee. Coffee? Had she overslept? Then she realized she was in her old bed. Back home. The pounding had stopped.

She took a deep breath and exhaled slowly. The pillow was soft but wet with sweat. She was warm. She listened. Someone was in the kitchen—her grandmother. Familiar sounds from years ago—the thunk of heavy ceramic plates set on the wooden table, the tinkle of cheap silverware, metal pans grating across the burners of a gas range.

She sat up on the side of the bed, stretched her arms over her head and felt the muscles of her back tense and snap, then relax back into place. She tested her right foot on the floor—stiff and sore. She rose gingerly, keeping most of her weight on her left foot and hobbled out the hall into the bathroom.

Looking in the mirror she saw a tired young woman, just 30, with short dark hair, dark eyes, bold cheekbones, and an aura of competence, even at this early hour.

"Breakfast, Kelly," announced her grandmother from downstairs.

"Be down in a minute," she replied cordially. She splashed cold water on her face, sat on the toilet, then returned to the bedroom to dress. She wore jeans, a tight sports bra, and a green T-shirt with "Marines" blazoned in black across the front.

"Thought I overslept," Kelly said as she sat down at the table.

"How can you oversleep—you don't have a job anymore," chided her grandmother. "Sleep as long as you need to; you need to recover."

Turning from the stove, she placed a plate with three pancakes in front of Kelly. "And now eat—you're nothing but skin and bones—didn't they feed you in the Marines?"

"They fed us just fine Grandma," she replied, dousing the stack with a small pitcher of home-made syrup and forking a wedge of pancakes into her mouth. In truth, she was lean and hard and strong, very strong, for her small frame. Regardless of the assigned task, physical toughness was job one for a member of the Corps. Even more so for Drill Instructors. Or now, a "former" Drill Instructor.

"Coffee black?"

Kelly nodded, her mouth full.

"I imagine you'll want to see some folks and get reacquainted now that you're back," said her grandmother, setting a steaming mug of coffee by her plate.

Kelly sipped the coffee and asked, "Was someone working outside—I thought I heard pounding?"

Her grandmother paused and unconsciously looked down at the dishtowel in her hands. "Oh, I don't think so. There may have been someone at the door. Maybe a salesman."

Kelly looked at her and paused a beat, then decided to let the subject drop.

"You know your great uncle is not well," her grandmother said, changing the subject. "You might want to see him before it's too late."

"Where is he—in Devil's Lake?"

"No, he used to be but they moved him to Bottineau into that new Regions Care Center once they found he wasn't going to recover from the stroke—it's like a swing bed and long-term care all in the same location. And a lot cheaper. He says he likes it there, closer to his family, closer to the Turtle Mountains. But he can't walk by himself anymore. Can't drive either. They wheel him outside in his chair sometimes but he'll never walk in those woods again. Some of the boys take him driving now and then, but that's about it."

"Who—Jamie and Rene?"

"No, not Jamie. Rene and Dylan, sometimes Cherie goes along too."

Rene, Dylan, and Cherie were her cousins, but she hadn't seen any of them since her mother's funeral.

"Do they still live in Bottineau?"

"Cherie and Dylan do. Rene says he doesn't like town, he has a place up north," her grandmother answered. Then her voice took on a conspiratorial tone. "You know your brother has gotten himself into a lot of trouble lately; he moves around. Was in Ottawa for a while and then somewhere near Grand Forks. I think he lives with a girlfriend now somewhere around here. Rene knows her."

Her younger brother Jamie had been in and out of trouble, and rehab, several times since high school. He had never been a good student and as they say, "fell in with a bad crowd". Kelly knew he spent some time in jail, but her mother never wanted to talk about it. He could never hold a job for more than a couple weeks before he was caught dealing or stealing. It made her sad to think about how he had let himself go.

Her grandmother still proudly displayed photos of Jamie in his dance competitions, back when he was thin and fit and costumed with his billowing shirts and the colorful Métis sashes of red and blue and green. He had been a good dancer, either solo or with his dance team of four. She could still see him tapping and skipping through the "Red River Jig" or the sash dance with a huge smile on his face. It was something he was good at and he had many ribbons and trophies to show for it. She imagined they were all in a box now in some closet. Every time she heard someone talk about him it was always about more trouble—with the law, his relatives, and his girlfriends. Such a waste.

"I want to visit the graves, then stop in and see Liz," Kelly said. "I'll try to visit Uncle Rodney maybe later this week." She added, "Would you like to come along?"

Her grandmother paused and considered. "Yes, Kelly that would be nice. I haven't seen him myself since Christmas."

"Can I use Grandpa's truck?"

"If you can get it started, go ahead. Nobody has used it since Dylan and Rene hauled firewood last fall."

"I'll get it going," Kelly replied confidently.

After breakfast she hobbled back up the stairs and into her room and painfully worked through a series of five stretching exercises, slowly manipulating her injured foot and ankle. Even now after nearly six weeks, her range of motion was limited. But she was improving and other than her ankle and stiff calf she felt good. She dug a large bottle of prescription pills out of her bag and popped one in her mouth.

It was good to be back in the shadow of the Turtle Mountains, a formation of forest and lakes straddling the North Dakota/Manitoba border. Generations of her relatives, Métis people, had called this region home. And it felt like home. Although just back a few days she was quickly reminded of the comfort, the caring, the slow pace.

When she left to see the world with the Marines, she was a young high school graduate who couldn't wait to leave. As a child, Kelly found delight in the Métis culture, with their dance and festivals and tales, but she found little of value there for her now. And obviously, it was no longer relevant to Jamie.

As a United States Marine, she had traveled all across the United States as well as to Norway, Germany, and Afghanistan. It was all new, and interesting if not exciting, but she never found anything in her travels which would tempt her to set down roots in some faraway place. But the Turtle Mountains and the prairies to the north, with their unforgiving winters and natural elements and forces on display, remained very appealing to her. Built in, she surmised. Part of her, and she a part of it.

Despite having sat in the cold for nearly six months, the old Ford truck started easily after she charged the battery for 20 minutes. She calculated it would take about an hour on the gravel roads to get to the cemetery outside Deloraine where her parents were buried, near Manitoba's Turtle Mountain Provincial Park.

After being restricted to hospital beds, wheelchairs, and crutches for weeks it felt good to drive again. She wouldn't miss the odors and sounds of the VA hospitals—competing scents of antiseptic, urine, and feces wafting throughout the hallways, punctuated by the groans and complaints of the luckless occupants. She lowered the truck window; now this was fresh air, scented of pine and silver maple and birch and the blossoms of chokecherry and plum. The landscape was vibrant and alive and growing. She hung her arm out the window and spread her fingers to feel the cool, moist air. It felt good on her skin.

She was happy to find the cemetery again. She knew one wrong turn on the unmarked roads would have turned her quest into a goose chase. Three years earlier, when her mother died, she had been in South Carolina. She returned for the funeral but had to leave right away. Ovarian cancer. Her parents' grave looked better than it had—more grass and someone had left a vase of plastic flowers. Unlike many cemeteries she had seen on her travels, this cemetery was well-cared for.

She paused. "Hello, Momma. I'm back again, maybe for good this time. I'm sorry I wasn't here when you left but I did what you told me—I've seen the world now, or at least a big part of it." She paused as emotion swelled in her chest. "I miss you," she said quickly.

Her mother had subtly encouraged Kelly to consider leaving her hometown since she was 14 or 15 years old. In the end, she nearly pushed Kelly out the door—military, out-of-state college or work program, Peace Corps, or job on a beach somewhere. Her mother didn't care where as long as Kelly got away from the Mountain and gained some perspective on life. Of course, her mother secretly wanted her to return again but left that to fate and her daughter's own good sense. In hindsight, her mother's instincts were correct. Jamie's failure was as much proof of that as Kelly's success.

She looked down at the gravestone and prayed the Lord's Prayer silently. As it always did, anger rose slowly through her sorrow, anger that her father had left them so early, a car accident cutting short an alcohol-fueled life predestined for tragedy. But she still missed him. A 13-year-old Dodge half-ton truck was no match for a 105-year-old white pine. He was killed instantly; Kelly was just eight-years-old, Jamie was two. She made the sign of the cross and then walked the 20 feet to her grandfather's grave.

"Got your truck, Grandpa," she said, forcing some cheer into her voice. "Still running good just like you said, 'long after I'm gone.' And you were right. I know Grandma misses you. We all miss you. I hope you're in a happy place."

Her grandfather had been a proud and able family patriarch. He was Métis through and through, could tell the stories of the great battle at Batoche, of his own father and mother living as squatters in a road allowance ditch, surviving winters by trapping, fishing, and their wits. Tough as a badger, his great white beard would whirl and his face contort as he cataloged the misdeeds of the Canadian government, deified Louis Riel as a patron saint, and warned of the ever-approaching social apocalypse which threatened to wipe the Métis off the planet.

At times the discussions between her grandfather and great Uncle Rodney would rise to such a ruckus that her grandmother threatened to throw them out into the yard. "*Kiiyaamaya!* (be quiet)," she'd scold. "Or it's the snowbank for you." Collectively, they were walking encyclopedias of family history and keepers of the family tree, itself a mixed bramble of Cree, Saulteaux, French, and Scot. While they didn't agree on everything, each reserved a special black corner of their hearts for the government which had taken the Métis land, closed their businesses, and scattered the Métis onto the cold Manitoba prairie with little more than the clothes on their backs.

Kelly plucked some grass from around each of the family headstones and said a quiet "goodbye." She then fished in her pocket and produced a bronze medallion: her Marine Corps Expeditionary Medal for Afghanistan. Just holding it in this cool, green place felt odd. She had earned it a half-world away on the doorstep of Hell. But now it seemed fitting to leave it here, as much a mark of accomplishment for her parents as for Kelly. She placed it atop their gravestone and quickly turned away.

She felt good; energized and refreshed, renewed in some way for visiting. She felt a connection, at least with her mother and grandfather, if not her father; with him, it was still resentment or disappointment.

She turned the truck south now, drove the perimeter of the park, crossed the border into the US, and a half-hour later pulled up to a modest rambler on the north side of Metigoshe. Liz appeared at the door just moments after she rang the bell.

"Kelly!"

"Hey Liz," she replied with a smile.

"Come in—I just put James down for a nap. I heard you were back, you look great!" Liz reached out and the two hugged briefly. "You are solid as a rock girl!" she laughed.

Kelly stepped inside the door and found herself in a modestly-furnished living room. She had graduated from high school with Liz, her best friend since childhood. While Kelly's features suggested a mixed French ancestry, Liz was nearly full-blooded Cree, with coal-black hair, broad facial features, and beautiful hazel eyes that danced and sparkled when she got excited. Kelly's mother had always said Liz was full of "spirit."

"Sit, sit," demanded Liz. "Can I get you something to drink? Coffee, pop?"

"No, I'm good thanks," Kelly replied, taking a seat on the sofa.

"So, my God, you're back—and look at your hair—it's so short! I love it."

"Well, this is actually pretty long for me. But once I decided to toss in the towel, I let it grow out. Besides, I might need some hair now just to keep warm."

"What happened, I heard you got hurt; are you out for good or what?"

"I was discharged, a medical discharge. So I guess I'm out for good. I was hurt in a training accident, but I was the instructor. Mostly my own fault."

"I didn't know you were a trainer, last I heard you were in Germany or something. Your cousin Rene said you were guarding an installation of some kind. I suppose it's all secret."

"Not really. Our bases are pretty well-established. Not a lot of 'cloak and dagger' stuff. I was in Germany for a couple years on regular assignment then was offered a promotion to Sergeant, a Drill Instructor. Did that for a few years, then Afghanistan, then back stateside for an advanced training position."

"You mean Drill Sergeant like those people who scream all day at new recruits off the bus, like the sergeants in the movies?"

"Yeah, we're called Drill Instructors or DIs," Kelly replied, still using the present tense.

"But then you got hurt?"

"Yeah, by one of my own recruits, during some advanced live round training. Shot in the ankle. Messed it up pretty good, six hours of surgery putting it back together, stainless steel pins. Lots of rehab.

13

Some doctors said I'll always have a limp, others said I might be good as new eventually."

Kelly still remembered the meeting with her Commanding Officer. She had not applied to be a DI, was happy enough just serving as a Marine. But she was asked to apply. "Your evaluations since Basic are exemplary Private Moreau—and your instructors feel you have leadership qualities. We're expanding operations to include more women and we need female Drill Instructors. Is there any reason why you shouldn't submit your application?"

"No ma'am."

That was the beginning of her promotion to sergeant, Drill Instructor training, and then personally training six different classes of recruits at Camp Pendleton, then being recruited again after Afghanistan to serve as a Marine Combat Instructor to train new "boots" (first year Marines) in actual combat conditions.

Even as a raw recruit she had learned early on not to volunteer for anything, but intelligence in the Armed Forces couldn't remain hidden for long. Like oil in water, it inevitably rose to the top. She found she was good at it, instructing, or what passed as instructing in the Marines—beat them down, break them, build a team. Make them Marines, make them lethal. She found, at least initially, she could easily turn it on and off—be overbearing, overwhelming when needed, but return to "normal' when off duty, or at least the Marines' version of normal. Without really understanding the "why", she found she had a reservoir of anger she could tap at will. She found most of the good DIs did.

Some instructors couldn't turn it off or took too much pleasure in creating pain, manufacturing misery. These instructors were soon rotated to the field where they couldn't do as much damage to those around them. But that didn't necessarily mean they didn't hurt themselves.

Her raw materials, new recruits, varied greatly. Maybe half belonged in any branch of the Armed Forces, with only half of those suitable for the Marines. They all came with their own stories—some were steered to the Marines by a county judge in some sweltering small-town courtroom, given an ultimatum by parents, or sought escape from abusive boyfriends, bosses or family members. Predictably, many were from rural areas of the south, or urban areas like New York or California; all lacked better options.

Once Kelly became self-aware of her own story, she wondered what category she belonged to; was she running or trying to find something? Becoming part of an effort larger than herself appealed to her. Her struggle as a Métis, who didn't quite fit in either the Indigenous or white world had always bothered her. There was no question that after Basic she became part of a family—the Marine family. As an Instructor, she had similarly ushered other women into that same family. But now she was left with some familiar doubts—like her biological family the Marines were not without their misfits and hard cases. She hoped she had not become one herself.

Kelly's instructor specialty, somewhat to her surprise, was edged weapons or knife work. For combat purposes, the Marines continued to rely on the "Fighting Utility" or Ka-Bar type knife – a blade designed to hack, puncture, slice or crush an enemy into submission, over and over again. It was a brutishly effective knife.

Once introduced to knife work during Marine Combat Training Kelly became fascinated with knives, especially finely-crafted blades. Old-time stilettos were her favorite, as well as certain throwing knives. It developed into a hobby; she would find old knives in her travels around the country and throughout the world—flea markets, roadside sales, pawn shops—choosing those of good high-carbon steel or Damascus, cleaning and then sharpening them to a razor-edge. Over her years in the Corps, she had assembled quite a collection. It was while conducting the edged weapon segment of Combat Training that she first encountered Private Zack.

15

She wondered how Jaysee Zack had come to be a Marine, how she ever got through Basic. Here was a woman who seemed continually surprised to find herself in the Marines. Kelly confided in her fellow DI Kristal Moore that Private Zack would kill somebody someday on the range, in the barracks or in the field. She was a certifiable screw-up and walking time-bomb. She should have never made it through Basic. Some DI or Black Shirt had dropped the ball.

"Basic is becoming too soft. They just need to keep their numbers up," complained Moore. "And now you're stuck with her. At least you have a shot at her—so she won't re-up."

Calling recruits and Marines "soft" was nothing new for Moore, whose threshold for physical pain and abuse was off the charts. Many still remembered her nearly running the nine miles back to camp after enduring the 54-hour test known as the "Crucible" at the end of Basic. Her feet were so swollen and bloody from blisters the medics had to cut her boots off. She had actually dragged and then carried another Marine nearly a half-mile during the final march. Afterward, she was on crutches for a week. But Moore was tough; she never complained.

Although extremely fit, Kelly had barely survived her own Crucible test, which combined survival skills, obstacle courses, combat simulations, and sleep and food deprivation. "Forged by the Fire" they called it. It was the ultimate test; you couldn't call yourself a Marine until you passed.

Now, sitting here, it seemed so long ago. And Moore had been dead for nearly a year.

"So now you're an ex-Marine," mused Liz.

"We like to say once a Marine always a Marine," smiled Kelly.

"Well, what do Marines who are no longer Marines do for a living?" she teased. "You have any prospects?"

16

"No, they have a job service for Marines who muster out, but I guess I really don't know where I want to live yet or what I want to do in the real world. I gave it a lot of thought while I was laid up but can't decide. I guess once my Mom died it threw a wrench into the idea of moving back here, at least permanently." Kelly paused. "Why did you and Jay decide to live here?"

"Well, he got the job cutting for the mill in Bottineau so it made sense for us to stay around here. And now with two kids, I guess we won't be going anywhere."

"Yeah," replied Kelly, considering the prospect of staying near the Mountains. She was single, had nothing tying her down. She had skills, was smart, flexible. At least she thought she was.

"But you have a lot of options Kelly," Liz continued, reading her mind. "I mean, your ankle is going to heal...right?"

"Yeah...yes." Then with more conviction, "Yes I'll be good to go."

"Well, you could go anywhere you want—Winnipeg, or Fargo, or even the Twin Cities."

"Yeah, half my relatives are in the US, and half are in Canada so I guess I have a lot of options. But I might need to stick around here to take care of my grandma, you know, now that Mom is gone, and it doesn't sound like Jamie is going to step up."

"So I guess this means you didn't find yourself a sweetheart in the Marines," said Liz with a mischievous smile.

"No," replied Kelly, more seriously than intended. "Not too many sweethearts in the Marines."

"Well, if you're ready to start working Jay says they're hiring at the yard in town—some type of computer work, not cutting or hauling, not physical. If you'd like he'll put in a good word for you. It'll at

17

least be something to get you started until you figure out what you want to do in the long-term. Not much for benefits but it's a good place to work."

Kelly considered it. "I'd appreciate that. I could get over there by the end of the week and at least fill out an application."

"Good, I'll tell Jay."

The conversation lagged and Kelly took advantage to take her leave. "I should get going Liz."

"Sure, but you have to come back sometime when Jay is home. He'd love to see you again."

"Yeah, I'd like that," she said, then paused. "You know I've only seen pictures of your kids. Could I peek in?"

"Sure, James will be asleep but it's about time for Kimi to get up." They walked down a darkened hallway to a single bedroom where both children slept. Three-year-old James was spread out on his bed with arms and legs stretched wide, a shock of thick black hair splayed across his thin pillow. He breathed peacefully. Nearby in a crib, Liz's 18 month-old daughter Kimi, lay silently on her stomach, eyes open, sucking her thumb, watching them.

Liz walked over and picked her up, cuddling her to her bosom and rocking gently back and forth as she walked back into the hall. "Hi Sunshine, can you say hello to Kelly," she whispered, then turned to Kelly. "Do you want to hold her?"

"No, she looks happy right there," Kelly replied. "She's beautiful. Where did she get that blonde hair?"

"There's some on my side and a bunch on Jay's. But I think it'll turn red."

"And what about those chubby cheeks?"

"That's just because she eats like a horse," smiled Liz. "Here's a little girl that will never turn down a meal."

Kelly smiled too. "Okay, I'm going to head out—say 'Hi' to Jay for me."

"I will."

Kelly drove away thinking Liz was happy, thinking she might never leave Metigoshe; two kids, husband, mortgage payment. It seemed boring, and she guessed it was —but maybe a good kind of boring.

Chapter 2

Jean-Luc Savard heard a shot and was suddenly awake, automatically reaching for the rifle by his side. It took an instant to realize he was in camp and another to identify the smoke from the cooking fires. A pot banged again, and he relaxed. Someone murmured as coals were stirred and the nearest fire snapped and emitted a shower of sparks.

The air was still and thick with moisture. Savard stretched and felt the muscles of his shoulders and back snap and shift and then relax back into place. He was stiff from sleeping on the hard ground and the hard riding of yesterday. He rose slowly from his bedroll and saw others near him still sleeping around the cold embers of last night's fires. Wood smoke hung in the air. Tipis were scattered in the distance, most still quiet as the camp slowly came to life. In the distance others slept under carts or staked canvas tarps, avoiding the morning dew.

They spoke softly in Mechif, a mix of French, Cree and English—the language of the mixed-bloods from the north. Their camp was over 200 strong, with nearly 70 hunters along with women and children and over 100 carts to carry their game, now some 14 days into their trip from southern Manitoba south to the *Maison du Chien*, or Dog Den Butte. They were on the Grand Coteau, the expanse of grassland, lakes, and small prairie ponds spread from the Canadian prairie southward to the Souris River. The area was roadless, marred only by rough trails cut from the hooves of bison and wooden oxcart wheels—a wilderness of grass, which stretched from one horizon to the next.

It would be another 10 years before the land would become known as part of the Dakota Territory, a moving storehouse of rich bison meat, hides, fat, and tongue. It also served as the rootstock for the

Métis pemmican trade which spanned hundreds of miles along the Canadian border.

He always slept in the open, where ducks and geese called and the blue-black sky offered sheet music for a chorus of wolves and coyotes and the quavering hoots of the owl. Under his blankets, with the thin wool pulled under his chin, he found no better feeling than surrendering his body to the tug of the land. Here the soil was life, with a hum and pulse all its own. He loved the open prairie; he loved how it felt and tasted and smelled—in drops of warm rain, cool creek water, and wind, which stung his eyes and filled his senses when he faced it.

Although he had never seen the ocean, at times he imagined the prairie grass to be an ocean, albeit at times an angry ocean with the wind cutting and carving the hills and buffeting the grass. But just as often a warm sunset and fair breeze ushered him to sleep amidst the soft rustling of a land trying to calm itself again.

Slipping on his unlaced boots, he walked stiffly to where the horses were tied, squared his feet, and let loose a noisy stream of urine against a purple thistle, the bulbous head nodding back and forth. A pack of coyotes squealed somewhere west of the camp, abruptly stopped, and were then answered by a pack far to the southeast.

At 19 years old and just over five and a half feet tall, Jean-Luc was lean and hard and square, with dark hair and a friendly manner. A product of a lengthy French lineage laced with his mother's Cree— but in truth he was of the earth—a divine creation of northwest gales, bitter winters, and the bright crocus which clawed through the frozen ground toward the sun each spring. Like all his people, he was resourceful, resilient, and expected the land to provide for those with the knowledge and skill to tame it. Theirs was a simple rule: you fed yourself on the prairie or you didn't eat.

He looked east and saw the dawn was still a half-hour from breaking, then glanced west, knowing he couldn't possibly see the camp some 30 miles away where his parents and sisters stirred in

21

their own tipis and bedrolls. The savory aroma of fried salt pork, bannock bread, and seared meat filled his nose as he buttoned his pants and quietly walked past his sleeping companions toward the cook wagon.

A stout man squatted by the fire clad in thin grease-stained pants, a faded red shirt, and dark vest. Henri Paquet's sharp knife moved in a blur as he sliced unpeeled potatoes on a board then tipped the slices into waiting cast iron pans, already sizzling with nuggets of pork fat. A squat brown hat covered the oily curls of his dark head, his face a fleshy montage of leathery skin laid on in deep furrows— the face of age, hardship, and wisdom. A black patch covered his right eye, lost during a tumble from a horse many years earlier.

"Bonjour Henri—how much sand in my potatoes today?" Jean-Luc queried with a grin.

"Extra sand for you—for sand in the belly," came the reply. Paquet had already been up for over an hour readying the fires, preparing camp breakfast, and collecting wood for the evening meal. "It's lucky the song dogs sing this morning or you would sleep 'til noon eh?"

"No need for songs—the smell of your breakfast wakes the dead!"

"They should stay that way," he muttered. "My pans feed only so many."

Jean-Luc loved this time before sunrise, before the camp was fully awake, a time of mystery and promise; what adventures would the day bring? He stopped, inhaled deeply, and filled his lungs with the moist air of first light. "You have hot coffee for the best hunter in camp?"

"The best hunter! It is dog piss for shooters like you...like the blind man. But I give you coffee. The bread is soon done and hot meat for the belly. Maybe today you shoot the fat cow?"

Jean-Luc began to respond but Paquet held up his hand to silence him. "Or *maybe*…"

Paquet stood now with a broad smile and clutched the knife flat across his chest while extending the other arm, then turned back and forth as if dancing. "Maybe you think too much about the young lady to shoot the straight bullet, eh?" His rough voice raised a pitch higher, "You like to dance Miss Lady, you like to dance?" Then he turned a full pirouette. Graceful, for a big man.

Jean-Luc burst into laughter at the sight of the stout old cook's whirling dance. He didn't mind being mocked for his dance with Elisa; he would do just about anything to dance with her again. "Be careful Old Man, if you fall into the fire no one will eat today." He smiled to himself and repeated the phrase in his head "Think too much about the young lady..." Not much got by the old rascal.

Paquet was a renowned cook, much in demand on their annual hunts. His mastery of preparing bison was widely acknowledged across the Métis camps. They had been fortunate to obtain him for their smaller hunting group, usually the larger party, the one to the west this year, laid claim to the better equipment and best cooks. But Paquet himself had chosen the smaller camp, perhaps in a nod to the toll the years and hard land had taken on his body. He was old now and slowing down. The larger camp had two cooks and a helper this year. Paquet didn't ask for help but Grace Snow, a young Cree girl whose parents had drowned in the Red River three springs earlier, was his assigned cook's helper on this trip.

Paquet had cooked over open fires for nearly 35 years; his subtly spiced and roasted bison hump fed body and soul, with the glistening fat dribbling down your chin as naturally as mother's milk. His roast bison calf, cooked whole until meat and bone parted ways, was a divine gift from the prairie—it was all he could do to fend the hunters off while it cooked. Once he gave the word, they fell on it like wolves.

Fish and fowl received similar treatment; the prairie was his larder. If it could be eaten, Paquet could prepare it. His *"tourtières"*—or meat pies—were Jean-Luc's favorite.

Part of the magic was a large, white canvas sack with drawstring top he always had within reach. The bag held mysteries and miracles: Paquet could "stop you up" or "get you going" if necessary, knock down a fever, cure the sniffles, assuage a headache. The sack held spices, powders, and potions collected over the years; it was a spice rack, drug store, dentist office, barbershop, and sometimes pillow. He reloaded it constantly with savory bits and mysterious paper packets each winter, gained in trade with other cooks and tinkers.

Jean-Luc smiled as he took the cup of coffee offered, the hot mug warming his cool hands. In the firelight, he examined the dried crimson blood lining his cuticles and lodged under his nails from yesterday's hunt. "No more old bull," he promised, looking off into the darkness. "Today…we find the herd," he said, nodding confidently. "Today will be our day."

They had seen only scattered bands of bison during the last week, not worth engaging except as camp meat. After a long trail day yesterday, they had come upon a solitary bull near their evening camp. A proven shooter, Savard had been tasked by camp boss Denis Granger to harvest the animal for their mobile larder. Rather than one of their quicker hunting horses, Jean-Luc had mounted his family's old sorrel cart mare Cheri and loped over the hill after the feeding bull. She was slow, but absolutely steady to the shot and did not spook at the smell of a carcass.

Riding as close as he dared, he crept forward and rested his rifle on a flat granite stone, cushioning the firearm with his hat. At 110 yards, it should have been a simple shot; a bull bison, at 2,000 pounds, made a big target. His .54 caliber gun, pushing out a heavy lead slug was the right medicine for making meat; this load would power through slabs of muscle, bone, and gristle to destroy vital organs deep in the bull's chest. When he squeezed the trigger the gun roared and he heard a deep grunt as the round smacked home. With the wind in his face, the sulfur stink of the rifle smoke blew directly at him and bit into his sinuses. As it cleared he expected to see the bull on its back, legs flailing, but instead saw it whirl and lope slowly over the rise.

"Damn." He reloaded quickly—pouring a black powder charge and seating a second slug down the muzzle of the barrel—all the while taking quick glances at the bull's progress. Then he ran hard after the animal. A second shot into the bull's neck at 20 yards put the animal down. It was meat, but he had wasted a second powder charge and slug to bring the animal down. Forgivable, but at the cost of ribbing from the other hunters and crew. Granger would not be so understanding; powder and lead did not come easy on the plains.

As he drank his coffee the sky brightened to the east, but the western sky remained pocked with brighter planets and countless fading stars. Shimmering, they were set, ageless, and at peace. They forced a man to consider his place in the world, and his world's place in the universe. They made him feel small, the way a sensible man should.

"*Mon Dieu* Henri," he said quietly, his head tipped back, peering straight up. "The stars and sky will swallow us whole… and no one will know we were ever here."

Paquet glanced skyward, as a courtesy rather than determining if the morning sky truly held something new. "You are right my young friend," he said, squatting again to loosen the bread from the pan banked against the glowing coals. "But the stars I think spit out this old man. I 'ave seen much – the sky black with birds, the white bear, the grand herds, but the stars see everything." He stood now and wiped his hands on his vest, then shook a finger skyward as if scolding a child and cautioned, "I think they *know* everything too."

"Well I don't think they know how many carts we will fill with meat today, and—"

"They know," Paquet interrupted. "And the *Maison du Chien*," he added, now pointing to the south, "she knows everything too. You be the careful one today—she is no friend."

Grace silently appeared in the light of the fire ring with a bucket of water she had carried up to the creek. "In the barrel," said Paquet, nodding toward the barrel mounted on the wagon. Wordlessly she hefted the bucket onto the top of the wheel rim, climbed up to the bed while balancing the load, and then poured the water in.

"Good morning Gracie," said Jean-Luc.

"Good morning," she replied softly, not meeting his eyes. Then she disappeared into the darkness again with the empty bucket.

Soon other hunters and their families stirred and began readying the oxen, horses, and carts for the day. He watched across the camp as the Ferguson family bustled around their wagon, the two Ferguson girls hiking their skirts and walking briskly beyond the glow of the fires.

There would be a quick meal, prayers and then they would collectively muster out, with scouts ahead of the wagons on each horizon, bearing south, toward the herds. But for the sloping hills and coulees they could make their way easily, even now in the hazy morning light they could see their goal – the dark hills of the Dog Den Butte on the far southern horizon.

After breakfast, the camp quieted as young Father LeSueur leaned into the morning prayers with more earnestness than required. At their core, the Métis were a humble group, respecting religion, the land, and the blessings of the Lord. They knew their place here and their continued survival depended on the vagaries of weather, luck, and skill as well as their relationships with the many tribes of the area, some of which were relatives. They knew too their ultimate survival all hinged on finding the bison, and a successful hunt. Sound preparation and the application of a discipline honed over many generations by their ancestors half a world away in European conflicts tipped the scales in their favor.

Father LeSueur raised his voice and lifted his hands and Bible skyward as he prayed. "We ask that you forgive us of *OUR* sins and ask for *YOUR* guidance and protection as these *GOOD* Christians go about their *DANGEROUS* work across this *HOSTILE* prairie." He performed his task admirably; comfort and assurance were fleeting and hard-won in this harsh, open land of wind and hostile forces.

Just 30 years of age, Father LeSueur was still inexperienced in the ways of the natural world. But they were glad to have him, and with him, they moved cloaked in a blanket of surety and righteousness. Theirs was a task ordained by the Word and consecrated by the blood of the Savior. And so they saw a clear path: Where the bison went the Métis would follow, hunter and beast swapping fates on a swirling dance floor of billowing grass and timeless stone.

Chapter 3

Kelly spent the evening after visiting with Liz going through a stack of mail that had arrived home before she did. Much of it was from the Veterans Administration. She opened several and found she had to pick a hospital for follow-up visits on her ankle injury. None of the options was close by—Minot or Devil's Lake were her best options.

The sole North Dakota Congressman had also sent her a form letter, albeit with an original signature, thanking her for her service. Nice touch. She got half-way through the stack and set the rest aside for later. With each envelope she found herself being further removed from the Marines and pushed closer to a civilian life she wasn't quite ready to embrace.

On Tuesday, Kelly and her grandmother traveled to visit Uncle Rodney.

The low-slung Regions Critical Care and Senior Living Campus in Bottineau was new but modest, running perpendicular to the frontage road off the highway. It faced southeast, with its rear toward the prevailing northwest wind. The only way patients or residents could get a Turtle Mountain view was to wheel themselves over to the small smoking patio outside the west doors by the large metal trash bin. The grounds were well-groomed and it looked clean enough.

They checked in at the front desk where the receptionist remembered Kelly's grandmother.

"Hello...Margaret right? So good to see you again," said the girl, of obvious Indigenous lineage. "When was the last time, Christmas? Rodney is still doing well. He has his good days and bad of course but he's a favorite of all the staff."

"I'll bet he is," said Kelly's grandmother with a smile. "He was always such a storyteller, mostly tall tales if you ask me."

"Let me ring his nurse," said the receptionist. "Please have a seat, it'll be just a minute."

They sat in two of the three green upholstered lobby chairs and waited less than a minute for a bright young white girl in pink scrubs to arrive. Her name tag said "Cammy, LPN."

"Hello," she beamed. "Here to see Rodney? He's just getting back from some PT. He hasn't had many visitors lately so I'm sure he'll be happy for some company. Are you relatives?"

"Yes," replied Kelly's grandmother. "He's my brother-in-law."

"Wonderful. Just follow me and I can take you back to his room."

They followed her down one hall and then took a left and walked down a short wing. Kelly's uncle was in the last room on the right. As they entered two young men in blue scrubs were wrapping a blanket over Rodney's legs and tucking the ends beneath him. The women waited just outside his room and then all three entered as the men exited

"You've got visitors Rodney," announced Cammy cheerfully, then, turning to Kelly and her grandmother added softly, "He's had a pretty bad day today but I'm sure he'll be fine." She then turned and leaned down next to him, "Just ring if you need anything, Rodney." He made no response. Then she quickly turned and exited the room.

Kelly had not seen her great-uncle since her mother's funeral, and she had never seen him like this. The man she remembered was barrel-chested with a full head of coarse gray hair and perpetually wind burned cheeks like her grandfather. Although her mother's uncle, Rodney had always been the "fun" elder at their family gatherings, never as serious as her grandfather and always teasing the kids or pretending he was a hungry bear out to get them.

She realized now how old he must have been back then when she was a child. This man before her looked ancient–haggard and spent. His skin had taken on a gray pallor and his breathing was weak and shallow. An IV fed into a vein in his left arm and a catheter tube emerged from under the blanket and hung down the right side of his bed, disappearing somewhere beneath it. Here was a man clearly not long for the world.

"Wa-a," he said, lifting his hand and reaching toward the bed-stand. "Wa-a."

"You want water?" asked her grandmother. He nodded weakly. Her grandmother picked up a covered plastic cup and straw and made a move to hand it to him. Then, realizing he could not hold it, she bent over him and moved the end of the straw to his lips. He sucked softly and then swallowed with great effort.

When he stopped, she set the cup down on the bed-stand again.

He looked at her face, trying to focus. "Maggie," he said quietly. Her grandmother turned and took hold of Rodney's hand.

"Yes, it's Maggie," she answered, smiling. "And this is Kelly, you remember Kelly don't you."

A look of puzzlement crept over Rodney's face as he repeated the name, "Kelly?"

"Yes, Marie's daughter, Kelly."

"Kelly?"

"Remember you used to pretend you were a bear and you would chase me?" Kelly offered.

"Marie," he said. "Marie."

"No, Marie is gone Rodney," interjected her grandmother. "Remember, she died several years ago."

Rodney remained silent.

"How do you like it here?" asked her grandmother, changing the subject. More silence. "Do you like it here?"

"Outside."

"You like it outside?"

He nodded twice and then closed his eyes.

Kelly looked around the small room with its one window and view of the parking lot and tried to imagine living here. Uncle Rodney had always been a man of the woods and prairie, like her grandfather, a true Métis. She guessed he had slept more nights outdoors than in, given all the logging and fishing and hunting he had done.

She knew he had run a winter trap-line for years and spent weeks at a time in small trapper cabins along the Canadian border in sub-zero temperatures. He said he loved it, returning each spring with hundreds of pelts in tow – beaver, mink, marten, fox, otter, wolf, and bear. The check from the fur buyer was substantial and paid for his living expenses for most of the year.

And he had his stories; twice he'd broken through the ice and nearly drowned when hunting by himself and once was chased up a tree by a black bear sow. He killed her with his knife as they tumbled out of the tree. He had her tanned pelt nailed to his wall for years. And now he was here.

They sat with him quietly for 20 minutes as he slept and then her grandmother pulled Kelly aside to the door. "Oh Kelly, it's so sad to see him this way, so sad," she said quietly, her eyes bright with tears. "This may be the last time we see him, dear—so you better say your goodbyes."

"I know Grandma," Kelly replied, squeezing her grandmother's hand gently, "I know."

They walked over to the bed again and her grandmother leaned over the bed. "It was good to see you again Rodney," she said loudly. "You must be very tired," then louder, "We'll come and see you again later." It was a commitment she was not sure she'd have the opportunity to keep.

He opened his eyes weakly and closed them again without acknowledgment.

Kelly sidled up to the bed beside her grandmother. "Goodbye Uncle Rodney, I'm so glad I could come to visit you."

He opened his eyes, then they saw him try to focus on her face. "Kelly," he said softly.

"Yes, Kelly."

Then a look of revelation came across his face as his eyes opened wider. "Kelly," he said louder.

Kelly glanced briefly at her grandmother.

"Yes," she replied. Her uncle said something softly, his eyes closing once more. Kelly leaned down to his face and gently brushed a lock of hair from his eyes.

"What is it, Rodney?"

"You go," he said softly, then more urgently, "You go."

"You want me to leave?" Kelly repeated.

He turned his head and said once more, this time as if a great burden, carried for many years, had been passed, "*You* go now." There was no smile, but a wash of contentment passed briefly over his pale face. Then he was asleep again.

As they walked to the truck in the parking lot Kelly asked, "What did he mean?"

"Did he say, 'You go?'" asked her grandmother.

"That's what I heard."

"Well, I don't know why he would want you to leave. I don't think he even knew who you were at first."

"I don't think he wanted me to leave either Grandma, I think he's out of sorts; he doesn't know what he's saying."

"Well, have a care; a Métis on their deathbed is washed in the light of the Creator. I wouldn't take it lightly. I just wish him a peaceful exit. Maybe that's all we can ever hope for, to die in peace."

One of her delayed Service checks had come through so Kelly took her grandmother out for supper on the way home. They rarely ate out and felt a little guilty doing so. But Kelly felt good about her visit with her great-uncle, perhaps because she could check off a family obligation, or perhaps because she knew she would truly miss him, or at least his memory when he was gone.

They did not stay out late as she needed to prepare for an interview at the mill the next morning.

Once home they sat in the kitchen while her grandmother made a pot of tea.

"You know I still have several boxes of your mother's things in the basement," said her grandmother. "I meant to go through them after the funeral but forgot all about it. It's really all yours now – since you have time now you should take a look. You might find things in there you want to keep."

Kelly dreaded the idea of going through her mother's possessions. In part, because she had streamlined her own life when she went into the military and now lived by the adage "less is more." Traveling light brought with it freedom. But she also didn't want to revisit the old Métis culture; she had burned that bridge once—a source of conflict with her mother—and did not want to stir those memories again.

Her mother had always encouraged her children to embrace their Métis culture, to be proud of their heritage. And so Kelly knew there were trunks of old clothes and costumes and a variety of colorful sashes and tops decorated with beadwork and quills. Her mother had even kept an old saddle. Although Marie Moreau had never owned a horse or used the saddle, she always kept it oiled and maintained it to be ready for use again.

The story handed down through the family was that the saddle had been hand-made by one of her great grandparents out of bison leather, possibly even used during the Battle of Batoche. Another version had it coming from Kelly's father who wanted his children to have it. At one point in Métis history, horses, specifically bison hunting horses, had been the most important possession a man could own. While other horses and oxen could be used for labor, the agile hunting horses were the key to the Métis bison harvest, which defined the early Métis culture.

Kelly assumed somewhere in her mother's boxes she would also find the moccasins. Of all her keepsakes these had been her mother's prized possession, two pairs of intricately beaded moccasins. They didn't fit anyone now—one pair too small and the other too big—but like the saddle, they had been handed down through generations of her family. How they came into her mother's possession was unclear, but they couldn't have found a better home; she cherished them. Now they were Kelly's, or Jamie's if he wanted them.

Kelly had no use now for sashes or dancing costumes or the moccasins. She had never danced like Jamie or her cousins and she couldn't play an instrument or dance a Scottish Reel if her life depended on it. And she wasn't about to begin now.

It had been a long day, and she was tired and her foot ached. She kissed her grandmother goodnight and gingerly made her way up the stairs to her bedroom. As she fell asleep, she puzzled over the comments Uncle Rodney had made. Why would he send her away? Or was he trying to say something else? She knew he and her mother had always been close. She also knew with her grandfather gone once Rodney passed away much of their family history would be gone forever. And although she couldn't say precisely why, she knew it would be a significant loss for her family, a break in the link which had bound her generation to its very origins, good and bad.

***

She arrived at the lumber mill office in Bottineau fifteen minutes early for her job interview. The yard was clean and well organized and smelled of sweet wet pine. The yard manager was a pleasant older man in his late 60s, thin and balding. She could tell he liked his work.

"So Kelly, you're a friend of Jay's?" he asked.

"Yes sir."

"Just out of the service?"

"Yes sir."

"Honorable Discharge?"

"Medical."

"Do you have your DD 214?"

"Right here, sir," she said as she handed over an application and military discharge papers.

"You're out now Kelly—you don't have to call me 'sir'. You can call me Dave."

"Yes...I mean OK. Thanks, Dave."

"Well, we're looking to take on a couple part-time inventory specialists—mostly working with our databases and doing a lot of data entry and number crunching. Doesn't come with any benefits until you pass a three-month probation." He paused and looked closer at the forms. "Says here you were injured. Can you tell me what happened?"

"It was a training accident. I was injured during a live-round session."

"Were you shot?"

"Yes sir, in the ankle."

"Most folks around here know how to handle a gun."

"I was a Drill and Combat Instructor, it was an accidental discharge by one of my trainees. It was really my own fault."

"So you were a Drill Sergeant?"

"A Drill Instructor yes."

"I see, I see," he said, now leaning back in his chair. "I was drafted in 'Nam, Infantry, barely survived the war. Hell, I barely survived Basic Training. I was real glad to get home again, real glad. I never thought I'd ever welcome a North Dakota winter but I'll tell you what, once I got back here I actually hit the ground and kissed the snow I was so damn happy. Got back in the middle of January— thought I'd never see my friends or family again. That damn war. Let me tell you young lady, it's all about family, that's the only thing that kept me going."

He paused. "If you were a Drill Sergeant or Drill Instructor, you must have good attention to detail. And I expect you're not afraid of work. No problem getting to work on time..."

"No sir," said Kelly, interpreting the last statement as a question.

"Well, I'm rambling. The job is yours if you want it. Always happy to help a vet. And I can't see a bum foot will be any problem. Won't be able to fill it for another few weeks or so; we're back-filling for a full-time gal that's going off and getting married on us. Gonna quit work and start a family."

"Thank you, Dave, I really appreciate it. Jay's wife Liz says he really likes working here. I've been looking at a couple different options though, can I think on it a bit?"

"Sure. Listen, you find something better out there—you go for it. We can't compete with the Oil Patch on wages but this is a good place to work, decent hours and we treat our people right. I gotta couple weeks before we need to start training someone in."

She left the interview feeling good but didn't feel she had accomplished much. Then she realized the yardman's crack about her "bum foot" had bothered her. It bothered her a lot. She didn't want to be "the woman with the bum foot". That afternoon when she returned to her grandmother's house she fixed a sandwich for a late lunch and then asked where her mother's boxes were.

37

Mad Grass

It was time to move on.

Chapter 4

He turned the big "King Ranch Edition" diesel pickup into the lot and parked between a Honda CRV with Montana plates and a gleaming black Suburban which had never seen a gravel road. A sign at the front of the lot said, "Two Hour Parking—Historical Society Visitors Only".

Carl Spoon was big, six feet tall, fleshy at 260 pounds, with a protruding gut on which you could balance a beer mug. He wore a faded light purple dress shirt with an open collar and buttons which threatened to snap off with the slightest exertion. Brown poly slacks were hitched with a black belt, hidden somewhere under his girth.

He was in Bismarck on county business, the annual meeting of North Dakota County Commissioners, held the third week of April every year. As the senior commissioner for Goodview County, he had the first choice on which meetings he would attend. Bismarck was always a good trip on the county's dime.

This year Carl was multi-tasking—he needed to talk to these State Historical people about his special project back home. They had broken early from the commissioners' meeting so he set up a meeting with one of the Society's reps.

He walked in, took off his Stetson, and approached the receptionist. "I got a meeting with a Professor Williams."

"Oh yes," she replied knowingly. "Would you please sign in?" she said, pushing a clipboard over the counter toward him. He signed, checked the time, and then looked at her again with eyebrows raised in expectation.

"Just follow this hallway down and to the left," she instructed, pointing down the hall. "Turn right by the Archives and you'll see his office next to the lab." He did as instructed, gazing at the extensive historical displays with envy as he worked his way down the hall. "*Lot of money in Bismarck*," he thought to himself. "*Getting to be a regular big city*."

Sakakawea, the young Shoshone woman who had guided Lewis and Clark on their expedition in 1804 was a prominent feature in many exhibits. In some displays she carried her infant son "Pomp" on her back; in others, they showed her with her French-Canadian husband Toussaint Charbonneau or the explorers Lewis and Clark. Even Spoon had to admit she must have been one tough woman.

Williams was seated at his desk, white shirt and tie, head down, reading a stack of papers when Spoon knocked on his open door. "Professor Williams?"

"Yes, and you must be Mr. Spoon," he said rising in his chair and holding out his hand. His handshake was firm. "Please, have a seat." Spoon sat in the only chair in the office not already occupied by a stack of papers.

"Thanks for meeting me on such short notice," began Spoon.

"No problem, always glad to help when we can. Now you were interested in the site of a potential Native American conflict in McLean County?"

"No, I'm with Goodview County, been a County Commissioner up there for 12 years now. But yeah our county people want to confirm some of the historical events which took place in our area."

"Do these involve construction at all?" asked Williams. "Because we'd have to schedule site surveys if they did."

"No, no," lied Spoon. "Nothing like that—we were going to put up some signs and interpol...intraprol..."

"Interpretation?"

"Yeah, that's it, interpretation, to explain what happened and things of that nature," he replied.

"Yes, there was quite a bit of activity in the McLean County area or the area which would later become McLean and Goodview counties," explained Williams. "One of our researchers Kari Miller did an extensive literature search of those activities about five years ago and documented sporadic conflicts between Native tribes, settlers, and the military beginning in the early 1800s through about 1880."

"We think our Goodview area might have also included a battle with the Sioux and the Métis Indians against the white settlers," said Spoon helpfully.

"Are you near the Dog Den Butte then? That butte served as a landmark and source of conflict for nearly 10,000 years. Many different indigenous people have occupied the area since prehistoric times—the Sioux, the Arikara or Ree, the Mandan, Hidatsa, the Assiniboines, Saulteaux, and so on. The Métis were more recent visitors to the area."

"Well, we're located quite a ways east of Dog Den, but I suppose it was all one big open frontier back then."

Williams continued. "Yes, before the military presence the Dakota Sioux controlled much of the area between Fort Totten, near present-day Devil's Lake, and Fort Stevenson, to the west on the Missouri. You mentioned the Métis. Ms. Miller's research indicates they made annual summer forays south from Canada to the Dog Den Butte area, east of the Mouse or Souris River, on bison hunts. These hunts took place in the 1840s through 1860s, at which time the US Military established a presence and largely put an end to the Sioux attacks

41

through the use of treaty and force as necessary. And of course, the bison were nearly eliminated."

"But the hunts might have taken place near present Goodview County too?" asked Spoon.

"Certainly, there were skirmishes everywhere along the Totten Trail, which ran east to west in that area. Travelers along the Trail were subject to constant attack from the Sioux, especially near the Dog Den Butte, which even the military avoided. But I'm afraid it's highly unlikely the Métis were involved in any attack on white settlers."

"Why's that?" asked Spoon.

"The Métis are a mixed race of European heritage, primarily French, and Cree Indian. They were often targets of Sioux attacks themselves as they pursued bison on their annual hunts. They may have been aligned with the Cree and Saulteaux, but not the Sioux."

"But they were half Indian right?" said Spoon.

"They were, and are, a mixed race of European and Native American heritage, that's correct."

Williams sat back in his chair now and considered Spoon—county representatives rarely engaged the State Historical Society unless forced to do so. He guessed there was another motive at work here. He also knew it was common practice to re-bury and conceal any old gravesites or remains uncovered on county road and construction projects—nobody wanted the added delays and expense which came with the documentation and preservation of history, leastwise a County Commissioner on a limited budget.

And Goodview County had a reputation statewide for harboring some of the last hard-boiled, tight-fisted pioneer families hailing from Russia's Black Sea and Volga River regions. Williams knew

Spoon already had the answers he wanted and didn't want to be confused by facts. Still, his job was to educate and preserve, so he would try.

"North Dakota was the site of many conflicts before statehood, much of it caused by the bison, or the lack thereof," Williams explained. "The government policy during that time was to eliminate the bison—once the bison were gone the Natives could not survive—at least that was the premise. But it worked, quite well actually. And with no bison for food and shelter the Native Americans on the Northern Plains, hostile and otherwise, were forced to turn to the government for support. One can imagine the Sioux, whose lifestyle totally depended on the bison, would resist. And so they were a hostile presence in the area for many years. Remember, many of those involved were actually fighting for their very survival." He paused to see if Spoon was following.

"The Sioux would attack any individual or small group which traveled in the area. They roamed the plains as predators, showing no mercy to their victims—which included white traders and settlers, Natives from other tribes as well as members of the military. After slaying their opponents they would frequently dismember their victims, and at times remove their heads, hands, or feet as trophies during conflicts. This was documented by the military outposts of the day. Of course, in many cases the Sioux just stole horses, mules or cattle, or counted coup," added Williams. "It didn't always end in violence."

"Counted coup?" asked Spoon.

"Counting coup would be—how would you explain it—a case where they merely struck their opponent and escaped, without killing them," he explained. "It was a matter of great honor or pride. But when they did kill, it seemed to be...overkill...if you will. Violence for the sake of violence. Appalling."

"When did all this happen?" asked Spoon.

"With the Sioux? I believe it was in the early to late 1850s" he replied. "I can find more precise dates if you need them."

"No, that's alright," said Spoon. He knew it was time to extract himself before Williams took an additional interest in their plans. "Well you've been a big help," Spoon began, planting his big hand on the desk in an effort to rise. "Would you mind if we ran some of our signs and interpretations by you before we have them made up?"

"No, that would be fine," replied Williams, producing a business card from his desk drawer. "If you'd like you can send us the text or any maps on e-mail and we could look them over and save you another trip down."

"That'd be great," Spoon said, accepting the card, then standing and shaking Williams' hand. "Thanks a lot Professor, we really appreciate it."

It was all Spoon needed; scattered skirmishes, Indians, or half-Indians, and brave settlers, conflict on the prairie. It was all good. Wasn't all of history just an educated guess anyway?

Instead of exiting the building Spoon now walked over to the State Archives. Had he missed anything? He wasn't much of a computer person, but he could paw through old newspapers and documents with the best of them.

"You'll need to sign in and leave your coat and hat here," directed the young male clerk. Spoon did so and asked where to find historical newspapers and documents related to specific counties. The clerk walked him over to a row of cabinets filled with microfilm.

"Which county?"

"Goodview," replied Spoon. The clerk opened a large flat drawer and motioned to a collection of microfilm rolls.

"It'll be these, from here to here," he announced, with a sweep of his hand.

"Thanks," replied Spoon, looking over the dates of the rolls. He selected two and then sat at a nearby microfiche machine and struggled to get the roll threaded on correctly with his stubby fingers. He finally got a roll started and began to go through it.

Three hours and four microfilm rolls later he was satisfied he had found what there was to find. And he was pleased with the result of his research. Any good lie starts with a grain of truth. "*We can make it work*," he thought.

He left the building and went back to his truck. He was tired, and in no mood to sit at the hotel bar with a group of commissioners who had gathered there. Instead, he waved and continued up to his room. Once in his room, he began making calls back home. "Listen, Royal, we can make this work..."

Carl Spoon had been raised on a small dairy farm in Goodview County with his parents, two sisters and a brother. He still had memories of hauling milk pails through the barn and pouring them into the large stainless steel bulk tank ("don't you spill one drop, that's money you're pouring boy"), pitching hay down from the loft with a fork, and shooting rats with their old single-shot Mossberg .22 rifle as they scampered around the granary. Milking was hard work, with chores each morning before school and each evening after school. Over time it was a business model which couldn't be sustained; with fewer and fewer creameries and larger and larger dairy farms, his family's small farm with 35 milkers would never get ahead.

There were positive aspects of course—they always had plenty to eat, with farm products supplemented by fish and game procured locally. And they had good schools. He had attended Goodview schools all the way through high school. No college, but he guessed he made out okay.

While the farm still existed, the dairy business was long gone, along with his siblings; his sisters had escaped to Chicago and Minneapolis, his younger brother to Denver. They all had good jobs, and families now. Carl had married his sweetheart from down the road and now they lived in the house he grew up in. He ran a small feedlot two miles down the road—buying steers, feeding them up and then selling them on contract to an outfit out of Napoleon, North Dakota, owned by somebody in Omaha. He also owned the used car lot in town. And he was a County Commissioner, which meant phone calls at all hours, lots of meetings and health insurance coverage paid for by the county. His wife didn't work but kept the books for both businesses.

He saw what was happening to the county—kids leaving, businesses rolling up, and disappearing overnight. And the brass in Bismarck and Fargo thinking they ran the whole state. He was going to show them, and those pansies in Medora too. Soon, there'd be no reason to travel west; Goodview was going to be the new "must-see" destination. Golf, history, cowboys, Indians, a big "shoot 'em up," real artifacts. Plus, used cars. They would come from Fargo, the Twin Cities, and Chicago. Medora could stick their "pitchfork fondue" up their ass—Goodview was three hours closer than Medora and was going to be just as much fun.

It irked him every time he drove past Casselton on Interstate 94. "Home of Five North Dakota Governors," said the billboard. Goodview County had contributed just one, back during the Eisenhower Administration. "We're going to change that," Spoon said aloud.

He made all his calls, ordered a $14 corned beef sandwich and an $8 bottle of beer from Room Service for supper…and went to sleep with a smile on his face. This was going to work, and they would have Carl Spoon to thank for it.

Chapter 5

There were three boxes in all; one file folder box full of papers, a plastic bin with a snap-on lid, and a battered shoebox that had originally contained a pair of size 10 men's brown wingtip shoes. Two faded red rubber bands now brittle with age held the shoebox and lid together.

"I don't know what's in there," said her grandmother. "I donated most of your mother's clothes and shoes to the Goodwill in Bottineau after the funeral. The rest of it I just boxed up and put down there on the shelf. I know there's a lot of papers, but I didn't go through much—there wasn't any life insurance and of course no pension or anything like that. As for the medical bills, I threw those out after a year or so."

"Well, I'll go through it and get rid of what I can," said Kelly.

"Jamie's old saddle and the decorated saddle are up in the garage loft," her grandmother continued. "I gave a lot of the dancing costumes and clothing to Cherie—her kids still dance. You didn't want those did you?" she asked hesitantly.

"No Grandma."

"I asked Jamie and he said he didn't want them either."

"That sounds fine," Kelly assured her.

She went through the plastic bin first. It held packets of photos—baby photos of herself and her brother, a school photo of her in grade school missing her front teeth, several photos of Jamie in his full dance regalia, he must have been about eight or 10 years old, and high school graduation photos of them both. She could not believe she ever looked so young. There were several photos of them with their father, a thin, handsome man; one during winter, maybe Christmas, and a couple at birthday parties with cakes in the background. The last photo in the stack was her mother's own high school graduation picture. She looked so young. So much promise.

Kelly next pulled out a long roll of dirty blue felt and unrolled it to reveal a Métis flag with a white infinity symbol, like a sideways "8" on the blue background. She had seen this flag before—her mother explained that the symbol represented the belief that the Métis culture would live on forever. Kelly carefully rolled it back up again and set it aside. Also rolled up were three wide sashes, two red and one blue. She re-rolled and also set these aside.

Four dance competition posters were plastered against the side of the bin. She recognized these as competitions that Jamie must have attended. His old dance group was advertised as one of the groups attending the competitions. They really had been very good.

At the bottom of the bin was a pair of small, well-worn mukluks, probably for a child or small girl. Maybe they were her mother's? The tops of the mukluks flopped over, but the leather soles appeared to be in good shape. Why would her mother have kept these? Had Kelly or Jamie worn them as a child?

She turned to the file folder box next. One file held birth certificates for her brother and herself along with vaccination records. Another folder held old purchase documents for a house and a parcel of land. Kelly could only remember living in this house, with her mother and grandmother, and did not know her parents had owned another home. Old bank records from long-closed accounts filled another folder. These had her father's social security number on them, so she set the folder aside to burn later. Other files held old tax records going back 10 years. These she would also burn. Another folder was marked "Appliance Warranties" but was empty.

Near the bottom of the box, she came to a worn yellow 9" X 12" clasp envelope. It felt thick with documents. She opened the clasp and found several smaller envelopes and a stack of folded papers held together by a large paperclip. She found one of the envelopes addressed to her mother at the old house. It was from her Uncle Rodney. Inside was an old faded blue mimeograph map of the State of North Dakota and another of southern Manitoba. Some handwritten notes written in pencil on the maps were too faded now to read. They may have been names or locations. Was this a vacation map of some kind?

The larger envelope contained a second, and larger map, folded twice over—this showing "Dakota Territory" rather than the state of North Dakota. But this map was not notated. A third large and folded map showed southern Manitoba with the towns of Batoche, Duck Lake and Fort Union circled. This map contained notes and dates, referencing a battle of some kind. It was all very cryptic.

She had no idea why her mother would collect maps or save these old versions.

At the very bottom of the file box was a small clutch of envelopes, all unopened and bound by a single rubber band. She undid the stack and slowly flipped through them. The postmarks were all from the year her mother had died. Two were from car insurance companies, one was a utility bill of some kind, one was for replacement house siding, one was a rebate offer on a new car purchase and two others were from doctor's offices. The last two were returned "Undeliverable" by the post office. One was addressed to "Rodney Savard." And one was addressed to her.

Her heart leaped when she saw the envelope addressed to her old Marine FPO address. She had not served at that address for over four years.

She knew by the date the letter had been written just before her mother had passed away. Her mother rarely wrote anything, having spoken Mechif most of her life and having little use for the written word. The words were scrawled out in long-hand cursive, which crept up the page as it was written.

> *"Kelly: You know how verry proud I am of you. You are Marines! It is important that you do not forget you are also Métis. I know I (illegible) away but I hope you know it was best – I hope you lern many new and wonder full things in the service. I know you will meet many new peepal. I hope you return to someday to our countree, here or in Canada. There are peepal who love you and want only the best for you. And I know you will do well, what ever choice.*
>
> *The docters say this desese will kill me, but I do not want you to wory. I have peepal who love me to. I have to favors to ask – first, take care of Jamie. I feer he is on a wrong trale wich leads to no good. Next, plese talk to your Uncle Rodney, he and your Grandpa know things about Métis you shood know to."*

She signed it "Love, Marie."

The call came in shortly after 11:00 p.m. that night. It woke Kelly who then heard her grandmother's muffled voice downstairs as she spoke into the receiver. Several minutes passed with her grandmother just responding, "Yes, uh-huh, okay." Then she heard her ask, "How much?"

She knew it was trouble when her grandmother called up the stairs, "Kelly."

It was nearly a three-hour drive to Williston. Kelly left at 5:00 a.m. and arrived at the Sheriff's office just after 8:00. She talked to the clerk, paid the bail, and waited by a side door for her brother to appear.

He was taller than she remembered, or maybe just thinner. He had let his black hair go long and now it hung halfway to his waist. His father's Cree features had won the genetic contest held within her mother's womb; Jamie would have looked right at home around the fire at a Cree fish camp 200 years ago. He carried an old green army surplus coat balled up under his left arm.

"Hiya Sis," he said cordially, although they had not seen each other since her mother's funeral nearly three years earlier.

"Jamie," she replied in recognition. "Let's get out of here."

They got in the truck and Kelly turned it east toward home.

"I need some cigarettes," he said.

"I thought you were living by Bottineau," said Kelly, ignoring the request.

"Was, but my girlfriend kicked me out," he replied, staring out the side window.

"So, what were you doing in Williston?"

"Trying to make some money."

"How?"

"There's a lot of money in the Patch."

"What's that mean? Jesus Jamie, are you dealing?"

"No," he replied emphatically, looking at her now. "No, not that."

"Then what are you doing?" she demanded.

"Just moving stuff around, making deliveries, things like that."

"And what were you busted for?"

"Possession."

Kelly sighed heavily in disgust. "Can you drive? I've been on the road since five o'clock this morning."

"No, I kinda lost my license last year."

"Kinda lost it or did lose it?"

"Lost it."

"Jesus, you know you're a real piece of work."

"Nice to see you too Sis," he replied, then pulled down the brim of his ball cap and went to sleep.

Chapter 6

Elisa Ferguson was her mother's first-born; impetuous, adventurous, and impatient in her pursuit of what her life would become. The blinders of youth had convinced her of one thing: The future was her friend.

She was quick with a smile or a pun, loved her mother and Daddy, was delighted in her young paint mare Sophie and served as best friend to her young sister Sylvie. Elisa was also an undisputed beauty, nearly 16, with a blush of face and figure which promised to all who might notice the pending arrival of a full-grown woman.

And Jean-Luc noticed, taking a keen interest in how her shawls and loose skirts of cotton failed to camouflage the molding of her bosoms and hips, images which even now formed the cornerstones of his dreams. Her cruel, selfish, wonderful smile, with lips of dark ruby, cut like a lance quick and sure, painless by its keen edge. Her blue eyes, colored as the prairie pasque flower, bore gently but surely into his very soul.

They had danced, the third night out, the whole camp danced and shouted and burst out with yelps and unrestrained peals of laughter. This was in the time of easy travel, before the shooting and killing, before the heavy butchering and cutting and lugging slabs of meat, before night watchmen were posted and point riders scanned the horizon for danger. This was before the hunt, a happy time—a time of anticipation. Henri and Guy and Jerome had loosened their fiddles and squeezebox to good effect, the sharp notes and low moans of the instruments saturating the camp and skittering across the prairie, to perplex the wolves, who sat atop nearby hills with ears and heads cocked in astonishment.

Jean-Luc danced too, if not well then with enthusiasm—with kicks and spins and the easy bounds of a spring colt. Then he was dancing with little Sylvie, just 10, whose wide-open smile of delight and happy shrieks as they twirled in the warm prairie night offered a thin promise of happy, sunny days forever. Now Elisa was there in blue calico and her hands were in his and they were soft and warm and moist and he knew then he would harvest the glowing moon, lace it with a garland of coneflower and place it at her feet if only to feel her soft bosom against his chest and the taste of those ruby lips.

This first was a chaste dance, but it was celebrated by the old men who recognized bits of their own sap rising in the loins of the young hunter. It was observed keenly too by the women, who traded gossip across camps as a commodity like beads or pelts. Grace Snow observed from her post by the cook wagon, watching the antics of Jean-Luc and Elisa closely, wishing she too could dance with the young hunter, so full of life. Unconsciously she pulled her arms to her chest and felt their warmth.

Denis Granger observed the festivities from beyond the light of the big fire. It was cooler here and the warmth of the prairie soil mixed with the growing dew, surrounding him in a bouquet of wet sage. Although hunt leader, Granger enjoyed the music and clapping and dance as much as anyone. The Métis penchant for labor must be leavened by play.

He knew the hard work ahead, hard backbreaking work, as did any hunter who had made the trip before. It was not without danger, so any chance at relief was welcomed, now before the hunt, and later, once they safely neared their home country along Canada's border again.

The squeaks and moans of the instruments brought a smile to his face as he watched the Métis and Saulteaux dancers whirl and stomp in their heavy boots and moccasins—this was a good group of men, with strong women. The Métis musicians were earnest if not talented—their early reel renditions were tentative but with the Duck Dance they found their level and then leaned into the Red River Jig with whoops of their own.

He was glad to lead them. They had already demonstrated they could work as a team by getting the oxcarts, hunting horses and pack animals hundreds of miles into unfamiliar territory. This same teamwork would now be critical to their success and safety. Each hunter and helper had a role, and each depended on the other.

The Métis hunted strategically, approaching each bison herd abreast of each other in long lines to maximize the point of contact between hunters and animals—at least until the herd broke into a run; then each hunter was able to shoot freely. Their goal was to kill the younger animals only—two to four-year-old cows—for their sweet, tender meat and soft hides.

In one good morning drive each hunter might drop six or eight animals. Many more could be taken in a day, but one family would have to work quickly to butcher more than eight or 10 animals before darkness overtook them. They generally passed on bulls, rutted up and rank tasting, with hide and hair so coarse it was worthless except for belts and ropes and such. And because they represented the future generation and future hunts, calves and yearlings were not harvested. Occasionally these young animals were trampled by the herd or the hunter's horses—these were brought in for camp meat, fodder for another feast of whole roasted calf.

The bison's loping gait was no match for the quick Métis horses; soon after the signal was given the hunters would race forward and the prairie would be filled with the low rumble of 10,000 hooves or more, then the roar of gunfire, billows of white smoke, and the whoops of the hunters shooting at will. As the balls and bullets punched forward the bison would bellow and roar and swirl and roll before collapsing heavily on the prairie, at times taking horse and rider down with them. It was a dusty, unpredictable melee conducted on uneven terrain—injuries were frequent, and few hunters survived the two-month hunting season without an assortment of bruises, concussions and broken bones to show for it.

Following the drive, which might last for a mile or more before the horses gave out or the bison scattered, the job of skinning and butchering the animals began, their carcasses throwing off heat and stink and steam in the cool morning air. It was an all-day affair, involving all family members as the animals were rolled onto their stomachs, skinned, deboned and the choice cuts of meat and hides loaded into carts for transport back to camp. A large bison might fill an entire cart, so a good day required multiple trips.

Once back at camp the work of preparing the meat began, or continued, as each family was processing multiple animals at any one time. Thin strips of meat were dried and cured in the hot wind and sun or over fires, then pulverized and stored in sacks made of hide for transport. This would later be mixed with fat and berries and formed into pemmican cakes, which would be sold along the Canadian frontier as a winter staple. It could be kept for years without spoiling if necessary. It took two to three days for the camp to process all the meat from one drive, assuming the northern prairie sun stayed high and the wind steady. Rainy days were days of rest.

Granger sipped from his cup and smiled again as he watched young Savard twirl the Ferguson girl. Savard was a good young man, would be a good hunter. Both came from good families. He didn't know how many more generations of Métis would follow the bison, but he knew the future was now in their hands. Strong and smart and sure—he was confident they would do well.

***

Jean-Luc struggled with his emotions. Father LeSueur's words offered much hope, much direction…but little comfort to a young man finding his way in the world. Could these feelings for Elisa be wrong? They felt as natural as the ripening of the Saskatoon berry or the creep of frost in the fall; timeless, inevitable, unstoppable.

As he lay in his bedroll each evening his only respite was to focus again on the hunt, visualizing the preparation of the powder and ball and weapons, the prayer as hunters knelt on the prairie with bowed head before each drive, and the skittishness of the hunting horses as their own anticipation rose.

He had two hunting horses along with old Cheri and her cart. His saddle, made of old bull hide stuffed with hair and fitted with wooden stirrups, had served him well for two years. At one time it had been his father's saddle—his mother had decorated it once with blue and white beadwork along the edging. Now it was stained rusty brown with bloodstains and worn smooth...but comfortable and cushioned in just the right places for the jolting ride across the prairie.

The Catholic Métis did not hunt or work on Sundays, keeping the day open for religious services and a day of rest and reflection. Jean-Luc looked forward to Sundays, but he could hardly rest or concentrate—this Ferguson girl was such a fine creature and potent catalyst to newly-awakened desires, a gift he held and turned over and over in his mind. And she was right here, right here in his camp; often asleep only a few strides away! It was almost too much to bear.

He always made an effort to talk to her after Sunday Services, cleaning himself as much as one young man could with a cake of lye soap and bucket of creek water. Elisa liked that he washed himself and combed his hair. Nor did she mind that he could not entirely remove the bison blood from beneath his nails—she was beset with the same problem. If you were Métis, you handled meat. He smelled good too or at least did not smell bad. A hint of chamomile?

Some hunters rarely bathed for weeks while on the hunt, counting on occasional creek crossings as their toilette. She wondered if Jean-Luc obtained lotion or cleansing salts from his friend Paquet, who always seemed clean despite his cooking duties.

She looked forward to his conversations following church services and their chance encounters at supper and the evening fires. She thought him handsome and felt both embarrassed and flattered at his attentions. Sylvie teased her about this earnest young man who took advantage of every opportunity to be in her presence. Her mother just smiled knowingly.

Once, after a long day moving south into a stiff south wind, a wind-burned and trail-worn Jean-Luc had rushed to her after the camp supper and presented her with a gift from the prairie—a large, weather-polished, purple agate. The size and shape of a summer plum, it was a beautiful stone laced with delicate lines and smooth clear surfaces of deep purple, crimson and white on three sides. She thanked him for the stone, a rare find on the prairie.

She liked this young man even more, and she began to think about where his kindness might lead.

Chapter 7

Jamie went directly to his old room when they got home and continued to sleep. Kelly was certain he was coming off some kind of bender or high. He had been released from court-ordered rehab three weeks earlier—his second stint—and had been kicked out of his girlfriend's apartment after she discovered him still using. Somehow he had hitched a ride to Williston and gotten hooked up again.

Kelly was angry at Jamie and had no intention of helping him clean up another of his messes. If it weren't for her grandmother she would have let him hitchhike back home. While he slept Kelly tried to focus again on the contents of her mother's boxes and the letters which had been undeliverable.

"Grandma, those letters indicate that Grandpa and Uncle Rodney...and my Mom...were looking for something. Do you know what was going on?"

"I really don't know Kelly but I can tell you your mother was always curious. When she was younger she liked to travel everywhere—it didn't really matter where she just liked to travel and meet new people. It stopped of course once she met your father and you two came along, but she was always fascinated by the stories your grandpa and uncle would tell about the old days."

"Did she ever go to Batoche?'

"Oh yes, several times. We went as a family back when your mother was young and I know she went by herself or with friends later at least a couple times. You know your grandpa never forgave the Canadian government for what they did there. He was bitter until the day he died." She shook her head, "Such bitterness. It's not healthy, you have to come to terms with it or it will eat you up."

59

"So she had visited the site of the Batoche Battle?"

"Yes, as I said."

"How about here in North Dakota, did she travel here?"

"Of course, she went to Minot all the time and Fargo many times—she wasn't a homebody. I know she also visited Mount Rushmore in South Dakota and traveled to the Twin Cities now and then. Your mother liked to travel."

"Her note said I needed to talk to Uncle Rodney about something. Do you know what that might be?"

"No, maybe they were planning another trip or something. What else did you find?" asked her grandmother.

"Mostly just junk, just stuff she collected," replied Kelly. "Some pins, a hair ribbon, dried flowers...an old broach. Some coins, some stones, and a flint arrowhead."

Her grandmother glanced at her and then pursed her lips slightly. Kelly could tell she was considering her next statement, something she was reluctant to reveal.

"Did you find a stone...the special stone?" she asked hesitantly.

"The special stone?" repeated Kelly. "What kind of stone?"

"Your grandfather carried around a stone for years in his pocket. Called it his "lucky" rock. He claims it came from his grandfather's mother. A real family hand-me-down. Too bad it wasn't gold—it might have actually helped us out. But it wasn't, it was just a stone. It had something to do with this big mystery; sometimes Uncle Rodney would just ask to see it. It wouldn't surprise me if it ended up with your mother."

"What did it look like," asked Kelly, remembering several stones in her mother's shoe box.

"It was actually quite beautiful. I can see it now as clearly as if I were holding it in my hand—it was purple and blue with beautiful lines, an agate. They call them Lake Superior agates. How it got here I don't know. Could be some Saulteaux from the east brought it for trade. I just remember it was quite pretty."

"Why was it special?"

"Kelly, your guess is as good as mine. And I guess that is literally a secret your grandfather or mother took to the grave. I think our family history is very important, and I admire your grandfather and Uncle Rodney for trying to find it again, and keep our history alive, but really, all this energy rehashing old conflicts or searching for lost relatives...I think we just need to move on."

"But Grandma, this could be important," countered Kelly.

"Well, I just don't know anymore. Keep whatever you like and toss the rest unless you think Jamie might want something. I don't need anything. You'll be going through my boxes soon enough."

"I thought you were tougher than that Grandma," teased Kelly.

"All Métis women are tough, and don't you forget it!" she laughed. "Don't forget how we made a living—a good living—on the open prairie living off the land. We fought the blizzards and cold and starvation and we nearly beat the government. And we're still here, which reminds me: Did your mother keep that old Métis flag?"

"Yeah."

"Good, you should keep that—that's us, we'll always be here, just like the flag."

61

Two days later Kelly returned to Bottineau to ask her great uncle about the letters. As she signed in at the desk of the Regions Critical Care center the receptionist looked up and caught her eye.
"Mr. Rodney Savard is getting a lot of visitors lately. Weren't you in a few days ago?"

"Yes I was," she replied. "How is he doing?"

"Not so well. His nurse can give you more information. Here she is now," she said, nodding down the hall.

Kelly turned and saw nurse Cammie walking toward the desk. "Here to see Rodney again?" she asked.

"Yes, is this a good time?"

"He's not too receptive today, but even if he can't see you it's always good for him to hear a familiar voice."

She doubted her voice was familiar to her uncle but saw no reason to argue with the nurse. As she was led once again to Rodney's room she saw a sheet with the bold letters "DNR" slipped into the chart slot outside the door. She thought she knew what it meant but wanted to be sure. "What's that for?" she inquired.

"Family was here yesterday," said the nurse. "They updated Rodney's living will..." she paused. "He has a 'Do Not Resuscitate' order now." She stopped, hoping she would not have to explain further.

"Oh, I see," replied Kelly, nodding knowingly.

"You can go right in. Let me know if you need anything."

Rodney lay in his bed, eyes closed. The IV drip and catheter tubes were still in place. A monitor showed his heart rhythms on the screen. He appeared to be sleeping.

She walked closer to the edge of the bed. "Uncle Rodney?" she said softly. No response. She grasped his hand and held it in hers; he felt warm.

She looked out the window into the parking lot, the sun shone brightly and it was growing into a beautiful spring day. She could wait.

She sat and took a packet of papers from the book bag she had brought with her and went over the faded maps again. From the letter it had been obvious they were searching for something...but what? More importantly, why did Rodney need his mother's help to find it? Now, with her gone, it was a question only he could answer.

Kelly sat with him for half an hour. During that time Rodney did not move other than once gulping for air in his sleep, after which his heart monitor beeped loudly twice and then settled back into its easy rhythm. She told him "goodbye" and let herself out of the room and limped toward the reception area again. Her ankle had stiffened while she sat. The receptionist was on the phone when she arrived at the desk. She waited.

"Yes," said the receptionist into the phone receiver, "we're open for visiting every day until six. Uh-huh...yes...no, flowers are okay but we recommend indoor plants. Okay, okay...we'll see you then." She hung up and looked up cheerfully. "Did you have a good visit?"

"He was sleeping most of the time," Kelly replied.

"Yes, of course. A lot of our residents sleep during the day—they need their naps."

"Did he have company yesterday?"

"Are you family?"

"Yes, I'm his niece."

'Well, I'm not supposed to give out any information except to family, but I guess you qualify. His daughter was here yesterday." She flipped the register back two pages, searched down a column with her finger, and then stopped. "Leona, his daughter Leona."

"Oh, okay thanks."

"You have a good day now," the receptionist offered as Kelly turned for the door.

"Thanks, you too." She had no idea who Leona was.

Her next stop was the Bottineau public library. It was small but modern, with a good selection of books and a small computer lab with four public-use computers. This library was one of several in the Bottineau County library system.

One of the computers was occupied by a homeless man. His clothes were soiled, his hair matted and he reeked of body odor. She moved to an empty computer two down from him and tried to access it but found she needed a password. A librarian noticed her attempts and asked helpfully, "Do you need to get in?"

"Yes, ma'am."

"Do you have a library card?"

"No, ma'am."

"Here then," she said, reaching out with a slip of paper. "Here's a guest code."

Kelly walked over, took the code, returned to the computer, and was able to get right in. "That worked," she said toward the direction of the desk so the librarian could hear.

"Good," she replied.

She wasn't sure where to start so she entered "Battle of Batoche." It refreshed with 76,000 hits. *"The Battle of Batoche in May of 1885 was the decisive battle of the North-West Rebellion, which pitted the Canadian authorities against a force of indigenous and Métis people."*

This history was familiar to her as the battle and the Canadian government's role in it to quash Métis efforts to retain their land in the late 1800s were common fodder for countless discussions between her grandfather and Uncle Rodney. The government suppression was brutal, and it marked the beginning of the end for the Métis culture. Once prosperous farmers and businessmen, their land was taken and they became scattered bands of outlaws, with no place to call home.

They would become squatters and schemers and survivors for nearly a century, living off the land and leveraging their knowledge of the land and their skill as interpreters between a wide variety of Indigenous tribes and the whites.

She dug deeper and found another battle—Fish Creek, in April of 1885, a major victory for the Métis over their Canadian oppressors. *"This made sense,"* she thought. The Canadians, embarrassed by their loss at Fish Creek, would intensify their efforts to punish the Métis in any subsequent conflicts. There was certainly bad blood between the Métis and the Crown. And the Queen was not in the habit of letting rogue elements run roughshod over the Crown's interests.

This really didn't help her solve the mystery of the letters though. What was Rodney looking for? And why involve her mother?

She went through all the maps again. She could only decipher one clear date on the map, 1851, so she typed in "Canada, 1851". Nothing related to Métis. She knew Manitoba had not been established until 1870 but she typed in "Manitoba, 1851."

Nothing. A dead end.

She drove back home and found her grandmother and Jamie in the backyard, planting tomato plants and onions in the garden. Her grandmother was on her knees in the soil while Jamie, clad in a dirty T-shirt and denim shorts, leaned on a hoe handle.

"Who is Leona?" blurted Kelly.

"Glad to see you too Kelly," replied her grandmother with a smile. "Leona is Rodney's daughter. How was Rodney?"

"He slept all the time I was there. Leona put a DNR order on him."

Jamie lit a cigarette and shook the match out. "What's a DNR?"

"It's a 'do not resuscitate' order," said Kelly. "It means if you crash they're not supposed to try to bring you back."

"Harsh!" said Jamie. "Why would anyone do that?"

"It's so they don't bring you back and hook you up to a machine for the rest of your life," said Kelly's grandmother. "I don't know of too many people who would want that, and certainly not Rodney. He would want to die with dignity. There is a man who loved life; he's got nothing to be sorry for, when he's ready to go he should go." She got to her feet and stretched her back.

"You mean like those people who are like…vegetables, like on TV, they're vegetables for years?" asked Jamie.

"Yes," said Kelly. "It's called a 'persistent vegetative state,' their body is alive but their brain is dead."

Her grandmother straightened and shook her finger at both of them, "Listen you two, don't you ever let me be that way—you pull the plug when I'm that far gone. You leave me in a coma I swear on your mother's grave I'll come back to haunt you. You hear!"

"Got it, Grandma," replied Kelly coolly.

"Yeah, I don't want to be a vegetable either," said Jamie.

"I had to fill out a living will in the Marines," Kelly offered. "It's in with my papers in my room now. But I said if I was deployed, I wanted them to do whatever they needed to keep me alive and get me back to the United States. After that 'no extraordinary measures.' Just let me go."

"So you wanted to die here?" asked Jamie, now intrigued.

"Yeah, I think it would be terrible to be killed and then buried in some foreign soil...forgotten. All those poor soldiers at Normandy from World War Two, that's just terrible."

There was a pause in the discussion. "So who's Leona again?" asked Kelly.

"You know Leona dear, she's Rodney's daughter. She used to play with you when you were a child. Don't you remember?"

"No," replied Kelly, then turning to Jamie asked, "Do you remember her?"

"Nope."

Kelly continued. "Well, she visited Rodney and must have talked to them about his Medical Directive or found the living will or something. How come we don't know her Grandma?"

"They've lived in Billings for years—I haven't seen her myself in a long while. I don't believe she and Rodney saw eye to eye on too many things. They didn't come to your mother's funeral but they were at Grandpa's. She's married to some government man—works for county extension or something. They had a couple kids but the kids moved to the West Coast, Oregon I believe. I still get Christmas cards from them."

It bothered Kelly that she couldn't remember Leona, and she wasn't sure where she fit in the family.

"So Grandma, would she be my aunt or some kind of cousin? I'm confused."

"She's neither Kelly," replied her grandmother. "Your grandfather and Rodney were best friends growing up, but Rodney is not related to us by blood. I thought you knew that."

"Then why do we call him Uncle Rodney?" asked Jamie.

"Well, he's close enough to the family to be like an uncle, but his family and ours are just good friends. Does it really make a difference?"

Jamie considered the question for a moment, "No, I guess not."

"All the Métis are probably related," her grandmother continued, "we have relatives from coast to coast, and I'm sure we still have relatives in England and France."

"Related to everyone but no place to call home," said Kelly derisively.

"This is home now dear."

"I guess so. I'd like to talk to Leona about Rodney. Do you have a phone number or address for her?"

"I believe I have both."

Later that evening, Kelly spread her mother's letters, notes, and maps from the file box out on the kitchen table and then called a number in Billings, Montana.

"Hello?" answered a man's voice on the line.

"Hello, this is Kelly Moreau, calling for Leona, is she available?"

"Just a minute."

"Hello?"

"Hi Leona, this is Kelly Moreau calling from Metigoshe in North Dakota, do you have some time to talk."

"Yes, I suppose, who did you say you were again?"

"Kelly Moreau."

"Marie's daughter?"

"Yes."

"Oh Kelly, yes, now I remember you. I was so sorry to hear of your mother's passing. We weren't able to make the funeral, but it was terrible she died so young."

"Thank you."

"Aren't you in the Army?"

"I was in the Marines, but I was recently discharged."

"And so...are you back living in North Dakota?"

"For now, still trying to figure out what I want to do now that I'm out. I'm staying with my Grandma Maggie. Actually, I'm calling because I went through some of my mother's things and found some items Rodney had given her. I heard you visited him recently at the nursing home."

"Yes, we were just there. I know we should have tried to stop in but it was a long trip and we needed to get back to Billings. We are terrible that way, but Dean no longer likes driving at night...."

"No, that's alright, I understand. Could I ask you a few questions about your Dad?"

"Certainly. It sounds like you visited him too?"

"Yes, I was there this morning."

"How is he?"

"Hanging in there, he was sleeping during my visit."

"Yes, I'm afraid he won't be with us much longer. The doctors say it's just a matter of time before his organs begin to give out. It may be days or possibly a few weeks," she said. "But how can I help you?"

"It looks like he gave my mother some maps, there are references to...to a battle."

"Oh good Lord, now you have those!" Leona exclaimed, laughing.

Kelly's heart sank.

"My father chased that dream for years—trying to find a hidden Métis battleground. He had heard this story from HIS grandparents, who heard it from THEIR grandparents or someone. And somehow he got your mother roped into this too. I actually think your grandfather believed in some of this too, Rodney was very passionate about it. To his credit, I've never known anyone prouder of their Métis heritage than my father."

"So he *was* actually looking for a battlefield. When was that?" asked Kelly.

"Oh, this was 25-30 years ago, but he gave up eventually, got your mother involved somehow and she helped out, but then she gave up eventually too."

"It wasn't the Battle of Batoche?"

"No not Batoche, it might have been the battle of the Duck Pond or something like that. I remember we visited a lot of supposed battlefields when we were kids, sometimes they'd be in some empty farm field or slough, other times there would be markers, but none of them was the 'right' one. One time we drove over 100 miles one way and do you know what we found?"

"No, what?"

"A parking lot! A parking lot of a gas station. I think that's when my mother put her foot down and said 'no more wild goose chases.' Dad refused to tell us exactly what he was looking for; I don't know if he thought it was foolish or what. But he must have told your mother, bless her soul."

"Why would he tell her but not you?"

"He said she was 'a responsible party.' I don't know if that meant I wasn't responsible or what but it didn't bother me—I didn't want anything to do with it."

"Hmm," responded Kelly. "He wasn't responsive this morning, and last week he asked me to leave his room."

"Well, don't take it personally, I don't think he knows what he's saying anymore. Did he give your mother anything other than the maps?"

"There were some letters between the two of them," replied Kelly. "But they didn't say much."

"I know toward the end they were trying to track down a priest, don't ask me why. It was some type of French name, I remember that. My father thought the priest could be important. The year 1851 was important too—I only remember that because I was born in 1951."

"Yes, I see the dates 1851 and what could be 1882, 1884, maybe 1885, but can't see any names on these documents. Most of the writing is faded but I'll take a closer look."

"Well, Kelly, I wish you the best of luck. You can do what you want of course but I'd recommend you just drop this and get on with your life. It's taken up parts of two lifetimes already—my father's and your mother's. Not sure it's worth it." She paused, collecting her thoughts. "I do want to thank you though for checking in on my father. I'm sure he appreciates your visits."

"Well, thank you, Leona, please stop in at my grandma's place next time you're in town. I would love to catch up and chat with you some more."

"We will try Kelly. You say 'Hi' to your grandma for us."

"I will."

Kelly hung up the phone and tried to absorb all the information she had been given. It was clear there was a search, there *was* another Métis battle out there. Winners or losers? She didn't know. But why was her uncle so intent on finding it? And what could her mother possibly have to do with it?

It was time to go thru the documents one more time.

Chapter 8

Despite a penchant for systematic cultural dismemberment, the Catholic missionaries did something right; they documented their travels, their goals and accomplishments, and the number of souls saved and lost along the way.

And despite her discouragement, Leona's information gave Kelly another line of inquiry—who was this mysterious priest, and what did he have to do with the battle? She scoured the maps and notes again—yes, there were several names scattered throughout the papers: Riel, Dumont, Heavy Bear, and LeSueur. She knew Louis Riel to be the famous Métis rebel leader, hanged by the Canadian government in November of 1885 for his role in leading Métis forces at the Battle of Batoche. Dumont had played a similar role at the Battle of Fish Creek. Neither were priests. Heavy Bear sounded like an Indigenous name. That left LeSueur as a possibility.

She decided to ask her grandmother. "Have you ever heard of someone named LeSueur, a Father LeSueur?"

"Well, if he's a priest he's certainly not one from around here. Father Daniels has been at our church for nearly 20 years, and Father Malloy is at All-Saints in town. No, I don't know of any Father LeSueurs. Why do you ask?"

"That name was written in Mom's notes, or Uncle Rodney's notes, whoever wrote them."

"I'm sorry dear," said her grandmother, "it's just not a name I know."

Kelly gassed up the truck and headed to the library in Bottineau again, this time searching "Father LeSueur, Métis, 1851". She could barely believe what appeared on her screen.

> *Report on the Missions of the Diocese of Quebec: An account of an excursion which Father LeSueur made in the summer of 1851 with the Métis on their annual buffalo hunt*

A Father LeSueur had accompanied Métis bison hunters from the parish of St. François Xavier in Manitoba on one of their annual hunting trips. The report, originally in French, had been published in 1853 by the Diocese of Quebec. The document had been digitized, translated, and uploaded in 2012 by the University of Manitoba library in Winnipeg.

In the report, Father LeSueur detailed a long-forgotten Métis battle, the Battle of Grand Coteau. As she quickly reviewed it Kelly realized she was looking at a blow by blow account, with the names of Métis hunters, their location, and the tactics they used during the battle. Was this the battle her uncle had been searching for?

She printed out the 1853 document and sped over to Regions Critical Care. She had to show this to Uncle Rodney. The receptionist recognized her but this time greeted her with a grim smile.

"I'm afraid Rodney isn't doing very well."

"Can I see him?"

"Yes, but he's been unresponsive for the last two days."

"Okay," responded Kelly impatiently, "but I still need to see him."

She went to his room, unaccompanied this time, to find him lying motionless on his bed. She leaned over his torso, motionless except for his shallow measured breaths, "I think I found it Uncle Rodney— I found the battle."

There was no sign he recognized her or heard what she said. But she felt it was important that he know.

She squeezed his hand. No response. "Rodney," she whispered louder. Nothing. Was she too late? Kelly walked back to the reception area. "Can I make a copy?"

"I'm afraid we don't have any copiers for public use," replied the receptionist.

"Please, it's just one page."

"Well, I guess I can copy just a page. Give it to me."

As she left the parking lot Kelly felt both a sense of dread and a spark of excitement; this was real progress. But what had she accomplished? Was this just another old document to add to the other old documents assembled by her mother and uncle? Still, it felt like she was closer, and that her mother and Uncle Rodney were closer, to...something. Something important, and she sensed, larger than any of them.

Rodney passed away in his sleep at 6:07 a.m. the next morning shortly after the nurses' shift change. On his bed stand lay a single sheet of paper, the cover from a report by the Diocese of Quebec: "*An account of an excursion which Father LeSueur made in the summer of 1851 with the Métis on their annual buffalo hunt.*"

Once she got home again Kelly pored over the document. Here were descriptions of the hunters and their families, the dates the group left Manitoba, the dates they met up with the second group of Métis hunters, and the route they took to the bison hunting grounds. Kelly took notes and began to cross-reference the information with the maps and documents she had found with her mother's personal effects.

Slowly the pieces began to fall into place. The group had set out in June of 1851 on their annual bison hunt. A train of wooden ox carts, oxen and draft horses, and a fine band of hunting horses accompanied some 150 Métis on their annual trek. Later, far from the land they called home, they would engage in a desperate battle with the Sioux lasting two days on the open prairie.

She spread the maps before her and considered their potential routes. The battle could have been nearly anywhere in a region which encompassed thousands of square miles. How to narrow it down? This was the same problem Rodney had encountered. And it had taken him a lifetime to run down hunches and clues and old map notations—all for nothing.

She retired to the backyard and sat on the garden bench to clear her head and think. She knew the early Métis operated with great efficiency; their goal would have been to harvest the maximum number of bison in the shortest time. Which meant the closer the better.

The wild card was the bison, which might travel over hundreds of miles in a single season. They would follow the grass. She sipped from a bottle of water and let her mind wander. If she could determine the North Dakota rainfall for a given year she could determine the areas with the best grass and subsequently the areas which would attract the most bison—and attract the Métis hunters. But rainfall maps didn't exist back then—North Dakota wasn't even a state in 1851.

Then she realized she was overthinking the problem—she had all the pieces she needed. This was just a simple orienteering exercise right out of her Marine field training textbooks.

She tore off a clean sheet of paper and began scribbling. By estimating the distance the Métis hunters traveled each day on the trail and projecting this week by week she should be able to determine how many miles they traveled before they reached the site of the battle, at least based on the battle dates of July 12-13. Assuming the basic directions were valid, she drew an arc on one of the maps from her mother's files, anchored by the town of St. François Xavier, just west of Winnipeg. The radius was nearly 150 miles. This was still a large area containing thousands of square miles but certain references to landmarks, creeks, and riverways gave her additional clues. As she looked down at the arc on her map Kelly was certain the battle had been fought somewhere within this sweep of prairie. Now to find it!

Kelly attended Rodney's funeral with her grandmother. She did not own a dress, so she wore her best pair of slacks and one of her two good blouses, black in color. Her injured ankle remained sore and slightly swollen, so she was forced to wear running shoes rather than pumps. The clothes were starting to feel snug on her, an indication that she was getting soft living as a civilian. Her grandmother wore a beige dress with a dark brown scarf. Jamie had begged off, promising he would attend but was getting a ride from a friend.

The funeral was held in Bottineau's only funeral home. It was well-attended, and Kelly visited with her cousins Rene, Cherie, Dylan, and Rose. It was the first time she had seen any of their children, a mix of precocious toddlers, preschoolers, and pre-teens ranging in age from two to 12 years old. They exuded energy and excitement, racing around the legs of the attendees, most not fully understanding the sad nature of funerals but feeding off the stimulation of a large, friendly crowd.

Liz and Jay were there with their two kids, but Kelly recognized few other faces. Seeing them in person, she was surprised to recognize Leona and her husband Dean from her childhood. Dean wore dark slacks and a tan western shirt with a big silver belt buckle. Leona wore a modest blue dress and black pumps. Both had salt and pepper hair.

After the funeral service, the crowd moved to the basement of the facility for a light lunch. Leona saw her across the room and must

77

have recognized her because she came over immediately and embraced her in a big hug.

"Kelly, it's so good to see you again. Thank you for coming and thank you so much for visiting my father when he was ill. I have to admit your call caught me off guard earlier but my…," she held Kelly at arm's length and smiled, "just look at you! You were a little girl the last time I saw you."

Kelly did not embarrass easily but she felt the blood rise in her face. "It's good to see you too Leona. It was a nice service," she offered.

"Yes, it was nice. I'm glad so many people showed up, quite a few made it down from Manitoba and even a few from Saskatchewan. I don't even know some of them, but Dad had a lot of friends."

"Was he the oldest?"

"Oldest what?"

"Was he the oldest still living on your side of the family?"

"I think so," Leona replied. "You know we have so many shirt-tail relatives it's difficult to keep track of them all. He had an older brother that lived in Danbury, Wisconsin—we were always going to visit him when Mom was alive but never did. But I believe he passed some years ago."

"Well, he was always my favorite uncle," offered Kelly, "although Grandma said we were never really related."

"I guess that's true but our families have been so close for many years. You were always like family to us. Your grandfather and my father grew up like brothers. And to hear the stories they would tell—my goodness, they were a wild pair. It seemed they were always getting into trouble."

"Oh yes, I heard the stories."

"But now what about you? I talked to your grandmother and she said you might be settling down here? She also said you had been injured in an accident – are you okay?"

"Yeah, I'm fine, I have a sore ankle right now but it's okay. They put a couple pins in there so now I just need to strengthen it and I'll be good as new," Kelly relayed optimistically.

"Will you be staying in Metigoshe?"

"That depends. I'm looking for work but don't quite know what I want to do yet. I have a couple leads in town here but I'm not ready to get back into it just yet."

"Well, you take your time dear, no need to rush," Leona said, and then leaned in and said quietly. "Now, have you given up on that nonsense with Rodney's letters and maps?"

"Well, they are very interesting," replied Kelly defensively. "And it was something my Mom thought was important."

"That's true, and my father certainly thought they were important," said Leona, "But young women like you— smart, young women— need to look to the future. What's past is past, and I can't see any reason to go back there."

Kelly appreciated her candor but wasn't sure she agreed. "I'm a little surprised to hear you say that," she said. "Aren't there a lot of people, a lot of Métis, who think it's important to know the past, to know where we came from?"

"Ox-carts creaking down the Red River trail, and fighting the government with rocks and sticks and getting scattered across the prairie like wild animals? I grew up hearing all those stories from my father; there's nothing there I care to revisit," replied Leona dismissively. She caught herself then, "Oh these are not things to

79

discuss at a funeral." She reached out her arms and hugged Kelly again. "I need to keep moving but you take care of yourself. I know your father and mother, rest their souls, must be very proud of you."

"Thank you, Leona," Kelly replied and watched as she made her way across the room. She found her grandmother again, who asked if she had seen Jamie.

"No, Grandma I haven't, maybe he's outside having a smoke." By now the crowd had thinned and people began saying their goodbyes.

Kelly searched around the funeral home and grounds, trying to locate her brother. She assumed if he had been dropped off, he would need a ride home. She looked everywhere except the Men's restroom.

"I can't find him, Grandma," she reported. "I guess he never showed up or got a ride home from someone else."

"I worry about that boy," her grandma said. "He stays out all night, sleeps all day. He should be looking for a job. What good is it to sleep all day? That's no good for anyone. He should have been here at Uncle Rodney's funeral. If you can't take time to pay your final respects to someone..."

"He's a grown man now Grandma," interrupted Kelly gently, "eventually he'll figure it out. Don't make his problems yours—he needs to figure this out himself. You can only do so much."

"Oh, maybe you're right, but your mother had such high hopes for him. He used to do so well in school, and she was so proud of his dancing. And he was good! He was really good."

"I know Grandma."

Her ankle throbbed now from standing so long and Kelly wanted to get home and get some pills. They drove home and pulled into the drive just as two men stepped away from the front door of the house. Seeing the truck pull in, they walked down the concrete steps toward the driveway. At the curb, their car, a rusted brown Lincoln four-door sedan, sat parked at high idle and spewed a steady stream of blue exhaust.

"Oh no," muttered her grandmother, placing her hand over her mouth. Kelly looked at her grandmother with alarm.

"What's wrong?"

"It's those men—I think they're looking for Jamie."

"Were they the ones knocking on the door the other day?"

"Yes, they've come several times I didn't want to worry you. I just don't answer the door anymore."

"Oh Grandma, you should have told me," Kelly scolded, then put the truck in park, shut off the ignition, opened her door and stood. "Can I help you?"

"Looking for Jamie," said the smaller of the two men. He was clad in a leather coat and soiled blue jeans despite the warm weather. His face was pinched and sported a handful of wispy whiskers. He reminded her of a weasel.

"Jamie's not here."

"Can you tell us when he'll be back? We're friends of his from rehab."

"No, sorry," replied Kelly with finality.

"Well listen, we got to talk to him."

81

"Does he know what this is about?" asked Kelly. Now her grandmother was standing outside the passenger side door of the truck.

"Oh yeah, he knows," interjected the larger man, whose bare arms and neck were covered with tattoos. "That prick owes us a lot of money."

"Well, like I said he isn't here, and we don't know when he'll be back," replied Kelly. The men walked to the front of the truck but made no effort to leave.

"Then why don't *you* just pay us and we can get out of here?" suggested the smaller man with a sneer.

Kelly knew where this was heading. "Grandma, why don't you go inside, I'll be right in."

"Oh Kelly..."

"No, it's okay, I'll be right in." Her grandmother clutched her purse and walked slowly up the stairs to the house, unlocked the door, and entered. Kelly waited for the door to close fully behind her.

Now she turned to the pair. "Listen, he's not here, we're not paying you anything so I suggest you just leave," she said evenly.

"Not before—," began the Weasel Man.

Improvise, adapt, overcome.

She was ready for this and so leaned forward and launched into them like snot-nosed recruits, "Listen you stupid shits, there's nothing here for you, you understand. Jamie's not here. So you need to leave NOW! And if I catch you here again I'm going to get really angry, and believe me when I say you don't want to see me angry because I can promise it's not going to end well for you."

Her DI voice. All that was missing was the Smokey Bear hat.

The effectiveness of such a threat rises exponentially if composure is maintained, and Kelly hadn't broken a sweat, or eye contact. The pair glanced at each other, then silently walked down the drive to their idling car and got in. The smaller man hit the gas and the old Lincoln lurched forward as the big man gave her the finger out his window. Fifteen seconds later, they were out of sight down the street.

Kelly felt good. She was angry about Jamie, about him bringing his problems to her grandmother's house, but happy with how she handled the incident. It felt good to blow off some steam.

Since becoming a Marine she had rarely felt fear. She had felt it in Afghanistan when she and Kristal Moore were cut off from their squad behind the school…when the shit hit the fan. But they had saved each other's lives that day and taken out three "enemy combatants" in the process. Kristal wasn't afraid to die—said she was "washed in the blood." Jesus had her back. It must have been true because Kelly had never seen what could be called "fear" in her eyes. Anger, defiance, compassion—yes. But never fear.

And once you had killed, and had processed it, and locked those feelings away in a place where they could no longer disable you, losers like Weasel Man and his big friend no longer scared you.

Kelly walked up to the house and went in the door. Her grandmother, whom she presumed had been watching out the window, was waiting to greet her.

"I've never heard you speak like that before," commented her grandmother cautiously.

"Well Grandma, sometimes you have to speak in a language that gets their attention."

"Jamie's in trouble isn't he?"

"Jamie's always in trouble," she said derisively, then turning to see her grandmother's worried look, she softened. "Yes, Jamie is in trouble."

Kelly went upstairs to change and get a pill for her ankle. Her pill bottle had been zipped in a side pocket of her day pack, which was now open, unzipped. She took out the bottle and checked the contents but could not tell if any pills were missing. It contained a 30 day supply but she had not been keeping track. She popped one pill, closed the bottle, and pushed it into a pair of socks in her sock drawer. Then she went downstairs and joined her grandmother on the sofa.

"The funeral was nice today, wasn't it?" said Kelly, trying to lighten the mood.

"Yes, it was. I believe your uncle would have been pleased. Leona said they're going to scatter his ashes in the Mountains. That's what he wanted."

"From dust to dust," said Kelly. "One minute you're whole and the next you're spread all over the hills." The conversation paused as they both silently reviewed the events of the day, highlighted by the soft "ticks" from the clock in the kitchen. "What do you think about that Grandma—cremation?"

In her mind's eye, Margaret saw her husband again, a stout young man with a sparkle in his eye and a ready smile. He had been her provider, protector, lover, and best friend for nearly 50 years. Stubborn but selfless, and passionate about a man's responsibility to his family and heritage. No task was too great, no burden too heavy. In her eyes there was no equal; she would not entertain the idea of such a man, or herself, reduced to a formless pile of ash.

"No, put me down in one piece next to Grandpa—the worms can have me. Then maybe I'll return as spring flowers."

"What color?"

"What color...what color?" repeated her grandmother with a confused look, then she smiled and reached for Kelly's hand. "What kind of a silly question is that?"

"It's not silly."

"Then let's make them blue, like pasque flowers."

It was a good choice. In her mind, Kelly saw clumps of pasque flowers dancing in the prairie wind, flowers which burst boldly and confidently from the prairie sod every year for countless millennia. These were flowers, like the bison, certain of their place in the prairie continuum.

Kelly wondered about her own place—where did she belong? Not in the Marines, that much was clear. Was it here, by the Turtle Mountains, or somewhere north, on the prairie? She only knew she was no longer certain...of anything. But it was time to find out.

Chapter 9

"Are you sure that's a wise thing to do?" asked her grandmother.

"If I don't do it now, I'll never do it," said Kelly. "This might be the only time in my life—like you said once Mom got married and had kids it was too late. And I don't want to be like Uncle Rodney, too old to do anything about it."

"Well, I can't argue with that. How long will you be gone? A week?"

"I don't know Grandma, I'll be gone as long as it takes. I'm going to give it one good shot and if I can't figure out what this is all about I'm done with it. I'm going to do it for Uncle Rodney and Mom."

Kelly's grandmother was confused, still trying to determine what brought on this sudden urge to leave. "So you're just going to take those old maps and start exploring?"

"I have a general idea of where this battlefield is, but it might take some time to figure it out. The maps will help, but it's been 165 years, any battlefield that old has probably been turned into a wheat field or something. It's hard enough to find a cemetery that old, much less a battlefield. I'll need help from the local people I'm sure."

"Is this up by Winnipeg, by Batoche?"

"No, I think it's south of here—about 100 miles."

"South? This place is in North Dakota?"

"Yes, I think it's somewhere between the Souris and Sheyenne Rivers in the central part of the state. There's a town called Harvey on the Sheyenne. It's about half-way to the South Dakota border."

"That's not Métis country, no wonder there was trouble. Is it a big area, this area between the two rivers?

"I suppose it's about 50 or 60 miles apart."

"Well, that's still a lot of area. But why did the Métis travel that far south? Weren't there problems crossing the border to hunt in the United States? Would the government even allow that?"

"That's where the bison were, and so that's where they went. And back then the area—the summer bison range—wasn't in a state or territory; it was open range free to use by anyone who wanted to use it. Can you imagine Grandma, traveling from Winnipeg or the Red River down into the middle of North Dakota with just oxcarts? And living off the land. Then hauling tons and tons of bison meat and hides back to Canada? It must have taken weeks."

"Well, I heard the stories about the pemmican trade. I just didn't know they traveled so far—goodness."

"They had to be tough as nails."

"They were Kelly, you remember that. Those were your relatives—that makes you tough as nails too."

"I thought the Marines did that," she laughed.

"It's always been in you. It's always been there. You're just finding out about it now."

"You might be right Grandma. I really feel there is something at work inside me, something that tells me I need to go, that this will be a good thing. I wonder if Mom felt the same way, or if she really did, why she stopped feeling this way?"

87

"Life catches up with us dear," said her grandmother. "Before you know it you grow old and someone else is taking your place. Your father's life was cut short, so was your mother's, maybe you're feeling a sense of duty to follow through with things they never had a chance to do. Just think how lucky you are to get this chance; you're young and still have your entire life in front of you.

"I know this, I know what your grandfather would say, what Uncle Rodney would say…what your mother would say. 'Go Kelly', go do this," and then she paused. "But don't do it for them, do it for yourself. You may find something you're not even looking for."

Kelly walked over and embraced her grandmother. "Are you the wise old Métis woman from the stories, or just wise and old?"

"Don't forget I used to be a young Métis woman too," she replied with a smile. "We all had our dreams."

Kelly updated her maps with the latest versions and mapped out several potential routes. After searching online she found a mini-version of a North Dakota gazetteer which broke the state down by county, township, and section. Many sections showed abandoned cemeteries, gravel pits, and creeks, which might help locate the actual battlefield. She printed out the pages for counties along her projected route. She hoped some of the local landowners or Historical Societies or museums would be able to help also, perhaps having found artifacts or other evidence of conflicts.

Now that she had a mission, she was happy again. For nearly 10 years she had always been assigned a mission: learning to be a Marine; providing a military presence at remote US or Allied installations; gaining the trust of foreign women and families in jeopardy, and training other Marines.

She would pack light and eat on the road as much as possible. She had some money but did not plan to carry much cash. She was used to roughing it and knew she could live cheaply. No firearms would be needed, but she would always carry her weapon of choice, a knife or two.

Worst case scenario she would head south and then crisscross the landscape between the two rivers using the clues from her mother's and uncle's notes. While it wasn't much to go on, she felt a confidence for reasons she could not quite articulate. Maybe the spirits of her ancestors would travel with her.

It was Friday and she was planning to leave Monday morning. She found a source at the Bottineau American Legion who could outfit her with surplus MREs, so she planned to pick some up Saturday. Plus, she wanted to attend church with her grandmother Sunday before leaving. She hadn't been particularly religious while growing up, neither were her parents, but she felt this was important.

Her grandmother prepared a huge dinner for them on Saturday night, roast venison, a braided French bread twist, potatoes and gravy, tiny carrots from the garden, fresh green peas with butter, and a homemade chocolate cake for dessert. Jamie had promised to show up for dinner so she made extra; when he did eat he packed away a lot of food into his thin frame. They waited for Jamie until 5:30 but he did not show for the 5:00 meal. While waiting, her grandmother had removed several platters and bowls from the table and put them in the oven to keep warm.

"Well, we might as well eat," she said finally, rising to retrieve the items from the oven.

Kelly rose quickly saying, "You sit Grandma, I'll get those," and hurried to the kitchen. She returned with the platter of venison and onions. It looked delicious.

"Cherie actually shot that one last fall," said her grandmother, nodding to the platter. "Rene says she's a better shot than he is." Kelly retrieved the rest of the hot bowls and then sat down. She did not want to discuss the trip for fear of upsetting her grandmother, so she focused on the food.

"Can you teach me how to make these bread twists?" she asked. The twists were golden brown on the outside and tender and moist on the inside. It was some of the best bread this former Marine had eaten in years.

"I didn't know you were a baker, Kelly."

"Well, I'm not, but what better time to learn?"

"That's very true. Have you ever baked with yeast?"

"No."

"Well, it's not that hard."

"Show me when I get back. I want to start learning to cook for myself again. This is the best bread I've ever tasted."

"I thought you said they fed you well in the Marines?"

"They did, but you cook circles around anything they made Grandma. The only thing worse is what I tried to cook myself."

"A Métis woman who can't cook!" exclaimed her grandmother with false alarm. "Don't tell anyone else."

"I was busy being a Marine. Besides, I don't consider myself a Métis woman."

"You hush Kelly," scolded her grandmother. "Of course you're Métis. Through and through. It's not good to forget these things, to forget where you came from. If your grandfather ever heard you speaking that way he would have given you a good thrashing. People used to call us "half-breeds" and "mutts" and all kinds of terrible names, and your ancestors fought for their very lives and survival because we were mixed. Don't ever forget that. Blood was spilled by your ancestors so you could be here today enjoying this meal."

"I'm sorry Grandma, I didn't mean it that way," said Kelly apologetically. "I just don't find much use for the old stories. Everyone is always angry. And they're never satisfied with anything."

"Of course they're angry, and with good reason. When I was a young girl Métis kids didn't play with the white children, their parents wouldn't let us. They thought we were drunks, squatters, and thieves—and some of us were, but it was for a reason. They tried to erase us, to pretend we never existed. And we were helpless to do much about it. But we burrowed in like ticks and refused to leave; yes, we were squatters, and we lived in ditches and pits and anywhere else we could. And we ate whatever we could catch or shoot and we worked terrible jobs for poor pay and if you were a woman you did what you had to do to survive in that situation," she said pointedly.

"And now I see this beautiful granddaughter of mine with so many options and choices, good choices, saying you don't have use for that history. And I see your brother, throwing his life away, a good boy who's lost his way and doesn't even know it, doesn't know he's squandering the pain and the blood of generations before him...well, it makes me angry. Not at you Kelly, and not at your brother, but angry that your parents and I didn't do a better job of preparing you. If all you heard from those stories your grandfather and uncle and mother told was anger, well then we failed. But know this—know the strength is in you. And it's there for a reason and for a purpose."

"The last thing I wanted was to make you upset," offered Kelly quietly.

"I'm not upset dear, not really, but maybe I'm starting to see some things more clearly now too."

The room fell silent again, as they both considered what had been said.

Margaret was tired of losing; she had lost her husband, a good man, an honest man she could rely on. She thought back on the frigid winter days he spent outside, cutting wood or fishing or tending their stock; some days it was 30 or 40 degrees below zero. But always he went, welcoming the work and the freedom to live how he chose. Then he would return to her, his face ruddy and frost-tinged from the cold, shedding layer after layer of clothing in order to warm himself by their fire. Happy, thankful…a simple but graceful life. Some days she missed him terribly and could not stop the tears.

Could she have done more as her daughter Marie and the father of her grandchildren were taken, much too early? She was just one woman, no match to cancer or alcohol. And now Rodney was gone.

She felt weary, tired of sacrificing loved ones to sickness, drugs, and the bottle. She remembered as a young woman the bad jobs, the mistreatment and disrespect, the slack bellies in winter and months of hardship. But her people were good people. She only wanted peace, and happiness for her family—a chance for harmony. Was that too much to ask? In her heart, she knew that's why Kelly, who had rejected her own culture in a rush to see the world, had been returned to them once more—Kelly was that chance.

And now it was clear, with the promises of the Good Book and the reassurance of fallen Métis elders ringing in her head, it was time for this old woman to act.

She leaned over the kitchen table and looked Kelly in the eyes. "Can I ask you to do me a favor?"

"Why Grandma, of course," she replied.

"Take him with you."

"Who?"

"Jamie, take him with you. He needs to get away from here, away from his friends and the drugs and the alcohol. He needs to find a way back to a real life."

"But he doesn't care what Mom and Uncle Rodney were looking for. He won't come. He doesn't care about anything but himself."

"If we both tell him he has to go he will," she said encouragingly.

"I don't know Grandma, he won't be able to keep up..."

"We're going to lose him Kelly!" she exclaimed. "We're going to lose him! Don't you see? I can't let that happen—I promised your mother I wouldn't. But now I know I can't do it alone. I need your help—you need to take him with you."

She saw her grandmother's hands tightly clenched around each other, her knuckles white, her face imploring. And she thought back on the letter from her mother—"Take care of Jamie."

"Okay, Grandma. Okay, I will."

Chapter 10

Granger knew this country southwest of the Red River was occupied by the Sioux, and the further south they traveled, the greater their chances of encountering them. Despite the great distances and seemingly empty prairie, word traveled fast on the frontier, so he knew their entourage—with squealing axles, braying livestock and clouds of dust—would be detected soon, if not already.

But they were well-armed, and each Métis hunter was a marksman in his own right. Among them were a handful of Saulteaux hunters as well, Métis relatives and allies from the east. The battle for dominance here in the northern plains east of the Souris had pitted the Métis and Saulteaux against the Sioux for years. There had been many incidents—theft, ambush, out-right slaughter—between the two factions, and would likely be many more.

The numbers, if not the odds, always heavily-favored the Sioux in these incidents, as they were wise enough to avoid attacking an equal or greater force. It was extremely rare for the Sioux to take on an adversary one on one, except by accident. Bravery in battle on the high plains counted little, but scalps and stolen horses merited great celebration. Of greatest merit was to count coup, or to strike your enemy and escape unharmed. Granger knew all these things as his party slowly rumbled and lurched along the oxcart trails deeper and deeper into Sioux territory.

He resolved the Métis hunters would not go looking for trouble, but if it found them they would respond in kind.

While his men were skilled hunters and marksmen, Granger took comfort too in knowing the women of the hunt—most of Cree heritage—were fully capable of staring down a sudden late spring blizzard or any man-made threat which came their way. Skilled with knives, they could reduce a 600-pound bison carcass to lean cuts and a fresh hide in a matter of minutes. Some could shoot, all could handle a knife or ax. With the added measure of their preparation and discipline, the Métis hunting corps was a formidable group.

This had always been a safe hunt; beyond the usual cuts and broken bones, they had harvested thousands of tons of bison in past years without incident. This year he was confident they would do the same. Still, Granger was glad the larger camp was not far away— together they were more than a match for any opponent on the prairie. But of course, they were not traveling together.

Unlike the creation accounts of other Indigenous people, the Métis were not created by animals or by spirits emanating from the heavens—they were created by commerce. Fur attracted white men to the North Country, specifically, beaver fur. Once there they lived among the Cree and other tribes in the land of the Red River near the Canadian Border, and a community of hunters, trappers, and traders was established.

As their circumstances would dictate, they were hardy men and the Indigenous wives they took were equally resilient. Many children followed and the Métis communities thrived, exploiting the niche between the Indigenous residents and newly-arrived Europeans. These mixed people, or "may-tee", had become a people onto themselves.

But being different came with a social cost; by European standards, the Métis were considered to be "Indian," while at the same time some Indigenous tribes considered them compromised by the blood of the whites.

In reality, the Métis leveraged the qualities of both cultures to their benefit. They were outstanding at fieldcraft and became accomplished hunters, trappers, fishermen, farmers, and horsemen. At the same time, they bridged the northern frontier's social and economic gaps by acting as guides, traders, and interpreters and provided for their own well-being through the use of modern weaponry and military tactics. At times this success bred resentment, for they moved easily between cultures and were quick to recognize and leverage opportunities when presented.

Despite appearances, their lives were well-ordered and strategic; Granger might have easily served as a military officer under different circumstances. The early summer and fall bison hunts were part of that strategy, part of that commerce; the sale of bison pemmican provided a major economic boost for the Métis each year.

Granger moved his camp along, traveling seven or eight miles a day while searching the plains for bison. Scouts would ride in each direction from the cart train daily, sometimes a half day's ride. When they found a suitable herd they would all travel to that location in their carts, each drawn by a single horse or oxen, set up camp, and prepare for a bison drive the next morning. Although Granger's hunting party was smaller than the second Métis group to the west, it could move through the hunting grounds quicker. He hoped this would result in more fruitful hunts and full carts.

He had been given his choice of routes this year and opted for the route closer to the *Maison du Chien*, the Den of Dogs, which lessened their chances of encountering the Sioux, who were thought to be closer to the Souris River to the west. The area between Devil's Lake to the east and the Souris was no man's land—poorly mapped and rarely traveled—which may have been the reason the bison gathered here still. It would be another decade before a military presence was established. No treaties held sway, just common sense, and prudence, driven by commerce and necessity.

He had hunted many areas south of the border but this area, near the Den of Dogs, was his least favorite. Although the Butte offered a solid landmark which could be seen for days, he felt from it an ominous energy...a malevolence...felt in his very bones. As Hunt Leader, Granger did not voice his concerns but knew others felt it too. Old Paquet had confided in him—this would be his last trip, next year he would tend potatoes in the north. Yes, Paquet was old and broken and weary, but the Butte troubled him as well. He would be glad to put its dark form behind them.

But they were Métis, after planting their spring crops they followed bison. That's what they did, and it allowed them to flourish, in relative terms. If the herds moved to the gates of Hell, the Métis would prepare to follow.

Granger hoped they were not there now.

Surrounded by this dark energy, he thought again of young Father LeSucur and was genuinely glad to have him along. LeSueur was a true man of the cloth, well-versed in scripture, always ready with the right word or phrase to encourage the righteous or soothe the sinner's soul. His Bible was his guide and instrument, to be used for good and to banish evil back to the depths of time. Dressed in his black Cossack, white surplice, and yellow stole, he was an impressive sight here on the prairie, weeks away from the nearest steeple or altar.

What Father LeSueur lacked in real-world experience he made up for in his unshakable belief that redemption awaited in the afterlife for all Christians who sought it. Left unsaid was that life on the raw northern plains was often only tolerable and in many ways a brutish existence, wholly dependent on what could be gathered or grown or killed from day to day. Was this life another penance, such as those handed out during confession, or a stepping stone to greater glory?

Granger did not let such philosophical considerations distract him; his job right now was to fill the carts with meat and get his group back to the Red River safely. He would let Father LeSueur sort out the rest.

Chapter 11

Jamie did not return Saturday night for dinner, or to sleep in his own bed.

After they returned from Sunday services around noon they found him in his room, asleep on a pillow stained with blood and mud and dried mucus. He was fully clothed except for his shoes, which sat at the foot of the bed covered in mud. His muddy tracks through the house and up the stairs had been their clue he was home. They let him sleep until 6:30 p.m. and then Kelly woke him for supper. He woke, swore at her, and fell back asleep.

She heard him get up sometime in the middle of the night and stumble to the bathroom and vomit in the toilet, then noisily drink two glasses of water, belch loudly and return to bed. He was still asleep when she awoke the next morning.

Rather than leaving on Monday per her plan, Kelly spent much of the day trying to convince Jamie to accompany her on the trip. As she anticipated, he didn't care about family mysteries or what their mother might have been looking for and he was too busy to go heading off on a wild goose chase based on a pile of old maps.

She pointed out he wasn't working, really didn't have a schedule to keep and that apparently some unpleasant people around town thought he owed them a bunch of money. He did not argue the facts but said he was going to come into some money soon and pay everyone off. He was not at liberty to disclose the source of this money.

Kelly worked on him all morning and then, exasperated, gave up, telling her grandmother, "See, I told you he wouldn't come."

"Let me talk to him," she said.

Kelly stayed in the kitchen as her grandmother left out the back and approached Jamie, who sat slumped on the backyard bench smoking a cigarette.

"Jamie, you need to go with your sister," she said firmly.

"No Grandma, I got way too many things going on here."

"That's just nonsense," she said, her voice tightening. "If your father or mother were here right now they'd be ashamed of you—you don't work, you're out all hours, and you treat our home like some kind of Bed and Breakfast where you can come and go as you please."

"Grandma, don't get mad..."

"I am mad, I'm plenty mad. And I can tell you this, it's going to stop," she said, her voice growing louder. "No grandson of mine is going to live this way, not if I have anything to say about it. You are either going with Kelly to straighten yourself out or you are moving out of my house right now. I mean it, I want you to pack your things and get out today." She was trembling now.

"But Grandma I don't have any place to stay. Rene kicked me out, my girlfriend kicked me out..."

"And now I'm kicking you out. Do you see a pattern here Jamie?" She was flustered and flushed, and stopped to calm herself, taking a deep breath. "Why don't you have some respect for yourself? You can't just give up on life, you're too young Jamie. I love you but I can't stand to see you like this."

In the end he gave in, largely because he really didn't have any other place to sleep but only agreeing to accompany Kelly for a few days; if they didn't find anything quickly she would have to bring him back. Kelly didn't comment but her grandmother took it as an encouraging sign.

Tuesday morning their grandmother made them a big breakfast of fried slabs of ham, eggs, crispy hash browns, and a dense homemade sweet bread made with Juneberries. It was a meal fit for the start of a big voyage. Kelly wanted to get an early start—in the Marines that meant 4:30 a.m., here, in a compromise with Jamie, it meant 7:30.

Jamie found his good hiking boots, which he hadn't worn in years, and piled several layers of shirts, blue jeans, socks, and underwear into a large zipped gym bag. He then produced an empty cardboard box and added a small radio, a knit cap, a baseball hat, a pair of tennis shoes, a carton of cigarettes, a clear plastic bag with three different colored pills, and two hot-rod magazines. On top of the magazines, he placed a box of pistol cartridges, .380 caliber.

He hauled the bag and box out to the driveway and set them on the ground next to the truck. Kelly came out wearing shorts, a light long-sleeved shirt, and high-laced boots. On her shoulder, she carried a tightly tied pack and in her hand, she held a smaller, empty pack.

"Are you sure the truck will make it?" asked her grandmother watching from the doorsteps. "That's a lot of miles down there and back."

"It won't have to—we're gonna walk," announced Kelly.

"Walk!" shouted Jamie incredulously.

"What are you talking about Kelly," said her grandmother, "you can still barely walk in the yard with your ankle. Don't be foolish."

Kelly turned to your grandmother. "Remember how tough you said we were Grandma, how the Métis suffered and spilled blood to find a better way for future generations? We used to walk hundreds of miles after bison. And you said it's in me—remember? Well, I'm going to find out."

Her grandmother began to speak, but then caught herself and remained silent.

Kelly turned now to Jamie and handed him the small backpack. "You can carry all that if you want but I'd suggest you only carry what you can fit in here." Then, looking down, she spied the cartridges and asked, "What're these?"

"Extras," said Jamie, pulling a small palm-sized semi-automatic pistol from a pocket of his cargo shorts.

"You need boot leather—not something that goes bang-bang. Give it here." He handed it to her without complaint and she expertly ejected the magazine and opened the chamber to check for a live round. It was empty. Then she flipped through the rest of the items in his box. "What are these pills?"

"Some stuff from rehab, so I don't go looking for the hard stuff again," he offered hopefully.

"In a zip-lock bag? Bullshit. You're leaving this stuff here. I have some ibuprofen if you need it. Get the rest of your gear repacked— we're leaving in 10 minutes."

She took the gun, box of cartridges, and bag of pills back into the house. "This is empty Grandma," she said, placing the gun on the end table. "Hide it somewhere safe until we get back. I doubt he has a permit for it. And you can flush these pills down the toilet. I'll put these pistol cartridges in the garage for now."

They were soon ready to leave. Before putting on their packs they both went to the house and hugged their grandmother goodbye.

"I love you, Jamie," she said.

"You too, Grandma," he replied sheepishly.

"Take care of him and yourself. Find what you are looking for," she whispered to Kelly as she hugged her. "And call me so I know where you are."

"I will."

"Do you have your maps?"

"Yes."

"Money?"

"Yes."

"Cell phones?"

"Don't need 'em."

"Pills for your ankle?"

"Yes, a few."

"Well, you know best I'm sure," said her grandmother. "Your Mom and Dad would be so proud of you two—they *are* so proud. God bless you."

They both felt foolish walking down the street wearing their backpacks. But Kelly knew the most difficult step of any journey was already behind them.

As they worked their way down to the highway around Lake Metigoshe and through the wooded hills they were stopped several times by curious friends and neighbors asking if they needed rides. Kelly kept her answers brief, not wanting to explain their mission or Jamie's presence. Given his "friends" from rehab, it was best he just disappeared cleanly for a while. "Just headed for a little hike," she offered, and that was explanation enough. Folks were friendly enough but knew not to pry.

Once out of the hills on the perimeter of the Turtle Mountains, they cut over to a gravel road which paralleled the blacktop highway south. Although there wasn't much traffic here, she didn't want to put up with the exhaust, noise, and swirling grit from the vehicles. It was much nicer on the gravel—few vehicles and quiet, except for birds. And Jamie. He had not stopped complaining since they left the block of their grandmother's house.

"I'm too hot," he said, sweating under the weight of his pack.

"Then take off some layers—a T-shirt should be fine for today." He stopped, dropped his pack, took off his hoody, and tied it around his waist by the arms. Kelly never broke stride.

"Slow down. I need to stop for a drink," he protested. Kelly stopped while he unsnapped an aluminum water bottle from a loop on his pack, unscrewed the top, and drank greedily, the water sloshing down his cheeks.

"You better pace yourself," said Kelly. "It might be a while before we can refill." They had only walked another 50 yards before he started again.

"This pack is too heavy. It's killing my shoulders."

She estimated his pack weighed only 30 pounds, maybe 35. In contrast, the larger pack she shouldered was pushing 65. During field deployments, she sometimes shouldered packs of nearly 80 pounds. "You'll get used to it," she said. "Your back and shoulders will toughen up."

They walked steadily for two hours straight then dropped their packs and rested under the shade of an enormous cottonwood tree in the ditch. Behind them to the north stood the dark hills of the Turtle Mountains, in front of them spread a great flat plain, broken only by trees planted in windrows and the glimmering spheres of water towers and grain silos on the horizon.

"What do we have to eat?" asked Jamie. Kelly handed him a dense nutrition bar and a small bag of dried fruit.

"Have some of this," she said. "We'll eat light during the day and have a good supper each night. It doesn't pay to eat too much while you're on the move, slows you down."

"Did you learn that in the Marines?" he asked smartly.

"No, in the movie '*True Grit*' – remember, all they had to eat during the day were corn dodgers."

"What the hell is a corn dodger?" he asked.

"Cornmeal, butter, and salt, with a little water to make it stick together. Sticks to your ribs and keeps forever. Like pemmican. Do you ever remember trying pemmican?"

"Yeah, they used to make it at the Red River Ex festival," Jamie replied. "We danced there a few times. But I didn't like it, tasted too dry. They said it was made out of meat and fruit, but I couldn't taste any fruit."

"Usually dried meat and Saskatoons or blueberries; they don't put apples or pears in it, usually just berries. And it was held together with fat. You know that's the reason we're here right now—pemmican."

"I thought we were trying to find a battlefield," Jamie said flatly.

"The main reason the Métis came south was to follow the bison, and after the hunt, they would make tons of pemmican. It was stored in leather bags. Would keep for years. That's what the Métis sold back then to make a living—pemmican."

"So what does your secret map show, where the bison were?"

"Well, it's no secret map but it does indicate the Métis traveled way down south from Winnipeg to find them, and that's where they got into trouble."

"And there was some kind of fight?"

"Yes."

"I thought all our ancestors were squatters and didn't have a pot to piss in. How could they afford to chase bison way down here?"

"This was before Batoche when the Métis were hunters and traders and owned their own businesses," responded Kelly. "There was a time we kicked ass on the prairie."

"Really?"

"Yeah, really."

They took up their packs and continued south, passing wide fields of canola and flax, not yet adorned in their blossoms of bright yellow or blue. Kelly wanted to get in 10 miles today, not a long stretch in terms of military marches but probably more than enough for Jamie on his first day out. Her ankle sent out a muted pulse of pain with each stride she took, and she knew it would stiffen up in the evening.

Her goal was to make it out of the county sometime tomorrow, putting them on track to reach their target area within six or seven days of steady walking, depending on the weather. She planned at least one day of rain. The wind they would deal with.

They stopped for the evening on a flat patch of grass between the railroad grade and the gravel road. It looked as if others had camped here based on some old coals in a circular fire ring made of fieldstone. There were old horse droppings near the edge of the grass; perhaps some riders had laid over here for a night.

Kelly prepared a stew of noodles, dried vegetables, and dried turkey from a freeze-dried packet and water from her container. She brought only one pan, along with two tin plates, four cups (for soup and coffee), and two sets of silverware. Their stomachs growled as the food in the pan simmered and steamed over the fire toward completion. It smelled delicious.

Finally, the noodles were cooked and the sauce thickened. Kelly tipped half the contents of the pan onto a tin plate and handed it to Jamie. He ate voraciously and looked for more. Who knew peas and carrots could taste so good. Afterward, he lit a cigarette and sat cross-legged near the small fire. He found he was tired and sore, but strangely content.

"So how far did we go today?" he asked.

"About eight or nine miles I suppose. Good start for the first day. You're going to be sore tomorrow, take a couple of these," she said handing him two tablets. "Ibuprofen."

There was very little wind, just a little breeze and as the sun slowly dipped toward the horizon it lit the western sky red, then orange and pink. Just over the rise to the south, a pack of coyotes began to yip and squeal. A chorus of crickets chirped in the ditch and peepers began their song further down the roadside. As it began to cool the moist air filled with the aroma of sweet sage. In the distance, they could hear the faint whine of trucks moving down the blacktop. Their small fire crackled and snapped in the breeze.

"Tell me why we're going on this trip," said Jamie. "It's not really to find some battlefield that Uncle Rodney once heard about is it?"

"Do you really have anything better to do?" Kelly replied, not answering his question. "I don't. I thought at one point I'd be a

106

Marine all my life, but it didn't work out that way. So now I'm back, the Marines weren't enough. I feel like I missed something. Maybe it's this battle thing with Uncle Rodney and Mom, I don't know." She watched Jamie for a reaction but saw none.

"Jamie, you were too young to know what it was like with Dad. He was angry, and drunk, all the time. Something was eating at him, some kind of sickness he couldn't deal with. Just being a Métis, and trying to live in two worlds is stressful enough; maybe he never came to terms with it. It just wasn't healthy to be around him as a little kid. And now, I guess I have something bothering me too. It's hard to describe. Is it something missing, or is it something I need to get rid of, some baggage I've been carrying around? I don't know. I do know this trip seems like something I should do now because I can. And I guess I'm doing it for Mom and Uncle Rodney as much as myself."

She wondered if Jamie carried a similar burden. "So what's bothering you?"

"Nothing," he muttered, toying with a stalk of grass.

"Then why the drugs and running around?" Kelly asked. "And what's with these thugs you're hanging around with? Do you know they wanted money from Grandma and me?"

"They did?"

"Yes, that's total bullshit. You gotta clean up your own messes."

"Easy for you to say, you weren't even around when Mom was sick, when she died."

"So what does that mean—that gives you permission to throw your life away and become a bum? Shit like that is supposed to make you stronger, not throw in the towel."

"Well, maybe you're just tougher than I am."

107

"Maybe that's because I got off the Mountain and did something with my life. You could have done the same thing."

"Okay, you're the perfect one, and I'm a screw-up, is that what you want to hear?"

"No Jamie no, that's not it at all. We're better than this, both of us. ALL of us. My God, at one time our people ruled the prairie—somehow we have to find our way back to that place. It seems like everyone wants to keep hauling all these excuses around; we've gotten too comfortable being victims. I don't want to be a victim. I won't be," she added defiantly.

"I don't know Kelly. If we ever ruled the land that was a long, long time ago. Too long."

They rolled out bedrolls around the fire and lay down without another word. Fifteen minutes later Jamie sat up and lit a cigarette. Kelly was already asleep. By now the stars were blazing overhead and he realized that in the scheme of the universe, his troubles amounted to nothing. The axle of the world would always be greased by money and inhabited by people scrambling to obtain it.

Although he would never tell her, he was glad to have his sister back. Since their mother had passed he had felt adrift. And while he truly loved his grandmother she couldn't relate to the pressures he felt of finding a job worthy of his best effort. He couldn't take the monotony of his previous jobs; in his opinion, only an idiot would do something they hated over and over for 40 hours each week. And while he did not agree with his sister on much, it was undeniable that they both shared a Métis perspective, which gave her contrary positions at least some grudging legitimacy. Curiously, he felt his last girlfriend Kara had also shared his perspective, but she rarely agreed with him either.

As he considered his circumstance he felt a presence near the fire. Peering into the blackness he saw nothing, then looking left he saw a pair of greenish eyes looking back at him in the edge of the fire's glow. They blinked once and appeared to swing away. He quickly turned to his pack and retrieved his small flashlight. He swung the light beam quietly around the whole camp but could not see anything. Turning off the light, he listened carefully for footsteps or sounds in the grass. Nothing. He placed the light on the ground next to his bedroll and flicked his cigarette butt into the ashes, then laid down again, chalking the visit up to a curious raccoon. Within two minutes he too was asleep.

The coyote returned a few minutes later and silently viewed the sleeping pair, its green eyes glowing in the dying fire.

Chapter 12

It was foggy at sunrise the next morning, a thick fog which soaked the tops of their bedrolls with dew. The fog filled the small ditches and depressions around them completely, spread there like frosting on an enormous dimpled sheet cake.

The pain in Kelly's ankle woke her, a dull ache with occasional spasms of sharp pain. She wondered if the pain was a sign the bones were healing. She reached into her bag and shook out two pills, followed them with a gulp of water from her container, then sat and flexed her foot back and forth with her hands before she tried to stand.

She rose slowly, balancing herself with her arms, and hobbled over to the grass to relieve herself. Twenty minutes later, by the time she had the fire going again and a pan of water on, the ankle felt much better. She knew it would be like this every morning, but it was bearable.

"Jamie get up," she ordered. "Breakfast is ready."

They ate hot oatmeal with tea and toaster pastries for breakfast, then broke camp and headed down the road just as the air began to warm and the fog began to lift. A half-hour later her ankle had warmed up completely and she felt no more pain or stiffness; the pills had helped.

They were on a two-lane blacktop now, lightly used but heading in the right direction. The shoulder was wide and firm, slightly damp from the fog. They had gone about two and a half miles when they came upon a wet smear of crimson with tufts of white hair in it. Whatever had been struck had either been pushed or dragged itself across the road shoulder and tumbled into the grassy ditch.

"Must be a deer," Kelly said, examining the hair. "S'pose someone hit it in the fog this morning."

"Do you think they killed it?" Jamie asked.

"Don't know," said Kelly, looking now into the grass. "Wait, I think I see it."

"Where?" asked Jamie, craning his neck now to survey the ditch.

"It's there," she said, pointing to a brown patch of color partially hidden in the green grass. "Looks like a little doe. She's not dead."

Jamie looked where she was pointing and saw the deer's head wobbling back and forth slowly as the stunned animal attempted to keep its head up. "Damn it. Now I wish I had my gun and we could put it out of its misery."

"Well, we can't just leave it," said Kelly, stopping short of voicing the solution she knew they had at hand.

"You could kill it, Kelly, with your knife," said Jamie, causing her to wince. Jamie knew of the solution too.

"I can't," she replied flatly.

"Why not?"

"I just can't."

"Well, then give it to me and I'll do it," he said, not pressing her further. Kelly took out her combat knife and handed it to him, handle first. He looked her in the eyes, then silently dropped his pack and walked down toward the deer. He walked up just a couple of minutes later.

"Do you have any plastic bags?" he asked.

"Yeah, I have one right here," she said, pulling a gray plastic grocery store bag from a side pocket of her pack. Jamie took the bag and walked back down the ditch. Then she saw him spread his legs wide and lean over.

"What are you doing?" she asked.

"Just wait," came the muffled response. A minute later he walked back up the ditch with something wrapped in the bag. He handed her back her knife. It was clean. "Fresh venison back straps," he said, holding up the bag. "These should keep until tonight," he said, tucking the bag into his pack, then wiping his wet fingers on the leg of his pants. "There was some water in the ditch there but you might want to clean your knife better – I just rinsed it off."

"I didn't know you knew how to butcher deer," said Kelly, with a look of puzzlement on her face.

Jamie smiled triumphantly. "I went with Rene and Dylan plenty of times while you were out playing soldier. I didn't hunt but always helped butcher and make jerky and sausage. I guess a Métis should know his way around an animal carcass."

"Well, you've got the job brother. It's all yours."

They continued walking another hour and then walked across a gravel parking lot at a bar called the Roundhouse. An old trackless railroad grade ran behind the bar, covered now with a robust stand of wormwood. Kelly didn't like the looks of the place but she needed to re-dress and re-wrap her ankle. Three dusty pickups and a beat-up Honda Goldwing with a cracked fairing were parked near the entrance.

"I gotta hit the head and take care of my ankle," she said to Jamie before they stepped in. "Why don't you get us a couple bottles of water if they have it…we're about out."

He held out the palm of his hand. "I'm gonna need some money."

She stopped and pulled some paper from the front pocket of her shorts and handed him a crumpled five-dollar bill. "This should do."

They stepped into the dark bar from the bright sunlight and waited for their eyes to adjust to the darkness. Two men in conversation were seated at a table to the left while three men stood at the bar directly in front of them, talking to the bartender. One of the men at the table glanced at them and then resumed his conversation. The men at the bar turned and stared at the new arrivals. Then Kelly saw them talk between themselves and they all laughed out loud.

"Didn't hear you pull up—you riding a horse?" said a big man in the center as his friends continued to chuckle. "How about I buy you a beer Missy and a soda pop for Chief Buffalo Hump there?"

Kelly looked at him without expression. "No thanks, just need to use the restroom and get some water." She glanced at Jamie, nodded toward the bar, and then walked toward a doorway marked "WOMEN" off to the right.

The restroom was small but relatively clean and smelled like concentrated orange zest. She hung her backpack on a hook, sat on the toilet seat, and removed her right hiking boot. It felt good to just air it out. She carefully unwrapped the elastic wrap around her ankle then removed the gauze pad which covered the top of her foot.

Although the scars from the surgery had healed, she found a hot red welt on the inside of her ankle which was beginning to blister. "Damn," she was afraid of that, afraid her foot, nearly numb from the surgeries, would develop blisters she couldn't feel while walking. She examined the gauze pad – nothing. Then she discovered a sharp burr clinging to the inside of the elastic wrap. Welcome to North Dakota, land of many burrs.

She picked the burr off with her fingernails and replaced the gauze pad, then carefully re-wrapped the elastic support bandage and laced on her boot. Standing, she stomped her foot and felt just a slight tingle of pain. She twisted her foot around. No more scratching. She washed her face, dried off with paper towels, and felt much better. "*No worse for wear,*" she thought as she looked in the mirror. Shouldering her pack again she opened the door—and ran squarely into the big man from the bar.

"Mebbe you and I got off on the wrong foot," he smirked as he extended his arm and blocked the hallway. His breath filled the space between them with an unsavory combination of tobacco, beer, and cinnamon gum. She estimated him at 6'2", about 240. He wore a red Case tractor ball-cap and a dusty white T-shirt emblazoned with a Chevrolet truck logo. A local.

Kelly felt no fear, just impatience, tinged with anger, and she let it rise in her slowly. Improvise, adapt, overcome. As an instructor, she had performed defensive maneuvers so many times in drills and demonstrations that muscle memory had taken over. No untrained civilian could match a professional soldier, and few professional soldiers could match a Marine.

This would not be another Private Zack encounter; she resolved to discipline herself, to use anger to her advantage. Quickly she found her center, found control.

She would handle this.

With an opponent outweighing her by 100 pounds she knew space was not her friend, so rather than backing off she quickly stepped forward, just an inch from his chest, watching his eyes flare briefly in response. She looked up dispassionately, directly into his eyes. Instead of fear or submission, he found an intense beam of discipline, preparation...and expectation. Her DI look.

"Mister, you need to know I'm not someone to mess with," she said quietly. "I'm not having a good day, and you are not helping. So I need you to help me by not being an asshole. Can you do that?"

"Listen you little bit—," he began but stopped abruptly as he felt a sharp object penetrate the fabric of his blue jeans and come to rest gingerly between his testicles. The fixed-blade stiletto Kelly carried was modeled after the classic V-42 Commando knife, but at eight inches total length, her custom model was four and a half inches shorter than the original, making it much easier to conceal and carry. As with the original, the tip of the blade was needle-sharp—built to penetrate helmets, skulls, and certainly any soft tissue it encountered.

"What's your name?" she demanded.

"Ha...Harlan," he stuttered.

"Well Harlan, stick out your right hand." He did. "Palm up." He turned his hand palm up.

She lowered her voice, nearly a whisper. "Harlan, I'm going to leave now with my brother. And if you or your pals out there give me any more shit, or try to follow us I promise you I'm going to cut off your nuts and make you hold them in that hand until they bleed out and get cold." She paused for effect and applied a bit more pressure with the knife. "Do you understand?"

"Yes ma'am."

"Outstanding, now you stay here until we're out the door. Got it?"

"Yes ma'am."

"Goodbye Harlan." She withdrew the knife from his groin, readjusted her pack and walked out of the dark hallway to the bar.

As she emerged it took just a moment for her brain to register the scene before her and decide on a course of action. Jamie was standing nervously at the bar, pinned between the shoulders of the two remaining men. On the bar stood two pint water bottles, a quart bottle of Jack Daniels whiskey, and a large cocktail glass nearly full of amber liquor. The bartender stood smiling halfway down the bar with his arms crossed.

The man nearest to Kelly turned toward her and laughed, "How about some firewater for you too sister!"

"*Seriously!*" she thought. "*What bad movie did these guys come from?*" But now she *was* angry. Without breaking stride, she let the pack slide from her shoulder onto a nearby table and mentally calculated her paces.

A good kick to the knee—a purposeful, disabling kick—should be directed "through" the knee as if attempting to snap the leg in half. While this rarely occurs, the strike is debilitating and can result in permanent injury. Kelly figured Carl here, or whatever his name was, probably needed both knees to farm or load hay or move cattle—and of course, to keep America strong in the process. So she planted her right foot and gave him just a sharp pop to the kneecap with the heel of her left foot, just enough to bend him over in pain and reach for the knee.

She blamed her bad ankle for her timing because when she followed up with the knee-strike to the side of his exposed and now lowered head, she hit a moment too soon. She was going for the ear but hit the jaw instead with her right knee, feeling the crunch of teeth on teeth. Carl went down moaning and sprawled across the sticky floor.

Kelly said nothing but just looked passively at the third man. He backed away and held his hands up in submission. "Grab the water," she directed Jamie. "How much do we owe you?" she asked the bartender, her eyes still boring into the third man.

When he realized she was speaking to him the bartender jumped involuntarily. "On the house," he blurted.

116

"Thanks," she said and turned quickly for the door. Once out in the parking lot, Jamie could not help but look back. Nobody followed.

"Jesus, you kicked that guy's ass," he said incredulously.

"Well, you ever hear the saying 'Don't mess with the Marines?'"

"Yeah."

"Well, we don't just make that shit up. It's best not to mess with us."

She wanted to reach Rugby before sundown; she had gone to school with the wife of a bar owner there and hoped they would put them up for the night. But now she doubted they could make it; a storm was approaching from the west and dark clouds filled the horizon. It looked like rain.

Instead, they got in another three miles before they felt the first raindrops. They stopped at a small grove of stunted popple next to an old cemetery. "We need to settle in for the night here before we get dumped on," said Kelly. She knew they would get better at making and breaking camp each day, but this was the first time they would camp in the rain so she took charge. Breaking out a two-man standard-issue Marine Combat tent from her pack, she had it erected in four minutes.

"Put everything in here," she directed as she moved their gear into the tent and under the rain fly. "It's gonna rain pretty good."

And soon, just as the sun set, it began raining steadily. With no fire or stove, there would be no venison steaks tonight. Instead, they dined on canned corned beef on bread with American cheese slices. For dessert, packaged oatmeal cookies.

"How am I supposed to smoke in the rain?" complained Jamie after their meal.

"If you want it bad enough I guess you just get wet," said Kelly.

Jamie flopped down disgustedly on his bedroll. For a moment neither said anything. It felt good to stretch out and just listen to the rain. Kelly was glad she brought the tent, despite the extra weight.

"Those guys, the ones that came to Grandma's looking for you, do you really owe them a bunch of money?" asked Kelly.

"It's complicated," said Jamie. "I was supposed to deliver something to them from another guy but I never got it from the first guy in the first place. They think I ripped them off."

"Drugs?"

"Yeah, some grass and pills, prescription pills. They resell them. I was supposed to get a cut after delivery."

"Get a cut? So you *are* a dealer. Take it from your big sister—you need to get past all that shit."

"I am going to get past it. I just needed some money. I don't ever want to go through rehab again."

"Hard to believe that. When's the last time you had a real job?"

"It's been a while. When are you going to get a real job?"

"The Marines were a real job, believe me. About as real as it gets."

"Why did you join—seems dumb?"

She had asked herself that same question, through Basic, through her deployments, and at times when she observed civilians just mindlessly going about their boring lives. It wasn't because she wanted "to serve," or to help people, or support "her country" or all

118

the other bullshit people told themselves. And she certainly had never wanted to kill anyone, but in the process of becoming a Marine whatever motivation you had was replaced by what the Marines wanted. As a DI she knew how it worked, what the Marines, what the United States, really wanted—they wanted killers. And if she did her job right, that's what they got.

And that's what she had become, someone to come in and clean up messes, usually of some politician's making. If they could do that with their "presence," fine, if they "consulted" or held hands or made nice with the locals, fine. But it always seemed to devolve into lethal force, and firefights and shit storms and bodies piled against walls and toddlers crying from the roar in their ears and women rocking and keening in the universal language of despair. Kelly had found the mourning of Afghan village women unsettling but did not deny them their well-placed grief; their world was being destroyed and they knew it wasn't coming back in their lifetimes.

She didn't answer Jamie's question but asked another. "You know what I learned in the Marines?"

"Aside from kicking people's asses?"

"Yeah, aside from that. I found out people are basically the same. Most everybody just wants to live their lives and be left alone. It's the same here as it is in Afghanistan, or anywhere else in the world.

"I also learned who you hang around with is a big deal—family, friends, the people you work with, the people you run with. Do you know why it's important?" she asked.

"No."

"Because every one of them gives you something and you leave something with them in return, whether you intend to or not," Kelly said quietly.

"I've seen a lot of bad in people and I've seen a lot of people that were just plain bad," she continued. "But now I want to find the good in people, because I know I'll be a better person because of it—the good will rub off, just like the bad rubs off."

Jamie turned and propped his head on his hand and elbow and looked at Kelly. "Well, I don't think Mom liked me, or Grandpa. Sometimes I don't think Grandma likes me. There's not a lot of good to rub off there."

"You idiot, I know for a fact Mom was very proud of you, and your grandpa really liked that you were keeping a Métis tradition alive in our family with your dancing."

"News to me."

"No, there's more to it than that. They were being forced off the land they settled. And so they fought back hard, so hard they ended up pissing off the Canadian government, so the Canadians brought in the military and military artillery. They even got a Gatling gun from the Americans. The Métis were some of the best shooters, best horsemen, best hunters on the prairie; people all across the border depended on us for food and trade goods. But what did we get for it? We lost our land. We were shot to pieces. We had to run. And we did, and so we survived."

"A Gatling gun is like a big machine gun right?"

"Yeah, back then those early guns would fire something like 350 rounds a minute, .45 caliber. A .45 slug is about twice as heavy as your little pistol."

She thought about the armaments they had unleashed on the Afghans. It was a sad truth of war that anything brought in for use against the enemy combatants was inevitably used against US forces and the civilian population. Even a basic M240 machine gun would put the old Gatling guns to shame; a modern Gatling gun, an M134, could fire 4,000-5,000 rounds a minute and hit targets over 1,000 yards away. It was insanity, how many rounds do you have to put through a human being to kill it?

"They still don't like us do they?" commented Jamie.

"Like who?"

"*Us*, the Métis."

"No, they would have been happy to have us disappear altogether. But here we are. Survivors."

"Is that why Grandpa and Uncle Rodney were always so mad?"

"I think so. I'd be pissed too; the Canadian government actually hung the Métis leader at Batoche by the neck, no better than the Americans hanging the Sioux for the uprising in Minnesota. Of course, there's nothing better than a hanging to get your point across. The Métis have been trying to get a fair shake ever since. But it's tough when you don't have a country to call your own. We're just a problem nobody wants. They'd still be happy if we just disappeared.

"But I'll tell you this: Grandma is right, it's not good to be mad all the time, eats you up. At some point, you have to make peace and move on. If you don't, you make yourself the loser."

The rain began to slack off, and soon it was limited to just a few drops, splatting heavily against the taut surface of the tent's rainfly. They both got up and went out to relieve themselves and then returned to their still warm bedrolls. Soon they were asleep, enjoying the deep sleep of exhausted wayfarers.

Kelly woke the next morning to a throbbing ankle and the sound of birds singing in the grove in the pre-dawn. As she glanced over she saw Jamie and his bedroll were gone.

Chapter 13

"What the hell?" said Kelly, trying to piece together the missing bedroll, her conversation with Jamie the previous evening, the darkness, and the bird songs outside the tent. Then the facts snapped in place logically and she realized the only real problem was that Jamie was gone. And she didn't know where or why. She dressed and then looked out the tent flap cautiously. It bothered her that he had exited the tent so quietly that she had not wakened. She was losing her edge.

She hobbled painfully out of the tent and looked around the campsite in the growing light of dawn. No sign of him. She looked up and saw the rain clouds had left and it was clearing. Then she smelled cigarette smoke.

She found him on the other side of the grove, on a strip of mowed grass on the cemetery's edge. He was sitting on his bedroll, legs crossed, absorbed in thought, smoking a cigarette. She walked up behind him quietly in the wet grass.

"There you are," she said, trying not to startle him. "I didn't know where you were."

"Been here for an hour or so, couldn't sleep so I wanted to lay under the stars after the rain quit, but there were too many bugs. Smoke helps."

The sky was clear and blue from horizon to horizon. "Looks like it's going to be a nice day," Kelly observed. "You should have just built a fire—that would have kept the bugs away."

"Would have scared away all the critters. This country is loaded with wildlife. I don't think the ducks stopped quacking all night, and you can hear owls and bitterns up to the north. I had a family of raccoons—a momma and three little ones—walk right by me about a half-hour ago, plus I saw five deer and a bison."

"You saw a bison?" asked an astonished Kelly.

"Yeah, he was by himself, over in that pasture," he said, pointing to a fenced tract across the cemetery.

"There aren't any bison here anymore. They've been gone for over 100 years," stated Kelly. "It must have been something else—maybe a moose calf? There are a lot of moose around."

"No, I know what a bison looks like, it was a young one, not a calf but like something half-grown, pretty shaggy, little horns."

"What did it do?"

"He looked at me for the longest time, then walked closer until he was just on the other side of the cemetery. Then he turned and walked away, the next thing I knew he was gone. Must have jumped the fence or something."

"Could have been a stray from some rancher's herd; I know a few people still try to raise them." surmised Kelly, looking across the cemetery. "Couldn't have been wild."

Kelly limped back to the tent. She saw their canvas water bucket left outside overnight was now half-filled with fresh rainwater. After a couple gritty days on the road and a clammy night in the tent, she was ready for a good scrubbing.

"You stay over there for a while," she shouted to Jamie. "I'm going to get a quick sponge bath." She heard a muffled "Okay" from Jamie's direction and proceeded to find a bar of soap, a small towel, and a dry top and slacks from her pack.

She walked down the small slope of the ditch with her clothing and water bucket and found a spot shielded from the road. She stripped, hanging her clothes on nearby branches still wet with dew. She splashed cold water on her face and neck then scooped handfuls of water over her chest, stomach, and legs. She rubbed the soap bar across her body and worked it up and down her limbs and torso with her hands. It was cold but felt good. She rubbed the soap in her short hair last and got a good lather going, then poured water over her head and down her body, rinsing the soap away.

She toweled off, starting with her hair and working down. She felt good, felt clean. She considered herself now; she was still hard and fit, despite the weeks away from the Corps. Her body was brown and taut, her breasts small and firm, her arms and shoulders and thighs well-muscled. It was a warrior's body; she would be sorry to lose it.

It had served her well on her deployments. She smiled; it had also served her well in a cool California hotel room some six months earlier. He was a Special Forces Sergeant she met at training. Theirs had been a brief but satisfying encounter—two hard bodies tumbling about a hotel room like dice tossed in a cup—spinning and crashing and careening, only to land, spent, face up on the bed. That felt good too.

She dressed quickly, dumped out the remainder of the water, and went back to the tent. Had Jamie really seen a bison?

She broke out a small fire-starter stick from her pack and soon had a good-sized fire going, albeit a smoky one with all the damp wood. She knew the fresh venison cuts from yesterday would go bad if they weren't eaten this morning. Slicing the venison loin into thin medallions, she sprinkled them lightly with salt and then speared the pieces on green sticks laid over the edge of the fire. They took only minutes to cook and were soon sizzling and smoking over the fire. She handed a stick full of meat to Jamie.

"Be careful, this is hot," she warned. He tore into it with his teeth, eating it like an ear of corn. The meat was deliciously rare and tender. They found they were hungry, especially for protein; Jamie finished off three sticks and Kelly ate two.

"You make a good breakfast Sis," Jamie remarked, wiping his mouth with his sleeve.

***

Forty-seven miles away the meeting took place in the basement of the Goodview County Courthouse in a room resembling a large walk-in vault, which it had once been. Even now the doorway was fronted with a massive cast iron door featuring ancient hinges and protruding bolts as thick as broom handles. The door was now permanently bolted into the "open" position.

The courthouse was over a century old, a fortress of stone block and brass rail and glass which anchored the commerce, rule of law, and history of a county set on the edge of the western frontier. Once proud, today it was a worn-out relic, offering only token resistance against the natural elements and little in the way of services to a dwindling population of county residents.

Years ago, before the 1st National Bank came to town, the courthouse had also served as the Goodview County treasury, and so a vaulted room was needed for cash, record-keeping, legal paperwork, and historical documents. Now, with little cash on hand, and the advent of digital records, the vault had been converted into a much-needed conference room.

"Jesus, I thought we had that air conditioner fixed!" said Commissioner Carl Spoon, fanning himself with a sheath of property tax reports.

"Still waiting for parts from Bismarck," replied Dorothy Carlson as she sorted piles of paper on the table. Although elected County

Treasurer, she still took notes and acted as secretary to the three elected County Commissioners. Today she wore a lemon house dress with white linen wrapped buttons and embroidered collar, circa 1955. White pumps.

Spoon sat heavily in the chair at the end of the table. Seated to his right was Commissioner Lyle Makarenko, a small, sturdy man of Ukrainian stock, just over five feet tall, peering intensely at a zoning request in front of him. His meeting dress never varied: white dress shirt, dark slacks, and scuffed black slip-on shoes. The third Commissioner was Royal Meyer, rail-thin, six foot three, white western shirt with brown beaded trim, jeans, bolo tie and cowboy boots.

Although by law open to the public, the monthly County Commission meetings were held in this room for one reason: It was very small, with room for perhaps eight people, if four of them stood. This served to discourage any lengthy public statements or appeals. Predictably, meetings were sparsely attended.

Goodview County, with 1,630 residents on a good day, was the third smallest county by population in the state of North Dakota. Only the county hosting the Theodore Roosevelt National Park and the county hosting the Painted Hill Reservation were less populated. With a landmass of over 1,000 square miles, Goodview County was among the least densely populated areas in the lower 48 states, with only two people per square mile. Over 99 percent of this population was white. And old.

It was a county easily overlooked by the state and largely abandoned by its residents, who served either as land accumulators or stubborn placeholders for a generation which left many years ago, never to return.

Two people sat outside the vaulted meeting room, waiting for their turns on the agenda. The meeting was called to order and, after reviewing and approving the minutes from the previous month's meeting, Spoon rang in new business.

"The first item is expenses," said Carlson. "They are as follows: $32.67 for Sheriff's office supplies—Costco, $43.07 for office paper and printing supplies—Costco, $500 consulting on Highway 200 project—PSR Engineering, $927.40 county shop, county courthouse, county extension office gasoline expense—Cenex, $4,022 county shop diesel expense—Kath Oil, $52.50, courthouse toilet paper and paper towels—Costco, $298 Commissioner's car allowance, $142.50 bagged concrete mix for curb repair—Farm and Fleet, $89.17 Sheriff patrol headlight and air cleaner replacement—Butte Repair, $125 reflective tape for parking signs—Wilson Graphics, $50 conference registration fee, 4-H adviser. Plus, we're still waiting for the invoice from Morris County for our share of the State's Attorney salary."

"How much is that gonna be?" asked Spoon.

"Should be about $1,800," Carlson replied, "depends if they charge us this month for his mileage."

"Damn, we didn't even have a court case," Spoon grumbled. "How in the hell are we supposed to pay for all this if we actually start arresting people?"

"Well, it would be about $1,800 regardless," Carlson explained. "We pay half his salary no matter how much time he puts in over here."

It was an old gripe, without an easy solution, and Makarenko was in no mood to rehash it again. "I move we accept and approve the charges as presented," he said to no one in particular.

Meyer looked at Spoon to gauge his approval. Spoon ignored him. "Second," said Meyer.

Spoon saw the next agenda item was the bid process on the highway resurfacing project, which involved the new municipal golf course project.   But he didn't like people waiting while they were in discussion, or voting, or really around at all during their meetings. If it were up to him these discussions would always be held behind closed doors, the only way to get things done.

"Let's jump ahead here, I see we have a couple visitors." Without waiting for agreement he turned toward the door, "Hi Jenny, come on in."

Jennifer Peters was one of just six teachers at the local high school. She taught English, Social Studies, Health, and Computer Science. By default, she also coached the girls' volleyball team in the fall, although she had never played the sport herself.

In her mid-30s, she was dressed casually in tan slacks and a supple brown blouse with pleated collar. She was thick but fit, her face inviting, her manner open and positive. With eight years in, she had seniority over most of the other teachers. She was also a transplant, having moved to North Dakota from Michigan after a couple years off following college. With a teaching degree in hand, she spent six months hitching across Europe with her boyfriend at the time, then lived in Florida and Utah with college roommates while job hunting.

She appreciated classical music, a nicely-balanced Cabernet, and the lessons of history—Biblical, Greek, Chinese. It was perplexing to her that history was largely ignored today. Moving to North Dakota for her first teaching job was exciting; here she found history, but she found it mired somewhere around the Kennedy Administration.

She entered the room and sat in the only empty seat, at the end of the small table.

"What's up?" asked Spoon simply.

"Hello Mr. Spoon," she said, then turning and nodding toward the other commissioners, "Mr. Meyer, Mr. Makarenko." They nodded in turn in acknowledgment.

"Hi Dorothy," she added, looking at Carlson. "Thank you for seeing me today. I won't take up much of your time." She laid several manila folders in front of her but did not open them. "As you may know I teach English and Social Studies at the high school and I've been working on a proposal, on my own time of course, for funding a public library in the county," she searched the commissioners' eyes for a reaction. Disinterested stares. "Goodview County is one of just three counties in North Dakota without a public library. I—."

"I thought we had the 'Borrow a Book' library on the curb?" interrupted Makarenko.

"We do," she continued, "but that really only contains about 20 books and as you know it's very difficult to maintain much of the year…especially during the winter months. It was actually knocked over by the snowplow five times last year. Four books were just found this spring, under a snowdrift." She paused. "They were ruined of course." The commissioners sat silently, consciously withholding any sign of encouragement.

"I was fortunate to locate a grant through the state library in Bismarck working with the Smithsonian in Washington to fund a small library here. It would pay for a few new books every month and partially fund the salary for a librarian."

Makarenko didn't wait for the other commissioners to respond. "Yeah, but where'd we put it—we got no room as it is for offices…you want us to rent another space? Who's gonna pay for that?"

"Well, there would obviously be some costs the county would have to absorb, based on my projections it shouldn't amount to more than $17,000 annually but—."

"We already got a library in the high school," Spoon interrupted, "why do we need another one? The high school is open to the public, they can use that. Seems like overkill."

"Sure," added Makarenko, sensing momentum building to shut down the request, "we can get a library started but there's no money to maintain it. Plus who's going to use it? I'm not hearing anyone say we need a library."

Peters steeled herself, took a breath, and continued. "Well, a library can be more than just a place for books, we could have a computer lab for those without an internet connection, we could have a meeting room for clubs and night classes, maybe career fairs…it could really anchor the community."

"Ya know these kids today, none of 'em read books anyway," proclaimed Meyer with a dismissive wave of his hand. "They got them phones and computers at home—they don't need no books."

Peters' eyes flared involuntarily and she leaned slightly toward him, trying to process what she'd just heard. At the same time, the other two commissioners thought Meyer had summed it up neatly and considered the matter resolved.

"Anything else?" asked Spoon.

She heard Spoon's voice but was still trying to mentally process Meyer's comment.

"Anything else?" Spoon repeated impatiently.

"Um…no, I guess that's it."

"Okay, thanks for coming in," he said conclusively, turning again to the door. "Troy, what's up?"

Peters gathered her folders, stood, and walked out the door, smiling weakly at Carlson, who returned a similar smile.

Sheriff Troy Lang stood, waited politely for her to exit, then entered the room and sat in the warm chair just vacated.

Lang was a fit man in his late 40s, 5' 10", 190 pounds with a dense, well-groomed reddish mustache adorning a ruddy face. He had been the Goodview homecoming king, captain of the high school football team, and a starting pitcher on the baseball team many years ago. Now he was just known as the Sheriff, having been re-elected several times to the post. He looked good in the uniform and wore it well. He was well-liked and respected, known to be fair, reasonable, and resourceful, given the minimal staff and financial resources with which he had to work.

But while the citizens of Goodview County elected him, the commissioners paid the bills. And they let him know it. And so he played their game, and he got by. Crime was growing here, but in many ways, Goodview County was still just the reflection of a sleepy landscape with lost cows, Saturday night bar fights, and the growing scourge of rural counties everywhere: homegrown meth labs.

He nodded at each of the commissioners and then began. "I know we're a little over from last month," referring to the previous month's expenses, "but we really need new tires on the patrol car."

"I thought you just got some last spring?" said Makarenko.

"That was on *my* car—Duane drives the other car—those tires have over 75,000 on them and we've patched them three times already."

"What's that gonna cost us?" asked Spoon, not looking up from a spreadsheet he was examining.

"Here's the bid out of Minot for four new ones installed," Lang said, placing a sheet of yellow paper in front of Spoon, who glanced at it and grunted.

"You get a bid out of Goodview Repair?"

"Yeah, the same tires would be $140 more."

"Mmm," responded Spoon simply, whose nephew owned the repair shop.

"Can't we just get some used tires now to get us by?" asked Makarenko. "They got plenty of used tires down to the shop."

"I checked," responded Lang. "Don't have the right size."

"Well, let's do this then," said Spoon. "We're not made of money and what we do have we like to keep local, so you get yourself two new tires from Goodview Repair and keep your other best two on the rig. That should get you by for a while. Will that work?"

Lang thought to counter, thought better of it, and responded, "Sure."

"Anything else?"

"No, thanks," said Lang, retrieving the bid from Spoon and exiting the room.

With Lang gone, the commissioners quickly moved to consider the bid for the long-awaited resurfacing of the highway heading west from town and a financial review of the recently opened municipal golf course.

'Say, Dorothy, could you run down and make us a fresh pot of coffee?" suggested Spoon. "Might take us a while to go through these next projects and I'm damn near ready for my nap."

Carlson pursed her lips but did not respond. Instead, she organized the papers in front of her into neat piles, rose, and left the room.

"Best leave the door open," said Spoon. "Don't want anyone thinking we're having a closed meeting."

With Carlson gone Spoon opened up another folder and passed out a short spreadsheet to the other two commissioners.

"Here's the costs for the Grand Opening and attendance," he said.

"You get these from Rhonda?" asked Meyer, referring to his daughter, the newly-minted Chair of the Goodview County Historical Society and part-time manager of the new golf course.

"Yeah, she had to get the final bill from the portable toilet guy but these are the expenditures and revenue to date," responded Spoon.

Makarenko set the spreadsheet down in front of him. "Not much of an investment. We're losing money big time—$7,200 for the Grand Opening, $1,250 for insurance, $2,900 for supplies, $1,800 for fertilizer…and none of this includes the construction costs for those first nine holes."

"Those are just up-front costs," explained Spoon. "Sure, it'll take a while for it to catch on but there's golfers out there every day now, and once families hear about the historic battlefield they'll be coming from all over."

Meyer held out the sheet, "According to this only 37 people golfed there the first two weeks."

Spoon began to get red in the face. "You guys are missing the big picture. Do you know how many people visit Custer's Last Stand every year? Guess. Take a guess."

"50,000?" said Makarenko.

"Not even close," Spoon declared. "It's over 300,000. Can you imagine what impact 300,000 people would have on *our* county? Let me tell you, this cowboy and Indian thing is hot—and the Custer deal don't even have a golf course."

"And you said the State Historical people were pretty sure the golf course was the site of that big battle of the Coteau?" asked Meyer.

"Yeah, yeah," replied Spoon. "This whole area was one big battle."

"But when folks find out we took the new shoulders off the highway project to pay for the golf course I don't think they'll like it," cautioned Makarenko.

"Well, sometimes Lyle you gotta do their thinking for them—we ain't never gonna put Goodview on the map without a good draw," replied Spoon. "Do you think people are going to drive all the way up here from Chicago to see some cow pies, or grass, or a...a...dumb library? No, they want some shoot 'em up, way out West stuff. And that's what we're gonna give 'em. The roads are always gonna need fixing. But years from now they'll look back on this and thank us for our vision." He searched their faces but saw his words were having little effect on their level of confidence.

"By the way," he continued, less animated now. "I'd like to vote on one more item before Dorothy gets back. My son says those golfers out there can't hit a golf ball worth a damn. They're hooking balls off the course right into my car lot—says eight cars have dents or broken windshields. Now my insurance will cover that to a point but I want to put up a big net to keep those balls off the lot."

"Well Carl, go ahead," said Meyer.

"It's gonna be around $4,200 bucks," he replied.

"You mean you want the county to pay for it?" asked Meyer.

"Well, of course, the county should pay for it—those are balls coming off the county golf course."

"Yeah, but you insisted the course go next to your car lot," countered Makarenko.

"Look, you didn't complain when your kid got the irrigation contract on the course—that was nearly $20,000," said Spoon.

Makarenko looked down at the papers again. "What are we going to cut off the road project to cover it?"

"We'll cut off a quarter-mile of length, that'll easily cover the netting and some of this Grand Opening stuff. We also need to talk to Rhonda about getting a nice sign telling folks we funded the project, you know, with all our names on it; I'm thinking brass," Spoon replied. The other commissioners shifted uncomfortably in their chairs. "All in favor?"

"Aye," said Meyer.

"Aye," muttered Makarenko.

Just then Carlson walked in, carrying a carafe of hot coffee which she set on the table. "Did I miss anything?"

"No, just discussing some of the construction jobs," said Spoon.

"No expenditures?"

"No," said Spoon.

"Well, what should I say in the notes?" she asked, setting down a stack of napkins and creamer packets.

"Just say...'Commissioners discussed funding options for county construction projects, then meeting adjourned' or something like that."

"That right boys?" he asked, looking at Meyer and Makarenko.

"Yeah," said Makarenko.

"Yep," said Meyer. "You want me to talk to Rhonda about the si—."

Spoon shot him a glance and then looked at Carlson, who looked back, slightly confused.

"We'll have to take that up at the next meeting Royal," Spoon said, giving Meyer a stern look.

"Oh yeah, right," he replied.

Chapter 14

Only two of the five bison scouts returned to camp. With them came the worst news Granger could have received—a large camp of Sioux, over 600 lodges, were camped less than an hour's ride from their location. Such a camp might contain 2,000 warriors, far outnumbering the Métis.

With less than 70 able-bodied men and boys who could handle a rifle, and a greater number of women and children to protect, Granger had no choice but to take a defensive position. He knew if the Sioux overran their camp it would be a slaughter.

The five Métis scouts had accidentally stumbled onto the Sioux camp and soon had a party of 20 Sioux riders on their tail. The Métis retreated toward their camp but the Sioux's fresh horses cut the distance and surrounded them, not far from Dog Den Butte. The scouts tried to confab and establish peace, but their mere presence had angered the Sioux. The gifts of tobacco were shunned.

Once captured, the scouts were quickly disarmed, but as the Sioux reached to secure the reins of their horses two scouts saw their chance to escape: They whirled their mounts, charged through the Sioux line and escaped to the Métis camp. Arrows and ball sent after them missed their targets but a far greater tragedy loomed—the Métis and their camp had been discovered.

The Sioux claimed this land, and the bison on it, as their own. And now, with a fully-provisioned Métis oxcart-train and a hundred horses, mules, and oxen stranded here on the prairie, they wanted much more from the trespassers than tobacco.

Granger swore an oath under his breath at the three scouts which had fallen into Sioux hands: Labide, the young Savard, and one of his best men Jerome Santerre. But he could not worry about them now, his duty was to the camp and the remaining hunters and families. The situation was desperate.

He immediately sent two riders to the larger Métis camp for help, several hours away. The riders would separate and ride as hard as possible without being detected or captured by the Sioux. Granger loathed sending two hunters but if he sent just one man—and he failed to get through—death was a near certainty for all in camp.

The chosen men were among their best riders—Georges Dubois and Samuel Campbell. The men cut two of the fastest horses from the Métis string—Granger's own big chestnut gelding and Jean Deschamp's little buckskin mare—walked them quietly north out of camp and then bore west toward the second camp. Granger knew the camp was safe, or would at least remain unharmed until the morning; it was too late in the day for the Sioux to gather their braves and mount a coordinated attack before dark. And the Sioux would not attack at night. The Métis had time to prepare a defense.

A quick meeting near the cook wagon was called.

The Métis traveled under the principles of military discipline, with each member having assigned roles and responsibilities. These rules were accepted by all members of the party. This framework, and the cooperation of all members of the Métis party, was crucial now. Granger knew what must be done and took control. They had very little time.

"You have heard the reports," he began. "Many Sioux camp near here. Perhaps as many as 600 lodges, 1,000 warriors…maybe more. They will almost certainly attack in the morning. We have sent riders on our best mounts to the St. Boniface camp for help but find no assurance there—our men may not get through. We must assume the worst and prepare for battle now."

Several women in the group gasped aloud or wept quietly at the news. The older women knew with certainty the brutality which awaited them if the group failed to repel the Sioux. At the same time, they were thankful the younger women and children did not comprehend the gravity of their situation.

"Lucien, you will direct the wagons into a circle with all the horses and stock within," Granger said, pointing to one man. "Once in place, we must all dig beneath each wagon for shelter of the women and children. Mark 10 paces outside the wagons and dig your rifle-pits there—dig them deeply and use the soil as your parapet for protection. The drying poles must go through the spokes of the wheels so they cannot be moved. Erick, you will gather all spare arms and powder and ball and cartridges—place them here for distribution. Henri, gather bandages, and clean water to care for any wounded. Everyone—we must gather all picks and shovels and axes, anything to dig. We must dig!"

"What has become of Jerome and Jean-Luc and Guy?" asked Paquet. The two returning scouts looked down, deferring to Granger for a response.

"They have been captured…but remain unharmed," Granger responded firmly. At this young Sylvie Ferguson burst into tears and hid her face in her mother's bosom. Elisa shuddered as if struck by a windblast but did not speak, then she too quickly buried her face in her mother's shoulder

"We must have as many shooters as possible—who among you women will take up a gun?"

Most women had little experience with the firearms but several of the younger wives raised their hands along with old Claudine, who had shot many bison and deer over her 66 years. "Erick, you will find them guns if needed."

Now he called on Father LeSueur. "Father, may we have your blessing before we begin our task."

Father LeSueur obliged. "Heavenly Father, please look down on your children and bless them as they prepare for battle, as David did in the valley of Elah and smote the Philistine," he intoned. "Give them the strength to complete their tasks and the courage to face thine enemy. We go forward knowing God is with us and our Father in heaven looks down in favor on his children. We shall fight these heathens and pray that with Your guidance our aim shall be true. Your grace Father shall be our salvation. AMEN!"

"Thank you, Father."

"I shall take confessions after our tasks of this evening are completed," LeSueur added.

Granger did not like the odds; a fight with the Sioux was a fight to the death. Once the Sioux overran their camp it would be a complete slaughter. Only the strength of their numbers had held back the smaller bands of Sioux hostiles, but now that advantage was gone.

The men, women, and children all worked quickly to complete their assigned tasks. Some found shovels and picks and took turns digging into the hard clay soil, others gathered the stock into a makeshift rope corral. It took the rest of the evening to organize the wagons and secure the stock inside. It was nearly midnight before the digging under the bright stars concluded and the rifle pits were finished. The group was exhausted and sweat-soaked as they gathered around the large single fire built within their garrison of carts and wagons.

Star Ferguson watched her daughters proudly. A full-blooded Cree, she accepted death as an equal partner to one's birth, and life on the prairie came without guarantees. She did not fear death but was saddened to think her daughters' lives may be cut short—and she dared not consider the violence which may befall them.

Elisa had worked tirelessly all day, grubbing and digging in the soil and dragging heavy hide sacks of dirt and stone around the hastily constructed compound. Her dark hair and fair features were covered now with dust and bits of yellow grass and prairie seed. Sweat streaked down both cheeks from her brow and trickled down her neck.

"Daughter," Star said, motioning with her hand. "Come." Elisa approached and her mother dipped the corner of a linen towel in a water bucket and wiped her face and brow. "Wash yourself. Tomorrow will be a great victory. Your father and the men are strong. The Métis will not be defeated."

"Jean-Luc has not returned."

"You must not worry, his battle is his…ours is here. It is in the Lord's hands now. We must trust in Him." Now an exhausted Sylvie came to her mother and collapsed in her lap without a word. Her mother gathered her, caressed her forehead gently with fingertips, and softly hummed a lullaby which her own mother had once sung to her.

Elisa took the towel from her mother, filled a small can from the water bucket, and walked from the fire into the shadow of the cart to wash. She removed her soiled blouse and hung it on the spoked wooden wheel. Their soap had been lost during the camp fortification so she simply scrubbed herself thoroughly with the wet cloth and rinsed with the cool creek water from her can. The thin white undergarment she wore was damp from the hard labor of digging but it cooled her as the warm July breeze moved through the camp.

She took little comfort in her mother's words—she could not bear to think of her happy suitor in the hands of the Sioux savages. She could see his smile now, and the awkward way he approached her to talk as if he had something terribly important to discuss—but he rarely talked about anything more than his latest hunt, or the weather. He simply MUST return to them tomorrow. Why did they hold him now? What was it the Sioux wanted?

These were questions she could not answer, she just knew she wanted Jean-Luc back. From her pocket, she pulled the slick stone he had given her. She could not see the beautiful delicate lines in the stone but she knew they were there. As she held the stone she gently rubbed her fingers across the smooth surface. The moon shone brightly in the clear sky and she knew Jean-Luc must see the same moon now. She prayed silently it would protect him through the night.

"*Viens et mange!*" Paquet called. It was time for the camp to eat.

As they ate a small meal of stew in the light of the fire, each of the adults excused themselves, in turn, to offer their quiet confessions to Father LeSueur, who had arranged two short wooden stools to one side of the milling horses and stock. Many assumed this was their last chance of confession and as such a wide variety of sins and misdeeds, some hidden for years, were revealed. All were granted absolution: liars, adulterers, thieves, blasphemers; all human frailties and temptations were exposed, considered, and forgiven. Father LeSueur closed each confession with a reminder of how blessed they were as God's children.

Father LeSueur waited a few minutes following his last confession and then rose to leave when he saw the bulky figure of Paquet slowly make its way toward him from across the camp. Father LeSueur sat back down and waited for the cook to do the same. Paquet had never offered a confession before but Father LeSueur was not surprised to see him now, given the circumstances.

"I am an old man Father," Paquet began, the words not coming easily. "I have no fear for death but I am afraid I will die an angry man."

"Angry? Do you have sins to confess?" inquired Father LeSueur.

"Many. Many sins," admitted Paquet. "But I worry about Jean-Luc, and I am angry at the Father God for taking him from us."

"You mustn't be angry with God—he is your friend and Savior. We shall see Jean-Luc and our other men tomorrow—I know it. The Lord shall protect us—we are all His children. You must believe that. Do you believe Henri?"

"Yaas, I believe. But I don't believe He protect Jean-Luc. I feel this here," he said, patting his big hand over his heart.

"Pray with me then Henri. Let us pray for his safe return." Father LeSueur bowed and placed his hand gently around Paquet's thick neck and quietly recited the Lord's Prayer and the 23rd Psalm, while Paquet mumbled along quietly. Then Father LeSueur leaned his face close to Paquet and whispered, "Go in peace Henri—a great Christian victory awaits us."

Paquet rose and slowly walked back toward the cook's wagon shaking his head, finding little comfort in the Priest's words. He still feared he would die an angry man. And only a foolish man died quarreling with the Lord. Like many of the Cree and Métis elders, he had long ago accepted death as the terminus of a hard life, but he would not willingly accept the sacrifice of the innocent.

That evening, as he lay in his bedroll he prayed again. He prayed that Jean-Luc and the others would burst into camp now under the cover of darkness, and they could all turn their guns on the Sioux in the morning. He prayed he would see him dance with the Ferguson girl again, and twirl and spin and laugh. He prayed that if Jean-Luc were lost, trying to reach camp on foot somewhere out there on the prairie, he would see the North Star and get his bearing and find them again. He asked God for all these things.

But then, as he peered skyward at the stars which would guide his friend, the moon slowly began to fade, and then finally disappeared. An eclipse. The date was July 12th.

Paquet crossed himself quickly. This was not a good sign.

Chapter 15

The first sensation Kelly felt was a throbbing in her ankle, she reached down and grabbed it with her hand and found it sore, and slightly swollen. Then she felt cold. She sat up, then realized where they were. The small campfire had long burned out and was now just a pile of gray ash. She looked at her watch and saw it was 6:12 a.m. but the morning was already bright. Morning storm clouds were building to the northwest. Jamie lay sleeping in a lump across the fire from her.

"Jamie," she barked. "Time to get up." He only moaned.

She tried to stand but could barely put any weight on her right foot. She sat again and slowly began to stretch out her leg, then calf and finally foot and ankle. Then she stopped, searched in her pack, and found her pills. She swallowed three and followed them with a swig of water. Then she went back to her stretching exercises. It was painful but the ankle was warming up.

"Jamie, get up!" she commanded. "We need to get going before it starts to rain."

Jamie stirred and then whipped off his blanket and slowly sat up. "Wha...what time is it?"

"Nearly 6:30, we've got to get going."

They broke camp quickly and after a breakfast of granola bars and the promise of a sit-down brunch, soon fell into a comfortable march down the road. Kelly limped slightly with every step but she knew her ankle would eventually loosen up to the point where the pain would disappear. She also knew there was a truck-stop about four miles ahead on the blacktop and a cafe where they could have a sit-down meal. Her goal was to make it there before the skies opened up with the rain.

They made good time, despite her sore ankle, and could see the truck-stop and small diner just a mile or so ahead when the rain began, first a sprinkling, then a light shower and then a heavier shower which came and went in waves. They walked on for another quarter-mile when a Sheriff's Department cruiser pulled up beside them. The uniformed deputy inside rolled down his passenger window and shouted across the seat, "You folks need a lift?"

Kelly leaned on the top of the car door and lowered her head so she could determine who was inside. Just the deputy.

"We were trying to make the diner before we got wet. Didn't quite make it," she said.

"I'm heading over there myself, trunk's full but throw your packs in the backseat and get in."

They helped each other take off their packs quickly and tossed them on the back seat, then Jamie got in and Kelly found there wasn't room for her. "Mind if I sit in front?"

"Sure, come on up," the deputy replied. She opened the front door and sat down as he removed a clipboard from the front seat.

"Thanks for the lift," said Kelly. "I'm Kelly and this is my brother Jamie." She wanted to get their names out without him asking, yet at the same time didn't feel it necessary to give their last name. The deputy didn't ask.

"Well, I'm Deputy Bauer, from Goodview County, that truck stop is just over the county line into McHenry, but the boys here don't mind if I sneak a meal over here now and then. Best hash browns this side of Winnipeg."

Kelly knew what the next question would be.

"So where you folks from?" he asked, eyeing Jamie in his rear-view mirror.

Kelly took the lead by default. "Up by Metigoshe, taking a little road trip." She also knew what the next question would be.

"Oh, so where you heading?"

"South," she replied, "going to look up some old relatives we haven't seen in a while, the Savards," she added quickly, thus avoiding the third question.

"Hmm, don't know of any Savards," he said. "Where abouts they from?"

"I think down by Harvey or Anamoose."

"Well, I know most families in that area of the county, but Savard is not familiar."

"They might have moved," Kelly offered.

"Well, here we are," announced Bauer abruptly, pulling into a vacant parking space in front of the cafe.

They thanked him and quickly unloaded their packs from the backseat and headed into the diner.

"I need to wash up," said Kelly.

"Me too," replied Jamie, then looking to the woman at the cash register asked, "Okay if we leave these here for a minute?"

She glanced down at the packs. "Sure, Hon."

They emerged from the restrooms a few minutes later and collected their packs and then looked for a table. Bauer saw them and waved them over to a table in a small alcove. All eyes followed them as they made their way through the diner. The alcove had been added onto the building years ago and the floor heaved a bit in the center and sloped slightly toward the outer wall. Like all of those who accept the chance of violent encounters as part of their profession, Bauer had chosen his table to allow clear sight-lines to the front door. It also afforded a modicum of privacy from prying eyes and ears.

Strange young man and woman—"Who, what, and why?" flashed across the synapses of 17 diners and wait-staff simultaneously. The entire process took about three seconds. The diners returned quickly to their conversations, although several snuck cautious glances at Jamie, trying to determine if an Indian had *REALLY* just walked into their café—and if so, what were they going to do about it? In that same instant, they realized he must be approved by Deputy Bauer, and so decided the prudent course was to mind their own business and drink more coffee. Which they did.

Kelly unconsciously conducted her own threat assessment as she walked through the room. Oddly, all the men in the café were seated around a center row of tables while all the women sat at a separate table. They were all white, dressed in a mix of faded bib overalls, poly slacks and western shirts, cotton house dresses, skirts, pastel blouses, blue jeans, heavy T-shirts, and a smattering of cowboy hats. Most had coffee cups in front of them, a few with dirty dishes showing the aftermath of eggs over easy, sausage links and toast.

In the opposite corner sat two younger women with a baby seat perched on the edge of the table. A young waitress was cooing over the baby, wash towel in hand.

Kelly wasn't sure what to make of Deputy Bauer but he didn't seem out to bust their chops. And he would have forced the issue of their last name if he had wanted to run them for wants and warrants. Maybe he was just a friendly cop giving them a ride in the rain.

147

After nearly 10 years in the Marines on three different continents, Kelly had gotten pretty good at reading people. She figured he was okay. She also figured he may be able to help them in their search.

"Jeez, is it okay if we sit here?" she asked quietly as they sat down in chairs opposite Bauer, glancing at the seating arrangements. "I feel like I just stepped back into 1952."

Bauer chuckled and replied softly, "Yeah, afraid most men here still don't know what a spatula is and most women wouldn't know what to do with themselves if they didn't cook all day," then added, "and have a bunch of kids."

The young waitress quickly approached their table with three coffee mugs, a pot of coffee, and two menus stuck under her left arm. "Will you be needing menus?" she asked, setting mugs downs in front of everyone.

"The usual for me Kylie," said Bauer.

"Could I get tea?" asked Kelly. "And I'll need a menu."

"Coffee and a menu for me thanks," said Jamie.

The waitress filled two mugs, displaying a small tattoo of a blue and white dove on her left forearm, then smiled and said, "I'll be right back with that tea."

Bauer shifted in his seat. "You hurt your leg there Kelly? I see you're limping a bit."

"Just out of the Marines, medical discharge. Injured ankle."

"Marines!" he said with a look of surprise. "You look a little light for that outfit. What'd you muster out as?"

"Sergeant."

"She was a Drill Sergeant," offered Jamie.

Bauer whistled softly. "I was glad I missed Vietnam, but I've known a few Marines, tough son-of-a-guns. Really tough. Did you see action?"

"Afghanistan, also Norway and several posts stateside."

"Norway? What were you doing there?"

Kelly smiled, "Classified."

Bauer smiled back. "Of course." Just then the waitress returned. Kelly and Jamie both ordered "The Ranch Hand" breakfast with extra pancakes on the side.

It was a huge meal: three eggs, a huge pile of hash browns, four links of pork sausage, steaming hot biscuits and jelly, and three pancakes as big as their plates. They made quick work of it.

In contrast, Bauer had a full platter of crispy hash browns and coffee.

After they had eaten Kelly suggested, "If we can't find our relatives we were thinking the county Historical Society might be able to help us."

"What was the name again?"

"Savard."

"Yeah, Savard," Bauer put his hand on his chin and rubbed it as if it might produce some information. "A better bet would be the county newspaper, they've been around for 100 years."

"Where are they located?"

"At the county seat in Goodview."

Kelly nodded her head. It was a good idea. "Do you know the name of the editor there?"

Bauer put his hand to chin again, "That's a...Cushman, Sarah Cushman. But she's very young. Last I saw her she was on her way to get a photo of the new paint job on the fire hydrant in front of the courthouse. That's what passes for news here. Nice kid but she's only been there about a year. They hire these kids out of college, don't pay them much but it gets them a newspaper job. Job, hell she's the editor. She'll be gone in a year or two like the rest of 'em.

"You really need to talk to the old editor, Anna Schenko," advised Bauer. "She ran that paper for over 30 years. Gave it up a couple years ago, health problems. Smart enough woman but I think she's pissed off just about everyone in town for one thing or another."

"Seems it'd be hard to be the editor of a small-town paper if nobody'll talk to you," Kelly said.

"Yeah, it was, but as I've said there's not much for news anyway. She just lives a couple blocks away from the Courthouse," he said, then sipped from his coffee mug. "I expect she'd talk to you."

"Would it help break the ice if we said you suggested we talk to her?"

"Nope, she's still pissed at my wife for writing a letter to the editor, which she refused to print, about a wind tower scheme they tried to push through a few years ago. Most news that's ever hit the county since the McClusky Canal—never heard a peep about it in the paper though. She and Margie got into it pretty good."

"So she's mad at you too?" asked Jamie, leaning in.

"Oh yeah, cross some people here and they never forget. We got families been fighting over a ditch or fence for three generations.

Most have been here that long—three or four generations—homesteaders. Their blood and sweat is part of the land. And let me tell you: They do not forget."

"Well, I can understand that," said Kelly, thinking back on the trials of the Métis people. "Maybe some things shouldn't be forgotten."

"Mebbe so. You gotta remember you're dealing with stubborn Germans and Russians and Ukrainians here. They eat hard work and misery for breakfast," he tipped his mug and sipped his coffee again. "My folks were the same way," he offered, matter-of-factly.

Jamie caught a glance from Kelly, who said, "Stubborn," with a faint smirk.

The checks came and they rose to leave.

"I'll get these," said Bauer.

"That's okay we can…" began Kelly but he cut her off.

"It's on me, and thank you for your service young lady. Now can I give you a lift anywhere?"

"Well, thank you, but we'd prefer to continue walking."

"Suit yourself," he replied.

As Bauer walked up front to pay the tab he yelled back toward the kitchen, "Lois, those are the best hash browns in the world. I don't know what you do but don't stop doing it." A laugh came from the back with a shout, "Okay Duane!"

They stopped by the cruiser in the parking lot, Bauer opened the door and then surveyed the landscape. "Well, it's quite a ways to Goodview, but I sense you know what you're doing," he said, then his voice lowered. "Now some folks out there might take exception to a couple 'Indian' hitchhikers if you catch my drift," he said

151

nodding at Jamie. "I expect you can handle yourself, but you take care now. Good luck with finding your people." They thanked him again and he got in his cruiser and pulled out of the lot.

"Well, that went well," said Kelly as she adjusted her pack. "Now we head for Goodview."

"I don't think so Kelly," said Jamie, standing in front of a bulletin board full of flyers posted outside the cafe.

"What do you mean?"

"Aren't we looking for the 'Battle of the Grand Coteau?'"

"Yes," she replied cautiously, now turning and walking back toward him.

"Well, hell, I found it. It's right here in...in...Harvey," he said, peering at one flyer in particular and placing a finger on the name.

Kelly looked closely at the flyer. "*Come join us for the Grand Opening of the Grand Coteau Golf Course, site of the famous Battle of the Grand Coteau. Free circus rides, golf simulator, battle reenactment with real Cowboys and Indians, free balloons, and hot dogs for the kids. Hours 10-4 p.m.*"

Then she looked closer at the date—the Grand Coteau Golf Course, on the site of the Battle of the Grand Coteau, had opened two weeks earlier.

Chapter 16

They set out early the next morning. It was a beautiful summer day on the northern plains…bright sun, modest northwestern breeze, bold meadowlarks warbling on scattered fence posts. It felt good to walk, to pump the cool, fresh air in and out of their lungs. Kelly found a good county gravel road that ran straight east toward Harvey.

She calculated it would take two days of hard traveling to reach Harvey, which lay on the very eastern end of her arc of possible site locations for the battle. She could hardly believe that the battlefield had been found by someone else, and now it was part of a golf course! She decided she would not believe it until she saw it with her own eyes. And saw proof. But what would that proof be?

The flyer had referenced the Goodview County Historical Society; somehow they must have dug into the history of the county and determined the site location. But still, after all the years, and all the time her uncle and mother had put into the search, Kelly couldn't believe it.

Jamie did not have the same problem.

"At least after this, we can say we've seen it and go home," he said. While he had adjusted well enough to their life on the road, it lacked the comforts he had grown used to like soft beds and regular meals.

"I won't believe it until I see it for myself," replied Kelly.

"Yeah, but they already had the Grand Opening and everything," said Jamie. "It's got to be the right place. They wouldn't make something like that up. Besides, it's right where you said it would be."

"It's in the target zone, but that doesn't necessarily mean it's the right spot. I wonder if they found graves or artifacts or did excavations of the site for proof. That would make sense; if they had a new golf course going in they would have to do an archaeology review."

"Well, there you go," said Jamie confidently.

"Still, you should never trust the government to do the right thing," said Kelly. "When the right thing does happen it's usually more of an accident than anything else."

"Yeah, but you *were* the government when you were in the Service."

"Yeah, and because of that I know better—so don't trust the government to do the right thing. If I learned anything in the Marines it's that sometimes you have to do the right thing on your own and say to hell with the government."

She thought back now to the Métis at Batoche, getting mowed down by bullets and shrapnel from the Canadian artillery, a civilian population chewed up and spat out by a military machine. She saw too the faces of the dead Afghan villagers, just chips in a war played in faraway places.

What hurt most though was the thought that her fellow DI Kristal Moore, a proud black woman, a woman warrior and true patriot who pushed herself to incredible lengths to maintain her personal integrity, could find no foothold in Marine regulations or brass to restore her dignity, her trust in the Corps family. *No, Jamie, you should never trust the government to do the right thing.*

"What's that ahead—a grass fire?" asked Jamie, pointing toward a plume of black smoke a mile or so ahead in the ditch.

"Not sure," said Kelly, squinting at the object and unconsciously checking the wind. It was at their back so any grass fire would be traveling away from them. Since the object was directly ahead of them, she added, "I guess we'll find out."

As they got closer they heard a roar, like a train passing or a huge engine racing down a track. Closer still, they found what they had thought were flames was actually yellow paint, from the body of a road grader. Heavy black smoke poured out its stack. The grader was tipped at a 45-degree angle down a steep ditch. The huge blade had dug into the shoulder, ripped out a barbed-wire fence, and uprooted a good-sized tree, which stopped the rig from rolling over. One set of rear tires hung off the ground and spun slowly in the air.

As they got up to the rig the sound was nearly unbearable. Kelly dropped her pack and put her hands over her ears, then motioned Jamie to join her in the ditch opposite the machine.

"I'm going to see if someone's still in there," she shouted. "You stay here." Jamie nodded in agreement.

Kelly sprinted over to the rig and made a quick circle around it, looking for an operator. She found him inside the cab on the lower side of the rig, plastered to the glass door, a heavy-set white man with a bushy mustache and greasy dark hair. She hesitated to try to reach him from that side because she would have no chance if the rig tipped over. Instead, she climbed up the outside of the cab from the higher side on the road and opened the door. It was heavy but she was able to hold it open with one hand while balancing on her waist. Reaching as far as she could, she stretched across the cab and turned off the ignition switch under the steering wheel. As she did the cab tilted slightly under her weight but the noise stopped as the engine quickly throttled down and died. Now she smelled a familiar odor but couldn't place it. She smelled diesel, smelled something like burned rubber, and then she identified it—alcohol.

"Hey Mister," she shouted, "Are you okay? Are you okay?" The cab and engine were quiet now except for the "pinging" of hot metal parts as they cooled. She wanted to see if he had a pulse but she could not reach him without getting down into the cab entirely.

"Is there someone in there?" shouted Jamie, still on the other side of the road.

"Yes, but I can't reach him," she replied. "I'm afraid if I get in the whole thing will tip over."

"Is he dead?"

"I don't know. I can't tell from here." Then she spied a half-empty pint bottle of Jack Daniels whiskey resting between his legs. The man snorted and then she heard him snore softly.

"You stupid bastard!" she shouted angrily.

"What's wrong?" asked Jamie, now standing on the shoulder next to the rig.

"He's drunk," she said, turning to him, "I risked my life for a goddam drunk."

She extracted herself from the cab and jumped down to the shoulder, brushing dirt and grass off her pants. Jamie cautiously walked around to the other side of the rig and saw the man was indeed sleeping peacefully against the glass door.

"He sleeping," he said. "What do we do now?"

"Some problems are ours and others are not. This is not our problem," announced Kelly. "Let him sleep it off." Without cell phones and no farms nearby, they really had no other options, so Kelly put her pack back on and they continued down the road.

"He's lucky it didn't catch fire," said Jamie, glancing back at the rig.

"Yeah, very lucky, he could have been toast, literally."

An hour and several miles later Jamie asked, "Do you think that guy in the grader is alright?"

"Well, he's obviously an alcoholic who drives heavy machinery for a living so I'm guessing his long-term prospects are not good," Kelly responded. "But this isn't the first time he's buried a rig in the ditch. He's probably home already trying to sober up and come up with an excuse."

As a Marine, Kelly had learned to compartmentalize her objectives, reducing them from overwhelming tasks to manageable pieces. She fully expected there would be obstacles in her path, obstacles that would prevent her from achieving her objectives, but only temporarily. Improvise, adapt, overcome. This same principle helped her cope with worry and stress. Once considered and acted upon, it was time to move on to the next objective. She had done her best to rectify the situation with the drunk man in the grader. Now it was time to move on to their next objective—closing the gap between their location and the battlefield. The man, the grader, the public at risk—were no longer her concern.

They walked on, directly east, with the setting sun over their shoulders. They made good time and soon came to a major powerline which intersected a shallow dry coulee. The powerline stretched farther than they could see in both directions, likely coming from the Missouri River dams to the west and heading east toward the Twin Cities in Minnesota. An old campsite at the edge of the powerline right-of-way was surrounded by buckbrush and hawthorn bushes.

"Camp here?" asked Jamie hopefully.

"No, listen," said Kelly.

"What?"

"Listen."

Jamie stopped and listened. "What's that humming?"

"It's the powerlines," said Kelly, pointing overhead. "Let's move down."

They moved down the coulee another 75 yards to a flat spot that overlooked the drainage. Thick clumps of olive-colored buffalo-berry lined the slope. It was a good spot to stop, breezy enough to discourage the bugs, secluded enough to give them some privacy from the road. There were plenty of old limbs from the shrubs and buckbrush for a campfire.

They set up camp and soon had a small fire going. Kelly dug two large potatoes from her pack and wrapped them in two thin sheets of foil, placing them on the edge of the fire to slowly roast. "Do you want some Spam with your spud, otherwise I have cheese and margarine too," she asked Jamie.

"What kind of cheese?"

"I don't know, it's cheese. You getting picky?"

"Not about my cheese, but can you make it without sand?"

"Without sand? Oh, I get it, *you're* volunteering to cook now. My, *this* is a pleasant surprise," she said with derision. "I can't wait to see what's for breakfast."

"No, no," said Jamie apologetically, raising his hands in submission. "I'm just saying I'd like to eat a meal or two without sand. My oatmeal had sand in it this morning."

"Guess what happened in Afghanistan?"

Jamie put his fingers to his forehead and closed his eyes as if concentrating. "Wait, wait...let me guess. You had...you had...sand in all your meals?"

"Pretty much. Anything outside had sand in it, half the stuff in our mess hall had sand too. We'd get sand storms and everything on the base would be coated with grit, would even get under the sheets. So, do you want Spam with this or not?"

"Spam, with a side order of sand, please. No cheese."

"Coming up." Kelly busied herself getting out the plates and dinnerware. The temperature had already begun to drop with the setting sun. The fire would feel good tonight.

Jamie sat on the ground near the fire and watched his sister cook. "So, did you ever kill anyone over there?"

"In Afghanistan?"

"Yeah, or did you kill somebody in Norway too?"

"Well, you're not supposed to talk about it. Some people get really upset."

"So that means 'yes.'"

"Yes. My friend Kristal and I got separated from our unit during a mission in an Afghan village. You would think the open countryside would be the most dangerous, but it was the villages. You never knew who was friendly and who wasn't. You had to assume everyone was a hostile, which is a hell of a way to live. Civilians were killed as often as the hostiles. The friendlies had to be nice to us and to the rebels to get by but eventually, they would say or do the wrong thing and get taken out by one side or the other. It wasn't fair, but once you're over there you do what you need to do to survive. Kristal and I had to take out some hostiles to escape."

"What happened?"

"We were helping some kids escape a friendly artillery attack—it was our guys firing. We got pushed down an alley and ended up in a room at the end and took incoming fire at both exits—the bad guys this time. It was a dumb move, going down a blind alley. Protocol would have had us leave the kids and extract ourselves. In the Marines one live American grunt is worth more than a whole roomful of foreign kids. But Kristal and I agreed we had to try to save the kids and so we got stuck in this room."

Kelly felt awkward speaking about the attack but then, as she relayed more and more of the story to Jamie, she felt an unseen burden lift and began to feel relieved.

"We could have tried to shoot our way out or we could wait until they breached the room and then take them out when they came through. That's what we did—Kristal took out two and I took out one. I don't think they were expecting us to be alive, and they didn't care about the kids. Two of the kids were killed and four wounded. We each carried two out on our backs when we retreated."

"That sounds terrible," said Jamie seriously. "Where did you hit your guy?"

"What do you mean?"

"Where did you shoot him?"

She played the scene out in her mind, the scene from her dreams, again; she felt the rough texture of the wall at her back, hot on the fingers of her open hand. Her gun was jammed and useful now only as a club. Kristal had a good angle and was able to take out the two hostiles who burst through the doorway she covered. It took just a second; two rounds and they were down. Kelly had the kids behind her, whimpering in fear, two of the girls had wet themselves, and she knew Kristal couldn't help her without exposing herself. She would have to do this alone.

160

She heard the steps approach her entryway, the soft soles crunching sand. She flattened against the inner wall, debating whether to swing her blade wide with her right hand around the door frame or swing close with her left arm in a backhand. The backhand would be a blind thrust but provided better cover—although she would have to wait until he was almost through the doorway. She decided to go with the backhand. Her heart nearly burst as she saw the muzzle of his rifle slowly inch around the corner.

Her arm was a blur as the blade "snicked" against the trigger guard of his gun and then sank in just below his throat. She felt it slide in, barely any resistance, and then hit bone. Then she jerked the blade toward her with all her strength. He dropped the rifle, and slowly began to fall forward and turn towards her.

"I didn't, I killed him with a knife it was…close quarters," Kelly said. "I don't want to talk about it."

"I thought all you Marines were badass killers," he chided.

"Jesus Jamie, it's not funny!" Kelly said angrily. "I'm just a girl that grew up in the Turtle Mountains!

"Remember when I said you take and give something to everyone you meet? It's the same when you're fighting for your life I killed a man, and it took a lot out of me, and it left me with some shit that will be with me forever. Kristal said she felt the same way. In a perfect world, no one should ever have to feel that way. But the world's not perfect, and now I have to think about this the rest of my life."

Jamie found he was genuinely sorry he had pushed her and for the first time in a long time, he considered Kelly's perspective—having to kill a man, up close, personal. He wasn't sure he could do it. Or if he could, could he live with himself afterward?

He considered the thugs from his rehab, thought how satisfying it might feel to take them out, but in his version, he would blast them with his pistol. They would die instantly and forever regret messing with him. But that's the point—they would be gone forever…because of him. Could he deal with that for the rest of his life? He knew he didn't want to. And he realized now his sister was much tougher than he would ever be.

Feeling bruised from their conversation, they ate their baked potatoes and fried Spam in silence. It was good; the meat was crisp on the outside and juicy in the center, it sizzled as Kelly forked the pieces onto their tin plates. Their meal done, Kelly put on a pot of water for tea and clean-up.

It was nearly 10:00 p.m. before the sun disappeared, but the western horizon still glowed with the remains of another prairie day. Somewhere far down the coulee a pack of coyotes caught their evening meal and erupted into a peal of excited yelps and squeals. It was tough being a coyote and Kelly didn't begrudge them an easy meal. She was massaging her ankle and about to settle down on her bedroll when a voice called out from the direction of the road.

"Hello the camp!"

Kelly and Jamie looked at each other in surprise, then Kelly called out, "Hello."

They listened but did not hear anyone approach. Suddenly an elderly Indigenous man clad in a long thin coat, faded trousers, moccasins, and long braids of gray hair stood at the edge of the fire circle. Even in the flickering firelight, they could see his face was creased and leathery from years in the sun and wind.

"*Tansi*," said the man in Cree.

"*Tansi*," replied Kelly. "Welcome to our fire."

"You are travelers," said the man, "as am I. May I join you a little while to chase the chill from these bones?"

162

"Certainly," replied Kelly. "Would you like a cup of tea?"

The man shuffled closer. "That would be very nice."

Kelly tried to determine the man's age; he moved easily enough, with a certain gracefulness or lightness, but his face was the face of wisdom, accomplishment, and if not confidence then contentment. She thought he must be somewhere near 80 years old.

Jamie peered behind him in the darkness, seeing and hearing nothing he asked, "Do you have a horse?"

"My best horse died many years ago and I will not have another. I walk where I need to go," the man replied. "But you walk also no? You walk to find something that the horse and rider would miss."

"We're traveling to find some relatives. Please, sit here," Kelly said, laying down her bedroll blanket, "we don't have any chairs."

"It is good to sit on the ground, to remind us where we came from. You are traveling east?"

"Yes, toward Harvey. Have you been there?" answered Kelly. Now they all sat down cross-legged around the fire. Jamie added two limbs to the coals.

"I know of it but my real home is to the north," replied the man dolefully. "People travel to many places, but you only belong to one place. My place is north, by the Red River. It is where I will die."

Kelly now noticed the beading of the man's moccasins was not just similar, it appeared *identical* to the beading on her mother's cherished moccasins, the smaller pair—with a bold red infinity symbol on a blue background framed by just three blossoms of pink prairie rose. How was that possible? As odd as it seemed, she considered now that perhaps this man's visit was more than just a chance encounter.

"Are you traveling back home now?" asked Jamie.

"Yes, but not so soon, not so soon. I have a task to complete first, then I will go home again."

"Would you like something to eat?" asked Kelly. "We have fruit."

"You have fruit? There is not much fruit in this country. My favorites are Saskatoons and the September plum, but it is too early for those. No, I am not hungry, but would you have any tobacco?"

"I have some cigarettes, but nothing for a pipe," offered Jamie.

"This fire feels good," said the man, ignoring Jamie's response and rubbing the heat into his shins. "It feels very good." Then he paused rubbing and looked up. "My name is Kitchi but I am known as Badger, what are your names?"

"I'm Kelly and this is my brother Jamie," said Kelly.

Jamie nodded in acknowledgment. "How did you know we were looking for something on our trip?"

"It is the way of our people on the prairie, always on the move, searching for food, better water, and more game. It is what we have always done, what we were meant to do," he replied with authority. "When we stay in one place…this is not good for us."

Kelly rose to pour a cup of the hot tea into a tin cup and offered it to him. "Be careful, this is very hot."

"Thank you, daughter," he said as he grasped it by the thin handle and immediately took a small sip. "You make good tea."

He set the cup on the ground in front of him and began to search his pockets, first inside the coat, then outside, then inside again. Then he triumphantly produced a stubby clay pipe with a thin stem. "Ah, here it is," he exclaimed, holding it for the pair to see. From his outer front pocket, he produced an empty leather pouch.

"You have tobacco?" he asked again, now looking at Jamie.

"Sure," he replied, fishing a cigarette from his pack. "Here you go."

Kitchi opened his pouch and rubbed the cigarette between his thumb and forefinger, sifting the tobacco into the pouch. Dropping the cigarette paper into the fire he then dug into the pouch again and began packing his pipe. Once packed, he selected a burning twig from the fire to use as a match. Holding it to the pipe bowl he drew in and soon produced thick plumes of smoke.

The aroma reminded Kelly of ripe autumn plums, a scent she had not encountered for many years. Had it been his suggestion? Or was he really smoking plum bark? Her thoughts were interrupted by Jamie.

"You said you had a task," said Jamie. "Can you tell us what it is? Maybe we could help."

"That is kind of you to help an old man, but I am not the one in need. It makes my heart glad just to see you here, a brother and sister, under the prairie sky. Too many families drift apart, and then they are nothing. To share your fire, and a cup of tea, it is enough."

"Do you have family up north?" asked Kelly, "Up on the Red?"

"All my people are there, some in the soil, others busy with the tasks and burdens which make up a life. My two wives have passed, my children have moved away," he offered sadly. "Where is your family?"

"We live near the Turtle Mountains, but our family is spread all over North Dakota and Manitoba," explained Kelly. "We both live with our grandmother near the Mountains, but we have other relatives near Bottineau and quite a few south of Winnipeg. Our mother just passed away a few years ago."

"You are Métis," said the man, a statement rather than a question.

"We are," said Jamie. "Our father was Cree and French, our mother was...what was she, Kelly?'

"I think she was French and Chippewa, or what used to be called Saulteaux. We are quite a mix."

"We are probably related then," observed Kitchi. "What is your last name?"

"Moreau," replied Kelly.

"I know of several Moreau families, it is not an uncommon name where I live. They are good people, hard workers, good family people. I do not know if they are Métis, but as you say it is quite a mix. Have you ever been to a Métis dance festival? I went to one with my granddaughter last fall when the maples blazed as if on fire—many fiddles and dancing, it was quite enjoyable to see the young people so happy. Of course, it made the elders happy too; nothing gives more happiness than seeing their children and grandchildren happy. Sadness can be shared by generations, but so too is happiness shared." He stopped and drew on his pipe again, then slowly exhaled. "Many of our young people have chosen a different path, but it seems to lead to anger and sadness."

"I used to dance," admitted Jamie.

"Did you? You have the build of a dancer, I can see it now. And do you still dance?"

"No, I gave it up a while ago."

"Do you teach then?" he inquired.

"No."

"He was very good," interjected Kelly. "My mother made authentic costumes and different colored sashes for each. He danced with one of the best groups in our area, they traveled everywhere to compete. They even won some contests in Winnipeg. He still has trophies in his old bedroom."

Kitchi removed his pipe and took a measured sip from his tea and set the cup down again. "But you don't teach?" he asked quizzically, looking at Jamie.

"No."

He drew deeply on his pipe and released a dense stream of sweet smoke which curled around his head, rose, and slowly dissipated before he spoke again. "When I was young my father taught me to trap the beaver, to hunt the birds and deer, and to fish for pike and whitefish. And we spoke in our native tongue. We sold furs, made jerky and pemmican, smoked the whitefish. It was a good life. Now my daughters live in the city and worry about paying for cars and what clothing they will wear."

He stared into the fire and drew on his pipe again. "They will never know how to skin a beaver or flesh a hide, and I have no sons to teach. My grandson is four years old now and I have never seen him. This makes me sad." He stopped and continued to stare into the fire as if receiving messages from it.

No one spoke as the fire popped and hissed, the smoke rising straight upward toward the black, moonless sky.

"Now I must go," Kitchi said abruptly and began to get to his feet.

"You are welcome to stay with us tonight," said Kelly, rising herself and brushing off her pants. "It's foolish to be walking around in the darkness. You might get hit by a car or something." Now Jamie stood too.

Kitchi smiled benignly. "Young people are afraid of the dark, while the hunter and the thief wait in it for their prey. But when you are old, the darkness is your friend, as are the stars and the sounds of the night." He leaned back and took a deep breath and then exhaled mightily. "It is a good night to travel."

He reached out to shake Jamie's hand. Grasping it he pulled him closer, "The coyote has no choice, it must kill to live; nor does the rabbit have a choice, it must run to live. But the Creator gave us a choice—to be strong like a predator or to be weak like prey. Each must choose their path. There are many ways to honor one's ancestors. Choose one and do it well. There you will find satisfaction."

Then he turned to Kelly and grasped her hand warmly in both of his. "Thank you for the fire daughter, you are a fine teacher. I wish you well on your journey."

"Goodbye Kitchi," said Kelly. He reminded her of her uncle.

Jamie watched as he turned and melted into the darkness. "Goodbye!" he said. They listened but could not hear footsteps or shuffling. He was simply gone.

"Well, that was interesting," Jamie remarked. "I thought *we* were crazy running around out here but he's doing it in the middle of the night. What do you really think he was doing? Was he gonna walk all the way back to Canada himself?"

"I don't know," Kelly answered. "I guess it might be cooler to walk at night, and you wouldn't be seen as much if you were trying to hide. But I didn't get the impression he was trying to hide. I wonder what this job was he had to do, the task he talked about."

She bent over and grabbed the blanket he sat on and shook it out, then reached down and retrieved his tin cup from the edge of the fire, still half full of tea.

"Jesus!" she exclaimed.

"What?" responded Jamie in alarm.

"Feel this," Kelly said, holding out the tin cup by its handle.

Jamie took the cup in his hand   it was as cold as ice.

Chapter 17

They made good time the next day and camped on State Forest land south of Rugby, lots of short logging roads, thick groves of popple, deer tracks, but for some odd reason poison ivy everywhere. It was a beautiful sunset, a North Dakota sunset, full of bold colors—blue and purple and scarlet all sweeping across the horizon as if competing with one another. The wind had died and it was quiet. They set up the tent to discourage mosquitoes.

The next morning Jamie rose from his bedroll to relieve himself around the bend of the forest road.

Kelly cautioned him as he left, "Be careful of the ivy."

"Yeah, I see it," he called back as he walked away.

It was a cool morning with low overcast skies, so with plenty of wood at hand and just a slight breeze in the shelter of the grove they enjoyed a morning fire. Kelly soon had their pot of water boiling briskly.

"You want raisins in your oatmeal?" she asked.

"Oatmeal again," groaned Jamie.

"Unless you're hiding some ham and eggs in your pack, then yes, oatmeal again. Have some tea," she said, as she poured him a cup.

"Yes, I'll take some delicious raisins in my oatmeal—wouldn't miss it. You should write a book, call it, 'Culinary Delights of the Northern Trail,' by Chef Kelly Moreau, or, 'Oatmeal 100 Ways.'"

"You sure complain a lot. Feel free to make your own breakfast; it won't hurt my feelings."

After breakfast, they snuffed out the fire, repacked packs, and walked out the short logging road to the county road. They walked for 40 minutes, following the twists and turns of the gravel road and skirting the perimeter of potholes and fields. After several more 90 degree turns Kelly consulted the maps she had packed.

"I'm not really sure where we are," she said, peering down at one of her maps. "We need to go south or southeast toward Harvey—do you think south is that way?' she said, motioning toward the right.

"No, that's southwest, we need to go straight—if we run into any more sloughs we need to bear left, that'll keep us going east."

They continued straight and then followed the road as it bore left, a mile down the road. A mile later the road bore right again and then ended at a cattle gate a half-mile later, which opened into a rough pasture. A prairie trail followed the fence line and in the distance they could see a blacktopped highway, some two miles distant.

They followed the grassy trail toward the highway but after a mile and a quarter the road went over a hill and then ended at the edge of a large pond. Actually, the road continued through the pond underwater; they could see it emerge 200 yards on the opposite side and continue straight, but they had no way to cross.

"Damn it," said Kelly. "This shouldn't be so hard. Let's take a break." She broke out her water bottle and sat down to look at her maps again. She looked around, trying to find a landmark, but saw only prairie hills falling away in each direction.

Jamie dropped his pack and sat down beside her.

"If we walk around this slough to the blacktop and take that east..." she began, pointing to the hills on the horizon.

"That's the wrong way," said Jamie. "That blacktop runs north/south."

"I thought that was east," Kelly replied.

"No, it's south. How did you find your way around in the Marines?"

"Let me get my compass out and I'll show you."

"Don't need it. You've got me. I've never been lost, doesn't matter if it's in the city or the woods, I can always find north. Every time."

"You never get lost…right," said Kelly skeptically.

"Well, take out your compass, and let's walk up to the top of that ridge. Harvey should be straight south of us, maybe a little east," Jamie said, pointing to a small ridge of land just behind them. "From there we should be able to see the Prophets Mountains again, which we know is southwest."

They walked up the ridge and Jamie pointed. "That way is west." From the rise, they could once again see the dark hills of the Prophets Mountains on the horizon, perhaps thirty miles distant.

"Lucky guess," said Kelly, consulting her compass.

"No luck involved," he responded. "Try me."

A breeze had kicked up now and the sky brightened as the cloud cover started to break up. The liquid trill of a meadowlark's song filled the air, with a second bird answering in the distance.

"That way's north, right?" said Jamie pointing northward.

"Yeah."

"Okay, I'm gonna close my eyes and cover them and you can spin me any way you want, and I'll still find north." He stepped in front of her and pulled his hat down to cover his eyes. "Spin."

"I am not going to spin you, spin yourself."

"If I spin myself you'll think it's a trick."

"That's true," she admitted. She grabbed his shoulders and pushed him away from her so he would turn in a circle. He spun on his own twice and then stopped.

"North is that way," he said, holding his arm out from his side and pointing—directly north.

"How'd you do that?"

He lifted the brim of his hat and smiled. "Human compass, I told you."

"Wait, you cheated," she said, unwrapping a bandanna from around her neck. "Let's try this again."

She tossed his hat on the ground. "Now, hold still, Tell me if you can see anything." She wrapped her bandanna across his eyes and secured it snugly with a single overhand knot behind his head.

"Can you see anything?"

"No…give it your best," he replied. This time Kelly walked behind him and turned him around twice then reversed a half-circle, then turned him opposite again in a 270-degree arc. She dropped her hands. "Okay, where's north?"

He lifted an arm and pointed.

"*Damn*," she thought. "*He really was a human compass.*"

173

Once they reached the blacktop they walked two hours along a good stretch of road with lots of wetlands and big open vistas, the kind that made you feel small but happy to be a part of it. The clouds had burned off now and the sun shone warmly. It was a fine day in the northern plains. Both sides of the road were planted to alfalfa, which buzzed and hummed with the flight of honey bees working the new purple, pink and white blossoms.

There was very little traffic, mostly pickup trucks with ranchers sporting cowboy hats, and a couple of quad-cab pickup trucks full of Hispanic bee workers. One of the flatbeds had a dozen hives or "supers" on it, which sloughed bees by the dozen as the rigs lumbered down the highway.

Kelly saw lights in her peripheral vision just before the North Dakota State Trooper's cruiser pulled ahead of them and, moving over to the shoulder, blocked their way forward. As the cruiser stopped, a nervous gadwall hen emerged from the cattails and quickly swam across a small pond on the side of the road with seven half-grown ducklings in tow.

The trooper opened his door and quickly exited the car, sliding a black nightstick into his belt ring as he walked. He was a tall, well-built, white man with clipped blonde hair. About Kelly's age.

"Hi folks, anything wrong?" he asked, looking them up and down as he approached.

They stopped. "Let me handle this," Kelly said to Jamie softly.

"No," said Kelly firmly to the officer.

"Can I see some ID please?"

"Why do you need to see ID officer?" Kelly asked.

"Just routine procedure, let me see your ID and you can be on your way."

"We haven't broken any laws officer, we're just walking on the side of a public road."

"Well, I'll need to see some ID."

"Are you detaining us?" she countered.

"No."

"Then I assume we're free to go."

The trooper appeared flustered for a moment, he was losing control of the stop. "Do you have any drugs or weapons on you?"

"We don't need to answer that. Are we free to go?" Kelly asked again.

That was enough backtalk thought the trooper—these were his assigned roads and he wasn't about to take any crap from a Rez runner. "No, you are not. Drop those packs and place your hands on the back of the vehicle."

Jamie fidgeted nervously and shifted his weight from foot to foot. Kelly sighed, then realized that by parking in front of them any interaction would not be captured by his dash camera…and he must have done so on purpose. Not good. She would try a new tact.

"Listen, officer, we don't have any driver's licenses on us because we are not driving a vehicle and we don't need them. You have no cause to stop us or question us. We are traveling for personal reasons we have no obligation to disclose. As they say, this is a free country. And we'd just like to be on our way."

"I'm ordering you to drop those packs and place your hands down flat on the back of the car," he barked, now taking the nightstick from his utility belt. "And keep both hands where I can see them." Kelly didn't move.

Jamie began to take off his pack. "C'mon Kelly, just do what he says."

"No," she scolded. "You don't need to do that—he has no right to stop us." Jamie took off his pack and held his hands up as if surrendering.

"You too," the trooper snapped at Kelly, his other hand covering the butt of his pistol now.

"*Damn*," she thought, this was headed in the wrong direction. She knew if it came to a defensive situation she would be much better off out of her pack, and she was damned if she was going to let this trooper bust them for "walking while Indian." Improvise, adapt, overcome.

She unbuckled her pack, slowly, and let it fall to the ground. It felt good to get the weight of the pack off her shoulders, and the sweat on her back began to cool immediately. She flexed her shoulders and worked out a kink.

"Now get *UP* against the vehicle and get your hands *DOWN* where I can see them or I'll be forced to cuff you," directed the trooper.

Jamie quickly complied and put his hands on the trunk. Kelly slowly did the same.

"Do you have any drugs or weapons on you?"

"We don't have to answer that," replied Kelly coolly.

"How about you Geronimo," he said to Jamie. "Any drugs or weapons?" Jamie just hung his head and remained silent.

The nightstick speared Jamie in the left kidney, and he went down in a heap, writhing in pain.

"I'm talking to you son," barked the trooper. "Don't you hear so good?"

"You son of a bitch!" protested Kelly, turning as the trooper wound up to deliver the next nightstick blow across her spine.

"*Don't use the blade*," she told herself. It would be easy but foolish to use the blade.

Because of her training, Kelly knew seven basic defensive tactics that could be used to neutralize an attack involving clubs and related items. Three of these countered attacks from the rear. She not only knew the techniques, but she had also taught them and had beaten down motivated Marines twice her size during training. And so she saw the trooper's actions now as if in slow motion.

She would make him pay for this.

She whirled and engaged: first the nightstick, then the arm, shoulder, and torso. With two quick twists and a leveraged turn, aided slightly when he stumbled over Jamie's legs, she slammed the trooper's face onto the trunk and wedged the nightstick across his neck, pinning him. She was sorely tempted to drive her left knee into his kidney as payback, but she maintained her composure. Still, she was disappointed; her plan had been to slam him down hard enough to knock him senseless, but he was still struggling.

She could fix that. Drawing a deep breath she slowly pressed three fingers of her right hand into the hollow behind the trooper's right ear. She focused, pressed harder, and then exhaled slowly through pursed lips as the trooper crumpled and slid into her. She eased him onto the ground and dragged him by his shirt collar between the cruiser and the ditch and placed him in the recovery position. Then she removed his pistol, a Glock .40 caliber, from his holster and released the magazine into her hand and ejected the round in the chamber.

She stooped again, found two spare magazines in his belt, removed them, and then threw all the magazines and the loose cartridge into the roadside pond. Then she replaced the gun in its holster.

Jamie was kneeling on the ground on all fours. "Are you okay Jamie?" she asked, pulling his shirt up to reveal a purple bruise near the small of his back.

"That bastard," he spat.

"Yeah," she agreed and then looked around to survey the area. "Listen, I hate to run but we're the losers in this deal any way you look at it. We have somewhere between five and 20 minutes before he wakes up, so we need to move. Do you think you can carry your pack or do you want me to take it?"

Jamie stood and rubbed his back. "How can you take it? You have your own pack."

"I've run with a larger pack and a Marine slung over the top of it. I think I can handle yours," she said confidently.

"No, no, I'm okay," he said, shouldering his pack with a wince. Kelly hefted her pack easily and strapped it on.

"Let's go," she said, then walked over to the driver's side door of the cruiser. She leaned in, removed the keys from the ignition, and hurled those over the top of the car into the pond as well. "Have fun trying to explain that asshole," she said with satisfaction.

Chapter 18

Their rifles gone, they were guarded by an old Sioux warrior with a crippled leg. Looking closer Jean-Luc saw the man's left foot was twisted, as if broken and poorly healed, his toes pointing nearly sideways from his body. As a result, he hobbled when he walked with his weight on his twisted heel. He pointed a double-barrel percussion shotgun at them, hammers cocked and ready to fire. Seated only 15 feet away, he could cut a man in half with one blast. Jerome and Guy sat next to him on the ground, their hands tied behind their backs.

Jean-Luc did not understand the Sioux language entirely but recognized a few words exchanged between the warriors. Although the Sioux riders had made out to be friendly initially, there was no doubt that the three Métis hunters were now hostages. They conversed between themselves quietly in their Mechif language and agreed they were being held in exchange for some type of ransom, or in trade for something else wanted by the Sioux. Otherwise, they'd have already been killed. The Sioux, members of Heavy Bear's band, already had their horses, which had been stripped of their saddles and tethered to nearby buckbrush, so they wanted more.

The sun hung low in the western sky now. They knew they were likely safe until morning. Jean-Luc could see Cherie 30 yards away calmly nibbling on tufts of grass. Their other two horses were tied next to her but remained skittish, responding with fright each time a Sioux shouted or cursed in their direction. There had been much shouting initially, and rough prodding with lances, rifles, and bows as the captured men were beaten, pushed to the ground and their hands tied. Now the warriors taunted them, pointing and laughing and pantomiming the cutting of their throats as they passed by.

Just before sundown, a thin, mixed-blood man wearing a long black ponytail approached them. His face was pinched and caked with

179

dust from riding. He wore threadbare linen pants several sizes too large for him which gathered around his waist and bunched over his ankles. A dark indigo vest with six large brass buttons covered his bare chest. From his belt hung a pistol and *parfleche* bag. Moccasins completed his outfit. His cheek was plump with tobacco, on which he chomped methodically.

He spoke in broken English, saying he was trading with the Sioux in their main camp. He had heard of their capture this afternoon. He spoke poor French but understood the Sioux language well. He did not offer his name.

"Heavy Bear says you are cowards, and…poor hunters," he related. "You steal his buffalo and deserve to die. If you wish safe passage you must surrender all your animals and arms."

Jerome, the oldest of the three Métis scouts, responded in a mixture of English and French. "The animals are ours. We have many guns and skilled hunters—many Sioux will die if they try to take them."

The thin man spat a stream of tobacco juice and looked at them quizzically. "*YOU* are far outnumbered sir. Heavy Bear has 3,000 warriors—fight 'em and they'll take your arms, your horses…*AND* your women."

Then the old Sioux warrior with the shotgun interrupted, shouting a phrase over and over.

The thin man interpreted. "He sez your blood will cover the ground and…dogs will feed on your black hearts." The warrior shouted something again angrily, emphasizing one word over and over as he thrust his gun violently at each of the captives. A bright stream of clear spittle ran from the corner of his mouth.

"He sez you're…worthless…not worth a…a bullet. He desires to drive a knife through your hearts and fly your scalps from his lance."

The man spat again noisily. "Can't though—Heavy Bear won't let him. Least not yet."

The Métis men doubted that 3,000 Sioux warriors were in the area but now the gravity of their predicament sank in. "Why are they holding us?" asked Jerome.

"You're to be traded for arms and horses tomorrow."

"If we give up arms we'll be killed."

"Heavy Bear'll give your group safe passage to the North. Sez you must promise to never return."

"We travel where we please," responded Jerome defiantly. "We follow the buffalo and take what we want. The buffalo are ours as well as Heavy Bear's."

"That so?" the man declared. "Mister you are a damn fool, they know you got only 75 rifles, and they know you got near 100 women and youngins...and over 100 horses. You can't protect everything. They been watching you for days."

The man shook his head sadly. "By now you probably sent a runner to the other camp to the west but I expect he's dead already." The man scratched his crotch area absent-mindedly. "You're all alone here friend."

He then squatted before them and calmly expelled a long stream of tobacco juice, as if considering the fate of a butcher pig rather than the lives of three men. "You know what'll happen to your women if they's caught..." He paused to let them consider. "They got blood in their eye now, I cain't see this working out. You Frenchies shoulda stayed over in that Red River country where you belong. Best give 'em what they want now and hope they let you git on."

Jean-Luc considered Elisa, and little Sylvie, and stopped himself from imagining the horrible fate which might befall them. He felt

181

anger replacing his fear—anger at this filthy little man, at the Sioux, at the bison which had tempted them to travel so far from home.

The man straightened now and stretched his back, then turned and looked toward the Butte, which loomed dark against the fading sunset. "Those braves will be riding up and down that damn rock all night long—it's big medicine. Good medicine for them...bad for you. They won't be singing death songs tonight, 'less they're for you." He spat again, barely missing his own moccasin. "You fellas might want to say a prayer."

By now it was nearly dark and the man hitched up his pants as if getting ready to go. "Anything you want me to pass on to Heavy Bear?"

The men were silent and then Jean-Luc blurted out angrily, "Tell him to go to hell!" At this, the thin man chortled and rocked back on his heels.

"Well, you might see 'im there!" he said cheerfully, then splashed another long brown streak of juice off a nearby rock. "Hell, this child'll see you there too." He then spoke several words in Sioux to the old warrior and departed.

As if reestablishing his authority, the old Sioux shouted angrily at them once again. A fire was lit now along with several others nearby. Despite being hidden in the brush they could hear more and more warriors arriving at camp, presumably gathering for the raid in the morning. Many men, many horses. The mood was jovial as if gathering for a coming feast. The Sioux were always happiest before a lopsided engagement and sure kill.

Hunger gnawed at the captives' bellies but the thirst was overwhelming—they had not been given anything to eat or drink since their capture late that morning.

Jean-Luc estimated they were no more than a mile or so from the Métis camp, although it seemed like 1,000. Still, if they could just free themselves and retrieve their horses they could make a dash for it. By the time the Sioux were aware of their escape, they would be half-way back to the safety of their camp. The men conferred quietly and agreed—an escape must be made. But escape under the cover of darkness might get them shot by their own people, mistaking them for Sioux. They would wait until dawn.

With a tremendous victory in the offing, none of the healthy warriors wanted to be left guarding the three Métis, so the aged warrior with the twisted foot remained with them much of the night. He was relieved for a brief time by a younger man clad only in a loincloth and an antelope skin vest, who said nothing but took the shotgun, spoke in low tones to the old man, and glared at them as he took up his guard position. The old man left and ate a meal, relieved himself in the brush, and returned about an hour later.

The camp quieted as some warriors slept, but most could not, the anticipation of a huge victory and many scalps would not allow for sleep. The thin man was right, they could hear the pounding of hooves as riders rode south up the Butte and back throughout the night, with distant whoops and yelps of excitement. Although the Métis could not know it, some 2,000 warriors had joined the camp and were poised to rub out the Métis entirely in the morning. They would sing about this great victory for many years.

The meal had made the old sentry comfortable and he began to drift off to sleep. During this period Jean-Luc moved closer to Jerome and began to untie his hands. It was a slow process as the cords were well-knotted and they had nothing with which to cut. He tried a sharp-edged stone but gave up after 20 minutes and began to work with his fingers again. As the sky took on the faintest glow in the east he freed Jerome's hands entirely. Now Jerome slowly worked on Jean-Luc, then Labide.

It was cool now and without wind, the air thick with moisture and dew. Morning birds had begun their songs an hour earlier and now were in full chorus—trills and buzzes and chirps and sweet happy songs—all punctuated by the faint quacks of ducks on a nearby slough, or possibly the creek. Through it all Jean-Luc heard the soft song of a dove as it cooed in the distance. Sweet wood smoke, which had always been a welcome aroma, filled the air from the Sioux campfires. Jean-Luc found no comfort in it now.

The captives were largely ignored as the camp began final preparations for the attack, but the hostages were quickly running out of time. The eastern horizon began to brighten; sunrise was near. It would be best to leave now before full light. They could see their horses still tied nearby. Unfortunately, the animals were on the far side of the fire and in the opposite direction of the Métis camp. Two Sioux ponies were closer, but the men doubted they could be easily ridden. The plan was to reach their own familiar horses and break for camp at top speed.

With the crippled guard still drifting in and out of sleep, they considered grabbing the shotgun, but that would cause noise and commotion, possibly alerting the camp. Better to leave quietly if possible. Should they slip away singly or together? One man would not attract as much attention as three. It was decided Labide would go first, then Jerome and lastly Jean-Luc, possibly the fastest man in the entire Métis camp.

They bid each other the Lord's blessing and then Labide rose quietly and moved toward the horses at a fast pace. As he reached the horses Jerome rose and followed in his footsteps. Jean-Luc slowly rocked forward and set himself as a sprinter on all fours while staring intently at the old crippled warrior for signs of life. His heart pounded in fear and anticipation.

It was the squeal of a Sioux pony, perhaps shying from a saddle some distance from their own fire, which gave him away. The old warrior's rheumy eyes opened and saw before him not three but one captive, this one in a half-crouch ready to bolt way. In the time it took the old Sioux to clear his throat Jean-Luc leaped across the space between them, grabbed the barrel of the shotgun, and struck the man a solid blow between his eyes with the buttstock. Even before he slumped to the ground Jean-Luc bore past him and dashed toward the brush and Cherie.

As he mounted he heard crashing in the brush and the heavy sound of hoofs biting into the prairie as Labide and Jerome spurred their mounts north toward the Métis camp. He turned Cherie and bore straight past the campfire they had just vacated, spurring her on, his face anchored to her neck, heels kicking her ribs.

The twilight had just given way to the first sliver of actual sunrise. Now Jean-Luc's best friend was the ground fog which swirled gently on unseen currents, filling the prairie's grassy dips and depressions. Ahead he saw patches of green and lighter patches of open prairie and heard Cherie's labored breathing intermixed with his own pleas and curses as she powered forward under the slap of his open hand. Had he been able to process his peripheral senses, he would have recognized dark movement around him as well as the whisk of arrows slicing through the air. Rifles sounded, both near and far, the sounds quickly absorbed into the mist—*boom, boom, boom...boom.*

Ahead of him, he saw Jerome and his mount scurry north, swerving back and forth then partially disappearing into dips in the landscape, only to appear again, much farther away and closer to safety. Suddenly Cherie shuddered under him and screamed as an arrow bit into her flank, then something punched a bloody hole through the base of her left ear. While Jean-Luc may have been the camp's fastest runner, the muscle-bound Cherie's best days involved pulling a cart, not running on the open prairie—she was much slower than the Sioux ponies.

He stopped trying to guide her now and just urged her onward. Then he felt a sharp sting in his left thigh and looked to see a brown and white arrow shaft waving stiffly from a deep puncture in his leg. Arrows struck Cherie again, then again and he felt her slow as the sharp arrowheads sawed back and forth, shredding muscle and digging deeper with each stride.

As he raised his right hand to smack her side again he felt a tug on his own shoulder and saw a crimson stream of blood running down Cherie's muscular neck. He did not know if it was his or hers. But he knew he must not fall.

He hung on now, clasping both arms around Cherie's neck, willing the horse northward, toward safety, his friends, Elisa. He did not see the Sioux riders approaching from the west, cutting off the angle of his escape. If he had he might have tried to veer east.

But then Cherie was gone, her right front leg snapped cleanly at the knee as it plunged into a deep badger hole. She went down instantly but Jean-Luc did not hear or feel it; he just realized she was no longer beneath him—and he was flying forward, toward the camp, toward the Red River country—toward home.

Chapter 19

They walked into an east wind all morning. The sky was gray and shapeless, rain clouds were building on the horizon. Despite the wind they moved at a good pace, eager to reach Harvey and the site of the battlefield. They reached the edge of town and stopped at a small municipal campground which featured eight RV hookup spaces and a small grassy area with picnic tables for tents.

At the pay station, they found an old plywood sign with a map of the entire city painted in faded reds, greens, and blues, likely an old Eagle Scout project. The town of Harvey, like many of these small prairie towns, was laid out in a simple grid. Someone had recently updated the sign, adding a large green space with a white golf tee flag in the center. Based on the map, the golf course was on the far side of town.

They filled their water jugs at the spigots and headed across town. Many of the town's old buildings had been re-purposed—a farm implement dealership was now an auto repair shop, old drugstore fronts now hawked insurance, a bank building on the corner advertised financial services, with a dentist's office downstairs. A large "Bakery" sign above one doorway invited visitors but upon closer examination, they found the store was closed. Other storefronts remained vacant, with "For Sale" or "For Rent" signs prominently displayed in the windows.

A train-yard and four sets of rails served as the town's northern border. It was busy and noisy. One trainload of oil tanker cars waited to be moved west—empty—while another moved slowly eastward—full. All in all, it was a clean little town, and despite a dying core the city fathers obviously weren't going to let it disappear without a fight.

They continued across town, walking past a hardware store, a feed store, a small supper club, and then arrived at a bridge that spanned a small impoundment—the Harvey Dam. Across the bridge, they could see a large sign for the new golf course and a large expanse of bright green. After miles of tawny prairie, farm fields, and rolling pasture it struck Kelly as terribly artificial.

"That must be it," remarked Jamie. "Sure looks like a golf course."

"But not a battlefield," replied Kelly.

"Nope."

The front of the course was framed by a large parking lot, a row of brand new forest-green colored portable toilets, several information kiosks, sitting benches, newly planted maple trees, and a huge sign with a diagram of the course. They headed there first.

There was a large portable diesel generator still parked in the lot and a closed portable food wagon advertising hot dogs, corn dogs and cheese curds sitting off to one side. Scattered across the lot were several muddied paper Indian headdresses made of blue and red dyed feathers. Programs from the Grand Opening two weeks earlier had been plastered by the wind and rain against a chain-link fence bordering the lot.

The largest sign said "Welcome to Battlefield Golf" and showed nine existing holes, "Phase 1" according to the diagram, along with the planned expansion of nine additional holes, a clubhouse, and storage sheds for golf carts. The expansion was "Phase 2." The sign also showed space for a kiddie playground on the other side of the parking lot and a baseball field; these were not assigned a phase.

"So where's the battlefield?" asked Jamie, looking up and down the range. Kelly was now reading the interpretive signs on either side of the "Welcome" sign.

"You're looking at it. Read this," she said dryly, pointing at a stout black metal sign erected by the Goodview County Historical Society.

Jamie read it aloud. "In July of 1851, the Battle of the Grand Coteau was fought on this site by members of the Yanktonai Sioux and Métis Indians led by Chief Heavy Bear for control of the hunting grounds surrounding the area. After a fierce battle over five days, the early settlers of Harvey successfully fended off a force of nearly 5,000 hostile Sioux and Métis Indians using just 100 guns against the mounted Indian warriors. The battle resulted in the deaths of an estimated 450 hostile Indians; the settlers suffered five wounded and a single casualty—Cramer Spoon, great grandfather of current Goodview County Commissioner Carl W. Spoon. In honor of their bravery and sacrifice, the Town of Harvey, the Harvey Rotary Club, and the County of Goodview have established this golf course to commemorate the battle. See interpretive signs at each hole for additional information."

"What the hell?" exclaimed Jamie. "What are they talking about? I thought you said we fought *against* the Sioux, not with them?"

"We did, it was a battle between us and them. The settlers weren't even here yet. And there were 2,000 Sioux against 100 Métis, not 5,000 Sioux."

"Well, who the hell is Cramer Spoon?" Jamie demanded.

"Someone's trying to make up history…maybe it's this Carl Spoon, the Commissioner," said Kelly disgustedly. "This is all bullshit. Let's see what the other signs on the course say. Maybe they're better."

There were just four vehicles in the golf course lot, three newer SUVs, and a black Cadillac sedan, their owners trying to get in some quick holes before the rain. Kelly could see them on the far end of the links, on the third or fourth green. They dropped their packs on a picnic table and started to walk out to the tees. She could see three larger signs but the remaining tees appeared unmarked. As they watched they saw one golfer hack at his ball and send it hooking sharply off the course, only to be caught in a large net on the course perimeter.

"You ever golf?" Kelly asked Jamie.

"No, it seems like a waste of time, chasing a little ball around the grass."

"Me neither," she said, watching as the distant golfer teed up a second shot and sent it sailing off the course again, except this time it cleared the net and landed atop one of the cars in the adjacent used car lot. "I don't know how you hit something that small and make it go straight—I guess that guy doesn't either."

A sign at the first tee explained how the Goodview County Historical Society had located several rifle pits dug by the plucky settlers to fend off the Indians. The sand traps on holes 1, 3, and 7 were converted pits, having been widened and filled with sand. Two other pits had been filled and incorporated into greens. All the greens were named, using some reference to the battle, e.g. "Settler's Revenge, Spoon's Surprise, and Red Man's Retreat." According to the sign, unmarked Indian graves were still scattered around the site.

"Seriously!" exclaimed Kelly. "They filled in the pits? The Métis dug those pits. They were 165 years old, and now they're part of a damn golf course?"

Near the middle of the course was a raised mound with a US flag swaying limply in the center. "Let's see what that is," said Jamie, pointing to the flag.

They walked over and stopped at the mound, which was surrounded by a black wrought-iron fence. It had a metal sign, similar to the one in the parking lot. Kelly read this one aloud.

"On this spot, brave patriot and settler Cramer Spoon was killed by hostile Indian forces during the Battle of the Grand Coteau. Spoon's heroic stand, at great risk to his own safety, saved the lives of countless settlers as it allowed them to retreat and await reinforcements, ultimately repelling the hostile Indian forces and driving them from the area." A tall gray tombstone topped the mound, with the name "Spoon" displayed prominently.

"Is this the guy Uncle Rodney was looking for?" asked Jamie. "I thought we were looking for a Savard or a relative. We're not related to any Spoons arc we?"

"No, I think this whole thing's a crock, I never saw anyone named 'Spoon' in Rodney's notes or Mom's things. And I never saw it in any of the research I did in Bottineau. I'm guessing someone's trying to spit and polish old Mr. Spoon's reputation and make him into something he wasn't. I doubt he was even around in 1851. Dammit!" spat Kelly angrily.

"Well, at least we found the battlefield," said Jamie.

"I don't know that we have...but if there were pits..." Kelly stopped then and realized her injured foot was throbbing. Did it throb when she got angry? Ahead of them was another hole, a water hazard with another sign. "Let's see what that next sign says."

They walked over and soon stood before a small, neatly manicured pond edged with short grass and goose droppings. Another sign provided the back story.

"Preacher's Pond" was a place where the wounded settlers had gathered to cleanse their battle wounds, bandage them and return to fight again. A courageous priest traveling with the settlers served as both their medic and spiritual guide; it was believed many wounded would have perished without his efforts.

"Well, they got some of that right," admitted Kelly. "The Sioux used the ponds by the battlefield to clean their wounds. According to the reports, the water was red with blood following the battle. But the priest, that would have been Father LeSueur, traveled with the Métis, not settlers. Damn it this is frustrating—I thought this was it, I thought we found it. But now I'm not sure. Still, the pits were here, and the ponds, that's right."

"And it's in the area of your map," offered Jamie helpfully.

"Yeah, it's in the right area. But it doesn't feel right. Remember what Grandma said, 'You'll feel it.' Do you feel anything?"

Jamie considered her question, then answered, "She told *you* that, not me. But no, I don't feel anything different."

Kelly sat down on a nearby bench to rest her ankle and thought silently for a moment. In her mind, she traced back the references to the site of the battle: the position of the field, the locations of the pits, the ponds. "*This could be it,*" she thought. After 165 years anything close, anything containing two or three of the basic elements of the location was probably the right site. Jamie lit a cigarette and watched the golfers work their way back toward the parking lot on the course.

"Let's head back to the old grave-site. I have an idea," said Kelly. They walked back to the fenced mound. "Wait here. I've got to get something from my pack." Jamie stood and watched her walk back to the parking area and dig through her pack pockets. Then she turned and began walking out toward him again.

"What'd you get?" he asked.

"This," she said, opening her hand to show him a stone. "This was a stone handed down through our family—Uncle Rodney had it, supposedly his Dad before him and someone else before that. At least that's what Grandma thought. I got it out of a box of Mom's things."

"Let me see it," said Jamie. She handed it to him.

"It looks like an agate, with all the lines," he said, holding the stone close to his face. "It's pretty. So now what?"

"It is an agate, a Lake Superior agate. I'm going to guess that if this is the right battlefield, the one Uncle Rodney and Mom were looking for, that whoever's buried here was related to us somehow. And I have a feeling this stone is supposed to be left here. I don't know why, maybe it was taken from the grave earlier, or belonged to this Spoon guy. I just don't know. But it doesn't make any sense for us to search for an old battlefield without a reason. Maybe this rock is the reason."

"So what're you going to do?"

"I'm going to toss it in there, on top of the grave. And then hopefully we'll feel something or get a sign.

"Do you have a better idea?" she asked sincerely. It was the first time she had asked for his opinion. "I'm out of ideas."

Jamie thought about her question. They had come far and experienced a lot since they left Motigoohe. And it seemed anticlimactic to just toss the stone and call their journey complete. He wanted this to work. Kelly had a lot invested in the trip; it was obviously important to her and he didn't want her to be disappointed. There might only be one chance to have all this make sense, and the stone could be that chance. And now, standing in the middle of an unnaturally green golf course outside of Harvey, North Dakota, he didn't have a better idea.

"Toss it."

Once tossed Kelly knew she could easily hop the fence and retrieve the stone but she knew psychologically it was a one-way street. She wanted to "feel" something—a sense of accomplishment, relief, completion, *anything*—anything to let her know she had not wasted her time and dragged her brother half-way across the state on a wild goose chase.

"Here goes," she said as she lobbed the stone over the short fence, seeing it bounce once near the flagpole and disappear in the green grass. Then they waited. The sudden appearance of a bird would do, or a ray of sun parting the clouds, a sound...anything. She glanced over at Jamie, who was likewise standing still, listening. Watching.

"Nothing," he said quietly. "You."

"No," said Kelly. A waste of time. "Well, we tried. Let's get our stuff and get out of here. It's a long walk back home." As she started walking back toward the parking lot she looked up and shouted in frustration, "I hope that's what you wanted Rodney. I hope that's what you wanted Mom!"

"You think they hear you?" asked Jamie.

"I hope so, I really hope this is what they wanted," she replied quietly. "They didn't give me a whole lot to go on."

They reached the parking lot and shouldered their packs once more. As they were buckling their belly straps Jamie looked down the fairway again.

"Hey Kelly, let's go talk to the people over at that car lot. Maybe they know something more about the battlefield—they would have been here all the time this place was being developed."

On the one hand, Kelly wanted this to be behind them, to just head home and admit defeat. They had tried their best and come up short—or maybe not, maybe this was all Rodney and her mother had set out to do. But Jamie had a point, they were here, so they may as well try to fill in more blanks if they could.

"Okay kiddo," she responded. "You lead the way."

Jamie led them down the sidewalk bordering the golf course and soon they were standing at the entrance of the "S&S Vehicle Sales" lot. The slogan at the bottom of the sign said "No need to Battle for the right price!" A second sign, nailed below the first larger sign said "Official Car Dealer of Battlefield Golf and Historic Site."

Steven Spoon was busy putting a length of clear packing tape over a huge crack in the windshield of a 2006 Toyota Tacoma pickup when he saw the pair approach. On the one hand, two people on foot might represent ideal potential customers for a car dealer, but on the other hand, if you couldn't afford a car at all you probably couldn't afford a newer car. And at least one of these two was an Indian; according to his father, Indians were always trouble.

Kelly surveyed the lot and saw five other vehicles with either cracked windshields or large dents on their roofs or hoods.

"Hi, how can I help you today," Spoon smiled, sliding into salesman mode. "My name's Steve, and you are?"

"Hi Steve, afraid we're not in the market for a car right now," said Kelly, ignoring his question. "But maybe you could tell us about the golf course and battlefield."

"Yeah, we saw there was a Grand Opening a couple weeks ago," said Jamie. "And you're the official car dealer?"

"That we are," Spoon said, "in fact, my great, great grandfather was killed in that battle—Cramer Spoon. He was one of the town fathers, put Harvey on the map."

"Yeah, we read that," said Kelly. "So would that make Carl Spoon, the commissioner, your father?"

"Right again," said Spoon. "Our family has quite a history in this area. Some of our other relatives chased those India...I mean hostiles all the way to Montana, where they got into it with Custer and, well, I guess everyone knows how that turned out. So, are you folks Sioux? I imagine you're interested in the battle."

"No, we're Métis," said Jamie.

"Oh, so your ancestors were involved in the Battle of the Grand Coteau too," said Spoon.

"They were," said Kelly coolly, debating on whether to educate him on the real battle, then concluding it would probably be a waste of time. The citizens of Harvey had arrived at their narrative and were going to stick to it.

"No hard feelings huh," said Spoon, still referring to the mythical Métis defeat, "I'd still be happy to sell you a car."

"Looks like you're about to have a scratch and dent sale," observed Jamie.

"Oh, we get a stray golf ball now and then," said Spoon casually, privately noting that today's ball raised the total of errant balls to 18, not counting the one that hit his salesman the previous Saturday.

"I could give you a great deal on this Toyota right here. It'll need a new windshield eventually but it drives great and only has…" he leaned into the cab and looked at the dashboard, "89,000 miles. Lots of miles left on this baby."

"We're not really interested," said Kelly.

But Spoon was not done. "Tell you what, I can give you a 30 day, 3,000-mile warranty, and finance the whole thing right now," then quickly added, "if you have good credit. And even if you have bad credit we'll work something out."

"We've got a truck already," said Jamie. "We just like to walk."

"Like to walk huh?" said Spoon, now realizing he wouldn't be reeling these fish in. "Well there's no denying walking is good for your health. But if we can ever help you in the future don't hesitate to contact me," he said, holding out his business card. "Steve's the name."

"Got it," said Kelly. "Thanks, Steve."

They quickly exited the lot before Spoon tried to sell them a different vehicle.

"None of that makes sense," said Kelly, walking steadily over the bridge back toward town. "The dates are off. Harvey wasn't settled until sometime in the 1890s, and the Battle at Little Bighorn wasn't until what...1876? Which would have been 25 years after the Battle of the Grand Coteau. Any Sioux warrior from that battle would have been an old man at the Little Bighorn."

"And the Métis didn't fight with the Sioux, we fought against them, right?" added Jamie, trying to keep the dates and participants straight in his own mind.

"Right. I think they just made half this stuff up to fit into their Battlefield Golf theme park or whatever this is supposed to be."

"But it's still the right location."

"Yes, it is," admitted Kelly. "Still...it doesn't seem right." She was tired now, tired of trying to make the pieces fit when maybe they never would, or maybe she had the wrong pieces to begin with. It was time for a break.

"How about we get a good hot meal in town before we head out? We deserve that much, don't we? I saw a Pizza Ranch on the way in."

"Yes! Let me at some hot pizza," said Jamie, "With or without sand, at this point, I don't really care."

"I'm going to call Grandma too and let her know where we're at."

Jamie glanced at her and then looked away, then casually said, "You know, now that we found the site, and left the stone, maybe we could just catch a ride back, you know, save some time."

"I'm the one with the bad wheel, are you saying you can't keep up with a girl on one leg? You're ready to give up? Don't you want to complete this trip on your own terms?"

"Yeah, but listen, Kelly, we've done what we set out to do—what Grampa and Mom and Rodney set out to do. We did it."

Kelly stared at him coldly. "Let me ask you—what have you accomplished in the last year? Actually accomplished on your own?"

"Well, I'd have to think about it."

"Yes, you would, because I bet you haven't accomplished much in a long time," Kelly retorted. "In the Marines we made new recruits make their bunks up perfectly every morning in Basic. And if it wasn't perfect they had to do it over and over again until it was perfect. Do you know why?

"Of course you don't," she continued, "you never make your bed. We did it because then they started each day with a small accomplishment. And once you have one out of the way it's easy to add another, then another. Pretty soon you're accomplishing big things, important things, every day.

"Think about it Jamie—if you can walk all the way down here and back like the Métis used to do chasing bison, you will have accomplished something nobody's done in over 150 years. Do you realize that? And *that*, little brother, is an accomplishment you can

198

be proud of, an accomplishment you can build on. Hell, anyone can jump in a car."

Jamie felt a little guilty. "Alright, alright, enough. I get it. And now that you say it that way it would be pretty cool."

They walked the length of the parking lot and had just stepped onto the street when they saw an old man with a cane, old-time fedora, and trench coat waddle slowly down the sidewalk and collapse heavily on a boulevard bench a half-block away. He leaned against the backrest, slowly lifted the cane and laid it on the seat. As they crossed the street Jamie could not help but glance back. He walked two more steps and then stopped.

"Hey, isn't that Kitchi, the guy from the other night?"

Kelly stopped and turned. "You mean by the campfire?"

"Yeah."

Kelly squinted across the street at the slumped figure. "Guess it could be. Looks like he's in tough shape."

"Let's go see," said Jamie, not waiting for her response. He turned and quickly strode back across the street toward the man.

Jamie got to him first; the man looked familiar but worn out from exertion. "Hey Mr. Kitchi, is that you?" he asked, lowering his head to look in the man's face.

The man shifted his shoulders and looked up at the young man. His face appeared sunken and hollow, and his skin had taken on an ashen tone. He did not look well. He sat up now, coughed a hoarse, rattling cough that came from somewhere deep in his chest, and smiled weakly. "Mr. Jamie," he said.

Jamie looked back toward Kelly, who was just now crossing the street and said, "It's him." He then turned to face the old man again. "Are you okay, you don't look well?"

"I am fine son," he said. "I am very glad to see you and your sister again. I was not sure I would." Kelly now walked up next to Jamie and looked the man over. His hands and knuckles were gnarled with arthritis, his hair greasy, his clothes stained; he smelled unclean. He seemed full of life and much healthier and stronger the last time she'd seen him at their campfire. Where they had once observed a wise elder, here was a hollowed-out old man. Had he changed that much in just a few days?

"Hello Kitchi," she said.

"Did you complete your search?" he asked in a wheezy voice. "Did you find your relatives?"

"We think so. But how did you get here? Did you end up walking all this way?

"Yes, I walked and now my journey," he looked up at Jamie and smiled weakly, "my journey is nearly over."

In response, Jamie said, "But you need to get back to the Red River, right? Didn't you say you wanted to get back to your land by the Red River?"

"That is true, and I will soon be back where I belong."

"Is someone picking you up?" Jamie continued, now concerned. "Do you need a ride?"

"Thank you, no, I do not need assistance."

Here was a man obviously in great need of assistance thought Kelly, and they couldn't just leave him here. "Well, let us buy you lunch," she suggested. "We were just going to get something to eat now—you can join us."

The old man struggled to sit up straight, and when he did so he took a deep breath, exhaled slowly, and looked her directly in the eyes. "Daughter, listen to an old man carefully. Your search is not over, your task not complete. Do you know you are not finished?"

Kelly was confused by the question. "I don't understand. What are you asking?"

"Do you know you are not finished?" the old man repeated.

Kelly looked at Jamie, who looked back at her with a gaze of anticipation as if expecting her to produce the tools to solve Kitchi's riddle. "*Not finished*," what did he mean?

Kelly looked back at Kitchi again but his gaze had not wavered, his dark eyes revealed no clues. She realized her frustration with the morning, the day—the entire trip—was not helping; it was keeping a solution from her. She inhaled deeply, exhaled slowly, and physically relaxed her shoulders. She willed her mind to clear.

Kitchi shifted on the bench and leaned back as he raised his arm and extended a gnarled hand toward her. He said nothing, but clearly, this was a lifeline, a way back to certainty, back to the answers she needed. She looked into his face and then gently grasped his hand in both of hers; it was hot and soft. She squeezed firmly.

A wave of insight washed over her as gently as old music, and she knew. She smiled. "Yes," she answered confidently, releasing his hand. "I know. I'm not finished."

"Good. You *will* know when you are finished. And now I rest," said Kitchi, closing his eyes slowly.

"Would you like to come with us?" Kelly asked softly.

He opened his eyes slightly, his lids heavy as if full of sleep. "You go. You go now. Leave an old man in peace." Then like a sweep of sunshine illuminating a dark prairie, the skin of his face brightened and relaxed. And as he closed his eyes, she saw peace wash over him. Kelly had never witnessed such a physical transformation before…or had she?

She had—Uncle Rodney.

"Let's go," she said to Jamie quietly.

"We can't go, we can't just leave him," he protested. "What did he say to you? Did he say you weren't done? What did he mean? I thought we were done. Kelly, what did he mean?"

"We're not done Jamie, that's what he said, and I think I understand now. We haven't found the site, we missed it. I think I wasted the stone. It's the wrong spot."

"We could go back for it."

She stopped and faced Jamie much as the old man had faced her. "It doesn't matter Jamie, this was never about a stone, I think it was about Mom, and now I think it's about me. Uncle Rodney wanted Mom to find the site, and once she was gone he wanted *me*." She looked down at the old man, now motionless on the bench. "Kitchi and Rodney both said the same thing—'you go.' They wanted *me* to go, myself."

"Go where?" asked Jamie, now thoroughly confused.

"We got off track here. We need to get to Goodview and talk to that newspaper woman. I have a feeling, a good feeling, that's the right track."

They crossed the street again and had just reached the opposite sidewalk when a Harvey Police Department car came down the street behind them. Jamie turned and held up his hand.

"What are you doing?" Kelly asked in surprise.

"I want to talk to them."

The car slowed, two officers occupied the front seat. The older one on the passenger side lowered his window. "Help you?"

Jamie leaned down, "Hello officers, we were just talking to that man over there and I think he's ill, he may need some medical attention," pointing to the bench where Kitchi sat in a slump.

"That guy?" said the officer who was driving, pointing with his thumb. "Don't worry about Old Savard there, he just about lives on that bench."

"We bus the Badger down to Tribal Health Services in Bismarck about twice a month but he always seems to make his way back here," said the officer in the passenger seat. "The Badger can take care of himself, don't worry."

The man in the driver's seat leaned over toward the passenger side window. "There's a guy that's waiting for a train that'll never come in," he chuckled.

"Would you please just check on him?" implored Jamie.

"Yeah okay, we'll check," said the older officer reluctantly.

"Excuse me," said Kelly, now leaning in toward the open window. "What did you say his name was?"

"Badger," replied the officer. "Badger Savard."

Chapter 20

It was a bright and breezy day as they walked into Goodview, a good morning for traveling. Many grain trucks were moving into and out of the elevator in town, and although Kelly and Jamie must have offered a curious sight, almost everyone waved at them as they passed by. A friendly town from all appearances.

Like many of these prairie towns, Goodview was a town hanging on by a thread. Empty city lots converted to gardens, abandoned homes and the sagging storefronts along Main sent the message as clearly as the front page news: Were it not for the courthouse and the county USDA office, Goodview would have gone the same way as nearby Kief, a ghost-town full of abandoned churches, houses and sturdy brick school buildings with broken windows.

They walked past the courthouse, an ancient building built around the turn of the century. Both the US and the North Dakota flags hung in front of the building. To the right of the walkway, a series of life-sized metal cutouts of soldiers surrounded a POW/MIA flag. Kelly had to admit it was simple but impressive. If nothing else, small towns were patriotic to the end.

A C-store stood at the end of the block, outside of which stood a relic from the past—an actual public telephone booth. Inside they found a ragged phone book with most of the pages torn or missing but were able to find an address for Anna Schenko. It was just a block away.

Her house and yard were neat, slate blue with white trim and short white garden fence. The sides of the concrete steps leading to the front door were also white. The driveway was cracked asphalt but, unlike those nearby which sprouted a spray of weeds in each crack, here the driveway was absolutely weed-free. A cast aluminum black mailbox confirmed this was the Schenko residence.

An empty city lot with an old house foundation abutted Schenko's yard on the right. On the left stood a house clearly neglected for many years. Torn sheets of plastic covered most windows and slapped rhythmically against the faded clapboard siding in the breeze. The yard was overgrown with tall grass and purple-topped thistle, the roof ridge sagged. A thick lilac hedge served as a divider and buffer between the two properties.

The door opened surprisingly quickly after Kelly knocked. Jamie, holding a folder containing the maps and letters, stood behind and two steps below on the concrete stairs.

"Yes?" said the woman who answered, just her head and shoulder peering out from behind the inside door.

"Hello," said Kelly, speaking through the screen door. "We're looking for Anna Schenko."

"Well you found her," Schenko said, looking past Kelly to Jamie. "Are you from the Reservation?"

The question caught Jamie off guard but he recovered quickly. "We live near Lake Metigoshe," he replied.

"We understand you used to be the editor of the county paper here," continued Kelly. "We..."

Schenko interrupted. "Are you looking for those lost Indian girls?"

"Indian girls?"

"Those Indian girls that went missing in the Oil Patch."

"No, ma'am. But we are trying to track down some people who may be related to us," acknowledged Kelly. "Would you mind if we asked you a few questions?"

"If someone's missing you should contact the Sheriff," instructed Schenko, still holding the inside door tightly between them.

"Well, they've been gone for a long time," explained Kelly.

"Over 100 years," interjected Jamie.

"100 years...well, that's different," said Schenko. "Who did you say you were again?"

"My name's Kelly and this is my brother Jamie."

She considered them both closely once again. "Did you two walk here?" she asked, observing the packs.

"Yes ma'am. We just walked here from Harvey."

"Don't you have a car?"

"We have a truck but we decided to walk instead, to take in the countryside," Kelly offered.

"Well, I haven't cleaned but you can come in. Leave your packs outside though, they look pretty dirty."

Schenko pushed the screen door outward and opened the interior door fully. "I wasn't expecting company so you'll forgive the mess."

They entered a small living room, sparsely furnished with nice, older upholstered furniture and a beautiful glass coffee table set on a stone base. The room smelled of stale air tinged with heavy perfume, such as that favored by a great-aunt. A thick, tightly-woven brown rug on the floor appeared freshly vacuumed, two stacks of magazines were set in perfect order on the table: *The Wilson Quarterly* and the familiar *National Geographic*. The room was well-decorated, with wall pieces, lampshades, and curtains in a complementary grassland theme. It was spotless.

"Please, sit," said Schenko, motioning toward the sofa. They sat gently on a pale green sofa. And now Schenko really looked them over in a hard glance: *Who were these people and what were they after?*

Schenko wore a tight pink newsboy cap on her head, which was plainly hairless. Her facial features seemed washed out and suggested a translucence, like the wrap of a fresh spring roll. On closer examination, Kelly could see her eyebrows had been applied with dark eye-liner. Cancer. She wore cream slacks and a loose untucked rose blouse. She was a bit overweight with a soft grandma belly, thick shoulders, and a pleasant, round face. Kelly put her age at 70, modest income, educated. A couple of kids. Husband…deceased? Out of the picture either way.

"This is a beautiful table," said Kelly, searching for a compliment before eliciting Schenko's cooperation.

"Thank you," Schenko replied. "The stones forming the base came from our farm south of town. We used to live on the farm, my husband and I. He's passed now but I wanted to have something here to remind me. It took us several years to collect them all. Are you familiar with glacial till?"

"I'm sorry, what?" asked Kelly.

"Glacial till," Schenko replied. "Are you familiar with glacial till?"

"No ma'am."

"Isn't that rock carried by glaciers?" interjected Jamie. "In high school, we attended a summer field camp in the Turtle Mountains where we learned about glaciers." Kelly glanced at him with surprise.

"Oh really?" said Schenko, now with a spark of engagement in her eye. "And did you continue in your studies?"

"No ma'am."

Schenko looked over at Kelly expectantly, eyebrows raised.

"Me neither ma'am—I joined the military out of high school."

Schenko regarded her again for an instant, then relaxed slightly before reciting an obviously familiar mini-geology lesson. "Yes, our area is full of glacial till, rocks and stones deposited here from Canada when the glaciers stopped. That's the same reason we have our ponds and what they call potholes—because of glaciers. I did a story on them once for the paper. We have all kinds of rocks here and other things...things which really don't belong here."

Neither Kelly nor Jamie knew how to respond, so they waited for her to continue.

"The stones here are a mix from our fields," she said, pointing to the different colored stones forming the base beneath the thick glass. "Here's granite, gneiss, limestone, and schist. I don't know what this one is but I think it contains a little gold."

"Beautiful," Kelly said again.

Schenko, a veteran of thousands of interviews herself, knew they had questions to ask and graciously dropped the subject. She guessed these two were alright. "And so how can I help you find your missing relations?"

Kelly shifted forward on the sofa cushion. "As I said earlier, we're looking for some people who may be related to us who traveled to this area in the 1850s. We believe their last name was Savard. We were told the current editor of the *Goodview Clarion* was new to the job and that you had much more historical knowledge of this area."

"Yes, she's sharp as a tack, but a Jewish gal from the Twin Cities wouldn't know anything about the history of Goodview County," Schenko said, taking some pleasure that she was recognized as a local authority. "We have archives at the paper going back over 100 years. They're not really indexed or cataloged properly...certainly nothing you could search electronically."

"*Not good*," thought Kelly, then quickly decided on a different approach. "You might be the best resource available then, with all your newspaper experience. The relatives we're looking for may have been involved in a battle that involved the Sioux, in this area, possibly around the Dog Den Butte area to the northwest. This would have been back around 1851. Can you tell us anything about that area?"

"Dog Den Butte? There's always been trouble out there," said Schenko. "Have you seen it? Nobody can make a go of it on that land, just abandoned farms in every direction. The Sheriff's office can tell you more I'm sure but there was always bad news from that area of the county—physical abuse, livestock neglect, and cruelty, drugs, storms, way too many vehicle and tractor accidents. You'd think people around here could handle driving up a hill. It's not like it's a mountain or anything, it's just a big hill, not even a real butte like you'd see out West."

Now Schenko paused, searching for examples. "In the early days, of course, there was always conflict with the Indians. I don't mean to be impolite but I assume you're Sioux—correct? Your people terrorized this area for many years. Even now most of the Indian stories around here involve drunks, stolen property, or casinos. They have casinos on the Missouri and Devil's Lake. But I suppose you know all about that don't you?"

"Actually ma'am we're not Sioux, we're Métis, from the Turtle Mountains and Canada," corrected Kelly.

"Métis? Yes, I know of them, but what were you doing way down here? I thought your people lived by Winnipeg and the Red River?"

"The bison," said Jamie.

"Oh yes," exclaimed Schenko, as if suddenly experiencing a revelation. "The bison, you came down for the bison hunts—I remember this now. And there was some type of conflict...I'm trying to recall where I learned about this...it must have been at a seminar or something. Nobody around here cares to hear about the Indians anymore, it's just acres and bushels and bushels and acres. No, they don't care about history, unless it's their own. What was the name again, the family name?"

"Savard."

"Savard," she repeated. "That's a far cry from all the Germans and Russians living here now. Sounds French."

"It is French," said Jamie proudly. "We were here before the land was even a state."

"We know there was a battle in this area between a small band of Métis and a large contingent of Sioux warriors," explained Kelly. "We think this Savard fought in the battle and may be related to us; there were casualties on both sides. We're trying to find the site of the battle."

"That's where I heard it!" Schenko proclaimed. "They just opened the Battlefield Golf Course in Harvey a few weeks ago. It was on the site of a Sioux battle. And they did mention the Métis were involved."

"We just came from there. We have reason to believe it's *not* the real battlefield," said Kelly.

"And they said the Sioux and Métis fought together against the whites in the battle," added Jamie. "That's not true, the Métis fought the Sioux over hunting rights for the bison. They got it all wrong."

"Hmm," said Schenko. "You may be right, there was no real European presence here on the plains until the Army arrived in the 1860s, after the Civil War. That's well-documented."

Kelly began to sense this was another dead-end. Very few records existed from the time before European settlement in the area. Newspapers did not yet exist. And those Métis records which did exist were housed somewhere in Canada or lost to time. The story of the Métis people and their conflicts were not an American story. She sensed this was a good time to end, on a note of cooperation. "Well, we've taken up enough of your time Mrs. Schenko. We really appreciate your help."

"Certainly," replied Schenko. "Your battlefield may well be out near the Butte but that was such a long time ago. I'm sorry I couldn't have been more helpful."

They thanked her again, stepped out the front door, and began shouldering their packs. Schenko watched them from the top of the concrete steps, her arms crossed. As they reached the end of her driveway she called out.

"Say, wait a moment, I know the head of the Velva Historical Society. They're located just northwest of the Butte. Would you like me to check with her? They may have local records or oral histories of the area. They had an old strip-mining operation there years ago and may have done some surveying or documentation before the dig."

Kelly stopped in her tracks and turned. "Really? That would be outstanding."

211

"I'll try to get in touch with her this afternoon. Do you have a number where I can get in touch with you?"

"We're not carrying phones, but how about if we call you a bit later? I have your number—it was in the book."

"That would be fine. Say can I give you a lift somewhere?"

"No ma'am we're fine, we're just going to do a little shopping in town."

"Okay then, I'll talk to you later."

They turned and walked toward the grocery store on Main Street. It was a beautiful day, with low humidity and blue skies. As they walked Kelly reached out and punched Jamie playfully in the shoulder.

"Hey, what's that for?"

"This could be it, mister," said Kelly, feeling a genuine happiness she hadn't felt in a long while. "I feel it. This woman in Velva is going to help us."

"I don't feel a damn thing, except I'm really dirty and could use a bath. Nobody around here cares about an old battlefield. At least not a *real* one. You heard her—it's all about acres and bushels."

"We care," scolded Kelly. "And we count. A lot. And your mother cared, and your uncle. We're gonna find it."

They bought a few really expensive groceries at the "Big Save" market on Main Street and walked down to the Goodview City Park and Pool. The park offered overnight camping and showers. With the bright sun, they took advantage of the heat to unpack their damp clothing, which they spread over a couple of empty picnic tables next to the outdoor pool.

"I'm getting a shower," announced Jamie, stripping down to gym shorts and a T-shirt as he walked over to the white cinder block building marked "Showers" in black paint. He returned a minute later. "Do you have any quarters?"

Kelly fished into her front pocket and pulled out the change from their grocery shopping. "Two quarters, dime, nickel, and two pennies," she announced and dumped all the change into his outstretched palm. "Go knock yourself out."

As Jamie showered she observed the three children in the swimming pool and the lifeguard. The children, two girls, and a boy all about eight or 10 years of age were playing a simultaneous game of tag and keep-away with a small yellow beach ball. She imagined two of them to be siblings and the third a friend. The girls screeched and shrieked as the boy either splashed them or hit them with the ball. It started early she observed; even at a young age boys and girls didn't play well together. The lifeguard, a young pink-skinned girl of about 15 wearing a blue, one-piece suit with white lotion on her nose paid little attention to their antics, her nose buried in a magazine.

Jamie soon emerged with wet hair wearing just his shorts and a wet shirt slung over his shoulder. "That felt good," he said with satisfaction.

"Get your money's worth?" she asked.

"Oh yeah."

"C'mon and eat," she replied, setting slices of rye bread and thin slices of ham and cheese on the table. A picnic wasp appeared out of nowhere and buzzed the selection but didn't land.

"No mustard," observed Jamie.

"Only if you brought packets from the cafe."

"Nope." He watched as she made a sandwich and spread mayonnaise from a small packet she retrieved from her pack.

"You've got mayo," he observed.

"Yep, brought packets from the cafe," Kelly responded with a smile. Jamie ate his sandwich dry.

After lunch, they spread out on the benches and let the sunshine and food usher them to sleep. Kelly was used to catnaps, a Marine survival tool. She woke after just 20 minutes. She stretched hard, feeling her muscles work against each other and observed Jamie still asleep, snoring softly. She began repacking her pack, making no effort to be quiet, and was nearly packed when he yawned loudly and sat up.

"Burning daylight mister, let's get packed up and check in with the newspaper lady," she said. Jamie packed quickly now and a few minutes later they marched toward the payphone at the C-store.

Now out of quarters, they had to break a dollar in the store to use the phone. Kelly dialed the number and Schenko answered almost immediately. Jamie could hear her speak excitedly as he stood behind Kelly's shoulder.

"Yes," said Kelly into the receiver. "Really...that's outstanding! No, no. We're at the C-store...okay." And then she hung up. Kelly beamed as she hung up the phone.

"Well?" asked Jamie impatiently. "What'd she say?"

"I told you I had a feeling. They think they know where the battlefield is, on a farm by the Butte. Schenko was really excited. She's driving over to pick us up now."

Schenko pulled up in a shiny black four-door Ford sedan three minutes later. "Get in," she called from the driver's side window. She popped the trunk open from inside. "Packs in the back."

Ten minutes later they were assembled in her neat living room again as she relayed the information from her contact in Velva. "They did mapping and surveys of the area around the Dog Den Butte, just after the World War," she explained. "The coal companies were buying up all the farms in the area south of Velva for excavation—this was strip-mining. But one farmer held out—more foolish than anything because the money was good for that time—he would have been rich. My contact says the records showed just a few landowners held out. Somehow one of those landowners came across an accounting of a priest who was with the Métis on a bison hunt, possibly on their land, in the 1850s."

"Father LeSueur," said Kelly.

"Yes, she mentioned a LeSueur."

"We saw that journal too, just recently."

"Then you know the Métis dug rifle pits to defend themselves from the Sioux."

"Yes," responded Kelly. "A dozen or more pits."

Schenko waited a beat. "They found the rifle pits on this farm," she said triumphantly.

"Damn," said Jamie, softly.

"There's more," Schenko continued. "The Historical Society has collected other information too, documented accounts from people who claimed to have been at the battle, both Sioux and Métis. They said there were many casualties on the Sioux side, but only a single Métis casualty—they believe his name was Savard."

Kelly gasped—Savard! Uncle Rodney must have been related to this man at the battle, the man who had been killed.

"By several accounts, his body was treated poorly by the Sioux but it seems he was buried right there at the site of the battle. My friend in Velva said she has more details. She knows the current landowners and would be happy to introduce you."

The pair were stunned by the news. For Kelly, it was "mission accomplished," they may have actually located the lost battlefield, and perhaps Rodney's relative. She had done it. For Jamie, the timeline was just too great to comprehend; he had been living day to day and week to week for so long that finding a foothold in history—his own history—some 165 years later was nearly beyond his comprehension. The idea rattled in his brain but could find no place to settle.

"Please let me drive you up there today," implored Schenko. "It will take you two or three days to get there if you walk; we can be there in just an hour or so in the car."

Kelly was about to protest when Jamie cut in on their behalf. "No thank you, ma'am, we've walked this far, walking a little longer won't hurt anything."

Chapter 21

It looked like an abandoned farm; the road ditch in front had not been mowed in years and was littered with old two and four-bottom iron plows, rusty hay rakes, dozens of old tractor tires with cracked and blistered sidewalls, and several old planters, all of which formed one end of an agrarian junkyard spanning some 75 yards between the ditch and a tangled tree grove. Tawny grass and dusky green wormwood grew around each discarded piece, which obviously hadn't been moved in years. Three strands of sagging, looped and broken barbwire clung to old gray fence posts on each side of the drive. These fences had not held anything back since the Eisenhower administration.

Like many old homesteads in the area, this one had two houses, the old abandoned one, from the '30s or '40s, and the new one from the '70s or '80s. They saw the mess from the distance and moved over to the far side of the road; many such eyesores featured junkyard dogs with temperaments matching their surroundings. As they walked closer, they heard a snapping sound that was hard to place. It wasn't as if two objects were striking each other, nor was it of equal cadence to be something mechanical. At times it sounded like a "snap," while at other times a lower-pitched "crack."

"What's that noise?" asked Jamie, irritated that he couldn't identify it.

"I don't know," said Kelly, crossing the road again and searching the farmyard for the source.

"Somebody's out back there doing something," said Kelly, nodding toward the newer house with sheets of plastic over the windows. Then, more clearly now, came the sound of another "crack" and the sound of hooves pounding the soil and frenzied snorts.

217

"What the hell?" said Jamie as he lengthened his stride and entered the yard. They walked down the short drive toward the noise and, once shielded by the house and out of the wind, heard a commotion clearly coming from behind an old barn. Four kittens with crusted eyelids scampered for cover under a dilapidated pump-house as they walked across the weedy yard.

Then they heard the high-pitched scream of a horse in distress.

They rounded the corner of the barn, which leaned well to the east, and saw a squat man dressed in a greasy white shirt and pair of stained blue bib overalls. His wild white hair was long, his beard greenish-gray. In his right hand, he wielded a long leather whip, some 20 feet long, which he drew back and lashed across the flanks of a frantic white horse.

Around the animal's neck and jaw was an old bridle, too small to begin with and now cutting into the flesh of the horse's nose. A short length of thick rope was tied around the horse's throat and snubbed securely to a wooden post.

In an instant the whip was raised a second time and lashed down again, this time leaving a blossoming streak of blood across the horse's croup and down its thigh. The horse reared and bucked its hindquarters away from the man, trying to rear its head but choking itself with each jerk. As the little man raised the whip again Kelly called out.

"Hey stop that!" The whip cut the air and fell again.

"Stop that!" she shouted again, waving her arms to get his attention. The man caught the movement and glanced back at the pair for an instant before laying the whip across the horse's bloody rump again. The horse kicked its hind legs out again in terror, striking at anything within reach.

"Kelly…" said Jamie, his eyes wide, his voice a mix of shock and pleading. He winced involuntarily each time the whip landed.

Now the man stopped, sucking in his breath and regarding them with a set of beady eyes and mouth slightly agape as if considering whom to whip next. Kelly's eyes, clear and piercing, bore into him.

"I'll do whatever I goddam well please to my own goddam horse on my own goddam property," he responded, showing a slick purple tongue between missing teeth.

Kelly didn't flinch. Glancing at the horse again she saw a puckered and weeping slash wound across its face and one eye, red-rimmed and milky blind. It was an ugly scar as if a whip had laid the skin open to the bone and healed poorly.

"You're trespassing on my property!" he exclaimed. "Didn't you see the goddam signs?"

"That's enough Mister," warned Kelly, ignoring his admonition. "You leave that horse alone."

"Goddam horse bit me. I'm done when I say I'm done." Now with an audience, he unfurled the whip again and increased the intensity of the lashing, taking sick pleasure in displaying one of his few apparent skills—meting out pain.

There were at least two possible ways to react to a scene like this: hysterically or professionally. Kelly didn't do hysterical, and under the circumstances, she felt no obligation to be professional. Few things seemed more unnatural to her than the application of punishment for punishment's sake. What she saw before her was not justified, necessary, or…natural.

"Kelly!" shouted Jamie again, his voice now laced with outrage.

Kelly dropped her pack and without thinking found her knife in hand. The violence before her opened a channel she had fought to keep closed. Every instinct told her to take out the abuser, and for a moment she saw a sweaty grunt groaning over the helpless body of Kristal, thrusting into her, punishing her, each thrust like the lash of the whip. She wasn't able to help Kristal, but she knew she could easily take this man out and end this. It was within her power. But she was disciplined.

Jamie was not.

And he had made a decision, or unconsciously, a decision had been made for him; the whipping would not be allowed to continue. Period.

He launched himself at the man, his long black hair streaming, his lean body still encumbered by his pack, shooting forward with no concern for the whip or his own safety, unleashing a hidden rage which had festered in him and clenched his heart. And he roared, an unnatural frightening roar which burst forth, unsummoned, from a place deep inside him. Kelly found the sound strangely familiar—it was a warrior's cry—and watched curiously as he speared the man squarely and sent him crashing through the air into a corral panel.

She had not moved but now calmly walked over to the prostrate figure and assessed his condition. She put her fingers on his neck, feeling for a pulse. "He's not dead," she announced coolly.

Jamie's heart raced but he ignored Kelly and the man and walked over to calm the horse. As he approached the animal tried to rear its head again and wheezed as its windpipe was cut off by the rope.

"Easy boy, easy," he said soothingly, reaching his hand palm up toward the animal. "Easy, now."

The horse stood now, stamping its front hooves nervously and taking him in with his one good eye. The eye flared at Jamie with each step he took. Closer now, Jamie could see the back of the horse was covered in welts from the whipping, some raised, others oozing, some split through the skin and bleeding. His neck and flanks were covered with old scars and cuts, some healed over and others crusted. One back hoof was packed with a clod of bloodied mud and encircled by a tangle of rusted barb wire; several barbs disappeared into the skin of the hock.

"We need to go, Jamie," said Kelly. "I don't want to be here when this asshole wakes up."

"We can't leave this horse here," he said quietly.

"Well we can't take him—we're not horse thieves. This isn't our business."

"You know this isn't right Kelly, this guy shouldn't own any animals. This horse is helpless, and he's torturing him."

Kelly knew he was right and shuddered as she imagined the animal snubbed to a fence post and then beaten, probably on a regular basis, with no escape from the pain. She wondered why it didn't run away but then realized it probably couldn't run. She wondered if it could walk.

As she looked at the horse she considered it as helpless, as hopeless, as the Afghan villagers she met while in the Corps penned in, captives in their own homeland, subject to torture and execution by forces they could barely understand much less overcome. Since returning home and finding some perspective she realized when she left that country she had not made any difference, no difference at all. The conflict and death and destruction would continue. At a great cost of blood and treasure. Here at least she could make a difference.

"Well, I'm not stealing a horse. You probably can't even get close to him," she said, now mentally considering their options.

Jamie worked his way around the end of the broken corral section until he was opposite the horse and protected by the fence. Then he

221

walked up slowly until he was just a few feet from the post where the animal was tied. The horse turned to face him and snorted and tugged as he inched forward. *"Easy boy, eeeasy."* Jamie held both hands palms up toward the horse to show he wasn't carrying anything to harm the animal.

"You're gonna get bit," cautioned Kelly.

"No, I'm not." He was now even with the post which secured the horse, which had backed as far away as the short length of rope would allow. "I need a knife."

Kelly unsheathed her combat knife and said "lookout," as she flipped it slowly end over end over the horse and Jamie, sticking it blade down behind him in the packed manure.

Jamie turned slowly to retrieve the knife then carefully reached around the post and in one movement sliced the taut rope securing the horse's neck. Kelly jumped behind the corner of the barn as the horse, now free from the post, reared slightly, snorted, and quickly hobbled out of the broken corral and headed for a small grove of trees near the driveway.

"Good," said Kelly, "now let's get out of here." As she glanced at the little man she saw he was still unconscious but seemed to be smacking his lips. It was time to go.

Instead of going back to the road they stuck to the field edge behind the house and continued in the direction of Velva. Kelly had wanted to avoid any trouble with the locals but maybe they had stepped into a mess now. Still, she was okay with it, secretly pleased that Jamie had reacted the way he did. Pleased that he cared about *something*. Good for him.

As they reached the corner of the field she looked back and looked for movement at the farmstead, now nearly a mile away. Nothing. The white horse stood out though—it had made its way to the ditch by the gravel road. Its head was down and it appeared to be feeding in the grass. She felt good about releasing it and hoped it would leave the area, far away from the man.

They kept moving, eventually taking to the gravel road again and putting about six or seven miles between them and the man at the farm. Jamie was in high spirits—none of the usual complaints about the walk, the road, the weather, or the sun. Their jaunt through the brush had come at a cost however as they found they were covered in ticks. Upon reaching the road they "de-ticked" themselves, but every now and then one or both would stop and reach under their shirt or pant leg to evict another of the pests.

"Damn ticks," remarked Jamie.

"We had 'em in Afghanistan," said Kelly. "Every camel or goat you saw had them. It was pretty disgusting. At least here we just have them in the spring."

They were both excited at the prospect of seeing the actual battlefield so they stepped quickly and made good time. The weather was hot, but as was typical in the high plains, there was no humidity. Ahead of them, they saw a lonely one-room country church—white, with a tall steeple and a dozen windows to the side. They had passed many such churches in their travels. Many were abandoned, with peeling paint and leaning steeples but, curiously, intact windows. Vandals on the prairie must have drawn the line at breaking windows at a house of worship, regardless of its current condition. Or more likely, Kelly thought, there weren't as many vandals about on the open plains.

As they got closer they saw this church had a newer metal roof and newer windows, with stone landscaping in front of gray marble steps and newer wooden doors, crimson in color. The small gravel parking lot beside it was well-used and currently held a rusty sky-blue mini-van, side door open, and toolbox on the seat. Nearby a workman dressed in faded jeans, gray T-shirt, and well-worn leather work boots flecked with a rainbow of paint colors squatted with a screwdriver near the church's front sign.

The man saw them approach and greeted them. "Good afternoon," said the man cheerfully, standing and wiping his hands on a rag. He was thin and fit, nearly six feet tall, late 30s or early 40s, sporting a three-day beard and short sandy hair.

"Good afternoon," replied Kelly. "Nice little church you have here."

"Welcome to St. Joseph's Lutheran," said the man with a flourish, sweeping his right arm upward, as if introducing a mansion. "I see you are travelers—looking for land, a lost dog, or the Lord?"

"None of the above I guess," Kelly replied, "just passing through really. We're on our way to the Dog Den Butte area."

"I know it well," replied the man, "I minister to a second church up there, St. Peter's." Then he stuck out his right hand. "I'm Pastor Joel."

Kelly and Jamie both shook his hand. "Nice to meet you, pastor," said Kelly. "I'm Kelly and this is my brother Jamie."

"You folks live around Dog Den?"

"No, we're from Metigoshe," replied Jamie, "you familiar with it?"

"Up on the border, by the Turtle Mountains?"

"Yep. Did you say you have two churches?" Jamie asked.

"Yes, two right now, keeps me busy on Sundays," he replied, then smiled broadly. "Guess you can call me a traveling preacher of sorts—have Bible will travel."

"Seems to be few people but a lot of churches out here in this country," offered Kelly. "A lot of them boarded up."

"Yeah," said the pastor, looking up and down the road. "We had five churches just in this township here, seven more in the township west of the Butte, down the tracks. Most are shuttered or falling in now. St. Joe's," he said, motioning behind him, "is the last active church around here. The Catholic, Baptist, and Presbyterian churches have all folded. They knocked the old Pentecostal church down a couple years ago. I heard at one time our area had more churches per capita than any other place in North Dakota."

"Really?" Kelly remarked curiously. "Why so many?"

At this, the pastor took off his gloves, propped his leg on the landscaping timbers, and braced his left elbow on his knee. "Came down to religious freedom I think. Most folks emigrated here from Germany or Russia at the turn of the century, and soon as they put down roots they started a church. I guess some of the churches just had a family or two, but they built them even if they couldn't really afford to, and they used them—at least until the families died off. Freedom to own your own land, worship in a church of your choosing. Those are powerful motivators."

"Powerful motivators indeed," thought Kelly.

"So, most of these churches just sit empty?" Jamie asked.

"Yep," replied the pastor. "They're just a maintenance nightmare now, with the winters and the wind. You can buy an old one-room church around here for a buck, just to get it back on the tax rolls. Some people convert them into houses, others just salvage the wood." The pastor paused and stood up again.

"You know it might not look like it now, but this area used to be the commercial center of the county. Lots of people here. Lots of energy. There were schools and stores and banks...car dealers, implement shops, restaurants...it all just petered out. Kief and Dog

Den, they're almost ghost towns. Everything's down in Goodview and over by Harvey now."

"Railroad stop running?" Kelly asked, knowing the location of rails often sealed a small town's fate.

"No, no...the railroad still comes through, just doesn't stop. No, something else changed. I think people just got tired of the hard times, started looking for someone to blame—spouses, relatives, neighbors, the State, or Uncle Sam. Focused on the bad instead of the good. Gave up. There's no denying this can be a hard, cruel place, especially in winter. My opinion? Folks just had enough, started to move away and the towns started to empty out."

Then, realizing he was failing in his role as accidental ambassador, the pastor quickly modified his recitation: "Of course we're still here, and we've got a lot of good things going for us, lots of kids in Sunday school, lots of people still excited about our community."

"Well, it's a really nice church," said Kelly, trying to help the pastor recover. "Thanks for the information."

"Say, we have Triple B here every Wednesday night—come on back sometime and join us," invited the pastor. "Then you can really see what our church is like."

"Triple B?" asked Jamie.

"Bingo, Baloney, and Bibles," said the pastor proudly, emphasizing the alliteration.

Jamie laughed out loud, "Ha, ha. So you win baloney at Bingo?'

"No, we sell baloney sandwiches; folks bring their own prizes for the Bingo. Kind of a fundraiser for the church. We begin each week with a new Bible verse."

"Sounds...fun," said Kelly graciously.

"We were gonna call it 'Quadruple B', because we actually do it in the church basement, but nobody liked the name," the pastor continued. "Wednesday nights, at 7:00. Everyone's welcome."

"Maybe we'll do that. Thanks for the invite," Kelly replied and began to walk away. Jamie didn't move.

"Say, Pastor Joel, does the last name Savard mean anything to you?" he asked.

"Savard? No, but I'm not the right person to ask, I've only been here a few years. Some of the other folks around have lived here all their lives. Are you looking for a Savard?"

"Yeah, we think we may be related to the Savard's, maybe by Dog Den, that's why we're headed up that way now."

"Afraid I can't help you. But if you're heading for the Butte that's quite a ways from here." He paused, considering something. "You're welcome to stay here tonight if you're camping, we have a little picnic area behind the church and the water spigot works. There's a restroom in the church basement. We never lock it."

Jamie glanced at Kelly, who nodded her approval. "We're going to take you up on that Pastor Joel, it's already been a long day. Thank you."

"You're welcome," he said as he began to load tools into the van. "But thank the Lord instead, it's all his, we just manage it for him. I have to head home now but you'll find what you need back there. Maybe I'll see you at Bingo."

The pastor loaded the rest of his gear, backed out of the lot, and was soon just a cloud of dust heading east down the gravel road. They went around back and found several wooden picnic tables and a small fire pit with a rusted wrought-iron grate over it. "St. Josephs" had been etched into a flat part of the grate with a welding rod. The grass around the tables was green and clipped short.

"No tent tonight," Jamie said. The sky was clear and the breeze sufficient to dissuade every flying insect save the June beetles, which occasionally hit the tabletop with a crunchy "splat". They washed, ate, and built a small fire with sticks they found in the tree line behind the church. The pit sparked and glowed under the evening stars. It was a beautiful night.

"Do you think we'll get there tomorrow?" asked Jamie.

"To the Butte? We can, if we push it, and don't run into any more problems," Kelly replied.

"What do you think we'll find, just pits?"

"I hope we find something. The battle was 165 years ago. It could just be a big wheat field now, or a parking lot. I don't expect there'll be a gravestone or anything for this Savard fellow if he was actually killed there. But for Uncle Rodney, I just want to be able to step foot on that soil, to say we found it. It was important to Rodney."

"Why was Mom involved? I don't get it," Jamie asked.

"I'm still not sure, but maybe we'll find out once we see it. It bothers me that Leona thought this was just some wild goose chase. I hope it isn't. Grandma said I would know. I'd know what this was all about if we found it."

"How's your foot?"

"Good, just a little stiff, but I think it's a lot stronger now. Well, I know it is. Doesn't really hurt at all unless I kick something."

"No comment."

"Go to sleep little brother."

Sleeping behind a church gave them a sense of security they hadn't felt in a while. They slept hard. Jamie arose at 6:04 a.m. and stumbled to the tree line in the weak light to empty his bladder. He looked up casually to see what the day's weather might offer and then peered through the thin line of trees to a long field of green wheat. Then he opened his eyes wide, squinted, and opened them again to focus. No, it wasn't an illusion.

Gazing back at him through the trees was a white horse.

Chapter 22

It had been a cool evening, as is typical even following a hot day on the northern prairie. And now the morning too was cool and damp. Birds sang sweetly in the nearby brush and ducks quacked noisily in the distance. There was no fire this morning, breakfast consisted of cold biscuits with Saskatoon jam and cool water. The hunters had no appetite but Granger exhorted them to eat: "Today of all days you need strength. Eat, you must eat!"

Elisa Ferguson sat with her mother and sister next to the wheel of their cart. Their father was already stationed in a rifle pit. The biscuit in her mouth was dry, crumbly and tasteless—she had not slept all night, her stomach sick with worry for Jean-Luc, who still had not returned to camp. Sitting with them was a young Cree neighbor from the north, rocking back and forth and nursing a four-month-old baby while tears slowly dripped from her cheeks. Her husband, Samuel Campbell, was one of the two men who had been dispatched to get help from the other camp.

It seemed foolish now for children to be along on the trip, but the Métis families had always traveled to the hunting grounds confident in their abilities to defend themselves. And wives, regardless of maternal burden, were needed and expected to work. No one could have expected an encounter with such an overwhelming opponent. Star Ferguson did what she could to comfort the young mother, but with two distraught daughters of her own, she had little to offer.

The shots at sunrise put the entire camp on alert; the women inside the cart circle grabbed the children and scrambled under the carts while the men in the pits prepared for the charge. Those within the circle poked rifles over cart tongues and through wooden-spoked wheels.

But no charge came.

Instead, they saw a single horseman and then another, on Métis horses, driving their mounts through the ground fog toward the carts.

The horsemen cried out as they rode but could not be understood. Pierre Grant, in the pit furthest from the carts, had been following the first rider in his sights and was ready to dispatch him when he recognized Labide and stood up.

"*Mon Dieu*! It is Labide, don't shoot!" he cried to the others. Jerome Santerre emerged from the fog on the second horse and the two escaped hostages arrived at the breastwork nearly simultaneously. The riders quickly dismounted and led their animals over the hitches and into the safety of the circle. The Sioux following them pulled up short, some distance away from the carts, and quickly circled back toward the Butte. Several more shots were fired in the distance.

"Where is Jean-Luc?" Labide asked the group which had gathered.

"He is not with you?" asked Granger.

"He was, he was to follow as we escaped," replied Santerre, still fighting for breath. "He may be coming still."

"Watch for Jean-Luc!" Granger cried out to the men in the pits.

"The Sioux number over 1,000 warriors," said Santerre gravely. "They will attack very soon. We must send for help."

"Dubois and Campbell left last night," Granger replied, leaving unanswered the question of their fate. The Métis had done all they could do, now they must fight or be killed. Rifles were produced for Labide and Santerre. They posted on the breastwork under the carts with the rest of the men and several of the armed women to await the attack.

Each of the men in the rifle pits outside the circle brought with them at least one rifle, some had two, along with knives, hatchets, and picks, which they simply stuck in the soil mounded around the pit for easy access. Each assumed they would be overrun at some point after running out of ammunition. The knives and hatchets would be used for hand-to-hand fighting. To a man, they vowed to take as many Sioux with them as possible before they perished themselves, as they almost certainly would. They were ready for battle, physically and mentally. They were ready for death.

They did not have long to wait.

In the distance, shrill shrieks and yelps announced the arrival of a group of some 40 mounted Sioux which burst atop a hill south of the camp and stormed toward the circled carts. The war cries sent shivers through the Métis women and tested the nerve of the assembled riflemen. Then the Sioux pulled their horses short, out of rifle range, as one young warrior continued, likely the self-proclaimed leader of this band, bearing his horse closer and closer until it was clear he was going to breach the barricade.

The Métis, showing composure and fortitude which would serve them well on this day, held their fire until Granger gave the signal. Then the young warrior and his horse fell under a fusillade of lead slugs and buckshot, his death wish granted.

The shooters reloaded quickly and again held their fire as the band of 40 and a second band of 75 Sioux converged on the fortified camp from both sides and began firing as they circled the perimeter of the rifle pits. The Sioux slugs and arrows found their marks, not in the flesh of the Métis but in the dense wood of the carts and wagons and in the packed breastworks of dirt. Several horses screamed as hot lead or arrows struck horseflesh, yet the Métis hunters remained unscathed by the first volley. The Sioux rode off, came together, and used the same tactic again, this time surrounding the camp and riding much closer.

"Courage brave hunters," shouted Father LeSueur as he raced up and down behind the Métis marksmen, gesticulating wildly with his arms and thrusting his clenched fist in the air. "The Lord is with us. The Lord shall smite thine enemy and deliver us to safety. Courage. Courage!"

Granger waited until the first Sioux shot and then gave the signal— 30 Métis rifles barked and nearly a dozen Sioux went down or slumped over their mounts. A second Métis volley dropped six more and the Sioux quickly retreated. The warriors continued to probe for a Métis weakness over the next three hours, each time circling farther and farther away but still falling to the marksmen.

It was clear now the Sioux, accustomed to shooting bison at near point-blank range, and skilled at close range ambush tactics, were no match for the disciplined Métis long-range shooters. Time and again the heavy-barreled Métis bison guns spoke and the slugs found their mark, at times taking both horse and rider down with a single shot. The Métis were holding their own.

Granger knew if the Sioux were to charge *en masse* they could easily overrun the Métis rifle pits and makeshift garrison, but they did not seem to have the stomach for it. It also seemed important for the Sioux to remove their dead and wounded warriors from battle. When one went down, he was quickly aided by another warrior who would drag the body or wounded man away. Some Métis waited for this and tried to shoot the second man but Granger put a stop to it—not because he wanted to spare the Sioux, but rather to conserve powder and ball for only the best shots.

"Sure shots only! Save powder, save your powder!" he implored the men. He knew their only hope of survival was to keep the Sioux at bay for as long as possible and as far away from the Métis barricade as possible. Beyond their own lives, their stock must be protected, for without horses and oxen they could never escape. By now he assumed his riders had not gotten through to the larger Métis camp, and so, this would be a battle of attrition.

"Father—how many have we wounded?" he asked Father LeSueur.

"By God's grace no one has been struck," Father LeSueur replied, then lifted his hands skyward. "Thy will be done, Father! Thy will be done!"

By now the children of the camp were beside themselves with fear, and more than one mother hid a knife in the folds of her garments in the event the Sioux did overrun the shooters and breach their defense. It was without question the wives and mothers, many of them Indigenous or of mixed-blood themselves would fight to the death. As necessary, they might take children with them, sparing them a worse fate at the hands of the Sioux.

The assault against the Métis continued as fresh mounts and fresh warriors poured into the battle, but the result was always the same— minor wounds for the fortified Métis, death for the Sioux. Now Father LeSueur redoubled his efforts, shouting a favored Psalm for all to hear.

"God be merciful unto us, *BLESS US* and make thy face shine upon us. Let us *PRAISE* thee, let all the peoples of earth praise thee. Though shalt *JUDGE* the people *RIGHTEOUSLY* and *GOVERN ALL NATIONS* upon earth. God shall bless us and all the ends of the earth shall *FEAR* him. We ask for your blessing Father and your *DELIVERANCE* from evil."

The combination of disciplined shooting and prayer was working in their favor. The tide had been turned, at least in the short term: For the Métis, confidence had replaced sure death; for the Sioux, a swift victory and the prospect of many scalps was now in doubt.

Granger directed three women to resupply all shooters with powder and ball or cartridges. The guns of two men in the rifle pits had misfired and now had balls stuck in the barrels, a not uncommon occurrence; with no time for extraction, the guns were replaced with working arms. The stock of a third gun had been struck by a Sioux round and splintered, sending wood splinters into the Métis shooter's face; the wound was minor, however, so his gun was replaced and he too resumed his position.

Having hunted bison many years for their livelihood, the Métis traveled well-armed. Their arsenal of weapons was surely superior to the guns of the Sioux, many of which were poorly-maintained trade guns. Captured guns from trappers and traders were of better quality but of many mixed sizes and calibers. As a result, a volley of shots from the Sioux might contain a mix of rifled slugs, round balls, arrows, and birdshot. The Métis returned fire with balls and slugs designed to quickly kill 1,500-pound animals. These projectiles, some as large as the end of a man's thumb, barely slowed as they passed through a man-sized mass. The Métis guns were powerful medicine.

Granger surveyed the damage: None of the Métis were seriously wounded, two horses lay dead within the stockade, and two others had arrows sticking into their hindquarters, one arrow flopping just barely through the skin, and one ox bled from a hole in his neck. He stood placidly, accepting his fate. They had been lucky so far.

The Sioux made two more charges, paying for it again in three lost men and two wounded horses. The Sioux chiefs soon accepted the fact their easy, overwhelming victory was not to be. Even now it was an embarrassment—this handful of Métis had stood their ground against over 1,000 Sioux warriors.

For the Sioux there would be no captured horses or mules, no victory celebrations, no stories passed down, no scalps dancing in the wind from lodge poles. There would only be defeat.

Following mounting casualties, the Sioux grudgingly admitted defeat and withdrew. It was a tremendous victory against long odds for Granger and his group of Métis hunters. Of nearly 150 Métis men, women and children, all were accounted for—except one.

Chapter 23

They left the churchyard after a quick, cold breakfast and continued north. As they traveled they looked back occasionally to see the horse; sometimes on a hill behind them, other times feeding on the edge of a hayfield. Then it would disappear for an hour or more and suddenly show up ahead of them, having found some cross-country shortcut. Late in the afternoon, they concluded it was following them.

They passed by several missile sites signed "A-6" or "B-4" according to some grid. Each consisted of two-acre gravel pads surrounded by menacing signs and eight-foot chain-link fences. Antennae arrays connected the sites to control stations that could control the missiles from remote, secure locations.

"What are those," asked Jamie, "looks like military stuff."

"Nuclear missile silos. There are nuclear missiles inside each one of those."

"Really? You ever have to work on 'em?"

"No, that's Air Force, not Marines. Those are all Minuteman Threes," she added casually, "I would not want to be around here during a launch."

"Well, how about that guy," Jamie said, motioning across the road at a working farmstead. "He can't be more than a quarter-mile from here."

Kelly glanced up and said, "I wouldn't want to be him either."

"So people are living here with all these nuclear bombs right next to them?"

"Yeah."

"If a war broke out they'd all be burnt to a crisp with these missiles taking off!" he exclaimed.

"In a real war, it probably wouldn't matter. Where do you think the bad guys are going to send their own nuclear bombs?"

Jamie thought for a moment, "Oh yeah, they'd send them here to take out these."

"Bingo."

"Seems like a waste."

"Most wars are kiddo. Let's change the subject. What are we going to do about that horse?"

"Do you think it's following us?"

"Yeah, it's following us, like a stray dog. It seems to like you though, I wonder if you could get close enough to get that halter and wire off of it. It must hurt with every step he takes."

"If he gets close enough I'll try."

His opportunity came later that evening as they camped at an abandoned farmstead a half-mile off the road. The yard contained a nice grove of tall cottonwood and elm trees, a hedge of lilacs, and a trio of stunted, gnarled apple trees. Within an hour of setting up camp, the horse came hobbling down the driveway and stopped at the edge of the yard.

"Here's your chance Mr. Horse Whisperer," said Kelly.

"Let me try an apple," Jamie said, searching the small trees. It was too early in the season for ripe fruit but he picked a couple small green apples and one mushy one from the ground beneath the trees. It looked like something had taken a bite out of it.

He approached the horse with the apples in his hand, palm up, and to his surprise, the animal immediately began hobbling over to him, then stopped 20 feet short and stared at him with its good eye. It seemed eager to eat.

"Here you go," said Jamie softly, holding the apples higher. The horse stepped forward slowly, then closer, closer, then craned its neck and then took one of the green apples from his hand.

"Don't get bit," cautioned Kelly. As she spoke the horse dropped the apple and seemed to spit out the hard green chunks.

"Too sour," said Jamie to the horse. "Try this one," now holding out the softer windfall apple. The horse stretched out again and took the apple, crunching it noisily as the juice dribbled over its lips.

"You're a natural Jamie," laughed Kelly.

"It's true, I'm loved by puppies, horses, and certain discerning members of the opposite sex," he replied. Fifteen minutes later he was cautiously stroking the horse's neck.

It was the first time he had gotten a close look at his condition. The animal's back and flanks were raw with pink and red whip marks and the milky blind eye wept constantly. His other eye was clear, bright, and exuded intelligence. The old leather halter was dried out and brittle and had bit into the top of the horse's nose and shaved the hair off the sides of his face. Physically he was in tough shape.

"I'm going to need a sharp knife to get this off," he said, calling out to Kelly.

"Then you're in luck because that's the only kind I carry." She walked up behind Jamie slowly and handed him her combat blade. "Maybe just try cutting the side and loosening it up," she suggested.

Jamie held onto the horse's mane loosely and slowly slipped the knife under a leather strap on the side of his face. The horse was having none of it and suddenly whipped his head back and jumped away.

"Damn."

"No, you got it," observed Kelly. The strap had been severed and was hanging loose.

"Damn, this knife really is sharp," Jamie said, looking down at the blade.

"Told you."

Now the horse pawed the ground and shook its head in a blur, with pieces of leather and metal rings slapping its face.

"It's off," said Jamie. The halter now hung under the horse's head, suspended by a single strap under its jaw. A bright red, raw patch was now visible on top of the horse's nose. Jamie moved toward it again, this time hiding the knife behind his back. "Easy boy, easy," he said, reaching out and again stroking the horse's neck. He brought the blade forward slowly; another "snick" and the halter fell to the ground. The horse was free.

"He's got to feel better now," said Jamie, lightly stroking the horse's neck again. "I wonder if he was following us because he wanted that off. Grandpa used to say horses were smarter than people."

"I guess even horses know when they need help."

They ate supper with the horse watching, another mix of noodles, dried peas, and sauce. Kelly washed it down with a pint of water.

"Guess I'll pay for that tonight when I have to pee in the dark," she observed. She did, about 3 a.m., under a sky blazing with stars and an endless Milky Way. She hadn't seen stars so bright, so clear, since Afghanistan. As she relieved herself she saw the horse watching her. "What are you looking at Mr. Troublemaker?"

The next morning they started out early again. Jamie found three more mushy apples and put them in his pack, but he needed no inducement, for as they left the camp the horse followed right on their trail. At noon they stopped and had a snack and he was able to slip a loop of thin rope around the horse's neck.

As long as Jamie didn't tighten it the horse would follow, clomping along on its three good feet and slightly dragging the fourth. If the rope tightened the horse reared back, or tried to with his injured back foot, and then planted his front hooves firmly.

"Kinda stubborn isn't he," mused Kelly.

"He don't like being told what to do," admitted Jamie. "As long as you give him some rope he's fine, otherwise you're in for a fight. I think he's doing well though, given what he's been through. I guess I'd be mean as hell if I got a whipping every day."

"Yeah, me too. I learned that in the Marines," offered Kelly, "Your true colors come to the surface under stress. Some soldiers rose to the occasion, others just got scared or mean. That horse must have a gentle spirit, but he doesn't want to be messed with." She thought again about the short rope which had tied him to the corral. "Must have been hell for him living on that farm."

"I don't want to even think about it," said Jamie, then found himself reflecting on the very subject. He had grown up with horses and knew them to be much like people—some smart, some dumb, some mean, others just lazy. To him, owning a horse was a partnership, with each contributing something to make a stronger whole. His high school horse Blaze would have made a good hunting horse—he seemed to know what Jamie wanted before he asked. He was fast and sleek and athletic, much like Jamie was in his dancing days. They made a good team. And now, for some reason, this poor battered horse had triggered a flood of happy memories—of trail riding through the Turtle Mountains, racing with his friends, and swimming on horseback across gin-clear, spring-fed ponds. He realized now he really missed his horse. And it wasn't at all clear to him now why he hadn't found another after Blaze died.

"You know we really need to do something about these cuts," he told Kelly. "They keep trying to heal but they open up again when he walks. They're never gonna heal that way. We need to grease him up with some antiseptic salve or something, if nothing else just to keep the flies off."

An hour later they had their chance.

Four horses watched them closely as they moved past a small pasture which paralleled the road ditch; three paints and a roan. An old farmhouse, barn, and worn corral stood back from the road a quarter-mile, surrounded by a thin tree grove. Several head of Black Angus steers moved slowly through the trees.

"They might have some salve or antiseptic here," said Kelly. "These must be horse people."

"Let's try," agreed Jamie.

They turned in and walked down the short drive to the yard. Now they could see a single line of electric fence circling a part of the grove. The Angus on the other side of the wire regarded them dully. They heard chickens somewhere in the yard and suddenly a compact, mixed-breed dog of about 45 pounds scampered out toward them barking dutifully, her tail wagging slowly as if still determining the threat level. She had a short red-ticked coat, possibly a Blue Heeler mix.

241

The horse startled and whinnied at the dog's approach and tugged against Jamie's rope, which brought the other horses in the pasture running over. Then a screen door slammed and a stout older woman stepped down from the back door and began walking toward them.

"C'mon Sally, that's okay," she called and the dog quickly scooted back toward her. "Hello," she said warmly, both a greeting and an invitation for them to state their business.

"Hello, this horse here ran into a fence and we're wondering if you might be able to spare some ointment for his cuts," said Kelly, trying to offer a plausible story to explain their intrusion.

"Well that's my husband's department," she replied. "But I'm sure we have something around." Then she stopped, looked closely at the horse, and frowned. "Oh boy, that back foot looks pretty tough, that wire's gotta come off there." Then she paused again and took in the sight of the two hikers, obviously Indigenous, and their backpacks. Satisfied they were not dangerous, she directed, "Come on over to the barn and we'll see what we have."

They walked slowly past the house and continued to an open barn door. "Eddie," she called inside. "Got company." An older man of about 70 stepped out in heavy leather boots, faded blue jeans and a wrinkled blue western shirt over a white T-shirt. On his head perched a red Case tractor ball-cap with a grease-stained brim. He didn't say anything but wiped his hands on a white rag and looked the pair over closely.

"Sez their horse ran into a fence, looking for some wound salve," explained the woman.

"Well, we use the pink stuff on our horses, buy it by the gallon," Eddie stated.

"That'll work," said Jamie approvingly. "We use that on our horses up north too."

"Oh, whereabouts you folks from?" Eddie asked.

"Metigoshe," replied Kelly.

"You're a bit far from the Reservation, aren't you?" he asked, looking directly at Jamie.

"We don't live on the Reservation but we live near there, in the Turtle Mountains," Kelly said.

Eddie stopped and slowly regarded them again.

"We're just trying to doctor up the horse and keep the flies off him," offered Jamie.

The man moved over to the horse and looked him up and down. "You say he ran into a fence?"

"Yeah," replied Jamie.

"Well, it appears to me this horse has been beat bad. Those are marks from a whip," he stated accusingly.

"We think so too," said Kelly quickly. "He was loose and following us, we caught him to doctor him up."

"A man who'd do that to a dumb animal should be whipped himself," Eddie added with disgust.

"And look at that back hoof," said the woman to her husband. "That's going rotten."

"Yep," he replied. Then he looked from Jamie to Kelly and back to Jamie again skeptically. "Exactly what you doing around here— hiking?"

"We're on our way to a place up by Dog Den, trying to track down some relatives," Kelly said.

"Well, you can nearly see the Butte from here," said the woman helpfully. "And we know everyone around here. What're their names?"

"Savard," said Jamie. "They were Métis hunters. Bison hunters."

"May-tee?" repeated Eddie. "Well, there haven't been any bison around here in 100 years. And I don't know of any Savards. Do you, Momma?"

"No."

"It was a long time ago," acknowledged Kelly. "But if you can spare some salve we'll be on our way."

"Let me see what I've got," Eddie said and disappeared into the barn.

"You drop those packs and come in for a drink," said the woman. "You must be terribly hot."

They were, and the idea of a cool drink was very appealing. Kelly's gray "Marines" shirt was wet and clinging to her back. They followed her to the steps of the house and dropped their packs on the ground.

"Well, come on in," the woman said, opening the door wider. As they entered she added, "Sally, you stay out," barring the dog from the doorway.

The kitchen was large and smelled of wood smoke, beef roasts, fried walleye, baked chicken, and...fresh bread—all these aromas becoming one with the woodwork over many decades of cooking. A red and white enameled metal kitchen table occupied one end, near a recently installed new picture window.

She invited them to sit at the table, removing two glass pans and a newspaper from its surface. The décor was late '70s supplemented with a few working antiques. A huge red tin rooster looked down at them from a shelf above the table. The heating element in the oven clicked and they heard a roast of some kind sizzle. It smelled wonderful.

"Would you like iced tea or lemonade?"

Regardless of their standing, friend or foe, everyone was offered refreshments upon entering a home on the northern prairie. Old Beelzebub himself could make an entrance on his way to collect souls, and he too would be offered a beverage.

"Tea would be great," said Kelly.

"Me too," added Jamie. "My name's Jamie by the way, and this is my sister Kelly."

"Very pleased to meet you, my name is Ellie Roth, and you met my husband Eddie. Ellie and Eddie, that's us."

Ellie Roth was in her mid-60s, she wore a faded white house dress in a daisy print, her long pewter hair pulled back in a loose ponytail. She removed a pitcher of tea from the refrigerator and poured two large glasses on the counter and placed them on the table. She then turned again and produced a tray with four small wedge-shaped pastries. "I just made these this morning, please help yourself." She then sat down at the table across from them.

"So, you're on a hike, walking all the way down from Metigoshe— that's the Canadian border right—looking for family?" she asked, subconsciously questioning the veracity of their story.

"I guess we're trying to recreate a journey our relatives took, and actually we were over by Harvey earlier, we had to backtrack a bit to get here," replied Kelly. "It's a long story but we're trying to find a site, a battlefield site, from the 1850s which may have involved some of our relatives. It's something our uncle started many years ago. We're trying to finish it."

"Are you...Sioux Indians then?" she asked politely.

"No, my brother and I, and our family are Métis."

"Oh yes 'May-tee,' you said that. I've never heard of the Métis Indians."

"Well, our families are a mixture of French and Scottish and Native American ancestry, Cree mostly."

"And you, or your relatives, were here hunting buffalo?"

"Yes ma'am," replied Kelly. "They used to bring long trains of ox-carts down to the Dog Den Butte area each summer and harvest bison to make pemmican."

"Oh I like pemmican, I had some at Frontier Days over at Fort Union but Eddie thought it tasted terrible—like sawdust."

Jamie, who had been silent to this point, now leaned forward on the table and cupped his open fingers to his lips, as if pondering a great question. "Lemon zest," he announced.

Ellie looked at him, confused. Kelly glanced quizzically.

"There's...it's lemon zest, you use lemon zest in these, right?"

Ellie recovered. "Why, yes."

"That's what I was tasting," said Jamie triumphantly. "And do you use Juneberries?"

"Saskatoons, yes," said Ellie, smiling. "We pick them wild up by the Butte."

"But how do you keep them from bleeding their color?"

"Well," she said, turning toward him now, "you freeze them before you add them to the batter. I keep some in the freezer just to have on hand."

"That's a great idea!" said Jamie. "You use a stone?"

"Yes! My, you do know your scones."

"I've tried. My grandma tried to teach me but my bottoms are always mushy or burned—we need to get a good stone. But these...these are really good."

Ellie was beaming now. "Why, thank you, Jamie."

The screen door squealed and Eddie walked in, carrying a pint jar of pink ointment.

"This is Kelly and her brother Jamie," announced Ellie.

"Pleased to make your acquaintance," he acknowledged coolly. "Got some salve." Then he noticed Kelly's T-shirt. "Got some relatives in the Marines?"

"I do," stated Jamie proudly, "my sister."

"*You* were in the Marines?" Eddie asked incredulously, looking at Kelly.

"Over nine years, mustered out last month," she replied.

247

"You serve stateside?"

"Yes, and Norway and Afghanistan."

"Combat?"

"Nine months in Afghanistan."

"I'll be damned," he said. "I was a jarhead too, in 'Nam. Drafted. We lost a third of our unit before I got out. That was hell."

"I lost some friends too," added Kelly ruefully.

"What unit were you in?"

"Second Division, Second Regiment. You?"

"Third Division, we fought at Tet. What did you muster out at?"

"Sergeant, E-6. I was a DI at Parris Island for 3 years."

"A DI? You don't look so tough."

Kelly smiled. "Don't try me."

"She got shot by one of her trainees," interjected Jamie.

"Shot?" Eddie exclaimed.

"Hit in the ankle," Kelly explained quickly. "Was my own fault."

"Well you seem to be getting around fine now," observed Ellie as she refilled their drink glasses.

"They put me back together with a few pins, I'll be fine."

"Well, let me shake your hand Kelly," Eddie said, stepping forward and offering a huge calloused hand with sausage-like fingers. "You must be one tough little lady."

"Semper Fi," said Kelly, returning the handshake.

"Semper Fi."

For a moment, the kitchen was filled with silence, then Eddie spoke again.

"Listen, that horse is in no condition to travel, why don't you leave him here for a few days while you do your business up at Dog Den then come get him. We need to get that wire off his back foot and get him cleaned up. Our horses won't like it but I can keep him in the barnyard corral for now."

"Jamie?" asked Kelly. "What do you think?"

"We tried to steady him to get that wire off but he won't have it," Jamie said, considering the offer. "I guess you're much better equipped to deal with it." He hesitated, "We can pay you for boarding him."

"There'll be none of that. Always glad to help out a fellow Marine. You just come back for him when you're ready."

They thanked the couple and walked out and down the steps and shouldered their packs once again. As they turned to leave they heard the screen door screech again and turned to see Ellie holding out a brown paper lunch sack. "Here," she said, pushing the sack toward Jamie, "take some of these with you for a snack later." Inside were four more scones. "I do hope you find your relatives."

With the long days, Kelly calculated they could get in several more miles before dusk. As they walked westward they saw the hazy dark form of Dog Den Butte set against the horizon. They were almost there.

"I've never had a scone before," said Kelly.

"Well, now you have, and those were good ones," said Jamie.

"So, you know how to make scones?" she asked curiously.

"I am a man of many talents," he answered without flourish.

"Really," she replied flatly. "Or maybe Grandma's just a great teacher."

"Whatever Sis. Man's gotta eat."

Chapter 24

They camped at a place off the highway called the Velva Sportsman's Pond. It was a peaceful setting, far from the traffic, and surrounded by huge chokecherry and Juneberry bushes. As they walked, blackbirds trilled and rooster pheasants cackled from somewhere far down the ravine. Unnatural hills of mine spoil bordered the site to the south, and they could see that the Pond itself had been formed by an earthen dam which plugged one of the ravines cutting through a mined area. The land at the top of the ravines was flat, planted to soybeans.

"Old open-pit mine," said Kelly, gesturing toward the spoil piles on the horizon. "Coal, I suppose. This must be the area Anna Schenko was talking about."

"You mean they dug out the coal and just left these piles here?"

"Looks like it."

"That should be illegal," Jamie protested.

"Probably is now, but those spoil piles have probably been there since the '40s. Just like those missile silos we walked by—this part of the country is important for national defense and in return, the local residents get, well, they get to live next to nuclear weapons and have these old spoil piles everywhere. Same with the oil out west. If nobody watches them the companies are going to get the oil out as quick as they can, and to hell with the consequences," observed Kelly, then added, "Seems nobody does the right thing unless someone's watching."

"Doesn't seem right," said Jamie.

"It's not. But the folks here just wave the flag and pretend it's all okay. And it's not just here—there are places like this all across the country. I heard there's a place right outside of Denver where the sites are so contaminated by the nuclear waste they can't be used for 10,000 years. They just put fences around them. It seems crazy what we do to ourselves."

As they sat near their fire they watched fish surface and splash in the pond. A pair of mallard ducks, a colorful drake and drab brown hen, swam parallel to shore nearby. "What kind of fish do you think are jumping out there?" asked Jamie.

"I don't know, I'm sure this pond is stocked with something. I don't think they'd be natural. You know Lake Metigoshe is probably one of the few really natural lakes in the state—those perch and walleye and pike have been in there for thousands of years."

"I like bluegills best. Grandpa and I used to catch a lot of bluegill," said Jamie. "He'd take the fins off and gut them and Grandma would fry them whole. You remember that? I'd scale them with a spoon."

"Yeah, I actually remember fishing with Mom and Dad a few times, but you were too young. We used to take a mesh bag with us and hang it over the boat and just fill it up with fish—bass, pike, walleye, perch—it didn't matter. Then we'd have a huge fish fry at the house with all our aunts, uncles, and cousins. Mom was a good fisher-lady, she always caught more walleyes than anyone in the boat; she had the touch."

"I wish we had some fishing gear," said Jamie. "I haven't had a good fish dinner since last fall."

That evening they dined on macaroni and cheese with packaged fruit bars for dessert. It began to cool as the sun lowered in the western sky so they made a small fire and enjoyed the end of the day. With the coming darkness, fish splashed constantly in the pond and pheasant roosters crowed from all different points on the compass. Just as the sun dipped to the horizon a coyote pack began to squeal and yip to the east, a second pack answered from the south, and then, far to the north, toward the lights of Velva, a third pack joined in.

Kelly thought back to what old Kitchi had said, how the predator waits for the darkness, welcomes it. The Sioux may have ruled the prairie before the Métis, and the Europeans after the Métis, but right now, on this plain, it seemed the coyotes ruled the prairie, at least in the darkness. What else had Kitchi said—"when you are old, the darkness is your friend?" Did he mean you were no longer afraid of the dark, or the unknown? In his case, she imagined he actually became part of the darkness, and perhaps fearless as well. She hoped he would find his way back to the Red River country before it was too late. She wondered if *she* would ever welcome darkness.

They went to bed early to get an early start at dawn the next day.

As they walked along the highway the next morning they passed a small construction camp full of cranes, huge coils of wire, several dozen utility and cement trucks, bunkhouse trailers, and small mountains of rebar. A half-dozen turbine bodies as large as school buses were lined up neatly against the highway. Nearby were dozens of blade sections. It didn't take them long to realize they had walked into the center of a huge wind-power project. Several turbines already crowded the horizon in various stages of construction— partially-erected towers, towers with turbine bodies, and completed towers and turbines with massive blades.

As arranged by Rose Dockter with the Velva Historical Society, they arrived at the back doorstep of the Whitney Ranch at the agreed-upon time of 10:00 a.m. A shiny red SUV was parked in the driveway next to the house.

The door opened quickly after Kelly knocked and the smell of freshly brewed coffee wafted out the door. "You must be the treasure hunters!" said a small, fit woman in her late 50s, smiling. "Welcome to the ranch! Take off those packs and come on in."

They dropped their packs on the lawn and walked into the kitchen. Another woman, mid-'40s, dressed in jeans, cowboy boots, long-sleeved tan blouse, and long auburn hair pulled back in a ponytail was already seated at the table; she rose to greet them. "I'm Kelly and this is my brother Jamie," said Kelly, offering the now-familiar introduction and gesturing toward Jamie.

"I'm Rose Dockter, with the Velva Historical Society," said the younger woman.

"And I'm Jennie Whitney, deputy calf wrangler and chief bottle washer around this place," said the older woman. "Please sit," she invited, gesturing towards the empty chairs at the table.

"I was so excited when Anna Schenko called," said Dockter. "McHenry County has been working with Jennie's family for many years to document the historic site on her ranch but we haven't been able to get much interest from anyone at the State. As you may know, Goodview County has concluded the Battle of the Grand Coteau took place near Harvey."

"Yes, we checked there first, by the new golf course," said Kelly. "But we're pretty certain that wasn't the actual site."

"Our family has lived on this ranch for four generations," explained Whitney. "We discovered some pits early on and did some research—we think they're rifle pits and we think the battle was right here, between the Sioux and Métis. I've come to this little adventure late myself, my grandfather was the one who started it."

"Ours too," added Jamie. "Our grandpa and uncle."

"Now...you're...your family are Métis correct?" asked Dockter. "That's what Anna Schenko said."

"Yes, we're Métis, from around the Turtle Mountain area and Bottineau," explained Kelly. "We also have many relatives in Canada, south of Winnipeg. Both Jamie and I live with our grandmother right now, just outside the Turtle Mountains. Our last name is Moreau, but we have some Gagne and Gibson in the family too. The relative or relation let's say, we think might have been involved in the battle was a Savard."

Dockter pushed a manila folder toward Kelly on the table. "I don't know if Anna told you but we found some oral histories from the battle, back before they started the mines south of here, and some survey notes. They seem to indicate the battle was located in this area, around the Whitney ranch, rather than Harvey. We also found an old roster of the actual Métis who traveled to this area in 1851, from church records—have you seen that?"

"No," replied Kelly. "My uncle and mother gathered a few names but I haven't seen a roster of any kind."

"Take a look at this," said Dockter, pushing a single page toward Kelly. "Look at the highlighted name," she added, with a look of anticipation.

Kelly glanced down the sheet listing 50 or 60 family and individual names and then saw the single highlighted name: "Jean-Luc Savard". Kelly's eye's widened briefly and her heart began to race. So it was true! She silently slid the sheet over to Jamie.

"There he is!" he exclaimed. "There's the Savard, just like Kitchi, and Uncle Rodney. We found him."

"Kitchi?" asked Dockter.

Kelly shot a glance over to Jamie then explained, "It's a long story. Kitchi, or Badger, is one more piece of the puzzle. I swear there have been a thousand pieces."

"Now I understand the two of you have actually walked down here from the Turtle Mountains?" asked Whitney. "Is that true or was someone just pulling our leg?"

"No, that's true," said Jamie. "We started a couple weeks ago. It was Kelly's idea, to take a journey like our Métis relatives did back then, chasing bison. You wouldn't know it now but Kelly has or had, a bad ankle; she hurt it in the Service."

"You were in the Service?" asked Whitney.

"Yes ma'am, I was in the Marines until earlier this year," replied Kelly. "I injured my ankle but the trip down here has really helped strengthen it." She added, "It's much better now."

"Well, I'll be happy to drive you out to the pasture where we located the pits," said Whitney. "Would you like to see them?"

"Yes ma'am, but if you don't mind we'll just walk out there," said Kelly. "It seems important that we do that now," glancing at Jamie, who nodded in agreement.

"Well that's up to you certainly," Whitney replied.

"There's more to Jean-Luc Savard you should know," said Dockter. "Based on the oral histories and church records it appeared the Sioux suffered as many as 30 or 40 casualties in the battle, but the Métis only suffered one. We think that was Jean-Luc."

"My research and the account from a Father LeSueur confirm there was just a single fatality and he was buried on-site," agreed Kelly. "There was some question as to who it was, but I think based on the description and the age it was this Savard fellow."

"Do you think that's what Uncle Rodney was looking for all along, this guy Jean-Luc?" asked Jamie, looking at Kelly.

"Could be," she replied, then addressed Whitney. "It would really be something to find the gravesite. Are there any markers like that out there? Have you looked?"

"We only found the excavations, which we think are the pits, the rifle pits the Métis used," she replied.

"There's more I'm afraid if this man was somehow related to you," added Dockter.

"More?" asked Jamie.

"You must remember the Sioux during that period, this was largely before the influence of Europeans, lived a very brutish lifestyle. They gave their enemies no quarter. By all accounts, the young Métis victim was...was, well..."

"Oh goodness Rose just say it," interrupted Whitney, "after all, this was over 150 years ago and these people have traveled a long way to find the truth—this Jean-Luc was dismembered. And he was impaled by over 50 arrows after he'd been killed. It was a terrible, violent death. Members of his party had to gather him up just to give him a proper burial. It sounds simply horrible. And to think this happened back there on our pasture, it's just horrible."

"My God," said Kelly, not because of the brutality of war, with which she was familiar, but by Jean-Luc's violent end and the denial of a peaceful passing. If this were true she knew his was a soul not at rest.

"They chopped him up?" exclaimed Jamie.

"You must remember times were different back then—this was 'no man's' land," offered Dockter. "People traveled here at their own risk, and often at great peril. It's a miracle more Métis were not killed in this battle—the Sioux numbered in the thousands while the Métis party was just 100 or so, including many women and children.

257

Those rifle pits must have saved their lives. I still don't know how they did it, outnumbered 15 or 20 to 1."

"They were tough," asserted Kelly. "They were marksmen and great hunters, and they feared nothing."

Dockter nodded her head in agreement, "The Métis continued to hunt here unimpeded by the Sioux for many years afterward, at least until the US military presence arrived some years later."

"And after the military arrived the bison disappeared, and then the Métis and then the Sioux," said Kelly. "And after the Métis retreated to Canada our trouble with the Canadian government began."

Just then a tall, gaunt man in a stained tan T-shirt and grease-stained blue jeans walked in the kitchen door, carrying an empty half-gallon plastic jug. His face bristled with stiff, gray whiskers. On his head, he wore a dirty green John Deere tractor ball-cap. He regarded the four of them seated at the table, then straightened and faced them. "Wondered whose car that was. Who are these people?" he asked, directing the question to his wife.

"These are the young people interested in the battlefield I was telling you about," said Mrs. Whitney.

He looked directly at Jamie. "Ain't nothing out there but some old buffalo wallows," he said. "Waste of time."

"Well we'd appreciate the opportunity to see them for ourselves," stated Kelly defensively.

"Those your packs outside?" he asked.

"Yes."

"You intend to camp out there?"

"No, we just came to visit the battle site."

"There's a wire across that section line back there, don't run over it with your car. And close the gates behind you."

"They're going to walk back to the pasture," explained Mrs. Whitney.

"Walk? It's over a mile back there."

"We'd like to walk, we've walked a long way already," said Jamie.

"Well, that's the damnedest thing I ever heard," spat the man. "Suit yourself. And don't listen to Jennie's stories about all the noises back there—she sees lights and hears noises all the time. Don't mean nuthin." He turned and filled the jug from the water faucet at the sink. "I'll be back at 12:30 for dinner," he said, then disappeared out the door.

An embarrassed silence lasted only a moment before Mrs. Whitney said, "Please don't mind my husband. He's still mad we didn't sign on to have wind turbines on the ranch, those that did are making plenty of money now, but then, of course, they have to put up with the turbines. This ranch has been in my family for over 125 years, and I want to keep it this way; some things are more important than money."

"Do you really hear sounds from the battlefield?" asked Jamie.

"Yes, I do," she admitted sheepishly. "But maybe it's just the wind or coyotes in the coulees. There are a lot of sounds in the darkness here."

Kelly had been patient all morning, now she wanted to see the site, to walk on the actual battlefield and feel the sun on her face and smell the wind, just like the Métis did over a century ago. "Can we see the site?" she asked.

"Yes, certainly, enough of this talk. Let's get you out there and see what you think. Rose and I can drive down with her vehicle and open the gates. We'll meet you at the site."

They left their packs where they had dropped them but before they left Kelly removed her sheaf of maps to bring along. A long straight two-track road continued out the back of the farmyard, shaded by trees here but then continuing between a field of canola on one side and pasture on the other. Ahead of them, they saw the small red figure of the SUV parked a short mile down the trail with the two women standing beside it. They walked as quickly as they could. Twelve minutes later they stood beside the vehicle and women.

"Now the site is just ahead, you'll see the pasture gate open on the left there," directed Mrs. Whitney. "If you go straight in and bear to the right you'll find the first depression there, about 100 yards out, then look to either side and you'll see others, about 50 yards apart."

"Aren't you coming?" asked Jamie.

Mrs. Whitney smiled. "I've seen them, and if you have a family connection to this site I don't want to spoil it. You go, take as much time as you like. We'll wait here."

"Thank you, Jennie," said Kelly sincerely. "C'mon Jamie," she said and stepped past the vehicle to the open gate.

The pasture was split by a fence into two sections; one had been grazed down by cattle while the grass on the other side of the fence was waist-high. A deep coulee cut into the landscape on the far side of the pasture cell in front of them. Kelly took one long stride onto the pasture and stopped, then turned to Jamie and smiled broadly. "I think we're here."

They walked out into the pasture and veered to the right and easily found a shallow depression, the grass had been grazed down so it stood out. Jamie immediately stepped down into the hole and looked around. "Where would the Sioux have come from?"

Kelly turned around and searched the landscape. "Those trees weren't there back then," she said, pointing to a grove 200 yards distant. "There," she said, pointing to the coulee, "that would have been a good recon spot."

Jamie flopped down and held his arms out as if holding a rifle, his lanky frame just fitting within the depression. "Damn, 20 to 1," he said, admiringly. "You tough bastards." Sitting up he asked, "Would they have all come at once, the Sioux?"

"No," replied Kelly. "If they had the Métis would have been wiped out. I'm guessing they held them back, probably 100 yards out that way or more. They were hunters and had to be good shots." Now Kelly worked her way off to the side, looking for a second depression. She found it. This one was still full of grass. She surveyed the entire field again and estimated the range of the depressions, some of which she could see because of the tall dark grass and wormwood growing within them. The Métis were smart, covering all the angles and digging in. Just like a military operation.

"This felt good," she thought. It felt right. She looked around the site for the ponds; there were two ponds at the scene of battle, which the Sioux had used to treat their wounded and clean the dead. The Sioux, despite losing many warriors, left none behind. They would be carried back for proper burials. She smiled at the irony; their warriors were brought back home, just like the Marines. In the distance, she saw what appeared to be a dried pond and a depression for another, which could have been the second pond. To the southeast, she saw the top of Dog Den Butte in a haze.

In her heart she wanted this to be the site of the battle, for her mother, her grandfather, for Uncle Rodney. Then she realized she especially wanted this to be the site—for Jamie. The site of a great Métis victory.

261

Still, something was missing. If this were all true—the battle, the overwhelming odds, the Métis bravery, the Métis victory—if this were true, somewhere here she would find Jean-Luc's grave.

They searched across the field for the better part of an hour, Kelly in one direction and Jamie the other. Every now and then he would shout, "Here's another pit" and wave, which she would acknowledge with a wave of her own.

They returned to the pasture gate where the two women were waiting in the SUV with the windows rolled down. They opened the doors and stood as the pair approached.

"Did you find them, the rifle pits?" asked Mrs. Whitney.

"Yes, we did," replied Kelly.

"Is this the battlefield then?" asked Dockter.

Kelly continued walking up to the pair and then stopped, "I think so, all the elements are here, and the location seems right."

"We found 10 pits and one, maybe two, in the center," said Jamie. "Plus," he added as he stuck a hand down his T-shirt collar, "a lot of wood ticks."

"There are at least 12 pits out there," said Mrs. Whitney, "we found others but they might be buffalo wallows or just odd depressions. Some of them are pretty slumped in, so it's hard to tell."

"The fact there's anything left out there at all after all this time is a minor miracle," said Dockter. "I'd like to get the University to sponsor a dig or grid search out here, but now everyone is convinced the battle was over by Harvey—can't get anyone interested."

"Have you ever had someone out with a metal detector?" Kelly asked Mrs. Whitney.

"Oh we did some of that years ago, and the grandkids have been out here, but all they've found are scraps of rusty metal and a few nails. You're welcome to try."

Kelly paused and looked at Jamie again. "I'd really like to find the gravesite, Jean-Luc's gravesite, if it's here."

"After all this time it would be one chance in a million; as you can imagine there are thousands of graves scattered across these prairies," Dockter said. "Many people died during settlement, and then with epidemics like influenza and childbirth and disease. But they're all gone now. Unmarked graves just become one more part of the prairie soil."

"Do you mind if we look around some more Jennie?" Kelly asked.

"Lord no dear, you've traveled all this way—look at much as you'd like."

"I know we said we wouldn't be staying earlier, but would it be okay if we stayed the night and took another look in the morning? Sometimes the morning light is best when you're looking for something. That okay with you Jamie?" Jamie nodded.

"Certainly, we can put you up overnight in the house."

"Thank you but we'd just as soon stay out here," interrupted Kelly, this time not conferring with Jamie.

"Really?" asked Mrs. Whitney.

"Yes, we don't want to be a bother."

"Well, okay then. I hope it doesn't rain on you tonight," she said.

"Wouldn't be the first time," said Jamie cheerfully. "We won't melt."

"At least let us give you a lift back to the house," offered Dockter.

Jamie looked at Kelly questioningly. "We found it, Sis, I think we can hitch a short ride."

"Okay," she said reluctantly.

They all got in the SUV and took the bumpy ride back to the farmhouse. Kelly took the opportunity to call her grandmother from the house with an update.

"We think we found it, Grandma," said Kelly into the receiver. "We're by Butte, south of the town of Velva. No, he's okay. No...it's good, no limp at all. We're going to look around again tomorrow early and then head back. We'll tell you all about it in a few days. Don't worry. What? Okay, hold on."

She held the receiver out toward Jamie. "She wants to talk to you."

"Hello Grandma," he said. "No...maybe a little. Yes...yes...yes." Then he looked at Kelly. "No, we're not fighting. Okay, I love you too. See you in a few days." Then he hung up the phone. "She wanted to know if I was losing weight," he reported sheepishly.

They retrieved their packs and began to walk back down the section line, but not before Mrs. Whitney handed them a large insulated cooler bag containing an entire fried chicken, steamed broccoli, and soft dinner rolls. "Just some leftovers I heated up," she said with a smile and wave.

They set up camp near the gate to the pasture. It had begun to cloud over and rain did seem likely so Jamie quickly set up the tent. Then they spread out the meal Mrs. Whitney had packed and finished every bit.

"That had to be the best chicken I've ever had in my life," said Jamie as he gnawed the last bit of gristle from the end of a wing bone.

"Hunger is the best seasoning," said Kelly. "We ate goat in Afghanistan and it was really good—but they know how to cook goat there. Had some kind of raw fish in Norway too; I'd have to say I still prefer it cooked."

They slept in the tent that evening, confident they were sleeping on hallowed ground.

Now to find the grave.

Chapter 25

They woke to the sound of a vehicle approaching at first light. Kelly threw back her covers and peered out the tent. A white Ford pickup truck was slowly working its way down the section line toward them, lights on.

"What is it," asked Jamie sleepily.

"Truck coming," said Kelly as she pulled on her cargo shorts and began lacing on her boots. She emerged from the tent just as the truck pulled up and stopped with a quick squeal of the brakes. The door opened and Mrs. Whitney stepped down from the cab.

"Good morning Kelly," she said brightly.

"Good morning Jennie," she replied cordially, stretching her back.

"I brought you some breakfast rolls and hot coffee."

"You didn't have to do that," protested Kelly. "We have our own food."

"I know but I'm so excited for you that I couldn't sleep, so I got up and made cinnamon rolls."

"Fresh cinnamon rolls!" proclaimed Jamie, now peering out of the front of the tent.

Mrs. Whitney walked up and handed Kelly a large paper plate covered with plastic wrap and a large insulated thermos.

"Thank you so much, Jennie, but you really didn't have to do that."

"It was my pleasure. I hope I didn't come too early but I figured you'd probably get an early start. Do you really think there's a headstone or old cross or something that might mark a grave here? I can't imagine how you'd find it."

Kelly nodded in agreement. "It's a long shot like Rose said, but we've come this far, so we have to try. Even if there were a marker initially, I imagine the bison, livestock, or weather would have destroyed it. Maybe it's a pile of stones or something. But then," she paused and gestured out toward the pasture, "there are a lot of stone piles out there too."

"Would you like a shovel, or a pick or something?" Mrs. Whitney asked.

"No, I wouldn't want to disturb anything—we're not archaeologists. I guess I'm hoping we'll just find something that 'feels' right if that doesn't sound too crazy."

"Well, Len thinks I'm crazy for hearing sounds out here, so you have company," she replied with a smile. By now Jamie had dressed and stumbled over to the pair.

"Did someone say cinnamon rolls?" he asked, eyebrows arched in a mock question, then he took a deep breath through his nose. "Ah yes! I'll take those off your hands, Sis," taking the plate from her and returning to the tent.

"We'll be up later this morning," said Kelly.

"You look as long as you'd like Kelly," replied Mrs. Whitney. "This mystery is over a century old, you don't have to solve it in one day."

Kelly looked toward the tent as the truck began heading back toward the house and saw Jamie wolfing down a second sweet roll. "Hey, save some of those for me!"

It was a warm morning, with hazy, blue skies overhead, and the aroma of bruised sage in the air, a day full of promise and anticipation. Standing here now, Kelly felt victorious, as if she had captured this sunny plot of pasture. This had to be the spot.

They strategized over breakfast. Each would work their way outward from the circle of pits, Jamie to the north and Kelly to the south, then east and west respectively. They would investigate any flat stones which might have been inscribed or groups of stones in a depression, such as a pile which may have been placed over remains which later formed a recess in the ground over the years. They would mark anything suspicious with a piece of orange flagging on a stick and investigate it together.

Two hours into the search, Kelly stopped, stretched her back, and wiped the sweat from her brow, surveying the pasture she had just walked—this was an impossible task. There was just too much ground to cover; it would take a team of a dozen searchers weeks to examine it all. And because much of it was similar, without a formal grid laid over the landscape there was a good chance they would miss something.

She looked in the distance and saw Jamie disappear over the edge of the far coulee. So far he hadn't found anything, and she had only found a couple of suspicious rock piles, neither of which seemed they would cover a body laid to rest.

She worked her way back toward the tent and began to pull out some lunch items. Five minutes later she saw Jamie emerge from the other end of the coulee and slowly work his way in her direction. She prepared sandwiches and set out some packaged cookies. It had been a disappointing morning.

"Find anything?" she asked as Jamie walked up, leaning on a makeshift walking stick he had found.

"No. There's too much here Kelly, and too much time has passed. All I'm finding are old bones and every kind of rock you could want. There's no way you'd find a pioneer grave unless you dug up the whole thing."

"Agreed. Maybe we need to rethink this."

As they sat and ate their lunch in silence, Kelly mentally went over the notes from her uncle and the journal from Father LeSueur. She thought too about what Kitchi had said—that they hadn't found what they were looking for, but she would know when they found it.

"Let's go over the battle details from the LeSueur documents," said Kelly, shuffling through a stack of papers on her lap. "I've gone over them several times but let me talk through it out loud and see what you think. Now that we're right here some things might make more sense."

"Okay, shoot," he said.

"The Métis dug in here, in the pits, and circled the oxcarts, just like in the movies. Three men had been captured earlier, one of them Jean-Luc, so the Sioux must have kept the hostages further away, in their camp. No that's not right, their large camp was a long ways off, and to the southwest, I think. This would have been a temporary camp, where they gathered before the battle. The temporary camp was between here and the Butte, which is there," she said, pointing, "to the southeast."

"I still don't understand why the Sioux just didn't kill the three men. Why take them hostage?"

"Maybe they were going to trade them for horses," said Kelly, "I'm not sure. But two of them escaped, they had better horses, fast hunting horses. I'm betting the Métis horses were much faster than the Sioux ponies; the Métis bred their stock for hunting. But the third horse was slower for some reason, and they recaptured the third man, which was Savard. The escaped Métis must have come in from

269

the south if they were on horseback, they wouldn't have been able to ride through those coulees fast enough. You're the human compass, which way does this pasture lie?"

Jamie looked up and around them. "Looks like it runs southeast to northwest, with the pits up here in the northwest."

"The Sioux forces would not have wanted to attack from the frontal position on the open prairie..."

"But they had no choice," Jamie interrupted, "because of coulees behind us. Wow, this was a great spot for a defense," he said appreciatively.

Kelly continued. "Yes, it was. The Sioux could have tried working closer by using the coulees but they were on horseback. Unless they dismounted that wouldn't work. And based on what I read, there wasn't a ground assault—it was all mounted."

"So," offered Jamie, "this area in front of us would have been full of dead and injured Sioux."

"And maybe on the sides since they tried to flank the Métis too, but that didn't work either."

"Wouldn't there be all kinds of artifacts then from the Sioux—beads and buttons and arrowheads?"

"Maybe, but remember the Sioux retrieved all their fallen warriors. They didn't leave any on the battlefield. But there's one thing they would have left."

"What?'

"You can't drag off a dead horse. Certainly, some of the mounts they rode would have been shot and killed and left out there."

"What about Jean-Luc's horse?"

"I thought about that," said Kelly. "If he was killed riding away maybe his horse was killed too during the escape."

"But there aren't any horse skeletons out there," complained Jamie. "I only found a few bones, some looked like cows and a couple deer."

"No, you're right. The bones are gone. After the battle, this land was covered with bison, and then bison skulls and bones after they were slaughtered. And now there's hardly a trace. Most of it was collected and sold for fertilizer. Souvenir hunters probably got the rest."

"Maybe they would have left horse bones, or at least the skull."

"Maybe," acknowledged Kelly. "But I think we've been looking too close to the pits. If Jean-Luc was held somewhere and then killed while trying to escape, he probably came from the south. My bet is he was held with the other two prisoners between here and the Butte, but that could have been anywhere from here to a couple miles away."

"Let's take a swing farther out," suggested Jamie.

Kelly nodded in agreement. "And let's start to the south and keep working our way southward."

They packed away their lunch snacks and headed across the pasture together toward the south end. The morning sky had given way to a deep blue now and the trill of meadowlarks filled the corner of the pasture. It was a bright day. To the west grazed a herd of Black Angus cows and calves on the other side of the coulee. One stout bull regarded them suspiciously as they walked, then discounted them as a threat and continued eating.

Kelly seemed to recall it rained during the day of the battle, or just after it. She tried to imagine what it was like for the Sioux, who must have ridden where she was standing now, preparing to attack the Métis fortification. Then she realized she knew, exactly, what it was like. A firefight was a firefight. She had experienced the same in Afghanistan—fear laced with raw terror, cloaked in a veneer of bravery. This was different though, it was personal, because the cause in Afghanistan, while it may have been American, was not her cause. But her kin had fought here, on the ground where she was standing, and perhaps died here.

The Sioux must have been angry. Angry at these Métis intruders, coming to take the bison they claimed as their own, on land they claimed as their own. *"I would have been angry too,"* she thought. That the Sioux would lose nearly everything in the end, and that the Métis too would be reduced to scavengers a few years later in their own homeland—was it ironic, or simply tragic? There was much anger to go around.

"I quit about here," said Jamie, pointing at a small clump of volunteer Chinese elm trees. "I'm going to head over to that hill."

"Okay," she replied. "I'll start here and work toward the southeast."

They walked the rest of the afternoon, crawling up and down slopes, through coulees, under trees, and over fences. They probed rock piles, sandy washes under old stream banks, piles of old lumber, and dried basins full of white alkali residue. Any flat rock was inspected, flipped, and inspected further. Old animal skulls were dislodged, probed, and inspected for extra holes or other curiosities. Soon the sun began to sink in the west. Kelly headed back toward their camp, soaked with sweat. Her eyes felt hard-used and full of grit. Jamie was already there.

"Anything?" he asked.

"I think I found one old bison horn and this," she said, holding open her hand. It was a small, broken arrowhead made of chert or flint. "Doesn't really prove anything, I'm guessing there are arrowheads all over this country. You?"

"Nothing but a lot of cow chips, a couple snakeskins, and more cow bones," he replied.

"Dammit, we're not going to find it," Kelly said angrily, rubbing her eyes. "It's just too late, too far, too long ago."

"Don't be mad. Look at how far we've come—Uncle Rodney spent a good part of his life just looking for this spot, Mom too. We found it in a couple weeks. You agree this is the spot—right?"

Kelly sighed heavily. "Yeah, these pits are too uniform to be anything else, and the site is in the right location. It sure as hell isn't in Harvey. But we're so close, and there's a reason we're here, there's a reason this kept eating at Uncle Rodney, and why he wanted Mom to look too. I just can't make sense of it."

"I don't know if it's supposed to make sense," offered Jamie. "Maybe it isn't, we're way down here away from home, away from where we belong remember Kitchi saying everyone belongs to one place. Could be it's just time to head back home to the Mountains."

"I guess you're right kiddo." In the distance, the white Ford pickup was coming toward them again.

"Here comes Jennie again. I'm going to ask her if we can stay tonight again and leave first thing in the morning."

"Works for me," said Jamie, "it's too late to move now and we're all set up."

The truck pulled up and this time Mrs. Whitney and Anna Schenko stepped from the cab.

"Hi Kelly, Hi Jamie. I didn't see you come through so I thought you might still be back here," said Mrs. Whitney. "You remember Anna Schenko don't you?"

"Yes, of course," said Kelly. "Hello Anna."

"Hello, I couldn't wait to find out what you found so I drove over myself," said Schenko. "Jennie says you think this is the site of the battle?"

"Yes, based on all the information we have, we're pretty sure this is it."

"Well, congratulations, that must be a relief, to finally step foot on the place where your ancestors fought. Did you ever find those relatives you were looking for?"

"No," Kelly admitted. "But it was a long time ago, we weren't really optimistic about our chances."

"Well, it's a great story anyway, traveling all this way, in the footsteps of your kin, on a search to find something lost over 100 years ago. If I were still at the paper I'd have to do a story on you."

"No need for that," said Kelly, "it's more of a family legend than anything else, and I wouldn't want to trouble the Whitney's anymore. By the way Jennie, I'm really sorry to ask but would you mind if we stayed here just one more night? We'll be gone first thing in the morning."

"Certainly," she replied. "But on one condition, you must come and have supper with us tonight at the house. I won't have you eating out here again."

"Jamie, what do you think?" asked Kelly, glancing at her brother.

"You don't have to ask me twice," he said, then turned to face Mrs. Whitney. "You make the best fried chicken in the country."

"Well come on then, we'll give you a lift," Mrs. Whitney said.

"We really need to clean up a bit first," said Kelly apologetically.

"Nonsense, grab some clean clothes and you can shower up at the house. And don't worry, Len had to go to Minot tonight for his Sportsman's Club meeting," she added. "Mr. Grumpy won't be around."

They grabbed a few items of clean clothing from their packs, zipped up the tent, and jumped into the pickup bed. Mrs. Whitney turned the truck around expertly and they were soon back at the ranch house.

Jamie showered first while Kelly sat in the kitchen with Schenko and Mrs. Whitney, who peeled potatoes while monitoring a beef roast in the oven. "Can I help with anything?" offered Kelly.

"No thanks, you rest, I just have these potatoes to peel."

"So what are your plans now?" asked Schenko. "Will you be heading back to the Turtle Mountains?"

"Yes, I suppose so," said Kelly, hesitant to reveal their plan to retrieve the gelding first. "I may have a job waiting for me there so I guess it's time to get back."

"And how is your ankle, that's what was injured right, your ankle?"

"Yes, I have to say it's much better. The walking, and the fresh air, seemed to do the trick. It's much stronger now."

"What kind of job do you have lined up Kelly?" asked Mrs. Whitney from the sink.

"There's a mill in town, a lumber mill, that's hiring some office staff. I interviewed before we started this little adventure and it seemed like it would be a good fit."

"They're still hiring in the Oil Patch too," added Schenko. "I hear it's a rough crowd but the money is very good."

"Remember she's an ex-Marine," chuckled Mrs. Whitney. "I think she's used to rough crowds." Then she turned serious, "How bad was the Service dear? Did you serve overseas?"

"Yes, I served in Afghanistan for nine months. It was pretty bad. I mean the mission was solid but the heat and the constant threats got to you after a while. You really couldn't relax at all. I was glad to rotate out."

"What did you actually do over there?" probed Schenko.

"We were in what's considered a Combat Unit, but my own unit served more as advisers. Our job was to establish relationships with Afghan women and families, to help them, show them the benefits of cooperating with Coalition forces. It was a tough job for us, but really tough on the poor families over there; they were pulled in so many directions. And they were really, really poor."

"Sounds terrible," Schenko said. "But it must have felt good to help them, I mean that's why we're there, right?"

"I don't know," said Kelly with a sigh. "We've been over there so long, and I'm not sure we're really helping them. We've lost a lot of, what do they call it, 'blood and treasure'? We've lost a lot of good people along the way."

Now Jamie came out from the bathroom in fresh clothes and a towel drying his long hair. "That was great, feel like a new man."

"I'd be happy to trim that hair for you young man," teased Mrs. Whitney. "Got my clippers right here."

"No thank you! This hair may come off someday, but *I'll* be the one to do it," he said with a grin.

"Kelly, get in there and shower up, and then we'll eat," said Mrs. Whitney with some authority. Kelly took a quick shower, as she always did, and 25 minutes later they all sat down together at the table.

The aroma from the roast was tantalizing. It occupied most of the platter but was crowded with glistening onions and bright orange carrots. It had been a while since the Moreau siblings had partaken in a sit-down dinner. Jamie sat straight and tried to remember how to act when dining as a guest.

"Would one of you like to say Grace?" asked Mrs. Whitney. The request caught them off guard but Kelly recovered quickly.

"Sure," she said as if it were the most natural thing she'd done all day. They bowed their heads as she began. "Heavenly Father, thank you for all the blessings of this day and all the wonderful food on the table. Thank you for keeping my brother and me safe on our journey and for meeting such kind friends who have helped us along the way. Please help all those less fortunate than us and help us to know and do Your will, in Jesus' name. Amen."

"That was lovely Kelly, thank you," commented Mrs. Whitney with a warm smile.

"Well, I have to admit we didn't pray that often in the Marines, but when you did you made it count. My grandmother is quite religious. I'm sure she's praying right now that we get home in one piece."

"And I'm sure you will," said Schenko. "I don't know why it's surprising, you're obviously two very bright and talented young people, but nobody walks around the country anymore. It seems like such an adventure, like it would be dangerous, but I assume it's been a lot of fun."

"We've bumped heads with a few people, but when you travel with a Marine, they pretty much take care of things," said Jamie smiling.

"I've got a pretty tough little brother too," offered Kelly, smiling back at him. "But it will be good to get back home."

They finished their meal with a thick slice of peach pie and declined a ride back out to the pasture where the tent awaited. It had been a great evening and now the stars shone brightly. With a full stomach, it felt good to walk.

"We could use a little moonlight to light up this two-track," said Kelly.

"No moon tonight, or what we get will disappear. While you were in the shower Anna said there was gonna be an eclipse tonight." They walked further and he added, "Hey, did you hear what she said about me?"

"No, what?"

"Bright and talented," he said proudly.

"You caught that huh?"

"Yes, 'bright and talented young person'."

"Well you are you big dope," she said and punched him in the arm, hard. "Does a stranger have to say that before you believe it? Mom told you that all the time. Grandma says it now."

They walked on in silence and listened to the night sounds. Somewhere out in the pasture, a Great-Horned Owl hooted softly.

Now long past sundown, the coyotes were quiet. Kelly knew they hunted silently, and now was the time of the hunt.

At one point a brown shape loped in front of them; Kelly recognized it as a jackrabbit, rare in this wooded environment. The rabbit gave no indication of seeing them but loped slowly down the section line in front of them. Somewhere in the darkness ducks quacked in alarm, maybe from one of the ponds in the coulee. She wondered if maybe a mink or coon had interrupted their slumber. It was the same old story, the hunter and the hunted, under the cloak of darkness.

"You out of smokes?" Kelly asked, knowing Jamie usually smoked after meals.

"No, cutting back," he said. "Trying to limit myself to five a day—one at breakfast, one at bedtime, and three in between. Plus, I'm running short."

"Well good for you, those damn things will kill you. I knew Marines that lit up first thing after a 10-mile march with heavy packs—dumb as a sack of rocks."

"Well, you've never been through rehab. When you're really hooked on something it's hard as hell to give it up," Jamie explained. "And then when you do there's an empty spot. If you can't fill it with something you just backslide."

"Yeah, sorry, you're right. Was rehab really tough for you?"

"Been through it twice, don't want to go through it again. I know some guys that have been through it five or six times. They're never gonna get clean."

"What about those guys at Grandma's, they said they were with you in rehab?"

"There's good parts of rehab and bad parts; they were the bad. A lot of guys can't make it and just want to drag you down with them. That was those two."

"You need to find some better friends."

"Yeah."

They reached their camp and turned in quickly. They wanted to get an early start in the morning, agreeing to pick up the horse at the Roth's and then quickly head north toward the Turtle Mountains. With any luck, they could be home in two or three days.

Jamie fell asleep almost immediately after sacking out. Kelly had become used to his snoring and wondered if she snored too. He hadn't said anything, but she knew other women, Marines, who snored in their sleep, but theirs was the sleep of utter exhaustion. She heard the owl hoot again, then remembered nothing more.

She felt the blade slide in, barely any resistance, and then hit the bone, she jerked back with all her strength and felt the blade moving toward her, watching herself from behind her shoulder, watching her wrist stiffen and her bicep contract. Blood spurted up and outward, hot across her fingers. She forced her eyes to watch as he turned toward her. Their eyes met and in that instant, their roles reversed, hers were now the eyes of the predator, his the eyes of defeated prey, even now reflecting the loss of his lifeblood, beat by beat, across her blade.

She shook her head and tried to shake away that look, the life draining from his eyes as it simultaneously dripped, hot and red, from her knife and clutched fist...

"Kelly...Kelly, get up," Jamie said, shaking her roughly. It was already light out. "The bison is back!"

Chapter 26

"Back, back, get the women back!" shouted Granger as he waved his arms over his head, his face red and eyes bulging.

The Sioux were now gone, but here in the buckbrush, their handiwork remained. Denis Granger was a hard man; many had died by his hand, both man and beast, but he could not have possibly prepared for this scene spread before him in the shadow of the *Maison du Chien*, this Den of Dogs. And now, for the first time in a very long time, he knew not what to do.

His was a world tempered by labor, discipline, domination, and achievement—leaving little room for compassion or mercy. There were words here he needed, but they would not come, his thought-process seized by the image before his eyes.

Then it came to him—he needed Father LeSueur.

"LeSueur!" he shouted. "LeSueur!" He swirled as he shouted, looking wildly in every direction as if Father LeSueur might suddenly materialize from the nearby brush. "LeSueur!"

Then Jerome appeared at his side, his dark eyes flaring as he glanced downward. Could Jerome help him? Yes, he would help. But Granger could not find the words to ask, no words would form, no words came to his lips. He grabbed Jerome, a fistful of shirt, and pulled until their faces were just inches apart, "LeSueur!" he demanded, the whites of his eyes bulging even wider. Jerome tore away and ran back toward the camp.

Moments later, he saw Father LeSueur moving toward him through the grass in short, quick steps as briskly as his long black cassock would allow. Now Granger heard the sounds, the sounds that had been there all the while but drowned out by the roar in his brain—the screams of women, the women of the camp, *his* camp—long wails punctuated with raw bursts of pain as the news passed among them. More men gathered now, following Father LeSueur, rifles, and shotguns at the ready. The old cook Paquet limped along quickly in the rear, bearing an ax in hand.

The young priest was emboldened, having just lifted the group through prayer to defeat the Sioux against all odds. Clearly, the Lord was with them on this day and the Lord would prepare him for whatever he was called to do now. He ran quickly and surely, knowing they were waiting, for something only he could offer. These were his people and he was theirs, to guide and support in their time of need.

Clearly, he was needed now.

As Granger saw the priest nearly upon him he felt only despair and resignation—he had tried so hard to avoid this outcome. But all the planning and precautions had not protected them. He had failed. As the full weight of the scene settled into his stomach he leaned and retched. Still bent, he reached out and spread his fingers, reaching for this young man, this priest, who could provide relief. "LeSueur," he croaked weakly. Then he fell down, bent on all fours, kneeling in his own vomit. "LeSueur." Hot, angry tears rolled down his face.

Like Granger, Father LeSueur could not have possibly prepared for this.

That the body of a man lay before him was difficult enough to discern—that the remains were that of young Jean-Luc Savard was unfathomable. Although the evidence was plain, it was also beyond belief. Father LeSueur took in the scene: The body had been crudely hacked and ripped apart…the torso here, the legs—there and there—the hands…missing. Where were his feet?

The savages had also left a calling card, dozens of arrows of all colors protruded from the dismembered torso. Iridescent blue bottle flies danced and spun among the colors and crawled inside the chest cavity, even now laying eggs on this rich feast which would feed their larvae. The stench of voided bowels hung over the entire site.

A solemnity settled over the scene. Decency demanded the remains be concealed from human sight, but the hunters were too stunned to move. The land too, despite an infinite capacity to absorb violence, seemed to have seized up momentarily; neither light nor shadow nor a cleansing breeze moved across the carnage. Indeed, each blade of bloodied grass around the site seemed to exude an angry energy...angry with their burden of splattered violence and eager to be shed of it.

No man could direct another to remedy this unholy butchery, to gather the severed parts and attempt to make them whole again. Granger remained incapacitated, unable to provide word or direction. But now Father LeSueur crossed himself, spoke a silent prayer, and suddenly found a strength and focus he did not know he possessed. This *was* his time.

Father LeSueur straightened, turned to the men, and exhorted someone among them to step forward for the burial detail.

"Our brave, young friend Jean-Luc, so full of life and promise, has joined the Father in heaven. We now must ensure his remains receive a Christian burial. Who among you will gather him so we may perform this blessed task?" One man who had not known Savard well stepped forward, and then a second. Father LeSueur pointed to brothers Guy and Andre Dupuis—"And you will remain here on guard." The men nodded numbly in assent. "The rest of you go now, and leave them to their task."

The half-circle of men slowly turned and began walking back to camp, mumbling and cursing the Sioux. In the distance, a knot of women stood peering in their direction and clutching each other while they wept.

The torso jerked roughly with the removal of each arrow—some tipped with bone, others sharp shards of metal, stone, or hammered brass cartridge cases. Father LeSueur sent a canvas sack and two shovels to the site with instructions to gather all the remains possible and bury them some distance away, then report back to camp.

The men used the shovels and dried buffalo chips to coax the dismembered limbs and organs into loose, dirty piles. They then placed them all into the sack along with Jean-Luc's clothing and two fist-sized rocks covered with gray matter. Each man then grabbed a corner and dragged it some 25 yards away from the site of the execution.

It took another 10 minutes to dig the grave, with the Dupuis brothers now helping excavate the hole. After interring the remains, the two volunteer undertakers walked down the slope to two small ponds nearby to wash, with the Dupuis brothers trailing behind with their rifles. Once at the edge of the pond they found the water red with blood. Tracks in the mud revealed the wounded Sioux had used the ponds to cleanse their own wounds. Upon realizing this the two volunteers quickly drew their belt knives and the guards held their guns at the ready, waiting for an attack. But the Sioux were gone, leaving no other trace of their dead and wounded.

The men rinsed off in the bloody water and hastily made their way back toward camp.

Granger had recovered now and once again took control of camp activities. After posting sentries in each compass direction to ward against a further attack he ordered the camp to be quickly broken down and made ready to travel. He also conferred briefly with Father LeSueur. The actions of this terrible morning had bridged a gap between this hard wind-burned man of the prairie and the young man of the cloth, each revealing a part of themselves previously hidden. They spoke now as equals and agreed a short funeral service was in order and then they must move toward the safety of the larger camp, quickly. The grave would remain unmarked.

As the carts were lined up to move, some 200 riders from the western camp arrived, having hurried the 40 miles from their camp to help fight the Sioux. Although too late to assist in the battle they were a welcome sight for the harried group. Jean-Luc's father was among them—he crumpled upon hearing the news.

However tragic, Jean-Luc's death could not be allowed to delay their hunt. They would press on and find the herd, for, like the Sioux, the bison represented their survival. It was agreed the women and children would leave now under escort and ride quickly to join the larger group to the west for safety, at least temporarily. The remaining men in Granger's group would follow with the carts, oxen, and stock.

As they gathered for a short funeral service at the site of Jean-Luc's burial, with Father LeSueur presiding over the ceremony, a light rain began to fall.

"We commend to your keeping, O Lord, the soul of your servant, Jean-Luc, and we beg you, Lord Jesus Christ, Savior of the world, who came on earth for his sake, to bear him aloft to the bosom of the patriarchs. Lord, let his soul find joy in your presence. Forgive his past transgressions and excesses which passion and desire engendered. For although a sinner he believed and faithfully worshiped God who created all things. Amen."

Elisa attended the brief ceremony with her father, along with 30 others in a small clearing amid the silvery buckbrush of the prairie. Jean-Luc would be left without a headstone, and his grave camouflaged with brush and stone to prevent the Sioux from further desecration. Little Sylvie stayed behind with her mother. Elisa stood tall, stoic, her eyes red-rimmed but tearless, as her father held her tightly, his thick arm around her strong, lean shoulders.

She mourned her young suitor and would remember him always. She would remember too the fragrance of the wet prairie on that day of his burial, a pungent perfume that rose after the rainstorm to sweeten and fill the air around his gravesite. It was the scent of the northern plains, which would remind her always of this tiny patch of forgotten prairie, and the promise hidden beneath. In her pocket, she carried a smooth purple stone.

They headed west now, angling away from the *Maison du Chien*, with its cuts and coulees hiding the unknown. As the last of the carts creaked and lurched across the prairie the afternoon sun and clouds shifted high overhead and licks of shadow and light played over the spot where Jean-Luc had drawn his last breath. Around the site lay 67 arrows, some broken, some tossed far into the brush in disgust. Surrounding the site lay bloodied clumps of little Bluestem grass, now splayed out flat and lifeless, despite the rain.

Much later, near sundown, the black shadow of the Butte crept silently and steadily across the prairie, painting over dried bloodstains in its path—and probing yet another unmarked grave for the crease of a soul.

Chapter 27

"What do you mean the bison is back?" Kelly asked, blearily searching his eyes.

"Get dressed," Jamie replied, ignoring her question, "Hurry before he's gone."

She dressed in the tent as quickly as she could as he excitedly explained what had happened.

"Remember you said we were here for a reason? Well, I couldn't sleep so I took my blanket out to the pits and just sat. The moon was coming out of the eclipse. I think my reason was to find the direction...no, I *know* it was my reason because I knew we had to look east, no that's not right, not to look east but to go east. And so I did."

"Slow down Jamie, slow down," urged Kelly. "So you walked to the east?"

"Yes, I walked east, across the coulee and over the fence and I saw it. I saw the bison."

"You saw the bison," she repeated. "Just one?"

"Yes, a young one just like before. It looked like the same one but I knew it couldn't be. It saw me and started to walk away. I started to follow but then I had to stop."

"What...why?" she asked urgently. "Why'd you stop?"

"I had to come get you. The bison wasn't for me...it was for you Kelly, it was for you. Don't you see?"

"For me...no I...what do you mean for me?"

"There's no time Kelly, this is it. We can't lose him this time!" He grabbed her by the arm and pulled her onto the pasture, then he ran.

Kelly stomped after him, trying to tie her boot laces as she followed. Jamie bore straight east, past the pits, over a small mound, and then down into the coulee. They both climbed up the other side and stopped at a three-strand, barbed-wire fence. Jamie stepped over with one leg and pushed the top wire down as far as it would go with the palm of his hands. "C'mon, over, quick," he urged as she stepped over carefully. "Keep going, east," he urged, lifting his leg over and then running behind her.

The landscape fell and rose again as they ran from the coulee. As they topped the next hill he stopped, breathless, hands on his knees, and then pointed. "There, there he is!"

Kelly just caught a glimpse of brown as an animal slowly disappeared over the rise. "Come on Jamie, there he goes!" But now as she looked back, instead of panic she saw a smile on Jamie's face, a look of contentment, the same kind of peaceful look she saw on Uncle Rodney...and Kitchi.

"No, you go now, Sis," he smiled, still bent over huffing. "This is all yours. You go."

A look of confusion came over her face and her mind raced. What was happening, what was he doing?

"Jamie!"

"Go!" he commanded, pointing in the direction of the animal. And she went.

Kelly raced down the slope and scrambled up the opposite side, topping the rise where the bison had been. She looked ahead, then side to side, not seeing any movement. Had she lost him? Her heart sank, he was gone. The land flattened here and the next hill was several hundred yards distant. How had he escaped?

Seeing no other choice she started for the next hill—then quickly stopped. There, sandwiched between a stout gray boulder and a patch of buffaloberry stood the bison, broadside to her, less than 100 yards away.

Suddenly it became perfectly clear to her why she needed to follow the animal.

She walked toward it briskly, not wanting to spook it, keeping her eyes on it at all times. As she drew closer it seemed to regard her without fear, standing in the same spot, tail twitching. She was less than 50 yards away when the toe of her right boot caught in a gopher hole and she tumbled forward. She quickly jumped up and brushed off—but now the animal was gone. She hurried to the boulder and searched the area. Nothing. Circling the bush, she scanned the landscape. It had disappeared.

She looked back the way she came, toward Jamie, but he was hidden now on the other side of the hills. She must be nearly three-quarters of a mile from their camp now. She was sweating and breathing hard. Damn, another wild goose chase. She glanced down, trying to find tracks from the animal, but the grass revealed nothing. Then as she turned to go she noticed a slight depression, where the animal had stood.

She froze, and a rush of emotion washed over her as she considered what it might be. Her heart, beating fast from exertion, now raced even faster. Could this be the resting place of a fallen warrior, a young Métis, far from his land, far from the place he called home?

She knelt at the edge of the depression, not large enough to contain a man, but yes, large enough to contain the broken pieces of a man. As she drew a deep breath the sunken stones on the surface of the depression suddenly blurred and her vision began to spin. Reaching out to steady herself, her hand landed on the top stone.

As her fingers made contact she gasped loudly and burst into hot tears as wave after wave of anger, sadness, and pain surged into her from the soil…and the shattered bones she now knew were there.

Moments later she found herself lying prone, pressed upon the stones with her whole weight, the rough grass scratching her face and absorbing her tears.

She recovered, and as she sat up felt only peace. "Jean-Luc," she whispered, resting her hand gently again on the top stone. "Jean-Luc, I found you. Rest, in peace."

Twenty minutes later she slowly walked up on Jamie, sitting, with his back against a gnarled aspen tree, calmly smoking one of his five daily cigarettes.

"You found it, didn't you?" he said confidently. "You found the grave."

She stood and regarded him; relaxed, confident, and comfortable.

"Yes," she said quietly. "I found Jean-Luc."

"The bison?"

"Gone, he disappeared. I don't think we'll see him again. Something happened at the gravesite, I can't really explain it but I think it's over—Uncle Rodney's search, our search, there was closure there, and peace. Jean-Luc's terrible death…it's okay now. There's peace. Remember Kitchi saying that some things, good and bad, follow from one generation to the next. Jean-Luc's death may have followed, may have haunted Uncle Rodney's generation. But it's over now."

"But why you?" asked Jamie. "This was something you had to do, not me."

"Maybe something followed our generation too, and Mom's generation before us."

They headed back to the opening in the fence, broke down their camp and began the hike back to the house. Kelly felt exhausted but content.

They knocked on the door to thank the Whitney's but nobody was home and all the vehicles were gone. They continued through the yard and began walking down the driveway when they heard someone shout, "Hey!" They turned to see Mr. Whitney waving at them.

"Great," commented Jamie sullenly as they stopped, turned, and began walking back toward him.

"Jennie said if you come through I was supposed to give you this," he said, waving a thin folder. "Copies of stuff from the Velva Historical," he paused and looked them up and down again. Two crazy Indians in backpacks. "So did you see any ghosts or Indian Chiefs back there?" he asked with a smirk.

"A lot of cattle and hoot owls," said Jamie. "No ghosts."

"Indian battles, that's just a lot of foolish talk, like I said." He handed the folder to Kelly. "Waste of time. Only thing that pasture's good for is running cows if a guy can keep up with the fence."

"We're sorry we missed Jennie, would you please tell her we said goodbye," said Kelly. "And we want to thank you for letting us on your land. You've got a very special place here. The site of that old battle was very important to our family, in fact, our uncle spent much of his life looking for it. He just didn't look in the right place."

"He did huh?" said Mr. Whitney, softening now. "Well, you're welcome. Guess it was no bother. You two take care now getting back home. Some folks around here don't take kindly to Indians snooping around."

They left and headed back east toward the Roth's farm. It would take them at least three hours of hard walking to get there. They were in sight of Dog Den Butte the entire time they walked, big and dark on the horizon. Nothing in the area approached it in size.

"How far away do you think you could see the Butte?" asked Jamie.

"Depends I suppose on how clear it was—on a good day I bet 50 miles. The border is about 85 or 90 miles from here, I wonder if you were on top of the Butte if you could see it. I imagine you could see the Prophets Mountains to the south, but there aren't any landmarks to the north."

"How about the Missouri River? That must be straight west of here."

"I suppose you could see over there, but I don't know if you could see the river; it might be hidden behind the bluffs. I bet a lot of people have climbed the Butte—the Sioux, our people, explorers, settlers—think of what they saw. Back then I suppose it was just an ocean of grass, in every direction. All these tree groves we see were planted later."

"And bison," added Jamie.

"Yeah, imagine the bison, herds of a 1,000 animals...10,000 animals...100,000 animals, moving in one huge mass over the prairie. Bison were life for a lot of people. Think of all the things we need, or think we need today. But back then, all you needed were bison to survive, they provided everything—food, shelter, clothing, tools."

As they worked their way east from the Butte the landscape flattened and they saw the Roth farm, with its dark tree grove, several miles away.

"You sure you want to bring this horse with us?" asked Kelly. "Technically it's not yours. Could be trouble."

"It was a stray found on the prairie, no brand, no markings. I'd say it was 'found' property. Besides, you don't want to see him go back to that vicious bastard do you?"

"No."

"You said yourself sometimes you have to do the right thing, even if it's not necessarily by the book—right?"

"You got me there little brother, I did say that," admitted Kelly, thinking back on the things she wished she had done differently. The right way, the wrong way, and the way of the Marines.

Dragging the kids to safety in Afghanistan, at the risk of her own life, had been the right thing to do, but counter to Marine directives. Now she wished she could have found more courage to help Moore, and not played by the Marine handbook. Now those kids were alive, and Moore was gone. It was difficult, but Jamie had reached the correct conclusion—do what's right and to hell with the consequences. At least you could live with yourself later.

They reached the Roth farm about 45 minutes later. The four horses were still in the outer pasture, by the highway, and they watched the two approach from the distance. As the siblings walked down the drive Sally came out running and barking again, this time wagging her tail in recognition. They looked around and once again saw the Black Angus fenced in the grove near the house. There was no sign of the gelding.

They both began to get a queasy feeling that the horse was gone— either escaped, confiscated by the authorities, or perished due to his injuries. The feeling disappeared as Ellie stepped out the back door and welcomed them warmly, "The great wanderers have returned," she said, smiling broadly. "To tell you the truth I wasn't sure we'd ever see you again."

"Took a little longer than we thought," Kelly explained.

"Did you find your relatives?"

"Yes," said Kelly simply. "Yes, we did."

"Is he still here?" asked Jamie anxiously, "the gelding?"

"Oh, he's here alright," laughed Ellie. "Eddie has had his hands full but he's really perked up since you dropped him off. Come around back and I can show you."

She led them through the old barn to a small corral off the back end and there the gelding stood against the far fence, looking for all the world like an abstract painting on four legs.

"He looks like you ran him through the dryer with a tube of lipstick!" Kelly exclaimed. The white horse was literally painted in pink, with two dozen streaks, swaths, and dabs covering his cuts, wounds, and partially-healed scabs.

"Eddie greased him up good alright," chuckled Ellie. "Got that wire off his back leg too—says it wasn't a cracked hoof, just blood from that fence wire cutting into his hock. It cleaned up pretty well."

They could see the clod of bloody dirt had been scraped off his hoof and the pastern and hock wrapped with a clean white bandage.

Ellie continued, "You'll have to ask Eddie what else he did, he's in town now but he'll be back soon."

"C'mere boy," said Jamie, holding out his hand. The horse dropped his head and slowly walked over to him, sniffing his fingers with a velvety nose. "Hi fella," said Jamie, gently stroking the horse's neck. The horse nickered and shook its head, then regarded him calmly with its one good eye. He seemed content.

"His nose looks a lot better," Jamie observed, nodding to the raw patch on the top of the horse's nose.

"Yeah, it'll be a while before he wears a real bridle again, but it's healing up nicely," agreed Ellie. "He doesn't put a lot of weight on that back foot but Eddie doesn't think it hurts—it's because he hasn't been able to use it in a while with that dirt caked on there."

"Did he give Eddie a lot of trouble, getting the wire off?" asked Jamie.

"Eddie's got a way with horses," explained Ellie. "I wouldn't call him a 'horse whisperer' or anything but he communicates with them at a deeper level than I ever could. This horse knew it needed help, and knew that Eddie could help it, so I think they came to an understanding. That wire had been on there for some time; he said the skin was almost growing around it in some spots. I have to tell you, Eddie got pretty upset when he found out all the abuse that horse had suffered. I don't know how a person could do that to another living thing. It's terrible."

"Yes. It's hard to think those people are walking around out there, but they are," agreed Kelly, then added ruefully, "there are some really bad people out there."

Eddie arrived within the hour and they revisited the horse again as Eddie cataloged its injuries and what he had done to treat them. Ellie insisted they stay for supper and then stay overnight before heading back. They agreed. That evening they had a simple meal of baked pork chops in mushroom gravy, green beans, and cornbread stuffing on the side. Dessert was chocolate cake with vanilla ice cream.

"It's good to see someone with a real appetite again," commented Ellie as she and Kelly cleared the table. Jamie stood at the sink doing dishes.

"Sorry I ate so much but that was just too good," said Jamie, somewhat embarrassed. "We haven't had too many square meals on the road, and Kelly's idea of a good meal is cold noodles for breakfast."

"Got me through the Marines mister," Kelly retorted. "And you don't seem to be blowing away in the wind anyway."

"When our two boys were home we'd have big meals every day—beef and potatoes and corn on the cob and fresh bread and pies for dessert," said Ellie, her voice fading in thought. "We had a bunch of layers back then; I'd cook up a huge platter of scrambled eggs and ham every morning. Those boys would go through it like nothing. But now with just Eddie and me, we don't eat much. Lots of leftovers."

"Where are your boys now?" asked Kelly.

"Gone, like the rest of their friends. Our son Curt lives in Fargo, Mason lives in the Twin Cities, Richfield I think. Got married last year, no kids yet. They couldn't wait to leave; neither of them wanted anything to do with farming. Their high school graduating classes were small, eight in Curt's class and I think only seven in Mason's. None of those kids still live around here. Some of them tried working in the Oil Patch, but even that has slowed down now. Those were good-paying jobs but the conditions were terrible—so many people getting hurt on the job. Makes me wonder who'll be living here when people like Eddie and I are gone."

They helped Eddie with some evening chores after supper and Jamie looked in after the gelding again. He seemed very content in the small corral and must have felt much better with all his wounds treated. At one point his ears perked up as a pack of coyotes howled somewhere in the distance, but it was a look of curiosity rather than fear. Jamie was glad they had rescued him, was glad they would bring him north.

Kelly walked up behind him. "Thought I might find you here."

"Just checking on him. Eddie did a good job patching him up."

"Eddie's a good man," said Kelly. "They're both good people."

"Nice place they have here," observed Jamie.

"It is nice," Kelly agreed. Both travelers felt safe here, and now as they approached the final days of their journey, the weight of their physical and psychological burdens began to lift.

"It's been quite a trip," said Jamie. "And to tell you the truth, I never thought we'd make it. If you would have told me a year ago we'd be here, doing this today, I'd have said you're nuts."

"We're not home yet," Kelly cautioned. "But yes, I know...quite a trip. I'm still trying to work through everything—the battlefield, the bison, the grave...trying to make all the pieces fit."

"How's your foot?"

Kelly stomped her foot down lightly as she leaned on the railing of the corral. "Never better. Can't wait to hit the road tomorrow and wrap this little adventure up."

Jamie slept on the couch while Kelly slept in the boys' old room upstairs. She had slept on the ground or under the stars for so long that the bed felt odd to her. The mattress was old and lumpy—and warm and dry; within minutes she was asleep.

The smell of coffee and pork sausage woke her the next morning. She rolled onto her back, stretched her arms wide, and shifted her back until it snapped and cracked. She felt totally refreshed as if she'd slept for days. No dreams, just rest. Her ankle was stiff, but no pain.

Jamie was already at the table eating with Eddie as Ellie served pancakes and sausages.

"Hey Sunshine," said Jamie, glancing up as he cut his pancakes into pieces.

"Good morning Kelly," said Ellie. "Sleep well?"

"Like a rock," she replied.

"Sit down and start eating," Ellie directed. Kelly sat and forked three pancakes onto her plate. An AM radio played softly in the background—farm reports.

"They said it might rain this afternoon," commented Eddie, as he cut a sausage link in half. "East wind; we're bound to get wet sooner or later."

"Liquid sunshine," replied Kelly as she poured syrup over her stack. "We can hole up in the tent if we have to."

"Been a pretty wet year overall," Eddie continued. "We need it, for the pastures. Those big cattle guys really need it. We came out of spring pretty dry, but I guess the crop guys liked that—they could get everything in sooner. Alfalfa crop looks good anyway. Wheat too. It's always a gamble. Don't know how those big guys do it— they have a quarter-million dollars in the ground with seed and chemical before anything even sprouts."

Kelly was hungry and worked purposefully cutting the pancakes on her plate.

"We got sprayed by someone south of here when we were walking on the road," offered Jamie. "Big boom sprayer, never slowed down, just turned at the end of the row and got us good.'

"That's terrible," said Ellie from the stove. "Did they do it on purpose?"

"I don't know, but we washed up good at the next creek we came to. It looked like a yellow mist."

"It's that glyphosate," said Eddie. "They spray that on everything. All the crops are 'glyphosate-ready' now—they just plant, hit it with glyphosate and it kills everything but the crop.

"What's more it's in all our food now. You know what they do with wheat? They spray it with chemical before harvest to kill it and dry up all the seed heads. Then they harvest it and sell it to the mills to make the flour and animal feed and it ends up," he slapped the table with his hand, "right here on your kitchen table. Probably in these pancakes."

"Oh Eddie, let them eat," scolded Ellie.

"Why doesn't the government outlaw it?" Jamie asked.

"The government says its fine for us," Eddie explained. "If you listen to USDA they'll tell you it's the best thing since sliced bread—growing more crops with less chemicals and all that. I'll tell you one thing, we never had all this cancer and these problems when we raised our own hogs and beef on the farm."

Kelly interjected, "Don't believe everything the government tells you."

"That's good advice Kelly," said Eddie, nodding in agreement. "Don't trust them further than you can throw them. I guess we learned that much during the war," then added, "or wars."

Ellie sat down now with her own plate of food and started eating. "Can you talk about something more pleasant, please? This is hardly the way to start a day."

"Well," said Eddie, pushing his chair back. "How about we talk about that horse?"

"Yeah," agreed Jamie. "That's some good news. He really looks better, looks like he's going to make it."

Eddie took a sip of coffee, squinted slightly, and leaned forward, "Now I'm not trying to intrude here, but you're not thinking of trying to find its previous owner, are you? 'Cause if you are we'd just as soon have you leave him here. I don't want to see him going back to that."

"He was just running loose," said Jamie, glossing over the whipping incident and how the animal was set free. He was trying to rationalize their next steps himself. "If his owner wanted to find him I guess he'd be out looking for him. We haven't seen anyone looking."

"Well, you do want you want. I know you're just looking out for this animal, and I trust your judgment, but I don't want his former owner to get him back. I'm afraid to say this, but the truth is he'd be better off dead," Eddie said firmly.

"We're all agreed on that point," said Kelly. "Don't worry Eddie, we'll take care of him. You've been very kind to help us get him back to health."

They packed, said their goodbyes, and left the yard with the horse following Jamie in a makeshift rope halter hung loosely over its head. Ellie had packed them a lunch of ham and cheese sandwiches, apples, and two big slabs of chocolate cake. They walked briskly. With nearly all their provisions gone their packs were lighter—and now they were actually heading for home.

Chapter 28

The weather was fair, the wind moderate and as they leaned hard into their northern journey the miles melted away. With all four feet unfettered, they found the horse could easily keep up with them now, although it was constantly trying to eat grass from the ditch.

"He must be feeling good, all he wants to do is eat," Jamie commented.

"He can eat all he wants tonight, but we need to get in some miles and find a good spot to camp before it starts to rain," said Kelly, motioning to the east, where the clouds began to get darker and darker. They ended up on a flat, largely treeless plain dotted with small dry depressions dusted with white alkaline powder. Small clumps of stunted popple trees dotted the landscape, and they chose a spot near one of these to make their camp. They had to open a gate to gain access but the pasture was not posted.

"I'll do the tent, you try to find some wood for a fire," said Kelly. Jamie took the rope halter off the horse and let him begin eating. The grass was sparse here but the horse seemed to relish it.

They made camp and got a small fire going before the first raindrops hit. Kelly quickly put on their small pot of water and heated it, even as the drops fell. She made instant soup in the pot; noodles with carrots, corn, and little freeze-dried bits of chicken. It was good, and after their large lunch of ham and cheese sandwiches, it was a good complement to the day.

While the rain continued, they crawled into their tent and stretched out on their bedrolls. The wind came up and hit the rain guard in gusts, but they were snug inside. The fire outside the door grew smaller and smaller as the rain continued. Eventually, it went out and just smoked. Kelly did not allow Jamie to smoke in the tent, so he crawled out to smoke his last allotted cigarette of the day in the light rain.

"Where'd the horse end up?" asked Kelly when he returned.

"He's behind us, went down to that other grove, more grass down there," replied Jamie. "I wonder if this rain will wash that ointment off."

"I don't think so," said Kelly, "that stuff is half grease."

"Eddie gave me a jar of it, I can grease him up in the morning again before we leave," said Jamie. "I offered to pay him for it but he wouldn't accept." He added, "They were really nice."

"Those were nice folks. Real nice to help us out, with a strange horse and all," said Kelly. "It's interesting how you meet some people who are very friendly and others won't give you the time of day."

"Why the difference you think?"

"If they perceive you as a threat, then they get defensive and hostile. If you're not a threat they'll help you, or at least not hurt you," Kelly offered, thinking back again on her time in Afghanistan.

"But why were those guys at the bar such assholes, or that cop who stopped us? We weren't a threat."

"Think about it from their perspective—a lot of these people have lived here all their lives, they grew up with everyone who lives around them, and they all look like them and think like them. Nobody likes change and anyone who doesn't look or talk or act like them represents change, and that's a threat. Then they act out of fear."

"But we were here, the Métis were here, long before they arrived. They're more of a threat to us than we are to them."

"And the Sioux and the Saulteaux were here before we were. It's a constant cycle; eventually, someone will replace all these farmers and ranchers too."

They were silent for a moment and then Jamie said, "Horse people are nice."

"That asshole who beat him wasn't nice."

"I wouldn't consider him a horse person."

"So," said Kelly, turning to him with a smirk, "Are you a horse person now?"

"I always *was* a horse person. I loved my horses when I was young."

"I thought you only had one horse growing up?"

"I did, but Rene's big paint liked me more than him. I think horses choose their owners, rather than the other way around. So I kinda considered him my horse too. I'm sure this gelding doesn't think the guy that beat him was his owner."

"Assuming we get this horse back in one piece, what are your plans?"

"I'll talk to Rene about keeping him out at their place. Then I guess I'd want to see what he can do. We don't even know if he's broke— or was used in harness. He might not be good for anything anymore; he's blind in that one eye and who knows how long he's been abused. I guess I won't know until I start working with him."

Kelly stretched atop her bedroll and yawned. "Kind of a gamble then?"

"Kind of a work in progress. It's just a matter of finding the good in there."

Kelly smiled, "What you gonna name him?"

"Don't know. I want to get him home first."

"Good plan, don't count your horses until they're corralled. I think we'll be good to go after tomorrow; we'll be back in our own country again. You know what old Kitchi said was true; everyone belongs in a certain place. And for us, this isn't it. But we'll be there tomorrow."

"It'll be good to be home again."

Kelly nodded her head in agreement. "Yes. I need to talk to Grandma some more, about what happened at the gravesite. I wish I could have talked more with Rodney, or Mom."

"What happened at the battlefield *was* weird," admitted Jamie, now flopping on his back. "All I can tell you is something got me out of the tent, and after I sat by the pits, I felt this overwhelming urge to go east. Then I had to find you."

"I'm glad you did," she replied. "You know what, I'm really glad you're here. Did I ever tell you that?"

"You are?"

"Yes, I am," Kelly said. "Tell me something—are you still angry?"

"Angry, about what?"

"About everything. Remember, you said nobody liked you and you didn't seem to like yourself. You were very angry."

"No, I don't feel angry now. Looking back I think a lot of the stuff I did was just dumb. I guess I was just being an ass—to Kara, to Grandma…"

"To me," interjected Kelly.

"Yeah, to you too."

"Who's this girl Kara?" Kelly asked.

"I met her at the DMV in Bottineau when I was trying to get my license back. Her folks have a place south of town. She lived in an apartment with another girl but her roommate moved out to be with her boyfriend in Williston. I moved in with her to help with the rent and … stuff like that."

Kelly smirked. "Uh, huh. So, why did she kick you out?"

"I guess I wasn't really helping with the rent, 'cause I wasn't working much. And…she said if I couldn't get my shit together I'd have to leave. Said she didn't have time for a slacker."

"Sounds like a smart girl," said Kelly

"Yeah, she is," he agreed ruefully.

They were silent for a moment, just listening to the steady taps of the rain on the tent fabric. They were dry and warm. It felt good to just lie back and listen.

Jamie broke the silence. "I have a confession—I'm glad you convinced me to come along with you Kelly. At first, I thought this was the dumbest idea…and then walking! Walking across the state, looking for some stupid battle? But I'm glad I came. I guess until you stand in the actual footsteps of someone who came before you, well you can't really appreciate what they went through. Those stories that Grandpa and Uncle Rodney told were true—we come from a line of crazy tough people who weren't afraid of anything."

"Yes, we do, and Uncle Rodney and Grampa knew that; I think they were trying to teach us that all along. But I have a confession too—I didn't want you here. Grandma is the one who insisted."

"Grandma?"

"That woman loves you more than life itself, and she's much sharper than she lets on. I guess neither of us really understands all she's been through. But I can tell you this—she was not about to stand by and let you ruin your life, not if she could help it. And I think while I was gone she tried everything she could, but short of lashing you to a fence post, you wouldn't listen. I know it hurt her, it hurt her bad. She was tough enough and stubborn enough to overcome everything that came her way but she couldn't save her own flesh and blood. That's why she insisted you come along. I don't know if it worked or not but I do know if you're not careful you *will* find yourself tied to a fence post. She's not going to give up on you—ever."

"Damn," he said. "I didn't know."

"That's because you didn't want to hear it. You don't always have to fight the world by yourself—not when you have a family. I know she came across as really angry before we left, but it's just love. It's really just love."

"Well, how about you Kelly—are you still angry?"

"Angry...I didn't think I was," Kelly replied.

"Seriously? You have nightmares, sometimes you shout and swear in the night, for no reason. I'd think you were awake but you'd still be sleeping. Aren't you pissed off that a trainee or whatever you call them shot you? Hell, why'd you go into the Marines in the first place? Nobody does that unless they're running from something, or angry as hell and just want to kill somebody."

She and Kristal had a similar conversation, in a tent just like this one, several years before. If she had a best friend in the Corps, it was this tough, strong, young black woman—loyal, ambitious, a perfectionist. Maybe too good for the Marines. In Kristal's case, Jamie was right. Kristal was running from something, and she was angry, and she chose the Marines to start a new life. But it hadn't worked; sometimes the old life hunts you down and you can't be rid of it. Or maybe it just stays within you forever, so you can't outrun it—it's there wherever you go.

Kristal had a terrible childhood, born to a 17-year-old single mother in a Section 8 apartment outside of Gary, Indiana. The bar was low for her mother's potential suitors—drinking, drugs, and womanizing could all be overlooked if they'd only provide, or attempt to provide, some modest level of household support for the family. After several boyfriends who couldn't meet even these minimal standards, her mother remarried when Kristal was 13.

James had a job, didn't do drugs but drank cases of beer like mother's milk. He was too drunk to womanize, but not too drunk to take an inordinate interest in his budding young stepdaughter. Kristal confided to Kelly that she had been raped repeatedly by James over several years. One night she confessed all to her mother. Instead of sympathy, she was scolded for accusing "this good man" who worked hard every day to "raise you and put a roof over your head." The next night he was there again, forcing his rough hands between her legs. She resigned herself to escape and on the day she reached 18 she enlisted in the Marines. The Marines were her new family.

Kristal Moore, the perfectionist, the bad-assed DI who never said never channeled her anger into something productive—she became a skilled warrior fighting for her country. And so it had taken four of them, four battle-hardened Marines to hold her down, and four of them, her brothers in combat, her family, four of them perforated her soul, one after the other, thrusting and groaning as the hot stuff of them spurt into her. And she screamed and twisted and bucked and writhed in rage. Semper Fi.

The Marine Instructor Kelly found the next morning was not the Kristal Moore she knew. What she found was a traumatized young woman from Gary, Indiana, terrified once more of the dark and the torment of a creaking door in the middle of the night. The trust, and Kristal's Marine family, was gone forever.

Despite Kelly's urging she refused to report the attack, although eventually the burden would prove to be too great for even Kristal to bear. Kelly knew Kristal was compromised now, knew she could no longer be a Marine. Kelly had seen it in her failed recruits and first-year boots as clearly as if a mental switch were thrown from "the hunter" to "the hunted." But she was afraid her stubborn friend would never admit this to herself.

Maybe Jamie was right, Kelly thought, maybe she was still angry. Her best friend was gang-raped and she couldn't find a way to help her. And after Kristal could no longer keep it inside, after the pain fed on her and then wormed its way out like a persistent maggot, after she reported it to her CO, her "family" wouldn't help either ("Do you want us to fight the enemy and ourselves too?"). And so her best friend in the Marines, who never said never, who saved her life and the lives of two strange children, did what no haji combatant could do—she used her own sidearm to take her life; one quick tug on the trigger stopped the pain and shame and guilt. Kelly never looked upon her friend's face again.

Yes, she was angry.

And she was angry because she pushed Jaysee Zack as far as she could but couldn't break her. Zack didn't belong in the Marines and Kelly pushed her harder and harder until they both found something to hate—each other. Kelly crossed the line; it became personal. Worse, she found she couldn't turn it off. Zack tapped a reserve of anger she didn't know she possessed, and once released it could no longer be contained. Was it even about Zack, or was it about Kelly's own Marine family, which had killed Kristal?

Zack beat her the day she carelessly swung her rifle barrel into Kelly while searching for targets downrange. Kelly knocked the muzzle away and screamed, "You want to shoot me? Is that it? You want to shoot me?" No sane Instructor would have done what she did next. She grabbed the end of Zack's barrel and pulled it to her chest screaming "Okay, pull the trigger! Pull the trigger, you stupid bitch!"

Zack showed no fear but then smiled cunningly—and in that instant, they both knew she was going to oblige. And in that same instant, Kelly swatted the barrel downward, sending the round through her ankle.

"I *was* angry at things out of my control Jamie. But now it's different, I realize I have at least some control of nearly everything. And that makes all the difference," she said. As she said it Kelly realized it was the first time she had put words to those feelings. It felt good; it felt like progress.

The next morning began cold and gray, but the rain had stopped, replaced by a strong northwest wind that pushed low clouds ahead of it briskly. They would be walking into the wind today. The gelding was a quarter of a mile away, just standing on the side of a small grove, watching them. Jamie waved his arms and whistled and the horse moved toward them at a fast walk. Upon arrival Jamie held out half a cherry toaster pastry; the horse sniffed it and then took it with his lips.

"Good boy, good boy," said Jamie softly as he loosely placed the rope halter over his head. "Let's see you," he said as he examined the horse's wounds. The ointment had not rubbed off his whip and wire cuts, although the wound on the top of his nose was open and bare, *"probably from grazing"* thought Jamie. He found his jar of ointment and gently coated the wound. The gelding was skittish and threw his head a couple times but did not try to move away.

"Don't expect there'll be much for flies out today in this cold and wind," commented Kelly.

"All the same, I don't want to see him lose ground. These cuts and sores are finally starting to heal."

They broke camp, walked to a crossroad, and turned north. This was aspen parkland, a flat, open landscape dotted with clumps of stunted popple, and lots of fence. Pasture land. Not really suited for growing much in the way of crops. Much of the pasture here was dotted with clumps of leafy spurge, a milky, poisonous plant with greenish-yellow stems and leaves unfit for grazing. Once established, it was very difficult to remove.

Kelly had heard that goats would eat it, but nobody in North Dakota was raising goats. She imagined her Métis relatives had passed through a similar landscape, minus the spurge of course, which was introduced from Eurasia. Had bison grazed these lands at one time? Certainly. And wildfires must have kept the trees to a minimum.

They walked on the shoulder of the highway and, despite walking into the wind, made good time. The cool weather was refreshing and their pace was brisk. They had gone nearly six miles by her calculation when they saw a car approaching in the opposite lane. There had been minimal traffic all morning—the usual farm and cattle trucks and some service vehicles. As it approached however she saw a light bar mounted on the roof and her stomach clenched.

Law Enforcement.

The Goodview County Sheriff's car passed them at highway speed and continued.

"Just keep walking Jamie," Kelly said. They did. After 30 seconds Kelly glanced back and saw the car had stopped about a half-mile down the road, turned, and was driving back toward them. Lights on, no siren. She imagined they offered quite a scene—two "Indians" walking with a white horse laced with pink. Might look suspicious to me too she thought.

The car pulled to a stop behind them and a white man got out; she recognized him, the deputy who had given them the ride in the rain. What was his name? Baker...Brewer...

"Hello, Deputy Bauer," called out Jamie, still holding the gelding's rope halter. "Nice to see you again. You remember us? You gave us a lift near the café, in the rain?"

"Well hello. I do remember, brother and sister team as I recall," Bauer replied.

"Jamie and Kelly," offered Jamie.

"Right, you were on a road-trip to see some relatives. How'd that turn out?"

"We found 'em. Down south of Velva."

"Well, that's fine, and you were walking all the way, from someplace up north—Metigoshe. Are you headed back home now?"

Kelly observed their interaction and saw no need to intervene. Jamie had taken the lead and was doing a good job of it. She just smiled at Bauer politely.

"Yes, we are," replied Jamie.

"And I see you picked up a horse along the way."

"Yes, we did."

Bauer walked closer now and stood next to Jamie. The gelding reached out its nose and smelled the deputy, then shook its head as if he smelled too strongly.

"Must not like my cologne," said Bauer with a smile, then became serious. "I don't believe I've ever seen a horse with that many injuries, not a live one at least. Bad foot too huh?"

311

"We're trying to doctor him back to health. He's come a long ways, health-wise, since we got him," said Jamie.

"Well, the reason I stopped is some fella down by Goodview filed a report saying a couple desperadoes came by his place and stole a fine white gelding right out of his yard. According to the report, it was a four-year-old cutting horse in peak condition, worth $15,000. To tell you the truth, I didn't know we had any $15,000 horses in our county, but that's what he said." Then he stopped and looked at the gelding again. "So, you folks seen anything around match that description?" He reached over and slowly stroked the gelding's neck. Jamie's mouth opened but he found his throat had turned dry and he couldn't speak.

"Son?"

"Sir?" croaked Jamie.

"Seen any horses like that around here?"

"No sir," said Jamie.

Bauer looked at Kelly, who pursed her lips and slowly shook her head.

"Nothing huh," affirmed Bauer, now nodding his head slightly.

Bauer stood tapping his fingers on his gun belt, obviously considering his next move. The gelding's ears perked forward at the sound and as it turned toward him with its weepy blind eye the Deputy winced involuntarily.

"Well listen," he continued. "If you do see anything contact the Sheriff's office will you. I'm guessing the owner may have already collected insurance on it, but we'll keep looking."

"Will do, thanks for the information," offered Jamie, recovered now. Bauer walked back toward the car and then stopped and turned toward them again, removing his hat and smoothing back his hair.

"Say, if you folks are looking for a nicer walk you might consider heading over a mile west to the section road there. I know it goes straight north nearly 15 miles to just east of Bottineau. No traffic, better scenery. We had to dig a lost hunter out of there last year. Might be a few gates...but like I said, straight shot...pretty country. You won't be bothered."

"Thank you," said Kelly gratefully. "That's good advice." Bauer got in his vehicle, turned off his light bar, did a U-turn on the highway, and continued south.

Kelly, Jamie, and the gelding headed west.

Chapter 29

Jamie had called their grandmother earlier so she was expecting
them when they walked into the yard, but she didn't expect them to
have a horse in tow. As with their departure, they ran into several
friends as they entered town who recognized them and pulled over
and then wanted to see the pink-striped horse up close. It felt good
to be back to familiar ground and familiar people. Despite this, they
both felt different as they stepped into their grandmother's house—
much different, although they had been gone less than three weeks.

It was almost two weeks later as Kelly emptied the last remaining
materials from her pack that she saw the packet of maps again and
the information from the Velva Historical Society. She had
processed their journey in her mind and accepted that she may never
know all the facts. By any measure, the trip was a success and she
was trying hard to be satisfied with the results.

But something—a connection, a relationship, a link—was missing.

She pieced through the pile of maps and came again to the roster
from the Historical Society. On it were the names of the Métis
hunters who had traveled south with Jean-Luc during the year of the
battle. She saw Jean-Luc's name highlighted again then went
through the remaining names one by one, speaking each to herself
softly.

There weren't any other Savards on the list, the rest of his family had
traveled with the larger Métis hunting group. And no Moreaus. She
saw Father LeSueur, Granger, and a Paquet, with the notation
"*cuisinier*" next to his name. There were some families listed, but
very few children in the group. The Ferguson family listed two girls,
another family was notated to include an "*enfant*."

She wondered if her mother or father were related to someone else on the list, or if there were another link, but the names and descriptions didn't help. Her only hope would be to find some new clue in the paperwork.

Kelly spent the evening going through her notes again, looking for a connection between her family and Jean-Luc's group and trying to put the battle, and the combatants to rest. No luck. She would sleep on it.

Jamie had already left for work the next morning as she shared oatmeal with her grandmother for breakfast. Her grandmother always rose early, often working in the garden right after an early breakfast. Kelly was a morning person too. It was bright in the kitchen and she could tell it would be a warm day later. She put a pad of butter, a shot of Half and Half, and a drizzle of honey in her oatmeal and mixed it in until the butter melted. It tasted good, much better than the plain oatmeal on the road.

"Say, Kelly, didn't you say you stopped at a golf course on your trip, by Hettinger or somewhere?" asked her grandmother, sipping coffee.

"Harvey, yes, a golf course by Harvey. The Métis battlefield was supposedly located there, but it was all a scam by the local boosters."

"Yes, Harvey, that was it. I saw last night on the news that MAGDA or somebody showed up and began digging up the whole thing—a big back-hoe digging up sections of the course. It was all taped off like a crime scene. Oh, you should have seen it," she smiled. "They showed the owner of the golf course hopping around like a wet hen."

Kelly pondered the information. "Well, the county owned the course, so maybe one of the County Commissioners got into hot water. But who's MAGDA?"

"I don't know," replied her grandmother, "I might not have the name right but it was something like that. It serves them right, they should be ashamed for trying to make-up history, especially Métis history."

"I'm afraid it happens all the time Grandma," Kelly replied.

Kelly would later learn that the county had been cited for potential Native American Graves Protection and Repatriation Act or NAGPRA violations. Because NAGPRA was a federal statute, and because Goodview County developed the golf course without any state or federal permits whatsoever, the US Bureau of Reclamation spared no expense in bearing down on the site with several teams of archaeologists flown in from California and Nevada and heavy equipment trucked in from Omaha to perform an emergency site assessment.

Strategic sample digs across the entire golf course revealed no Native American remains, funerary objects, or cultural artifacts. In the end, the supposed grave of local pioneer hero Cramer Spoon was also exhumed, revealing only 118 bovine bones, 16 malt liquor beer cans, and the steering wheel from a 1976 Chevrolet Monte Carlo sedan. The County was presented with a bill of $196,658.67 for the assessment. This did not include the expenses of Special Investigator Rosemary Red Horse who flew in from Washington, DC, to begin investigation prep and interviews with Commissioners Carlton Spoon, Royal Meyer, and Robert "Lyle" Makarenko; those expenses would be covered by the Department of Interior.

Goodview County Treasurer Dorothy Carlson was the only public official present at the next County Commissioner's Board meeting, along with nearly 200 angry residents which filled the small meeting room, the lobby, stairwell, and the sidewalk outside the Goodview County courthouse. Sadly, Carlson explained, the Commissioners all had "other obligations" and were unable to attend. Recall petitions were circulated around Goodview the following day.

When Kelly informed Jamie of the developments he seemed genuinely relieved and quipped "See, sometimes the Government does do the right thing!"

Kelly took the truck down to the library in Bottineau the next morning, telling herself this would be the last time. On the seat beside her were all the papers she had assembled, both before and after the road trip. She had a few more names and locations now and she wanted to conduct searches on them. What she really wanted to know was how she or her mother were connected to the battle. Her experience at Jean-Luc's gravesite had defied explanation. What was the connection?

Three hours later she gave up. The LeSueur document remained the most complete description of the battle and its participants. Indeed, the jumble of names, dates, and locations contained in other historical accounts often conflicted with each other. She could only be certain of one thing: The unmarked grave contained the remains of Jean-Luc. While she had no proof to back it up, her heart told her all she needed to know.

As she drove home she realized again that she and Jamie had accomplished something extraordinary—they had found the missing battlefield, the site of a tremendous Métis victory. Rulers of the prairie! Yes, if only for a short while, but rulers nonetheless.

Upon returning home she found her grandmother in the living room, reading a gardening magazine. Kelly sat heavily on a love seat and placed the stack of documents she had been carrying down on the coffee table. She sat back with a loud sigh.

"Hi Grandma," said Kelly.

"Hello dear," she replied, looking up from her reading. "You sound tired. How is your ankle?"

Kelly flexed her foot back and forth. "It's fine. Stiff some mornings but really fine."

"You know both you and Jamie are on the prayer list at church. Maybe it's time to take you off?"

"I think you're right. I'm good now, and I think Jamie has turned the corner."

Her grandmother continued to read as the clock ticked loudly in the silent room. Kelly sat up, "Grandma, can you do one last favor for me…from our trip?"

"If I can, sure."

Kelly thumbed through the papers in the top folder on the coffee table and extracted the roster of names she had received from the Velva Historical Society. "Do any of these names look familiar to you?" she said, laying the two sheets of paper on the table.

"What is this dear?" asked her grandmother, picking up the first sheet and looking at the names written there.

"Remember the Métis people who fought at the battle, at the place we visited? This is a list of those people, not necessarily those who fought, but those who went along on the bison hunt that year; some were just babies or kids."

"These are the people from 100 years ago?"

"Yeah, about 165 years ago?"

"I can't believe you and Jamie tracked them down Kelly, that is so impressive," said her grandmother, smiling proudly as she held the roster.

"Well, Mom and Grandpa and Uncle Rodney did a lot of the work. And now with the internet and some local records from down there, it was much easier," explained Kelly modestly.

"But still, and you walked all that way! I'm very proud of you. And your Mom and Dad would be so proud, especially of Jamie. You know he's a changed man since the two of you got back."

"Thanks, Grandma, but the list, do you see anything on there that sticks out?" Her grandmother put the two pieces of paper in front of her side by side and slowly began reading down the rows, tracking with her index finger on the paper.

"We have the Moreaus, the Gibsons and the Gagnes in our family tree, but I don't see any of them here. You know there are still quite a few Grangers around," she said, pointing to the name on the list. "I think Rene lives next to a Granger up north. It sounds familiar."

"We met an old man in Harvey, they called him Badger but his Métis name was Kitchi. He said he knew of some Moreaus up by the Red River country, several families," said Kelly. "He said we're all related if we go back far enough."

"There aren't that many Métis in the world Kelly, so he's probably right," said her grandmother, now gazing at the second page of the list. "Well, here's a name I recognize—Ferguson. Your grandfather's kin were Fergusons, on his mother's side. His grandmother I believe. I remember from when we were first married. Now there was a woman with some grit, little bitty thing but tough as a nut. She buried two husbands and was still going."

Her grandmother pushed the roster over to her, pointing with her finger, "Right there."

Kelly looked at it, "Joseph and Star Ferguson. But if she was at the battle *and* Grandpa's grandmother she would have been over 100 years old."

"Oh she was over 90 when she died, still living in the same little two-room house where your grandfather was born," said her grandmother. "But her name wasn't Star, it was something else. Let me think…"

The timing doesn't work, thought Kelly. She looked across the roster and saw two children listed under the Fergusons. Could the missing link be one of their daughters? "Was it Sylvia or Elisa?" she asked curiously, her own finger on the names now.

"No," said her grandmother, now looking down and concentrating intensely. "It wasn't Sylvia, Elisa sounds close but it wasn't Elisa...it was...it was...Lizzy!" she declared triumphantly. "That's right, everyone called her 'Old Lizzy,' oh she was a tough one. Grandpa said she nearly beat her second husband to death with his own boot. Caught him sneaking around. Took out two teeth and broke his nose. I believe she had a sister that died of influenza. She was Grandpa's grandmother so she'd have been your great, great, grandmother," she said hesitantly. "Yes, your great, great grandmother."

"My great, great grandmother," repeated Kelly, looking again at the name and doing the math in her head, "Elisa Ferguson." She was at the battle at Dog Den Butte. She would have been a bit younger than Jean-Luc. And tough as a nut. That was it; Lizzy was the final piece. Kelly smiled and exhaled loudly, although she didn't realize she'd been holding her breath.

"So we *were* related to her. We were related. I want to tell Jamie about this," said Kelly. "Is he at work today?"

"No, some kids from the dance class wanted to see the horse, he took them over to Rene's," her grandmother responded.

Kelly smiled and thought, "*Dance class. What do you think about that Lizzy?*" She walked over to her grandmother and wordlessly planted a solid kiss on her forehead.

"My!" she smiled. "What was that for?"

"I'm just glad you're here, Grandma," Kelly replied. "I'm really glad you're here."

Epilogue

On Friday, July 13, on the 167th Anniversary of the Battle of the Grand Coteau, a writer scaled North Dakota's Dog Den Butte in the predawn and greeted the new day from atop its northern slope.

The view here elicits many emotions, not least of which is the raw beauty of the prairie dawn. Then one realizes how truly unique this landscape is—not just because of the native plants and animals which still exist here and occupy its slopes, but for the stability of this landscape, however accidental.

One can stand near the site of the battles (there were several encounters over at least two days), with a clear view of the Butte, although a recent wind-farm mars an otherwise pristine view. Had one actually sought to preserve this setting some 165 years ago the prospects of success would have been predictably slim. Yet here it is, a setting largely left plain. Perhaps nowhere east of the Missouri River has a landscape remained so unchanged over 165 years as the 100 mile stretch of rolling prairie between North Dakota's Dog Den Butte and the Canadian Border.

As the weight of this conflict and similar conflicts settles in, one feels the dull ache of history atop this little prairie mountain. There are many stories here, why does this story—of a young Métis man executed near here, his remains impaled by 67 arrows—still matter?

In an era where we are bombarded with frivolous stories daily, there are still some stories that deserve to be told, and some of these over and over again. The Butte has given us one of them—a story of displaced people, traveling far from home, living by their wits, doing what was necessary to survive. Such stories go back to Biblical times. Sadly, cruelty is a cancer of which we may never be rid; we hear of new atrocities occurring around the world regularly. But stories of courage and sacrifice and daring, these are stories worth repeating and appreciating, wherever they are found. The story of the Métis is one such story.

The Battle of the Grand Coteau was one of many similar ambushes and battles which took place within sight of *Maison du Chien* or Dog Den Butte, going back to the 1700s and continuing through the 1870s. While such geographic formations may lack relevance for current area residents—those leaning on "bushels and acres" rather than bison for their livelihoods—the tremendous Métis victory at the Battle of the Grand Coteau against incredible odds remains an inspiring story.

While many tribes were involved in the conflicts, history tells us that members of the Sioux nation were most often the aggressors and the casual reader may find it easy to place blame on them for the bloodshed.

Yet, what landowners defend today with laws and litigation and attorneys, the Sioux protected with arrows and lances and clubs—protecting their property with the tools and methods available to them at the time. It mattered little that legally this land belonged to the French or English or the United States (which it did at different times in history). From their perspective, it was Sioux land and they defended it, albeit with a cruelty we find abhorrent by today's standards.

Upon climbing Dog Den Butte and sitting on its rounded shoulders, one familiar with its often violent history might expect to feel a sense of malice or foreboding. Instead, you hear the buzz of grasshopper sparrows and the warble of meadowlarks while the morning sun warms your face and rising updrafts circulate a perfume of red ripe wild raspberries. Hardly the malevolence one might expect.

Today, a handful of radio towers top the Butte, and each evening their lights blink a warning across hundreds of square miles of dark prairie: I am here, I am here.

And here, more stories await, simmering just below the surface.

Acknowledgments

First and foremost the efforts of the late Dr. Allen Ronaghan must be acknowledged for locating the actual Grand Coteau battlefield some 135 years after the fact. My thanks also to the late Lawrence Barkwell who documented the site and pulled together many historic references of the battle from Métis, Sioux, and Canadian archives. My communications with Mr. Barkwell before his passing provided key insights into the battle and its participants.

I would encourage anyone seeking more specific information on the battle, as well as on Métis culture and history, to seek out Mr. Barkwell's work. He has provided a true gift to all historians.

It is also fair to say without the timely encouragement and support from my editor, K.J. Wetherholt, this novel would not exist.

Thanks too to Bill Thomas of Prairie Public Radio, and the Indigenous participants in Prairie Public's, "Ask A Native American" program.

In addition, the staff members at Fort Stevenson State Park, Fort Totten State Historical Site, the North Dakota State Archives and the Historical Society of North Dakota provided valuable background information and context to early pioneer life in North Dakota.

And finally, thank you to my early readers Neal Feeken, my son Benjamin Sobieck, and to my wife Jeanie for their reviews and advice along the way.

About the Author

Daniel Sobieck's work has appeared in many national periodicals and major daily newspapers across the Midwest. Sobieck and his wife reside on their ranch in central North Dakota near Dog Den Butte, the site of the Grand Coteau conflict.

Mad Grass: A Warrior Returns, is his debut novel.

Made in the USA
Monee, IL
30 August 2020